Day by Day Armageddon
Origin to Exile

J.L. Bourne

GALLERY BOOKS
New York London Toronto Sydney New Delhi

Gallery Books
A Division of Simon & Schuster, Inc.
1230 Avenue of the Americas
New York, NY 10020

This Gallery Books trade paperback edition September 2011

GALLERY BOOKS and colophon are registered trademarks of Simon & Schuster, Inc.

For information about special discounts for bulk purchases, please contact Simon & Schuster Special Sales at 1-866-506-1949 or business@simonandschuster.com.

The Simon & Schuster Speakers Bureau can bring authors to your live event. For more information or to book an event contact the Simon & Schuster Speakers Bureau at 1-866-248-3049 or visit our website at www.simonspeakers.com.

Manufactured in the United States of America

10 9 8 7 6 5 4 3 2 1

ISBN 978-1-4516-3303-0

These titles were previously published individually.

Praise for J.L. Bourne's page-turning
novels of the zombie apocalypse

DAY BY DAY ARMAGEDDON

DAY BY DAY ARMAGEDDON: BEYOND EXILE

"There is zombie fiction and then there is crawl-out-of-the-grave-and-drag-you-to-hell zombie fiction. *Day by Day Armageddon* is hands-down the best zombie book I have *ever* read. *Dawn of the Dead* meets *28 Days Later* doesn't even come close to describing how fantastic this thriller is. It is so real, so terrifying, and so well written that I slept with not one, but two loaded Glocks under my pillow for weeks afterwards. J. L. Bourne is the new king of hardcore zombie action!"

—Brad Thor, #1 *New York Times* bestselling
author of *The Athena Project*

"An excellent addition to a zombie section of a library, or anyone's home collection."

—Bret Jordan, *Monster Librarian*

"A dramatic spin on the zombie story. It has depth, a heart, and compelling characters."

—Jonathan Maberry, Bram Stoker Award–winning
author of *Patient Zero*

"A visceral insight into the psyche of a skilled survivor. . . . Claws at the reader's mind."

—Gregory Solis, author of *Rise and Walk*

Contents

Day by Day Armageddon

Origin to Exile

Day by Day Armageddon

THIS BOOK IS DEDICATED TO MY BROTHERS AND SISTERS IN THE U.S. MILITARY THAT HAVE FOUGHT AND CONTINUE TO FIGHT THE GLOBAL WAR ON TERROR IN IRAQ, AFGHANISTAN, AND THE REPUBLIC OF THE PHILIPPINES AS WELL AS THE OTHER DARK AND UNFAMILIAR CORNERS OF THE EARTH.

In this world, I am no more.

I am a decadent monument of
humanity.

I must strive for survival
alone, afraid and vulnerable.

They are cold, recalcitrant
and lethal, but I am alive.

                    ---unknown survivor

In the Beginning...

Happy New Year to me. After a drunken night of fun, I sobered up and headed back home. I am so tired and bored of being home on vacation. I'm thankful for the break in training but Arkansas gets old quick. All my good friends are still drinking the same beer and doing the same thing. I will be extremely happy to get back home to San Antonio. *New Year's resolution: start keeping a journal.*

January 2nd

1100 hrs

My hangover is finally gone. I like to watch the news when I am near a television, but out here at my parent's house it seems that all they get are the local channels. I'm not going to attempt to try the dial up connection, as it will only frustrate me to the point of madness. I guess I will just check my e-mail when I get home. It seems that something is going on in China; the local news reported some type of influenza virus sweeping them over there. The flu season was bad here this year. I received my flu shot on base, avoiding the shortages of vaccine. I'm glad I get to go home tomorrow and get re-connected with my nice high speed Internet connection and digital cable.

My damn cell phone doesn't even work in this desolate place. The worst thing about being here is knowing I'm going to have to do a lot of flying to get back up to speed. When I signed up for

7

naval aviation I didn't think it was going to involve constant work and studying just to stay competent.

January 3rd
0609 hrs

My grandmother called this morning to tell mom that we were going to war with China and to try to talk me into going to Canada to desert the military. I honestly think my grandmother has lost it. I turned on the news half expecting to see some kind of bullshit trade embargo deal with China. The news went on to say that President Bush has agreed to send medical military personnel over to China for *consultation* purposes only.

Makes me wonder, what do we have in America that a big bad country like China would need? They have all the natural resources anyone would want. I keep thinking I may have kept a light on in my house back in San Antonio. I have two small solar cell panels on my roof but I am wired to the electric grid. I just use the panels to sell electricity back to the utility company when I'm away on deployment. They have already paid for themselves.

January 5th
2004 hrs

After a nice ten-hour drive from NW Arkansas, I made it home yesterday. I received a satellite radio for Christmas and activated it for my trip home. I listened to BUZZ, or FOX all the way home with some music from my MP3 player thrown in every now and then. Wish I would have thought to hook the satellite radio up at my parent's house because I am almost certain that it would have worked out there even though it's in the middle of nowhere.

This China situation is starting to heat up. The news reports that we have lost over ten medical personnel to this China "bug." The other "military consultants" that are still in China are going to have to be quarantined prior to getting back to the United States.

Talk about a pain in the ass. You go over there to help someone out and all you get in return is a prison sentence.

Today was not a bad Monday. Had to go fly a few sorties for training. The EP-3 is basically a C-130 with a lot of antennas. It's somewhat non-maneuverable, but it can receive some valuable data from 20,000 feet.

My friend in Groton, CT called today. Bryce is a Navy submarine officer. He really helped me out on a great deal on salvage parts off the old diesel boats when I was installing those panels in my house a few years back. He said that he was finally getting a divorce, she admitted to cheating on him. I kind of had a feeling about this girl, but I never said anything. Don't think it would have mattered if I did. We talked about this China thing for a long time and he seems to think it's some bad flu bug. I kind of think the same thing.

January 9th

1623 hrs

TGIF.

My mother called today on my cell worried asking me if I knew anything about what's going on overseas. I had to once again explain to my mother that just because I'm an officer in the Navy does not mean that I know who killed JFK or what happened in Roswell, NM. I love my mom, she just drives me nuts. I comforted her the best I could but something just isn't right. This nonsense is getting too much coverage in the news. I know the reporters smell a rat by the questions that they are asking FEMA and the White House and Homeland Defense.

The President made a speech (only available on AM band radio, probably to avoid too much publicity) and told the people that there is nothing to worry about and that the Army/Navy medical team in China had to send one of our doctors home because he was too ill to be left with the inadequate care/facilities in the location he was in. Another strange thing is that my squadron was scheduled to go to Atsugi, Japan next month for training in the Pacific and it was cancelled.

I asked my skipper about it, he just told me that they were trying not to take any chances with anything, and that there were rumors of "sick persons" in the Honshu, Japan area. He gave me the nod and told me not to worry. Something doesn't sound right about this whole thing and it's starting to mess with my mind. I have a feeling I might want to go to the store and get some bottled water and things of that nature.

January 10th

0700 hrs

Not much sleep for me last night. I kept the news on all night just in case I missed anything. "I can assure the American people that we are taking every effort to contain this epidemic within the borders of China." Go ahead; say it in your best southern accent. I went to Wal-Mart today and bought a few things just in case I had to stay indoors to avoid getting sick. I bought some bottled water, canned beef stew and went by the base to chat with my supply friend at the warehouse. He told me that he could part with a few cases of MREs for a new nomex flight suit. Didn't bother me, I have a couple dozen of them. I picked out one of my lesser-worn flight suits and brought it to him. At least I will have a little variety in my diet if I need to stay home despite the fact that MREs are not an optimum bug out food because of how much they weigh and the excess space taken up by the packaging.

Vance (my supply connection) informed me he saw on an on-line government invoice, that a few thousand cases of MRE food were shipped to NORAD and a few other locations in the north-west. I asked him if it were normal, and he told me that these facilities haven't requested this much of a food supply since the Cuban missile crisis. I am thinking that if this is serious enough for the big wigs to want to lock themselves up for a few months it is more serious than I thought.

1042 hrs

I unloaded my "meals ready to eat" and noticed that one of the packages was busted. The smell of "Case A" MRE filled the air and reminded me of all of them that I had eaten when on station in the Arabian Gulf area on a ridiculous ground assignment. I hated it over there. It was so damn hot all the time, and when I had to embark on the ship it didn't make it any better. I checked my battery bank and all six batteries were in the green. Made me think of Bryce, and the "steal" I got on those old submarine batteries.

Back when submarines were diesel and not nuclear, they ran on batteries when under the water and when they surfaced they charged the batteries with a diesel generator. Some countries still use the old diesel boats. I thought this was a good idea, however, charging them with solar panels takes considerably longer, ten hours instead of three but the sun is free.

I miss my sisters, Jenny and Mandy. I haven't seen much of them since I have been in the service; they have sort of grown up on me. I called my dad's house and spoke to Jenny, the youngest. She was still half asleep when I called. I used to pick on her badly when she was little. Oh well, I love the little shit, and it builds character. Mandy is living back home, until she can get back on her feet again. Mandy has never been one to open up and talk to me about anything. I wish things would have been different, or that we would have been closer in our childhood.

I really need to clean my guns. Especially my CAR-15, she is really dirty. Might as well clean my pistols while I'm at it. While I'm on the subject, a few hundred rounds for the carbine is not a bad idea since it's so cheap. I don't exactly like looters, and if any of this quarantine shit comes this way, I want to be on the ball.

1436 hrs

Ok, I'm starting to worry, the Atlanta Center for Disease Control has reported a case of this "disease" at the Bethesda Naval Hospital in Maryland. Since there are no communists here to hush the news, the report got out. Apparently this disease causes the victim to lose some motor function, and also makes the victim seem to act erratic. I called in to the squadron to ask some questions. They told me that it's possible we might get Monday off so the Department of Defense can assess the threat to armed forces personnel inside the United States.

My mother also called about the news report and told me that the Bethesda Naval Hospital was the same hospital that they took Kennedy to when he was shot. I laughed at my mom's conspiracy theory attitude and told her to look after her husband (my stepfather) and try to avoid town if they already have enough supplies to stay put. I'm off to the local H.E.B. grocery store to get some stores, oh yeah, bought a thousand rounds for the carbine. Had to go to a few different stores to get them all. No one wanted to sell me that much all at once. It was probably some kind of liberal law that I didn't know about causing the red tape, or it could be a worried gun shop owner conserving some for himself and trying to keep his customers happy at the same time.

Almost out the door when I got the call to get in uniform and report to squadron H.Q. More to come.

1912 hrs

Just got back from my meeting at my squadron on base. I'm a little troubled. We got word that we have an important mission to fly tomorrow, on a Sunday. Apparently we are to fly recon over Atlanta, actually Decatur, Georgia. We are to focus on a specific area, namely the area around the CDC in Atlanta. It's nothing serious, we are just ordered to be a check and balance for the "G-men" in Washington, to make sure the CDC isn't hiding anything. It is just a photo recon, and signal recon mission.

Reminds me of the time I listened to my ex-girlfriend's phone conversation when I was flying training missions around the San Antonio area. I love the signals intelligence (SIGINT) equipment as it saved me a lot of money and time with that woman. Also in the news, one of the reporters was really punking out the Bethesda public affairs officer for not allowing press passage into the hospital to ask the medical personnel questions. O'Reilly was asking . . . "What are you people hiding?" The young officer held her ground and insisted that it was just for the protection of the press corps that no extra personnel be admitted to the hospital, and besides it was not public property, it was a U.S. Government military hospital. Sort of odd that such a low ranking officer would be giving this type of interview.

January 11th

1944 hrs

I don't know what to think now. We were on station, sent to spy on our own government (CDC) at 0816 this morning. We started tuning our equipment to intercept any cell phone/land line/data transfer in or out of the CDC. I almost couldn't believe some of the things that were being said. There was an FBI agent on board, which is very unusual. During the brief prior to flight he stated it is technically illegal under Posse Comitatus for the military to be deployed inside the United States for official missions.

The agent was to be the official mission commander of the aircraft as to circumvent the military from being implicated for breaking any laws by operating inside the U.S. We were getting broken transmissions between the different CDC compounds about the virus being difficult to contain, and how the director of the CDC doesn't wish to look bad or in a bad light in front of the President. They were being as confidential as possible about this problem. They were using Secure Telephone Units (STU phones), but we had a little help from the National Security Agency so breaking the code was as easy as hitting decrypt on our proprietary software.

They went on to say that one of the infected males that they had quarantined had bitten a nurse in a fit of rage when she was trying to feed him. They had strapped him to his bed and put a mouthpiece in his mouth to avoid any further problems. The nurse wasn't doing so well and he had started to run a fever over the last few hours. The CDC voice also said, "Jim, (person on the other end) you won't believe the vital signs we are getting from the male." Jim said, "What do you mean, can you give me specifics?" CDC voice, "no, no specifics over the phone."

That is enough to start worrying for me. After we landed, I

was forced to sign a non-disclosure agreement then I promptly broke it. I called my parents and told them what I thought they should do, then I started my own preparations. I found out we were not coming in tomorrow and that we were only required to call in by 0800 hrs.

I already cleaned up my rifle, so it was time to take care of the pistols. That brings my weapon number up to four firearms and a good knife. Went up on the roof to clean my solar cells, they were dingy and dusty. I also pulled up my notes on switching power from the power grid to submarine batteries, as it might prove useful in the future. I loaded all my magazines (10) for a total of 290 rounds. I never like to load the full thirty per magazine, as this could cause an inadvertent weapon jam.

My bottom floor windows are only double pane, so I went to the local super hardware store to purchase some DIY window bars for the two windows I have that are chest level. All others are too high to effectively reach without a ladder. I am going to install them now.

2354 hrs

I installed the bars using a tape measure, pencil, 5/32 drill bit, and a square head screwdriver (proprietary screwdriver that came with the bars and it's supposed to be difficult to get the screws out without using a drill.) If a looter is good enough to drill out my bars and take my shit while I'm still sleeping, I'll fucking load it on his truck for him.

While doing a quick walk around my yard perimeter, I have decided that my rock wall is not nearly high enough. Any able-bodied man could easily jump it. I had the wall built with the house. I have broken some bottles that I had in the spare room and I used some bonding cement to glue the shards around the top of my wall perimeter every foot or so. At least it might slow someone down. I was listening to my headset radio while I worked and now that I am more informed, I can only see the situation getting worse.

The radio says that the president is issuing a statement in the morning at 0900 EST. Down the street in the distance I can see a family packing up the SUV and leaving. No one takes vacations this time of year so I can only infer that they are bugging out. I'm going to get more supplies tomorrow after I listen to the president's speech and call in to my squadron to check in.

January 12th

0934 hrs

All I can say is, wow. The President pretty much said that the disease is highly contagious and there is no cure at this time. He said that Americans are encouraged to stay indoors and to report anyone with *"suspicious symptoms"* to the authorities at once. One of the press cronies managed to get a question in and asked, "Mr. President! Mr. President! Could you please elaborate on *suspicious symptoms?*" The President replied that we should be on the lookout for person or persons acting wildly and looking ill.

He also said, *"It is extremely important that if any of our family members have these symptoms it is paramount that you give them no special treatment, turn them in just as you would a stranger with the same symptoms."*

A 1-800 number flashed on the screen and he then said:

"I urge you to call this number in the event that there are any outbreak symptoms in your community. We have specially trained men and women to handle the situation, we will take your loved ones to a suitable medical facility for treatment."

The President also said that he is ordering a full withdrawal of American military and civilians in China, Iraq, and Afghanistan. He commented that he was considering withdrawing troops from the DMZ in South Korea. A video clip played in the background showing the U.S. Embassy in China being evacuated under the close supervision of heavily armed U.S. Marines. One of the clips showed three Marines taking down the American flag to signify that the embassy was officially decommissioned. A scene not unlike the fall of Saigon flashed on to the screen. There were mobs of U.S. citizens being evacuated via helicopter from a random rooftop in Beijing. There were sounds of automatic weapons in the background but the people on the roof didn't seem concerned, they just wanted out. I'm off to get supplies.

1522 hrs

It was a total mad house. I got into an accident in the parking lot at the hardware store, and some lady almost fought me for the (4) five gallon barrels of water that I bought at Wal-Mart. I also bought some more 9mm rounds while I was there. I am happy that I have a few cases of MREs and enough water to sustain me in case this gets worse. I also bought some cheap throwaway facemask to wear in case there are any outbreaks at my location. I bought what was left on the shelf in the canned goods section. I purchased fifty cans of different soups. I can't believe this. I haven't felt this surreal since 9/11.

My parents are safe out in the hills of Arkansas, I advised them to stay home and don't go into town for anything. They always have a freshly stocked freezer, and water is not an issue since they use well water. They have a small generator for electricity in the winter when the power lines freeze and break.

I bought some hardware at one of the major hardware chains; some boards for general purpose and some heavy steel brackets and bolts to install a primitive barricade on my front and back doors. It was just a simple 4 x 4 board sliding into a rest on the inside of my door to keep anyone from smashing their way in. I think that if I ration myself to one liter per day and 1000–1500 calorie diet, I could last for at least five months on my current supply of food.

I also turned on the citizen band radio today to see who was on. I selected channel nineteen to hear what the truckers had to say about all this. They were generally angry about all the roadblocks and cargo searches they were experiencing. Apparently the CDC and INS were concerned about semi trucks carrying a truckload of illegal immigrants in the trailer over the border. Something about it not being safe and that they had an incident of a case of this bug when an INS agent opened the gate to the back of another trucker's trailer.

According to what I was hearing, they had to quarantine the whole truck and the agent on duty because every damn person in the back was infected and one of the infected immigrants attacked the agent, probably scared of going back to Mexico. I'm going to call one of my Marine buddies out in San Diego to see what he is doing about all this.

1854 hrs

I just got off the phone with my buddy Shep in the Marines. He said that there were armed National Guardsmen on the street corners in San Diego and that he was being called in to be a part of his base's security team. He told me that he was told to move his wife on base to the cold war shelter that was being reopened and that they were going to close the gates and quarantine the base in the event that there was an outbreak in that area. The sun is down now. I have motion sensor lights on my house around the perimeter. In the event a looter sneaks over and tries to steal anything, at least the light will go on. When I go to sleep tonight, I will sleep with the Glock under my pillow and the CAR-15 next to my bed.

The news is going on about reports of strange phenomenon reported in the major cities, apparently some cases of cannibalism have been reported. That is America for you. The shit hits the fan and everyone goes crazy. Since I happen to live in the outskirts of the eighth largest city in the nation, this news isn't good news. I hear police and ambulance sirens going up and down the street outside my wall. I'm hungry but I have already had too much to eat today. Celery fits the bill I suppose.

2113 hrs

CNN is reporting with a web camera in Times Square. Apparently they own it and the feds haven't thought to have it shut down. They are panning it around and the grainy images are showing armed military troops shooting civilians. Damn, there are going to be some lawsuits over this one.

The image was quickly cut-off by the emergency broadcast system. After a few minutes the picture came in as the Secretary of Homeland Defense stepped up to a podium marked with the seal of the President.

"America, I'm sorry to report that despite our best efforts, this disease has broken the bonds of our containment measures. It is no longer safe to inhabit larger cities. Safe zones are being set up on the outskirts of high population areas and will be open to those not infected with this disease. Please try to remain calm, as what I'm about to say will sound quite abominable. This disease is reportedly transmitted by the bite from one of the infected. We are not sure if this is linked to saliva, blood or both. The infected soon succumb to their wound and expire, only to rise within the hour and seek out living humans. It is not known why those who die of natural causes are returning; however this is also the case. I apologize that the President could not be here, as he is being transferred to a secure location. May God be with us all in this trying time. I now turn you over to General Meyers."

As soon as the Homeland Defense Secretary began to close his folder, he was bombarded with questions from the press corps below the stage. It was more like Wall Street trading than a press conference. Even though you couldn't see the crowd of press in front of the podium, you could feel them there by the ambient noise, camera flashes, and garbled voices. One of the particularly alarming question and answer included one of the reporters asking how the Secretary knew the creatures were dead or if they were merely infected with a disease. The Secretary replied by saying, "Living humans don't have ambient body temperatures that match the ambient air temperature. This morning we locked one of the creatures in a lab reefer. We have recorded a sustained body temperature at 40 degrees Fahrenheit for over twelve hours and counting."

The crowd gasped at this in disbelief and more questions poured toward the podium. "What are the chances of being infected by a bite?" The secretary took a deep breath and said, "So far the communicability of this disease is one hundred percent post-attack if the skin is broken by a bite." I can't fucking believe this is happening. I am calling my family.

2200 hrs

After trying to call for over thirty minutes, I realized that that's exactly what everyone else in the United States is doing. The phone lines can't handle that kind of usage. I tried my mobile phone. Same results. "Network busy." I also listened to what the General had to say during my redial attempts.

"The best defense in this situation is to remain in your home and await the evacuation teams. Avoid infected personnel at all costs. If you are forced into an altercation with one of these individuals, the only thing that will have effect is trauma to the cranium. If you are unfortunate enough to be forced to defend yourself from a loved one, do so with the same vigilance you would a stranger, as that is what he or she is. Try your best to avoid getting bitten as there is no way to avoid infection by these means.

The reports coming in from our troops returning from China indicate that the creatures are primarily attracted to loud noises. It seems they use this as a primary method for finding prey. I must stress that it is in your best interest to remain indoors and to remain quiet and calm. Our best guess from our CIA human intelligence (HUMINT) operators on the ground in China is that the disease has been rampant in China for more than three weeks and they are in a state of disaster. If we don't do things differently than the Chinese, we could be doomed to the same fate."

The General was then ushered off the podium and given a stern glance by one of the civilian government officials. What followed next was an attempt by one of the speakers to apply a calm tone to what the General had relayed.

I'm scared . . . I really don't know what else to do other than turn the lights out and sit here and write . . . my rifle is slung over my shoulder even as I sit here . . . There is a knock at the door. Back soon . . .

2350 hrs

One of my fellow officers from the squadron came over to tell me about the rumors he had heard from Jake, our mutual friend, when Jake had returned from a mission over one of the outbreak areas in Atlanta, GA. During the mission Jake said that he had seen numerous infected corpses walking the streets in the south part of town. He said he could see the stray dogs barking at them in the streets and watched as the infected tried to lunge at the dogs. He was using the camera pod to digitally zoom in. To him it seemed like some of the younger gang members were trying to take the law into their own hands by shooting the infected corpses.

From what my friend said, Jake was as white as a ghost when he landed, not believing what his eyes had transmitted to his brain. Chris, my midnight visitor was scared from what Jake had told him, I could see it in his eyes. He asked if I wanted to come with him and stay on the base in the shelter that they had organized. I knew what he was talking about. On the base there are numerous cold war bomb shelters still active and mostly being used to store civil defense food and water and various medical supplies. I looked at Chris and told him that he would be ok, just keep a level head and watch his back.

I told him that I was going to stay here alone and try to keep out of view of anybody and anything. He asked me if I was sure, I told him yes. He left and I'm tired. Going to lock it up and watch some news then TRY to get some sleep. I still can't believe this. Part of me wants to see for myself, part of me wants to just hide under the table with my guns and shiver.

January 13th

1143 hrs

No sleep came for me last night. I kept hearing police and ambulance sirens and fire trucks. Very disturbing. Thought I could hear gunshots in the distance, but it could have been vehicle backfire. Got out of bed at 0500 hrs. Went to the garage to get the fluorescent bulbs for perimeter and inside lights. I normally use regular bulbs because they are a little brighter, but given my situation, I may have to temporarily live off solar/battery power if any fires knock out the transformers or power grid.

The news is only portraying death doom and destruction. The news is now saying that every major city is reporting cases of the dead walking. This morning I began boarding up all my windows, even the ones that are not on ground level. I also boarded up the two vulnerable windows that I recently installed bars on, just in case. I feel pretty safe about the windows. I put the efficient bulbs on my perimeter lights.

Disadvantage: It takes them a couple of seconds to come on when the motion sensor trips.

Advantage: Will not drain my deep-cycle batteries as quickly.

I'm concerned about my safety, but I am taking every precaution to ensure that I am doing ok. I'm making a new section for supplies so that I can keep track of the amount of water and food I am consuming. I also checked the acid level of my batteries. They are good to go. Should last through this, unless . . . well I don't want to go there in my mind right now.

1555 hrs

I finally got through to my Mother and Stepfather (Dad). Mom was hysterical. I had to talk to dad to get any words in. He told me that things were fine and that they were as safe as possible. They hadn't seen any signs of the disease, but told me that there were reports in town of a possible outbreak (10 miles away).

They had the guns and dogs ready for looters if the situation should arise. I asked my stepdad what his plans were if things got too bad at home. He said that he and mom and the dogs would probably head out to Fincher cave if things got too bad. It is just a small cave that I used to play in when I was young. Old man Fincher used to threaten to shoot me with his rock salt loaded twelve gauge if I kept trespassing in his cave without my parents. That seems like ages ago. I was only twelve then. I told them that I would stay in touch as long as the lines were up. It was no use with the cell phone as it was already dead. The high maintenance services would be the first to go.

1910 hrs

The lights were flickering today. Not a normal occurrence here. I was cleaning my rifle when it happened. I thought they were going to go out, but they held. Sirens and gunshots can be heard in the wind. That sums most of the sounds I heard today. After I got off the phone with my family (decided to call my dad, no answer), I also started preparations to keep my house from looking too inhabited.

I took the staple gun and some extra blankets and gunned them over my re-enforced windows to make sure no ambient light gets out when I check the TV for news or turn on a light, or use my computer. I have a couple old batteries left over from my last laptop. Not the same model as my Apple, but I could get it to work with some electrical wire if I had to. I'm just thinking worse case. I used some duct tape and wired my web cam to overlook my front yard so instead of opening curtains to look outside, I could just look in my screen.

When my computer is in sleep mode (clamshell closed), I can't even see the needles move on my drain gauge of my battery bank. I had to use my extra USB cable from my printer, but who really cares about printing anything at a time like this. It's not like I'm going to be printing pizza coupons. I sent out some e-mails but got them all back. There were numerous error messages stating that server (insert random IP) was down. It's dark here now.

I would get my camera out and take a picture outside my upstairs window. I'm just too scared.

2319 hrs

I woke up to the sounds of gunshots nearer this time and turned the cam on. Looks like a green Army transport truck parked under a street light on the corner in front of my house. There are soldiers loading a body in the back of the truck. I have to sleep tonight. Perimeter is secure . . . I just took the risk of taking an off-the-shelf sleep aid (just 1/2 dose) to try to cut the edge off. The news says that martial law is in effect in the inner city. I'm on the outskirts. It could be put into effect here too if these Army guys keep showing up. Oh yeah, I got a call from the squadron today, I didn't answer. It was my Executive Officer telling me I had to report to the shelter and to call him immediately upon receipt of his message. Yeah right, fuck you sir . . . feeling the effects of sleepiness . . .

January 14th
0815 hrs

I fell asleep to the sound of ocean tides on my mp3 player. I turned it up to drown out some of the noise. Woke up around 0300 to take a piss. I actually forgot what was going on. It reminded me of my childhood and early adulthood when something bad would happen, like a death in the family. There were brief moments of levity where my mind would forget the tragedy and then the cold hard facts would hit me. The second my hand reached out to turn on the television the tragedy returned to my conscious thought. I watched as endless talking heads were giving their theory on the cause and effect. The stock market is to the point of non-recovery.

The Coast Guard's helicopter fleet has been reassigned inland to aid law enforcement and military personnel evacuate some of the harder hit areas. A news clip that really got to me in particular, showed a group of survivors on a rooftop in San Diego. The helicopter was circling the roof of the building and I could see the wind from the helicopter rotors blowing the people's hair and clothes around. The people were trapped on top of a large air conditioning unit; apparently they had climbed up there to escape their pursuers (a dozen walking corpses). A particular shocking image was that of a mother and her daughter. The mother had her daughter's mouth taped over and her hands and feet bound. She wasn't one of us anymore. The daughter was dead. The mother just couldn't let go. The poor ignorant woman.

I don't know how to react to seeing the world crumble. There are countless cities scrolling by on the news tickers. Even my own city made its way across the bottom of the screen. There are no commercials on the television, only the talking heads.

Reporter: *"The following scenes display material that is not suitable for young children."*

The scene showed a group of reporters in their news van driving through downtown Chicago. The camera was pointing to the driver and you could see that he was visibly shaken and trying his best to keep the van on the road. The camera then panned to a frontal view. There are seas of figures in front and on the sides of the van. I could tell the van was moving as quickly as it could. You could hear a male voice crying from the back of the van. The driver did his best to weave in and out, but there were just too many bodies walking into the van to avoid. The camera panned back to the rear seat to get a shot of the female reporter.

She said, *"As you can see, it would be SUICIDE to enter the city of Chicago, may God help us all."*

She then made a "cut-throat" gesture and the camera cut out. The screen went back to the reporter. He made a half-hearted statement about hoping they would return safely, all the while trying to keep up a fake smile. I turned off the TV and made my own assessment outside my house.

0900 hrs

→ Perimeter wall: solid

→ Street view: Emergency vehicles only. I see some
  human figures, but can't tell friend or foe.

→ Threats: I see a fire burning in the distance about a mile
  up the road. I can tell by direction of smoke that it's
  blowing away from me.

2212 hrs

I came across a post on a survivalist forum online. I guess the
news isn't reporting the whole truth. A sailor holding out on a
U.S. Naval warship posted today. Apparently he is living off fish
and seagulls. I hope he makes it. This just reassures my thought
that the government is and will continue to hide the facts. This
brings up a question. What government? I haven't seen any repre-
sentatives of the White House on the TV in over 24 hours.

I spent the rest of the morning and afternoon prepping my
backpack with a "bug-out" kit, in the event I have to get the fuck
out of Dodge, and also filling up the bathtubs in my house. The
water hasn't shut off yet so I'm going to start drinking out of the
tub to conserve my bottled water. I began rationing food today.
Only had a can of stew and a banana. Might as well eat all the fruit
now because it will be useless within a week (sans the apples).
I checked the perimeter again, and decided that I will keep my
flight suit on at all times and remain as camouflaged as possible
when I go out.

I have a nomex mask and gloves and ten nomex flight suits. I
think it's a good idea to wear these because:

1. They are fireproof, and
2. They are one piece and no hassle, which means less to
   get snagged on shit if I have to get on the run. The only
   bad thing is that I need to be in a very safe place if I
   need to use the head.

25

I fashioned a pretty good washboard from the grill part of my propane grill. Had to wire brush it clean, but it will serve a good purpose in keeping my clothes clean and giving me less of a chance of catching disease or rash. I'm going to shave every other day to save on razors.

2350 hrs

I heard movement outside my gates and disabled the motion sensor lights while putting on my mask and gloves. I grabbed my rifle and went outside to investigate the area. I saw a strange man in civilian clothes stumbling up the street bumping into my rock wall at random intervals. Looked a lot like those corpses on the TV (the way he walked). I'm not taking any chances, nor am I going to get "commando" fever. I shall remain silent to avoid being seen or heard by anything alive or dead. Besides, it was too dark to tell whether or not he was alive or dead. I feel like a fucking idiot for not stealing some NVGs from the squadron when I had the chance. They would be handy in this situation. Good night journal.

January 15th

2237 hrs

I spent the whole day monitoring the situation outside my home. I saw some of the poor bastards shuffling up the street around 1045 this morning. I used my binoculars to get a decent view. Some of the ashen bodies looked normal, some of them not so normal. One of them had its throat torn out. Very unsettling. My phone rang today around noon (it was out momentarily earlier). I had set it to quiet mode a couple days ago. I was sitting next to it, so I decided to pick it up, half expecting it to be one of my superiors wondering why I'm not on the base in the shelter. It was one of my squadron buddies, Jake. We went through Officer Candidate School together.

Surprisingly enough, we both picked the same profession, and ended up the same places. He was telling me the situation on base, and I can say that I made a good decision by staying here. He told me that he was sent to pick up some blankets from the base storage units near the west gate. When he arrived he said that the military police were constantly shooting over the fence at the creatures in an effort to weed out some of the mass before it was too much for the gate to handle. A Humvee with a .50 cal was dispatched to deal with the crowd but they had to retreat when the gunner almost got pulled off the vehicle.

He said he didn't know how long the gates would hold, but he was sure that they couldn't get by the concrete bomb shelter. I asked him from where was he calling. He told me that he was using the base's DSN lines (lines strictly for DOD use). He said that the officers were all heavily armed in the bunker and that he thought they had enough food for at least a few weeks. I told him not to worry about me, and that no one knows I'm even here. Instant Karma was playing in the background. That is all for today, journal.

January 16th

2200 hrs

The phones are dead again. At least the broadband is still working. All the news websites have stopped putting up the nice colorful flash images and are just sticking to basic tickers. I suppose they don't have time to be fancy. I spent the day preparing, loading up some bottled water and one case of MREs to the attic just in case. I also took some plywood from the garage and made a temporary floor up there big enough to sleep on. No emergency vehicles today. The air was thick with smoke from fires in the city. I can see the fires outside now even through the rain. All the lights are off in my house. The electricity kept flickering again today. If the electricity goes out altogether, it will take me at least twenty minutes to set up for solar/battery power "off grid."

The news isn't even broadcasting live anymore on TV. It's obvious they are controlling the broadcast remotely because all you see are street corner cameras that are only connected to the world through the WWW. Oh, and the tickers on the screen keep rolling by showing government shelter centers. Half of it is misspelled and hastily typed, not unlike this journal. One camera of particular interest was a traffic camera pointing at a random interstate in California. It showed those dead bastards trapped in their vehicles with their seatbelts still on trying to scratch and moan their way out. From the looks of it, they died in an accident and came back only to be stuck in a car with no motor skills to unfasten the seatbelt. That makes me feel better, because if they can't un-click the belt, they can't turn the doorknob.

> *Theory:* Phones down, Internet up . . . why? I think it's because most of the lines dealing with the Internet are buried or satellite. Most of the phone lines are above ground and susceptible to fire and weather.

January 17th
1424 hrs

The sun is out. It is getting hot indoors. I don't want to run the air conditioner out of fear of the noise it will make. Electricity is intermittent. Water pressure is failing. I'm keeping the tubs filled up as I drink water. I'm not risking a shower or bath because I will have to drain the water to do this and I might lose total pressure. Using a bucket and sponge to take a bath. Trying to shave every other day to keep my morale up. The same news keeps flashing on the screen. No reporters in two days. I'm trying to establish a routine as to maintain sanity. In the early AM I am walking the perimeter before the sun rises as to avoid attention from those things. Later in the AM I intend to work out by doing basic calisthenics.

I had a real scare this morning. A cat had jumped my fence in order to avoid being killed by one of those things. I didn't think much of it until the cat had ran off and jumped the fence opposite the side it came in on. That's when the thing that was pursuing it decided it wanted to keep up the chase. I could only see its hands as it groped over the fence feeling for the cat. It just kept cutting itself on the broken glass that I had glued there a few days earlier. I guess these things have no fear of pain.

I think it got angry because it started beating on my wall. I could hear the thuds from the other side. Let it thud away I suppose it's going to take a lot more than that to tear down my rock wall. There are four or five of them in that area now. They are shambling around. I get a feeling they sense I'm here, but I cannot be sure. If it gets too bad, I will have to deal with them. I was thinking I might get my stepladder and some of my reserve kerosene and put it in my pesticide sprayer. I will climb the ladder and spray them down then light a match and burn them to death, again. It's much quieter than shooting them I suppose. At least this way I will be able to get a good look at one of them. I'm off to make preparations for this.

1600 hrs

I cannot begin to describe how disgusting these things look. I am a believer now. They are certainly dead and certainly want me to be dead with them. I quietly went to the garage to get my kerosene, ladder and sprayer. I set the ladder up first. Went over to the section that I thought they were near. I could hear footsteps where I placed the ladder.

I wanted so bad to see, but I was scared to look. I went back to the garage, and picked up the rest of my death squad gear. I could have easily shot them, but I don't want to make the noise, or waste the ammunition. I filled the sprayer up and climbed the ladder. First rung . . . I could see the tops of three of their heads . . . second rung, they noticed my presence and this awful gurgling moaning sound erupted from one of them. Sounded like, well I don't know what it sounded like. I got to the top of the ladder and there were six of them gathered around my position on the opposite side of the wall.

I pumped the canister to get pressure to the sprayer and doused the bastards with kerosene. They were fucking pissed, or hungry, or both, I don't know. I lit a match and threw it at the closest one, no dice, didn't ignite. I repeated this three more times as these vicious things kept clawing at the wall trying to get to me.

29

Finally on the fourth attempt one of them caught fire. I knew I had to stay there on the ladder so I could make them bump into each other and spread the fire.

Finally when they were all up in flames, I stepped down from the ladder and put away my gear. I could hear the popping sound of burning fat for the next two hours. I'm glad it had rained for the past few days, or I wouldn't have even thought about doing this. I really have to start making a backup plan in the event I get SNAFU'ed here at my house.

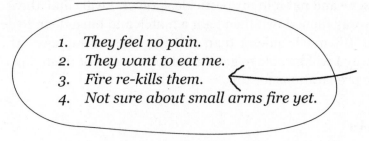

1. *They feel no pain.*
2. *They want to eat me.*
3. *Fire re-kills them.*
4. *Not sure about small arms fire yet.*

1815 hrs

The sun is quickly going down. From my laptop web cam, I can see numerous figures up the street gathering around another house. I wonder if someone is alive in there? I hear birds going crazy in that direction. Not sure what the deal is. I hope if someone is alive in there, they have the common sense to stay quiet, because I really don't want to find out how gunfire affects them just yet. I don't want to be a hero today. I miss the world already. I miss flying. I miss being a Naval officer. I guess I still am, but I'm not sure if there is even a government around to recognize my commission. I sharpened my knife to a honed perfection today. It was sort of a relaxation technique. Also cleaned my carbine, although she didn't need it. A visual inspection was made of all weapons.

The solar panels are running efficiently. I dread going on the roof to clean them, because I'm sure I will be spotted. I should do it at night. That's a ways off. I heard the sound of a helicopter today, didn't take the chance to go outside and look even though those things can't spot me from ground level. Maybe they can smell me. It makes me wonder what senses they lost or gained from dying and coming back. I think it probably took longer than normal for the ones that I burned to die, as compared to a normal human.

I saw the caps of the flames from my house over the wall stumbling around for at least three minutes. The average human would collapse from pain in less than thirty seconds, I would guess. When it gets dark, I am going to use the Laser sight on my pistol to try to signal the house up the street. At least that way the creatures will not see the signal, only the recipient will if they exist or are even alive.

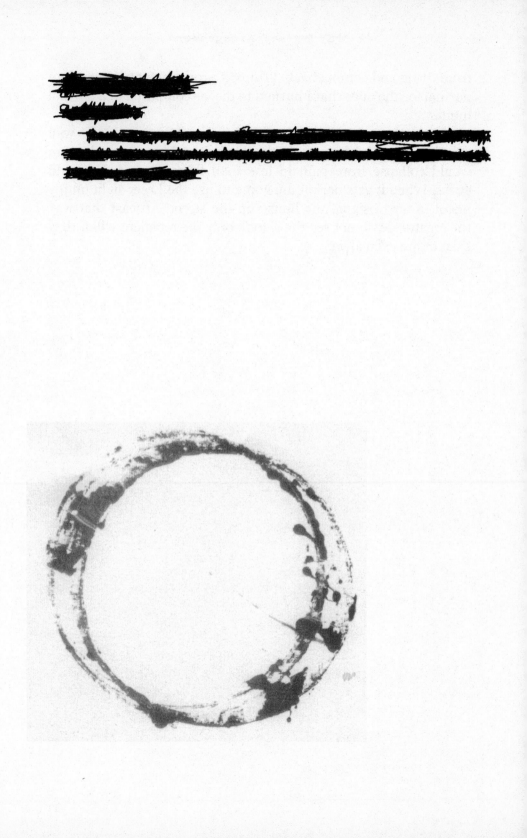

John

Using my pistol LASER sight, I made the attempt at signaling the house that the creatures were gathering around. At first I just aimed the "dot" at every window and shook it around. After about five minutes of this, I saw the faint glow of a flashlight in the upstairs window. Whomever it was started flashing the light. "Dit-dit-dit-da-da-da-dit-dit-dit." It was SOS in Morse code. I learned Morse code a few years back at a military radioman school I attended and was pretty good at visually interpreting and pretty shitty at interpreting it through audio means.

This time I was in luck. I grabbed a pencil and some scratch paper (bills that I will never pay) and gave the signal that I was ready to copy. The things weren't reacting to the other person's flashlight, so I decided to use my L.E.D. light because of the 25 hours of battery life, unlike my pistol laser sight. I started to copy the Morse. At first it was slow going because I had to signal him/her to repeat the signal. I got into the groove after a couple of sentences.

> O...K...(break)
> H...E...R...E...(break)...N...A...M...E...(break)
> ....J...O...H...N...(break)...
> Y...O...U...? (interrogative)

I told him my name and that I was OK also. I also told him to be quiet, the things like sound. He understood. Not bad communication for being a hundred yards away. He signaled and said that his house was secure and that he had a plan to make communication faster, but it would wait until tomorrow. I asked him what the plan involved his reply was:

R...U...B...B...E...R...B...A...N...D...(break)
...W...A...L...K...I...E...T...A...L...K...I...E...(break)
...S...L...I...N...G...S...H...O...T.

Uh...

I told John that I sort of understood. He signaled that it was time for him to get some rest. I let him go after that. That was over an hour ago and I still cannot fathom what he intends to do with a rubber band, a small radio and a slingshot. I can't think of a sling shot big enough to propel a handheld walk & talk one hundred yards to my house and even if it could, it would break into a million pieces if it did make it over here. I guess at least I have something to look forward to for tomorrow.

January 18th

1012 hrs

I woke up at 0605 and went to look out the upstairs window. Sat there for a minute with my light and then began to try and hail John. I kept flashing my light at the window. No answer. I started thinking the worst. I just sat there for a few minutes feeling sad, knowing that in half an hour it wouldn't matter anyway because the sun would be too bright for us to see each other's flashing signal. That was when I saw him. I saw movement on the roof, the silhouette of a middle-aged man in a plaid button up red and black shirt and jeans. I grabbed my binoculars ran back and started flashing my light.

The sun was starting to shine so I was not sure if he could see the light trying to compete with the sun's brightness. He looked my direction and waved. Then he held up this long green elastic looking thing and what looked like a short stubby metal coffee thermos.

He then proceeded to wrap one end of the green band around the chimney and the other around his exterior attic fan, forming a primitive sling. He put the thermos in the sling and started walking down the other side of his roof, out of my sight stretching the green-looking band. It seemed like a long time. Finally, I saw the band snap upwards, then less than a second later, when the sound caught up, I heard the snap.

The thermos that John had cradled into the band was shooting at a trajectory that would put it roughly somewhere in my yard. The ten or fifteen undead that were shambling around John's house took no notice as John's package sailed to its target.

I heard a loud *KA-THUMP* as the thermos hit one of the stepping-stones in my yard.

The package had made it over 100 yards inside the perimeter of my fence. Not without cost though. The sound was loud and two of the things turned from John's house, as if they heard it and started walking in my general direction. I wasted no time and immediately put my gloves and mask on and grabbed my pistol. I didn't feel it necessary to bring the rifle for a front yard expedition.

I made it to ground zero in less than fifteen seconds, picked up the dented thermos and ran back inside waving at John. He could see me and I could see him, but the things could see neither of us from our positions. When I got inside I opened John's package and found two packages of eight triple 'A' Duracell batteries, and the following two items: a note from John, and a two-way radio.

NEIGHBOR,
Signal me back
on channel Ø7.

—John

P.S. I told
you it would work!

It also came stuffed with packing foam peanuts.

The corpses finally made it to my general area, but the sound of the impact was so brief they had no idea what specific area to go to. I loaded the batteries (takes 4 AAA) into the two-way radio and put the ear bud on. John was already trying to get me on channel seven. We talked for a great while. He told me that he used his wife's yoga resistance band to slingshot the thermos. We both laughed at that. I was afraid to ask him about his wife so instead I asked him if he had lost anyone in all this, he simply replied, "I think everyone has."

I didn't probe any further. I asked him what his plans were, and what his supplies looked like. He told me that he was still formulating a plan of survival and a backup of escape, and that he had plenty of food and water. He also told me that he had a semi-automatic .22 rifle and a couple bricks of ammunition. Hell, that's more ammo than I have.

I asked him why all of them were gathered around his house and he told me that it was because of his dog, she started barking at a group of them so he had to muzzle her. I asked what kind of dog he had, and he told me that he had an Italian greyhound (tiny version of regular greyhound) named Annabelle. I was jealous of the companionship he had. My busy Navy schedule kept me from getting a pet, because I would deploy at odd times. I told him that I had another friend named John back at the squadron. He said that we should conserve battery power and think of something useful to chat about in the evening and that he would be back on at 1800 sharp. I agreed and we both signed off.

(1.) Supplies: status <u>GOOD</u> !

1950 hrs

John was on the air and ready at 1800 just like he said. We spoke about our current situation and came up with theories of how it began. I asked John if he knew if bullets could kill them, he was not sure. I told him about my little campfire yesterday and he told me he saw the fire after they had succumbed and wondered what happened. He finally broke the news to me about his wife. His son was away for college at Purdue when all of this hit. His wife was a victim of one of those things. It had attacked just before sunset days earlier as she walked out to the shed to get some nails for the boards they were putting up. It was a bum that had died the night before after taking refuge in the backyard shed. By the time his wife called out, it was too late. When he arrived with a baseball bat she was gripping her bloody arm and running toward him with the creature behind her. He killed it with the bat.

He said that the bite on the arm immediately showed signs of infection and swelling. Black and red vein tracks were spreading toward her shoulder within an hour. He applied first aid and kept her comfortable, but there was nothing else he could do. He started to cry, (I could hear his tears through the tinny transmission of the 2-way) and I tried to change the subject, he said *"I had to put her down, it hurt like hell, but I had to."* I told him not to think about this and try to keep his head in the game for the time being. He agreed and we kept talking.

I told him that I had seen numerous postings from survivors all over the United States on the Internet, but none from our allies overseas. He asked me to read them to him so I did. I told him that one survivor was in southeast Texas, so that means that he and I weren't the last survivors here. I read about the survivor from New York and John told me in a distant voice that he had family there. We both went off the air for a couple minutes to get our road atlases.

We got back on and started to discuss escape routes should this area become infested and uninhabitable. He suggested the Alamo because it's only a half a day's walk from here. I told him that I thought it would be suicide to enter the city now. I suggested that we "borrow" a sturdy vehicle and head east to the Gulf of Mexico and find an offshore oilrig.

John said that his power had been flickering on and off in the past few days and he wasn't sure how long it would hold. John had a Honda generator in his basement, but he told me he refused to use it unless he had to, because it might be audible outside. We decided not to waste too much battery power on these two-way radios. I only had three other sets of triple A's.

I tried the CB radio on every channel, only static.

I'm hungry.

Thought: I still have my satellite radio in my vehicle. Satellite = no lines to catch on fire. If the uplink station is still operational someone could uplink from the WWW, and transmit. I will go out tonight and get the radio and UHF antenna.

2334 hrs

John and I decided that if we needed to talk to one another we would be at the window at the top of the hour to flash our lights. We decided to make a deal to go to the window and check on each other every hour, until we signaled it was time for bed (5) flashes. No light means there is no need to waste our two-way radio batteries. I checked my radio. It seems to work fine; unfortunately every station that is active is playing a constant loop. Some of the news channels are broadcasting stories and news from last week. Old news. I will continue to monitor when I can. I checked the CB radio again. I could have sworn that I heard the faint signal of a human voice. I called out and tried to get a response, no joy.

Looking out the window, I see at least a dozen fires in the distance, and every now and again, I think I hear gunfire. I imagined for a moment that it could be the last survivors in the big city. I bet it is a war zone there. I feel dirty, but I just don't want to waste the water. That reminded me to check the water pressure. Still some left. I haven't left the confines of my domicile for five days I think (sans the bonfire and slingshot incident). It feels like a month.

I wonder how other countries are holding up. I bet Eskimos and some of the small islands in the Philippines aren't really affected by this. Lucky bastards. I wonder if the walking dead are cold to the touch? That would lead me to believe that they don't generate body heat therefore they are much like a snake. I theorize that if it gets very cold, they may slow down. Tomorrow is Sunday. No church for me tomorrow. I guess he wasn't bullshitting about the Omega part in the book of Revelations. It's almost midnight, so I'm off to give my (5) flashes to John.

January 19th

1659 hrs

I woke up this morning to no power. It was around 0730. At 0800 sharp I went to the window to signal John. He was already there. He told me that the power went out last night at about 0330. I slept right through it. I don't know what it is, but I have just been able to sleep a little better since I met John. I guess it's the feeling of not being alone. Being in the military I never got a chance to make many close friends because I would always be on the move. That was the case here. I had this house built because I thought it would be a good investment and because I knew I would be here for a couple years.

John said that he really didn't need any power to do anything. He had a propane cooker and plenty of water. I told him that I was using solar power with deep cycle submarine batteries.

My broadband connection is running through the buried cable lines, and it still seems to be unaffected. There is also power to the phone grid because when I pick the phone up, I get the quick busy tone telling me the switchboards are down, but the lines are not out. I told John that I would be back soon and that I had to go to the garage to switch from the power grid to my own power supply (wouldn't want the power surging back on and damaging my battery banks).

After I switched power to solar/battery, I got back on the horn with John. He asked if there were any new survivor entries on the online forums and I read them to him. People from all over the US were sounding off. Some sounded bleak, others sounded hopeful. I guess reading the survivor entries to John was sort of an outlet. John and I discussed travel. I told John that I could fly. If I had a way to get an operational aircraft, we could make it pretty much anywhere in the US, as long as we had the charts so that I could find airfields with fuel. We were both getting cabin fever and it showed. We were just thinking of excuses to leave this dead place.

1920 hrs

Gunshots outside. It's too dark to see John's house without the streetlight. I turned my radio on and waited for a few minutes. I was sure John was in danger until I heard him crackle in. "Don't worry, I'm safe, I had to shoot some of them because they were starting to pile up onto each other and form a human ladder." I asked him how they were affected by the shots. He said that he shot twelve of them in the head using only the moonlight at close range and killed them. That's good news. I know that those shots are going to attract more of them, so I will be sleeping extra softly tonight. Suggested to John that he be ready at first light to kill twice as many as he killed today.

2311 hrs

I can't really sleep as I keep thinking about all the people left alive and struggling to survive. A woman in Oklahoma is trapped with her children, and asking for advice on the online message boards. What grief it would bring me to find out that my advice doomed someone to being destroyed by a crowd of those things? I know that if I was in a situation . . . trapped . . . with the undead increasing in numbers daily around my perimeter that I would have no choice but to leave. I'm thinking of short-term safe havens as we speak. Water towers, train cars (with roof exits), roofs of buildings with limited roof access come to mind. I just wouldn't want to be somewhere surrounded with no way out. If there are any prisons or military facilities, I might choose those. They are defensible if, and only if you can clear them out. The more I think about it, the more I realize that my situation could become much like hers quickly if I don't stay in the game. I don't feel it prudent to give others advice, as I am no expert. I just hope that we all survive. There doesn't seem to be much chance for most of them.

The Marriage of Figaro

Situation, *dire* . . . John and I woke up today and started communicating on the two-ways. What I saw out the window was almost too much. It was 0700 hrs and there were approximately one hundred of those things on our street forming a human moat around John's house. I grabbed my carbine, checked its action, holstered my side arm and prepared for battle. I donned gloves, hood, and flight suit, and John's radio with ear bud. John had no idea that his previous efforts to clear them out would lead to so many following the noise here. I told John to stay put and I unbarricaded the back door, stepped through and jumped my fence, avoiding the glass by throwing over an old bath towel.

Taking careful aim with my weapon I started aiming for the nearest ones first or the ones on the outside of the circle, thinking that this may slow their pursuit down as they trip over their slain. I only had four magazines, that is 116 rounds. I shot round after round into the skulls of those things. One would think that it would bring instant death. This was not the case. Even some direct hits didn't hit the brain, but skirted along the outside of the skull only to pass through on the other side. For every ten I shot, I only killed eight or nine.

The lumbering mass of ghouls chased me as I tripped over the corpse-laden ground. I had no choice. I had to flee. I ran for blocks only to find more of them. I knew this was a dead place. I could feel it in the air and the vibrations of their moans hit my chest like a cheap band in a local nightclub. I was being hunted. The nearest immediate shelter I could find was a gas station. My body was full of adrenaline. I knew they would consume me if I gave quarter.

I climbed a pipe on the side of the gas station wall and stood flat-footed on the roof. I could tell by the moans and movement in the distance that I was a dead man and lived on borrowed time. I had around thirty rounds left (one magazine and some change). So I decided to take one out of the magazine, and save it for myself.

I started shooting. Trying for headshots. Hitting some and missing more, the fog of war was taking my aim or maybe it was the depression I was feeling, probably similar to someone that just found out they were HIV positive.

That is when I heard my savior. I caught glimpse of a car coming from the direction of my street. I kept shooting. The car took notice and headed my direction. It was John. He haphazardly pulled his car around the side of the gas station. There were five of them closing in. I took three of them out before I ran out of rounds. I had to go for my sidearm. I quickly jumped down from the roof, walked up and killed the last two at point blank, executioner style. A dark brown mist permeated the air behind their skulls. I stayed clear of it fearing infection and jumped in the car with John. We skipped shaking hands and John asked me if I wanted to go home. I told him that if we went back there, it would only lead them to us. He agreed. That was when I came up with the plan. I asked John if he could part with his car. John smiled and said, "What's your plan, sailor?"

I told John to keep driving. Those things were following us. I navigated him to a place not far from our homes. I asked John what type of music he had in his car. He was a conservative man. Looking through his CDs, I found what I was looking for. It would be perfect for the job. We made it to the place—a large parking lot next to a run-down factory. We parked the car and I told John to keep it running. I put a CD in, rolled the windows down and opened all the doors. I turned everything on, even the wipers. Then I turned the volume up as loud as it would go without blowing the speakers. John and I grabbed our weapons and headed to a safer rally point a quarter of a mile away from his car.

The *Marriage of Figaro* was filling the air of the parking lot and surrounding area. The mass of the undead finally rounded

the last corner and came into plain view of the car. Their shambling pace quickened as they saw what their glazed white eyes
wanted them to see. They surrounded the car, and took it over.
John and I wasted no more time. Once we saw that our plan
worked, we headed out.

On the way home, I told John that I wasn't sure that even *they*
could survive that music. He laughed and we kept moving. We saw
a dozen of those things as we made our stealthy way back. None of
them detected us. A half a bottle of whiskey later, here I sit. Staring at the bullet I saved for myself . . . —*Is life worth living?*

January 21st

2143 hrs

I have re-gathered my thoughts and recovered from yesterday's
catastrophe and this morning's hangover. John and I have decided that it's better we stay in separate houses because it's "never
good to put all of your eggs in one basket." We don't want both of
us dying because one house is under siege. The events that trans-
pired yesterday really hit me hard. I almost died out there. If John
hadn't found me or had chosen not to, I would have spent days up
there dying of dehydration, listening to the moaning of the dead,
until I decided to end it.

There must have been five hundred dead swarming the car
when John and I left it there in the parking lot. Last night lying
in my bed, I could hear the faint sound of Mozart in the distance
when the wind blew just right. I can't hear it now. I can only
imagine how long it took for the car to run out of gas on idle, and
the battery to drain from everything that I had left on. The streets
are clear now, but there is no way to know for how long. When the
sound stopped drawing them near the car, I am sure they spread
out again. It's only a matter of time until the law of averages puts
them back here.

John and I talked. Last night before we left each other to our
solitude (after the Figaro incident), John ran inside and handed
me a few more packages of batteries for the 2-way radio. I could
tell he wanted to talk. It wasn't until today that I got around to

it. John knew I was messed up. Today I got to know him a little better. John is an engineer (explains his wacky plan with the yoga band). He has a Master's in mechanical engineering from Purdue. Told me that he worked for Execu-Tech.

He expressed his guilt about his son's probable fate, and that he felt like he pressured his son to go to the same college as good ole' dad. I told John that it really wouldn't matter where in the world he was when this happened. Apparently, it's just as bad everywhere.

After the debacle that I witnessed yesterday, I know that not many would or could survive this. I'm down to 884 rounds of .223 ammunition. I think that anything below 500 is critically low considering that they probably out number me thousands to one. Maybe even more. This can't be a battle of attrition, as a pyrrhic victory is not an option.

John and I are meeting tomorrow, providing the street is clear enough. We are going to discuss an exploration attempt and see what type of supplies we can gather. It's quite possible this could be our last few days here. I firmly believe that the government has collapsed. We basically canned the oilrig idea, as it would put us through countless miles of terrain ruled by the dead. When/if we bug out, it's going to have to be both a realistic plan and defensible location.

It would be impossible to close off the neighborhood with those things running around. The only thing I could think of would be to somehow drive a few tractor trailer rigs to each end of the street and use one to pull another trailer over on its side (to prevent them from crawling underneath). Then we could use smaller vehicles to fill in the gaps. This plan is lunacy. Before we even put one semi truck into place the street would be swarming with them. What I wouldn't give for a seaplane with a full tank of juice right now. I wonder how my base is holding up. I bet the gates are still holding. Worst case, the large planes (737s) carried survivors to a safe place long before they got in. I need time to brainstorm. Goodnight journal.

January 22nd

2240 hrs

John is here now. We decided it best to plan in person rather than try to coordinate this effort over the 2-way. He is in the kitchen feeding his dog. John and I are going to attempt to locate an aircraft suitable for flight. We spent the day packing our essentials, and we are going to head out at first light. John is going to leave his dog in the basement with enough food and water for five days. The bonus is she can't be heard if she decides to bark while she is in the basement. I feel sorry for her but this is no world for man's best friend. While I'm out, I'm going to attempt to locate more weapons.

One thing of particular interest that I will be bringing is a car battery jump kit. My car just isn't going to cut it. The plan is to leave in the morning in my car, (since John's car is useless to us now) and immediately look for alternate transportation. Any type of military vehicle would be best. An armored car would be optimal, but the chance of that happening is about the same as monkeys flying out of my ass. I am wondering if the GPS satellites are still functioning without human intervention. If we do happen to find an aircraft, I wouldn't mind having GPS as a backup navigation tool. I plan to keep writing in my journal while I am away. I think that we will be back in three days, nothing further than three hundred miles. We plan on heading to a location near the outskirts of Austin, TX. We won't be going into the city, especially after my fiasco at the convenience store a couple days ago. I still start shaking and smelling gunpowder and sweat when I think of that.

January 23rd

0600 hrs

John and I are off. Change of plans . . . back in two days not three.

1000 hrs

We departed this morning at around 0600. We are currently in Universal City. I packed my car while it was in the garage to avoid any unwanted guests then turned the ignition over, it sputtered but started. There is not much room in the Volvo, so our first mission was to find suitable transportation. We made it to the 1604 loop. I have never seen so much chaos. The road was littered with abandoned vehicles. I used my binoculars to survey the area. Panning the binoculars left to right, what I saw was disturbing. Reminded me of the traffic camera I saw before (seems like weeks ago). Some of those things were trapped inside with seat belts on. It looked like some left their windows down and were attacked and left to re-animate. We found what we were looking for, although the color wasn't ideal.

A canary yellow Hummer H2 was sitting crossways on the loop with the driver's side door open. John and I parked the car out of view, took our weapons and car jump kit, and slowly skirted the knoll near the edge of the 1604 loop. The only movement we could see were a few of them walking around a good distance away and of course the movement of those trapped in the vehicles.

As we neared the H2, I saw something that I will never forget. A car seat strapped in the back. I told John to stay put while I approached. I didn't want him to see this, since I know he is or was a father.

I opened the back door of the vehicle. There it was, a shell of a human infant, writhing in the seat reaching for me. The black circles around its eyes looked like orbs. I wanted to cry as I unfastened the seat and set it on the ground a safe distance away. Just as I sat the car seat down and bent back up, I saw her. A woman, badly disfigured, wearing a pear of jeans and a t-shirt and boots was slowly moving around not more than a few meters up the road.

She caught glimpse of me and started walking toward me. A high shrill moan escaped her decomposing frame. I desperately tried to figure out a way to quietly dispose of her. I knew we were going to have to jump the Hummer (causing noise) because the driver side door had probably been open for days, if not weeks, leaving the dome light on.

She approached slowly and steadily. I looked inside the Hummer. There was a pillow in the passenger seat. I quickly grabbed the pillow, took off my belt and wrapped the pillow around the muzzle of my CAR-15, fastening it tightly with the belt. She was on me so I had no choice but to fire. Just as her gnarling lips curled over her yellow teeth, I pulled the trigger on my carbine.

The weapon made no more noise than popping popcorn as the monster's head exploded in feathers and a dark mist behind her. She was no more. I knelt down to the small infant. I sat there and meditated over what had to be done. I prayed that if there were a god, I would be forgiven. I dispatched the young one with my knife. No further details about that need to be given.

After the previous encounter, I threw the pillowcase over the car seat and signaled John to come over. I didn't see any immediate threat in the area, sans one of them in a car twenty feet away thrashing about. John brought the portable jumper (basically a charged battery with cables to connect to the dead battery). I unfastened the hood restraints, leaned in the driver's door and popped the hood and went back into the car to check for keys. No keys. I sat there and reasoned for a minute.

What happened to the driver of this vehicle? Would he/she be so selfish as to leave their infant to die here at the whim of those things? After careful thought, I realized that maybe the parents didn't leave the infant. Checking the interior of the vehicle, I noticed a pink pine tree air freshener hanging from the rearview mirror. I then looked down on the ground at the ghoul thing that I had just killed. I checked her pockets and found the keys to the H2 as well as her driver's license. Sorry about your baby Ms. Rogers.

I took the keys and tried to turn over the ignition. Just as I thought. Dead. I took the portable jumper and hooked it up while John turned the key. She roared to life. Checked the gas. It was running off fumes. John jumped in the passenger seat and we were off. We did sort of a u-turn and drove back in the direction of my car. On the way up the embankment, I looked in the rear view and I could tell instantly that we had gained some unwanted attention. I would guess a score of them were lumbering toward our vehicle about three hundred yards off. I stopped the Hummer next to my car and quickly loaded the supplies into the back of our new vehicle. We then headed to the nearest location that we could get fuel. John and I knew that the pumps would not work without electricity, so we brought part of a garden hose to siphon the gasoline.

After about two miles of driving and weaving in and out of wrecked traffic, I spotted a side road and took it. We drove for a half a mile before we found a car that was old enough to probably not have an anti-siphoning screen. Its hazard lights were blinking dimly, probably been flashing for weeks. We checked the perimeter and didn't see any threat. I parked the H2 in a position that would make siphoning easier. We drained every drop from the car, but this only put us at half a tank. It would have to do as the gas stations are all closed.

Blue Light Special
Aisle 13

2243 hrs

If there was hell on earth, I found it today. I am thinking about just throwing my camera away, as I don't think anyone would ever want to see these pictures even if mankind somehow survived this ordeal. All I see are images of death and destruction.

I drove most of the way. After we left Universal city, we headed up I-35 toward San Marcos, dodging in and out of cars and those fucking puss sacks. It is taking its toll on me. I have a newfound respect for combat veterans that saw death every day. I don't see how they did it. I could see the smoke over Austin well before we even got to San Marcos. We needed gas, so I took exit 190 and veered off, taking a right into a long-abandoned Wal-Mart parking lot.

John kept a lookout while I relieved myself in the ditch. I did the same for him. We pulled the Hummer near some cars so we could siphon more needed gas. At least this time we found a late 80's model Chevy Blazer that had a full tank. We filled the Hummer up to over 3/4 full. I was sitting somewhere around 880 rounds of .223 and 300 rounds of 9mm. John had two bricks of .22. I approached John and asked him if he felt like doing a little shopping.

The door was locked when we got to the front. I went back to the Hummer to pull it up front and check the tool kit for a pry bar. I found what I was looking for and commenced to try and pry the door from its lock. I got good leverage and put my back into it. John was watching the parking lot to make sure we didn't have any surprises. I kept tugging. All of the sudden I felt a thud on the door. I looked up and much to my chagrin; there he was . . . —A corpse in a bloody blue Wal-Mart vest pawing at the glass door drying to get out. The thing walked right into the door and bumped into the door latch on the inside.

The door came open slightly as the thing tried to ease itself out to us. It poked its head out and I took that opportunity to drive my tire tool into its head through the eye socket, killing it instantly. I held the door open like a gentleman and let the corpse fall out onto the sidewalk. I opened the door fully and placed the trashcan there to keep it open.

I told John that I thought that there were probably more inside. We pulled the Hummer so close to the entrance that no one could get in, and no one could get out unless they went in the driver's side door and climbed out the passenger door. It was my idea in the event some visitors decided to show up during our shopping spree. I showed John how to handle his weapon inside close quarters conditions. I call it the recon glide as I had picked it up from one of my marine friends. John and I eased through the aisles . . . goddamn it . . . why does Wal-Mart always have to put sporting goods in the back?

I motioned to John to look where I was looking. It was another worker that must have been killed during a shift. It slowly walked toward us. I gave John the signal to shoot, because his weapon is much quieter than mine. With a careful aim, John took the creature out and it lay lifeless on the floor.

Thank god for the skylights because without them, this idea could kiss my ass. John and I continued to the back. We made it to sporting goods and found that many of the guns were either sold out or looted. There were many boxes of .223 ammo and also many boxes of twelve gauge shells. There was one gun of particular interest left in the cases; —A Remington 870 twelve gauge pump. I saw fit to break the glass and give it to John since he was lacking in the firepower department. We took the shells and rounds for the carbine, and started to make our escape.

John and I were constantly scanning the aisles for ghouls. Just as I rounded the corner from sporting goods, I was pulled off my feet by a female corpse. I hit the ground hard and felt a tug at my ankle. I felt a hard pinch as the thing tried to bite me through the heel of my combat boots. I gave her a hard kick to the nose and heard the cartilage snap as I hit home. I got up and stepped back, checking my heel for wounds. Thank goodness for Altama boots. She didn't get up, as her back had been broken by a large shelf that had fallen on her probably weeks before. She snarled at me. John took aim . . . I signaled him not to shoot. I walked up to her and brought my heel down on her temple as hard as I could. She was no longer a factor.

We made it to the front and just as I thought, a welcoming committee was there to greet us. I stood and counted thirty of them. John climbed through the window over the driver's seat and I did the same and sat driver. I started the ignition and rolled up my window. We would have been in a pickle if we hadn't wedged the H2 inches from the open door to the store. As we pulled out into the parking lot, I lost all care and just mowed them over. John was busy pulling the stickers and tags off his new Remington.

It was time to find shelter, as the sun was starting to get low. We got on the service road along I-35 north and started to look for a spot to stay. I recommended to John that we find a semi-safe spot and just sleep in the Hummer. He agreed and joked, "The motel six isn't exactly open anyway."

I kept driving, until we reached a small town called "Kyle" just south of Austin. There was a sign that read; —Kyle, Texas "Welcome Home." That was when I noticed the spot. There was a large hay field with a fence around it and no sign of any of those things shambling around. I pulled into the drive and picked up the t-handle that held the gate in place. Motioned John to switch seats and pull through so I could secure the gate again. We pulled the Hummer in between four round bails of hay. The bails covered up the sides of the vehicle so that if anything approached, it would have to do so from the front or the back. John and I made sure all doors were locked, and John went to sleep. It's 2330 now, so I suppose I should do the same.

January 24th

1534 hrs

John and I awoke at 0615 this morning to the sound of a rooster crow in the distance. I started the H2 up and pulled out from between the hay. We pulled over to the gate, and looked down the road from the direction that we came. There were a lot of them in the distance. Couldn't tell if they were heading our way. Could it be possible that they heard our vehicle and were following the sound this far? I hope not.

We arrived at the outskirts of Austin, TX at 0705. The smoke was almost unbearable. Visibility was only at around a hundred yards. Every now and again when the wind would blow just right, I could catch a glimpse of the taller buildings in the distance. One of them looked like a torch, as its tip was burning brightly. To the right I could see what looked like an airport air traffic control tower. John and I took the next road to the right toward the tower.

We made it to the outer perimeter fence. It was a small private airport with a few Cessna aircraft and two small jets sitting inside open hangars. A section of the fence was destroyed so we drove right up onto the tarmac. We surveyed the area and didn't see any immediate danger. I tied off a rope to the front nose wheel of one of the Cessna 172 (picked out the best looking one) and opened the cockpit door. To my surprise, sitting in the passenger seat, I found the aircraft pilot's kneeboard, flight computer and chart.

I climbed in the cockpit and yelled at John to take it slow and easy and to pull us over to the refueling station. I shut the door and concentrated on the checklist so that I could turn the aircrafts electrical system on and check the gauges for fuel or anything out of the ordinary. Every few seconds I felt the aircraft tug, as John towed the aircraft and me to the pumps. After checking the gauges, I was happy to find that both wing tanks were full, so I opened up the door, jumped out and ran ahead to tell John to flip a bitch and pull the bird back to the tower.

At the tower I used the aircraft checklist to do a walk around inspection. I didn't fancy the idea of losing my engine over a heavily infested area. I prepped the bird for flight and discussed with

John our next plan of action. We took out our atlas and looked for the nearest airport to our homes back in San Antonio. I looked and looked and all I could find was the international airport in the center of the city. That was unacceptable.

John bent down and had a puzzled look on his face. He asked me if I had ever been to the "Retama Park Racetrack" off of I-35. He told me we passed it on our way out of town. I had never heard of it since I hadn't lived there long. John asked how much length I needed to land the plane. I went out to the cockpit and looked in the chart compartment. I couldn't find any info. Some of the smaller planes I have flown needed maybe 1,000 ft if I used beta. This bird didn't have beta controls. I had to take a guess. I would probably need 1,500 ft minimum. John said that he thought it might work.

John and I brought our weapons up and carefully approached the tower entry doors. John opened the door and I took point. The elevator was obviously out so we had to take the stairs. We shut and latched the door behind us as we quietly ascended. There were windows at the top of every flight overlooking the runway. I heard and saw nothing until we got to the top of the stairs. I saw a coagulated pool of blood sitting in front of the tower control center door.

I motioned for John to look. I walked up to the door, slowly opened it, and jumped in ready to blast. I didn't expect to see this . . . One of the controllers had taken out four of those things and then probably out of despair had turned his pistol on himself and did the same. I opened up the doors to the observation deck and John and I threw the bodies over the side, opposite the side the aircraft was on.

John and I went back down stairs to unload the H2. We brought everything into the tower just to be careful. I locked up the Hummer and went upstairs to plan.

John expressed to me that he would not leave his dog in the basement to starve to death. I understood. John told me that he would take the H2 and meet me at the racetrack and then we would both go to the house in the H2 together. I would have to fly the bird and land safely at the track. I had many hours in military aircraft, but never in a Cessna. It was going to be risky, but necessary.

I calculated that it would only take me around 35 minutes to do the startup checklist, get airborne and be over the track. This meant that in order to conserve fuel, John was going to have to leave before I did. It was a two-hour trip for him. I showed John my calculations and he agreed it would be best he leave first.

2243 hrs

Dark outside. Only fires can be seen in the distance. Found some airport departure/approach plates for this airstrip. It was a good thing too. Because of the documents, I found out that there is a water tower two hundred feet high off the departure end of the runway. I would never have seen it in time with all the smoke. Now at least I know what general direction to fly when I get off the ground. It's time for sleep now.

January 25th

0700 hrs

It was time to fly the coop, literally. John and I went outside this morning and looked down at the base of the tower. Apparently we had made too much noise. There were ten of them walking around the tower, bumping into it, making metal tapping sounds. I distracted them as John threw the non-breakable supplies to the ground so that we would not have to make multiple trips. John came over to me and handed me his .22. I told him I would take care of them while he consolidated the supplies. Visibility was still only around 100 yards.

I shot the creatures and quickly helped John with the last of the supplies. We made it down the stairs without incident. I took what I needed for the flight, i.e. my guns, some food and water, and left John with the rest. I asked John if he were sure. He said yes. I told him I would meet him at the track at 0930 hours. Last night we took a portable radio from the tower, so John could reach me on 121.5 when we needed to talk. It was the aviation distress frequency. Doubt anyone would mind.

John got in the Hummer and drove off. I got in the aircraft, and locked the doors, and started checking everything I could for the wait. All the smoke in the air and poor visibility must be fucking their senses up. I figured that those gunshots would have attracted more. I am getting scared, and am leaving now . . .

0812 hrs

I'm in the air now. The aircraft is trimmed up (so I can go hands free) and I am headed back to the track. Decided to do a little recon mission since I was in the air so early. This plane is relatively easy to fly. I thought it would be more trouble than this. After taking off, I decided to head toward the base and see if the walls were still intact. I remembered the VOR frequency, dialed it in to the navigation aid and followed the needle. My heart sank as I descended through the clouds at 2,000 feet.

I flew right over the base, as low as I could and saw the horror. Every building was either on fire, or destroyed . . . —Looked like an air strike. That might explain what happened to Austin, TX. I pulled the aircraft around into a shallow fifteen-degree angle of bank and headed toward the gate. The gate was totally destroyed, and through the smoke, I could see thousands of walking dead dominating the landscape inside the base. I then brought the bird on general course to make rendezvous at the track.

2356 hrs

I am home.
    Don't feel like writing.
    The dead are the lucky ones.

Hindsight Is 20/20

Yesterday was a hard day. I made it to the track with plenty of fuel to spare. The fence was intact and there were no creatures present. Looked like I was going to have enough room to land, but noticed that the track was uneven and it looked like about a ten-degree grade. I was going to have to show some good aileron control to keep both wheels solid when I landed.

I came over the northern end of the track at 85 knots. Pulled back power, flared, touched the back two wheels . . . eased the elevator control and brought the nose down. Pulled power back to idle, and let her roll to a stop (no breaks, since the track was dirt). Looked down at my kneeboard and flipped the pages to the engine shutdown checklist, I shut her down after I taxied her to a less visible spot on the back end of the track.

Now came the waiting game. It was 0930 when I set down. I didn't see the H2 anywhere, and it would be difficult to miss a canary yellow H2 even at two miles visibility. If John came, he would see the bird, and know I was near. I decided to try and find something to cover the plane up with so it would be less noticeable to anyone . . . living or dead. This was a racetrack, so I was sure there is some type of tarp somewhere. I took my rifle and headed for the maintenance area. Outside the chain link fence of the track, there were numerous undead walking around. Some of them were rapping on the fence, angry at their inability to walk through it. I knew that if enough of them came, they would do just that.

I approached the maintenance area with caution. I stood in front of the steel door and listened . . . I could hear the sound of banging metal. Sounded like someone was using a hammer on the floor inside . . . My philosophy has always been stealth over confrontation. I walked around the building looking for windows. I found one in the rear, about eight feet off the ground. The only problem was that there was a corpse shambling about on the opposite side of the fence. It couldn't get to me, but I concluded that it would make a lot of noise if it saw me. Window was a "no go." I quietly hugged the wall back to the door.

The sound had stopped. This was really fucking with my head. I couldn't take it anymore so I eased the door open and looked inside. It was dark, except for the spear of light shining in through the window that I had seen. I could smell rotting flesh.

I shut the door again. My instincts told me, fuck the plane cover; it's not that important. For some reason I ignored that completely logical thought process. I took out my LED light and tightened it on the light mount of my rifle. I switched the light on and opened the door again. Put the muzzle of my weapon in so that I could light up the dark garage. The smell was almost unbearable.

The source of the noise became immediately apparent. A dead mechanic, crushed by a hydraulic lift was lying there on his back, re-animated, and banging a torque wrench on the ground. A low grunt came from his badly mutilated body as he tried to look up at me. He was reaching for me. It was then, *all in the span of a second* that the following happened:

I saw the bite marks of the flesh that had been torn away on his face and neck. I knew that he didn't do it to himself, and deduced that there was another dead fucking corpse in the room. Last but not least, the door flew open and I was tackled by one of them (best guess, the same one that had the mechanic for lunch).

The only thing that was keeping this stink ridden shit ball from biting my nose off was the fact that I had my weapon wedged between us. I pushed it off, and it (couldn't tell male or female) grabbed my wrist. I gave it a nice rifle butt to the head and it fell back. I immediately got to my feet and popped a round in its miserable head. I wanted to just fucking mow it in half, but the reasonable half of me kicked in and I told myself not to waste the ammunition.

The door to the garage was shut, and it was going to fucking stay that way. I could hear the sound of fists on the door, and I knew that there were more inside. I went back on the side of the garage where I saw some oil drums and rolled one of them back around to the front, to put in the doorway and prevent whatever was behind that door from opening it and ruining my day.

No more exploring. I carefully started walking back toward the plane. I noticed that I had gathered an entourage of fans on the other side of the fence. I guess they enjoyed my little execution. They were gnashing their teeth on the metal wire and groaning and beating on the chain link fence. Watching this motley crew of gray evil made me very uneasy.

About that time, I heard a vehicle approaching. I hid behind one of the concession stands and watched. The ugly yellow confirmed my suspicions. It was John. I ran up to the gate to let him in. It was locked.

Reluctantly, I pulled the carbine up to fire, aiming for the part that touched the chain and not the actual lock . . . Three rounds and the lock fell off the chain. I was thinking to myself that shooting locks only worked in movies as I yanked the chain off and pulled the gate open. John came screaming through. I quickly shut the gate, wrapped the chain back around the gate and ran over to the aircraft. I remembered seeing a c-clamp in the cockpit clamped to a headset. I quickly unscrewed it and ran back toward the gate. There were a few of them already within a rock throw. I put the c-clamp through both ends of the chain and tightened it down. Wouldn't stop a living person, but I doubt these miserable shells of human beings could figure it out.

I walked back over to the plane where John was parked. I looked at him. His cheek was bleeding. I asked him what happened. He told me that he had to make a stop to siphon some gas and ended up having to shoot three of those dead people. He killed the first one and on the second shot, he missed and the round ricocheted off a concrete embankment, hitting him in the cheek. He killed the last one and got the fuck out of there. Luckily he was finishing up the siphoning when this happened.

When I first saw him, I thought he had been bitten or scratched and my only friend in the world was going to be one of "them."

I told John that I probably had about two hours worth of fuel left, (roughly 190 nautical miles at max cruise speed of 95 knots).

. . .

The plane was ready to fly. John and I decided it best to leave the plane and head home to figure things out from there. We were only maybe a twenty-minute drive from home. I collected my things out of the plane and put them in the Hummer. We were going to have to distract those things if were going to get back out the way John drove in.

I walked over to the gate, and got their attention. I used myself as bait (they were on the other side of the fence) and lured them to follow me while John got ready to make the escape in the Hummer. They followed me to the other end of the fence. This gave me two hundred yards to sprint back, open the gate, get in, drive through, get out and shut the gate back. No problem. It went exactly like that. John and I drove toward our home, dodging, surviving.

This was becoming second nature. John took a back street when we got to my neighborhood, and parked the vehicle in an empty building lot. We took our weapons, and essentials, and made like shadows back to John's. We avoided being seen by few of those things along the way. We jumped John's wall, and he rushed in to check on his dog, and I secured the rest of the house. His dog came running upstairs, jumping up on John and licking his face. I told John that since I had power we should use my house as a base. After all, if were going to die, might as well be together. It's funny how attitudes change.

Today, we spent moving John's gear over here, one trip at a time, avoiding being seen. I had a feeling we would be taking to the air sometime in the nearer future.

January 27th

1713 hrs

I'm glad John is an engineer. He thought of a way to make an alarm device that could save us in a pinch. We thought of it today when we had to go out and quietly put down one of *them* that was beating loudly on my back gate. I killed it with an ice pick taped to a metal pipe with duct tape. It was then that John asked me what I thought of his plan. He wanted to wire a battery-powered radio to the mailbox of a house two doors down. He said that he had quite a bit of wire in his basement and that it would work. We slipped over to his house to gather some supplies and the wire. His basement was full of Annabelle dung.

He took his battery powered alarm clock radio and the wire, and a simple light switch (that we cannibalized from his house), and made a sort of remote alarm. Our thinking was that if those things got the jump on us in the night, and there were too many of them, we could flip the switch, turn on the radio and use the noise to draw them to the mail box across the street and a few doors down.

John wired it so that the radio/alarm would fit inside the mailbox, thus using the metal box as an amplifier. We tried it out for a second, and it was definitely loud enough, although we had to use the alarm function, as there were no more stations broadcasting. We wrapped the wire around the pillar of the box, and tucked it along the curb out of sight. The problem came when we had to get it across the street and into my wall for easy access. We brought the wire across the street and John and I took shovels and piled dirt over it so that those things would have a hard time tripping over it and yanking the connection loose. All in all, it was over 100 yards of wire.

I mounted the light switch for the alarm to a junction box using a kitchen magnet.

I will be spending most of the night figuring out where to go next. We might end up staying here for a while, but then again, the mood I was in yesterday might take over.

After our little invention was complete, I used my binoculars to check on the Hummer. From my vantage point, I could only see from the side view mirrors to the front. I could see 3–4 of them curiously wandering around it. I made sure to take a mental note of this.

247 nm
32 nm
———
279 nm

January 28th

2039 hrs

While monitoring the citizen band today, I made a startling discovery. I intercepted a recording being transmitted out on CB channel nine for survivor volunteers to be members of the "new military." The broadcast was a recorded loop dated yesterday. The recording was calling for responses at the top of every hour. Something didn't sound right. If this was a band of leftover military and they were calling out for replacements, what happened to the original members? Slain? Executed? No chances. I turned it off until about ten minutes shy of 1800 hours. I then listened in for any others out there that might volunteer.

*"**static**, Shane Stahl here, Concord, Texas.*
Anyone there?"

"Yes, this is Captain Thomas Beverly formerly of the 24th
special tactics squadron, it's good to hear your voice."

The conversation went on, and the two exchanged information and decided upon an extraction point not far from "Shane's" house, near a water tower off the interstate. John and I discussed this new development, and decided it best to continue monitoring and gathering information, until it could be discerned that this rogue group was in fact a benign group of leftover volunteers.

Spent much of this morning reading over the aircraft manuals and emergency procedures. I wanted to be knowledgeable of this aircraft's systems the next time I took her up, just in case.

John and I discussed numerous destinations for our next outing. We had one of two options. Continue to stay here, and hope we don't get overrun, or take the bird and what we can fit inside and head southeast to the islands off the coast of Corpus Christi. There is a Naval air station in Corpus, and I'm sure there is plenty of fuel, and maybe even a better aircraft.

If we chose the bug out option, careful consideration would have to be given as to what equipment stays and what goes with us in the plane. John and I have a combined weight of 360 lbs.

Add fuel and luggage to that, and we can only afford to fly with four hundred pounds of supplies. That was also pushing it, and that wasn't much when you added it all up. We began to make a list of things we absolutely could not leave. John listed, "dog, 20 lbs." I told John, not to worry, Annabelle was coming with us.

We wouldn't be leaving today, or tomorrow for that matter. I told John that I did not wish to die on my birthday.

January 29th

1250 hrs

A group of bikers came roaring through our neighborhood thirty minutes ago. John had to put the muzzle on Annabelle to keep her from barking. I doubt they would hear the bark over the roar of their engines, but my motto is "no chances." I counted 70–80 bikes as the convoy rolled past. Many bikes had passengers. Most bikes had long rifle/shotgun holsters mounted on them complete with weapon.

I noticed something that I don't think you would have seen before this epidemic. There weren't just cruisers, there were also racing bikes (crotch rockets) in the convoy. I bet they used the racers as recon scouts. Again this group looked rough and I didn't see it necessary to alert them to our presence.

1847 hrs

The sound of moaning, shuffling dead is almost unbearable. Three hours after the bike convoy came through, the creatures that were no doubt following them began their slow parade into the neighborhood. John and I are maintaining our silence. In the fading light there are too many of them to count. This could easily turn into the worst-case scenario. I do not think that they are alerted to our presence, but I cannot be sure. I can see them periodically looking in this direction, and walking into my wall, but I do not know if they are trying to get in, because of the noise.

I went to my gun cabinet and pulled out two sets of yellow foam earplugs and handed one to John. I told John that if we had to make a break for it tomorrow, we were going to need our rest. John stuck them in his pocket and nodded.

2213 hrs

We got our things ready just in case we had to make the great escape. Many of the ghouls have continued on their path in the direction of the bikers. Many more undead are seemingly lost and confused and have camped out here on our street, just walking around bumping each other and changing directions. It reminds me of my college physics class years ago. The molecules were bumping into each other in unpredictable patterns and just milling about on the slide. I would say a safe estimate puts the count at 85 walking dead. I can only go off the moon and starlight for my estimations.

Note to self: Find some NVGs most ricky-tick.

If today were a normal day, my fellow squadron officers and I would be getting shit faced at a random bar on the river walk. It was my birthday and I know they wouldn't allow me to stay inside like this. Well, I guess the celebration would have to wait. I had a shot of whiskey with John and toasted to survival. Goodnight.

Proverbial Beans

Bad news. While monitoring the television, and radio, John and I came across the first government broadcast in weeks. It was being transmitted over every available TV channel as well as over the AM bands. I think this might be because AM carries further than FM. It was the First Lady. In a solemn voice she relayed to what was left of the United States that the President had perished in an undead attack and died a week earlier. The armed forces were now in the control of the Vice President. She went on to say that the VP was in a secure location and that she hoped the best for America and the world.

She warned of rogue military factions that had deserted over the past weeks, and hoped that they would come to their senses and return to fight for their fallen Commander-In-Chief.

She saved the best for last.

She asked that anyone able to hear the following announcement, to do their best to spread the word, as she was sure that not many survivors had electricity, or access to a TV or radio.

She then spilled the proverbial beans.

"The President has authorized the use of *tactical nuclear warheads* on all major cities. On *February the first* at approximately 10:00 AM Central Standard Time, a strike force consisting of Joint Navy/Air Force bombers will deploy high yield tactical nuclear warheads on major urban centers. We believe that this retaliation strike will give us the advantage we so desperately need to take back our country and eventually our world. The use of our Global Hawk and Predator UAV drones has revealed major populations of the undead in and around the targeted cities. If you are able to travel, and can hear this message, I urge you to *make preparations to evacuate.* We will now broadcast the list of designated target areas. Please look closely at the bottom of the television screen."

I could now see tears rolling down her face.

Nope, she wasn't bullshitting. They were going to do it. I watched and crossed my fingers. I knew my city was the 8th largest in the United States. I didn't kid myself. As the "letter R" cities rolled by, John and I held our breath. There it was . . . —San Antonio. John and I have been designated as a nuclear target. I live eighteen miles from the Alamo. The Alamo is in the center of San Antonio. The blast radius would be at least twenty miles, depending on the warhead. I bet they weren't taking any chances, meaning the blast radius would probably be more like fifty miles.

The instant that thought crossed my mind; I watched as the doomed cities rolled by on the bottom of the screen, a precautionary tutorial was being displayed. "Minimum safe distance is 150 miles from ground zero." This would mean that the government is using their mountain buster nukes and are pulling all stops.

I looked over at John and said, "I think it is time we thought about leaving this place."

January 31st

2341 hrs

Situation is not improving. John and I loaded up the Hummer for our trip to the racetrack. We will be flying out tonight. The moon is out so visibility will be great for flying. The text on the emergency broadcast is warning survivors that bombers will be dropping electronic sound decoys in the center of the designated cities to draw the undead in so that they will maximize the effectiveness of the explosion. The warning also made sure to mention that this would cause much more activity within the dead ranks. The jets flew overhead today at around noon and dropped their payload. I know it must be loud if I can here it from this far. It is sort of a high-pitched, oscillating whine. Annabelle doesn't like it but she is getting used to it, despite her hackles being perpetually raised.

It's hard to believe January will be over in a few minutes. John and I had to use our "mailbox sound device" today while loading the H2. This was a couple hours after the military dropped the sound decoy. The things were coming out of the woodwork and many of them were milling around our street. We made four trips until the things destroyed John's noisy invention. One of them finally yanked it out of the mailbox and used it as a bludgeon, denting the mailbox top. We loaded everything up and it's almost time to leave. It's dark outside and I have turned the lights off so that when we leave, our natural night vision will be already adjusted. John and I will be flying east in our small aircraft. I have studied the manuals over and over. Not much else to do besides count down hours.

I think we may be a little overweight on the bird. Oh well. I will get her in the air. Ten hours until the end of the world.

Nuclear Winter

The three of us (including Annabelle) slipped out the back last night and made for the Hummer. Our eyes were adjusted. Apparently Annabelle's were also as she warned us of a ghoul lurking in the shadows. John told me he felt the hair stand up on her back (he was carrying her) and we could both hear her quiet barks through the muzzle. I dispatched the creature with an aluminum bat and continued on to our vehicle. There were a few lurking around behind the vehicle, but they were a safe distance away and we were able to make it inside. Even through the window we could hear the oscillating whine of sound decoys. The unearthly moans of the dead in the distance seamed to rise over even the decoys.

The drive to the racetrack was pretty much uneventful. I drove slowly and kept my headlights off. Other than the occasional thump, of one of those things off my fender, there was nothing. The moonlight showed me the way.

We pulled up to the chain link gate that led to the track. I turned on my headlights and the c-clamp was still there just as I left it. My rifle and me exited the Hummer and went over to the gate and unlatched the clamp. Although I didn't see any of them around, I could smell them and sense their presence in the distance.

After pulling the Hummer in, I reattached the c-clamp. A hundred yards off I could faintly see the outline of one of the undead. No matter. It would take at least a hundred of them to breach the fence.

69

John and I unloaded the Hummer and packed up the Cessna. I performed the preflight checklist and got her ready to take to the air. I got in the cockpit and performed the engine start checklist. She started with no difficulty. Checked the fuel pressure and quantity and it was all in the green. John and I both latched our exterior doors and I turned on my landing/takeoff lights. It was then that I had remembered my gruesome discovery a few days before, the poor mechanic that been crushed under a lift and dined upon.

I also remembered my encounter with one of them, and how I killed it and put a 55 gallon oil drum in front of the door to keep whatever else was in there from getting out.

My landing lights were pointing at the garage door. The door was wide open; the barrel was tipped over on its side. It was at that time the garage's mystery resident showed itself. A loud thump on the pilots side window and then the thing was there . . . drooling and pressing its lips to the cockpit glass like one of those algae suckers in a fish tank. It scared the shit out of me. I can't believe I forgot about the garage until I was in the plane. That could have been my demise. I started to taxi to my takeoff area; —The thing was shuffling after the plane. I tried to avoid hitting it with my propeller, as I didn't want to risk any damage.

I pushed the throttle to full power, and fed a rich mixture of fuel to the engine. We started to lurch forward. My anti-collision strobes were making the stadium look like it was in a thunderstorm. I looked in my rearview mirror and could see two ghouls inside the perimeter shuffling toward me.

50 knots . . . 60 knots . . . 75 knots . . . I pulled the controls back and started to climb. It was going to be close. The engine strained as I put her at max blast. I could almost swear that I felt my main landing gear touch one of the bleachers as I cleared the top row of seats.

We were airborne, and flying SSE in the direction of Corpus. Earlier, before we left for the Hummer, John and I checked the TV/Radio and checked it twice to make sure that there wasn't a nuke on its way there with our names on it. The same cities were scrolling across the bottom of the screen. I guess Corpus just wasn't big enough. Damn, I know they have enough nukes . . . but somehow I bet they were running low on pilots to drop them.

En route, we could make out the faint signs of headlights on the interstate. I wondered if it were other survivors evacuating. I could do no good and would probably get both John and I killed if we attempted to land on or near the interstate.

I was flying at 7,000 feet in accordance with Visual Flight Rules (VFR) out of habit. Somehow, I don't think an airborne collision is likely since I'm probably the only manned prop plane in the air in all of North America. I'm certain that there were probably several Predator drones patrolling the skies, giving status reports on the multiplying dead below. Halfway to Corpus I saw something I didn't expect . . . —Lights, actual electric lights. Yes, fires were commonplace since we took off, but not electricity.

According to my charts we were approaching "Beeville, TX." There was a small municipal airstrip there. I checked my fuel, and knew it would be close, so John and I decided to buzz the airport, since it had lights and see if we could land safely. I was flying southeast above I-37 when I broke off for Beeville municipal airport. Miraculously, the GPS satellites were still working and I keyed the coordinates into the GPS (28-21.42N / 097-47.27W). The green LCD was pointing in the same direction that I was headed so I knew I was on course.

We arrived at the airstrip about eight minutes later, just like the GPS indicated and I lowered my altitude to 800 feet, to check the runways. The runways ran NW to SE. I decided to flyby runway 12, since the wind would favor my landing there. The directional beacons were still on, so I knew I could make the landing as long as there wasn't something parked on the tarmac. After one flyby, I brought her around for a landing. On my first pass, I saw a fuel truck sitting next to the taxiway.

I landed the plane, and taxied over to the fuel truck. I left the plane running and walked around the back toward the truck. My rifle was at the ready in case anything was to go wrong. I turned my LED light on and its bright beam illuminated the area around the truck. I forgot to turn off the anti-collision strobes when I got out of the plane, so they were flashing brightly, giving me snapshots of the area every two seconds.

I walked over to the hose, pulled it off the rung and checked the pressure on the fuel pump. Looks like it was never shut off. No matter, it wouldn't drain the battery unless it was constantly pumping. There was enough fuel in this truck to fly cross-country two or three times. Too bad I couldn't take it all. I walked over and unlatched the fuel cap on the wing with a wood block that was inside the door. I didn't want to take any chances with spark. I normally wouldn't leave the engine running to refuel, but hey, I wasn't taking any chances of this bird not wanting to start. I filled the tanks up until some of it started splashing out on the wing. I returned the hose to its cradle on the fuel truck and started to walk back. I couldn't hear anything over the engines. As I walked back to the plane, John was frantically trying to signal me. He jumped out and started running toward me. I turned around and instinctively raised my weapon. Good timing.

I squeezed off a round and decapitated the creature from pretty much point blank . . . Glad I had John with me, because this seven-foot puss sack was the right height to bend down and just take a hunk out of my neck before I knew what hit me. The thing was just a convulsing maggot pie on the ground now. John shot me a worried glance and got back in the bird with Annabelle. She didn't like flying, and puked twice since we took off.

Got back into the air and continued for Corpus. Checking the chart, Corpus was 144 miles from San Antonio. We needed 150 miles safe distance. It was 0315 when we were back airborne. That meant 6 hrs and 45 minutes until they dropped their payload. An hour after taking off from Beeville, we were over Corpus airspace. Our destination would be the Naval Air Station east of the city. It would give us our minimum safe distance. Naval Air Station Corpus Christi is a training base. The aircraft there would be of no tactical importance, just single engine reliable training turboprops.

The lights were still on at the Naval base. They must be using an onsite generator. Most bases have alternate sources of power in the event of enemy attack on the power grid. As I flew over the base, destruction was apparent. The base perimeter was destroyed and there were hundreds of them on the base. Same routine . . . checked the airfield. The tower beacon was still operational and flashing its white/blue signal.

The lights inside the tower were on and I could see no movement inside the airfield perimeter as I made my pass (there was a separate fence for the airfield and admin/tower buildings). I could see 50 or 60 single engine prop aircraft on the taxiways parked. T-34c Turbo mentors, and T-6 Texans made up the bulk of them. That was more like it. I was familiar with the T-34c, and I knew they all had parachutes (unlike the Cessna). John and I decided to land near the tower and use it as shelter for the night. We landed the plane and quickly shut the engine down near the tower so as to avoid attracting too many of them. The door to the tower was unlocked but it was shut. Just as I suspected, the tower was abandoned. No sign of life or death inside. John and I took our food/water and weapon and ammo inside for the night, locking the door behind us. It was a heavy steel door and I knew it would hold.

Ground Zero

John and I finally got to sleep around 0540 this morning. The tower was clean and quiet and safe, and that felt good. I set the alarm on my watch for 0930, to give me thirty minutes of prep time for the show. We turned on the radio; the same message was being looped from the other day. Around 1005 I knew it happened. The blast wave must have been traveling at immense speed. The wind picked up and I could see the trees blowing toward the east, not swaying. My eyes were trained northwest toward the direction of San Antonio. I saw it. It was small from this distance, but it was there.

We witnessed a bright orange mushroom cloud on the horizon. Damn, they must have really dropped the big one for me to see and feel the wind from over 150 miles. It was a clear, calm day. I knew the wind would not be radioactive from this distance, but the force that pushed the wind was. I just hope that the gas cloud didn't drift this way.

I noticed something else that was odd. Houston was northeast of me. John was checking that direction. There was no blast. Granted it was 217 miles away. Just odd. I wondered if they were running late.

The tower has electricity, water pressure and radios. I think I am going to stay here and ponder what just happened.

February 2nd

1435 hrs

I woke up this morning and grabbed the binoculars to survey the area. The first thing I checked was the windsock. It was blowing west. That was good news. I wouldn't be glowing in the dark today. The airfield was secure. All Naval air stations have eight-foot high chain link fences to keep unauthorized personnel off of the flight line. There were numerous dead around the perimeter in the distance. They were paying no attention to the fence; they were just there.

Annabelle was whining. John was monitoring the radios, so I decided to take her out (it was the "I have to pee" whine). Walked her down the stairs and took her out to a patch of grass on the side of the tower opposite the runways. She did her business and sniffed the air. She is a small dog, but she has a good sniffer. The hair on the back of her neck was standing up again. I took her back upstairs and shut the door to the tower behind me. The tower had a 360-degree view, so I walked around the center over to the grassy side to see maybe if I could catch a glimpse of what was pissing her off.

There was nothing. It is probably the wind carrying a bad smell to her. She was happy again, and I poured her some water and gave her some dog food. John was wearing headphones, listening. In the control towers everyone used headsets because it would be chaos if every radio played out loud. John was clearly listening to something besides static. I walked over to his panel, checked his frequency and went to another terminal to listen.

There were two pilots talking to each other. One of them asked the other if they had both made the best decision. They must have been near our tower, or we wouldn't pick them up. They probably thought they had all the privacy in the world right now. As far as they knew, no one was alive to listen to them in this area. I wondered what they meant. Were these the same pilots that dropped the nukes? My question was soon answered. As their conversation went on, I discovered that these pilots refused to drop their ordnance. They didn't see it as a good decision, so instead of following their orders, apparently they chose exile.

I really can't blame them. They were human, just like me. I am not sure I could have dropped it either. I wonder which cities were spared. My guess was that one of them was Houston, or maybe even Austin, although the San Antonio blast might have taken care of them.

John and I couldn't carry all of our food and water on the plane with us. Water wasn't a problem right now, but I would say in a couple weeks food would be. Last night the fire to the northwest was bright. Every thing that could burn was probably burning. I bet my house was nothing but dust now.

2143 hrs

After rummaging through the tower, John and I came across a large aluminum case with a master lock attached. We were able to pry it open with a set of bolt cutters from the maintenance closet one flight down. The case was a foam padded equipment case used to store night vision goggles. There were four sets inside, monocular type, using civilian AA batteries. I should have known. Tower controllers use them at night to warn pilots of obstructions on the runway. Most military airfield towers have them. Now John and I had them. They were shit for depth perception, but hey, I felt better with them.

I tried them out. John and I turned off all interior lights. I adjusted the focus and starlight power. The airfield was bathed in a green glow. These were going to be really useful. I could even see field mice scurrying on the runway, near the planes. Tomorrow, I'm going to go out and check the planes for myself.

February 3rd

1523 hrs

I went out this morning to check on a few of the aircraft and pick out the best one in case John and I had to leave. These turboprops were much more reliable than the Cessna, and I at least had some hours in them. I knew they were all in working order, but I carefully screened the one I thought looked the most maintained. It was aircraft number 07. John and I are going into the hangars today to find some equipment.

While I was out this morning, I carefully walked the perimeter fence staying clear of areas where they were lurking on the opposite side. It was a big airfield. On the ground, using my binoculars, I could see movement inside one of the administration buildings on the third floor. Alive? Not sure. I quietly moved back to the tower and alerted John of my find. I was starting to think that the only way to defeat these monsters was to just wait them out. It was like a long prison sentence.

I hadn't thought about my parents for a long time. My hopes weren't too high as to their fate. I thought about taking one of the birds and landing it in a field near my home just so I could get some closure. I could never ask John to come along. It was just a passing thought.

February 4th

~~1447~~ *1447 hrs*

We fueled one of the T-34s up. Checked the engine, showed John how to work the APU (auxiliary power unit). The T-34c can perform a battery start; it's just best to start it from the external gas powered auxiliary unit. After this, John and I locked Annabelle in the tower and got ready to check out the hangar for any equipment that we may need.

John and I were getting adept at this. He would open the door and I would clear the room. It was a ghost town inside the hangar. John and I edged our way to a room marked, "flight equipment maintenance." The door was halfway open and the lights were on inside. I rushed into the room, weapon ready. I almost shot a dummy that was standing there modeling its flight gear. To small for me, but looked like it would fit John.

After clearing the room, and shutting the door, (just in case) I told John to strip the dummy and try on the flight suit and helmet. I grabbed a helmet off the "maintenance completed" rack and walked over to the test radio to test the boom microphone. It worked fine. We grabbed a couple survival vests, equipped with the bare essentials, as well as one of the wooden model T-34s that might prove useful if I had to explain how something worked to John. There were also sets of keys marked "fuel truck key" hanging on a rack.

After getting back to the tower, I started showing John the basics of flight. I used some flight manuals and the wooden model to give him some idea on avionics and how aircraft control surfaces work. I asked John if he would like to go up and check things out, sort of a recon mission. He agreed and we suited up.

1932 hrs

John and I took off around 1545. We flew northwest at over 200 knots to survey the blast damage. It only took us 40 minutes to get to the outskirts, and that was close enough. The city was rubble. We were at high altitude (over 10,000 ft) to avoid any residual radiation. Decided it best to head back. As soon as we were out of danger we dropped down to an altitude of 2,000 feet. It was a clear day and the sun was at our back. We followed the interstate.

John asked me to roll us over so he could get a good look at the ground. I rolled over about 30-degrees. John and I gazed down to the interstate. These things were making a mass exodus out of the city. I wondered how effective the nukes were on those not in the immediate vicinity. I doubt radiation has any effect on the creatures. Only the heat from the blast could have destroyed them. Minimum safe distance for a living human being would be 150 miles, but not for them. I bet they could survive within twenty miles.

John snapped a digital of the "ghoul's retreat" from the city. We touched down, just as the sun was starting to set, and taxied back to our parking spot near the tower. It truly was a dead place. We saw no sign of life, only thousands and thousands of them walking the landscape. The lights of Corpus Christi would eventually lead them to the city.

February 5th

2201 hrs

They are increasing in number at the west side of the fence. That side is approximately 1/4 of a mile from the tower. Using night vision goggles, I can see them shambling in the distance. The green grainy image is very surreal and disturbing. John and I turned the lights off when we noticed them earlier today. I have a feeling they are the first wave, pushed out of the major cities. Damn, a Geiger counter would have been a good Christmas gift last year. No more frivolous trips in the aircraft. Don't want them getting worked up. I'm going on a scouting mission tonight to the admin building where I saw movement the other day. I have the advantage of night vision, so I think I will be fine. Plus, I need batteries.

February 6th

0430 hrs

I went alone last night to the admin building. John stayed back in the tower. As soon as I left the top floor of the tower, I shut the door and switched to NVGs. The familiar green, grainy image faded in. It made me feel invisible. The building was a good three hundred yards from the tower. I took my rifle for a main weapon, and the Glock for backup. Only took 58 rounds of .223 for the carbine (29 rounds in each magazine). I wasn't heading out to fight a war, just to scavenge. I also took some heavy-duty black zip ties and some rope that I found in the tower. For some reason, I don't think the "me" of a month ago would have left the tower tonight. In the back of my mind, I keep thinking . . . what is left to live for?

Carefully approaching the front door to the administration building, I began to methodically check the windows for movement. Because of the NVGs limitations, I couldn't see inside the windows until I was close enough to almost hit the building with a thrown rock. I couldn't tell what was moving up on the third floor. I thought for a second that it could be the shadow of an oscillating fan, backlit by a hall light of some sort. That is what I wanted it to be. I was at the front door. It was unlocked. Carefully stepping in,

I listened for any possible sound. Reminded me of all the hearing tests I had to take in the military. It was quiet, like a soundproof room inside. After stepping through the second set of doors, I walked into the center of the room and noticed a large staircase that I assume led up to the second and third floors. I took another step and heard a loud crunch beneath my feet. I stepped on a piece of broken glass . . . an especially loud piece. It was then that I started hearing it.

Sounded like a group of four or five on the floors above me. Low moaning and slow moving feet could be heard moving over the debris above. I knew what it was. They had heard me, and they wanted to come downstairs and dine on my flesh. I quickly spun around and headed back toward the door. Behind me, I heard the sound of one (or more) of them falling down the stairs. Sounded like a garbage bag full of wet leaves.

I sprinted as fast as I could for the door. After making it through the first set of double doors, I quickly pulled out a couple large black zip ties and secured the door. I ran through the next door (outside door) and did the same. They were hard plastic, and I knew they would only slow them down. I put four of them on this door. Just as I was stepping away, they broke through the interior door and started banging on the door I had just secured. I started running back to the tower. I heard the loud, frustrated thuds as I made my escape.

Then the loud crash of shattered glass. I looked over my shoulder and saw one of them falling out of a third floor window. All the noise must have excited it. I made it to the tower, and ran up the stairs to the top door where John and I were staying. I knocked and yelled through to John to dim the lights and put on his NVGs. After seeing that the crack below the door went dark, I stepped inside to see if the fallen ghoul had chased me.

No sign of it. The door was locked below. I would hear if it tried to gain entrance. We are safe for now.

1534 hrs

John was listening to the radios (he has become depressed over the death of his wife the past few days), and scanning channels when he called me over to check something out. He told me that there was something crawling under one of the planes, but he couldn't see it anymore. I grabbed the binoculars and scanned the area that John was pointing at. It was the corpse that had fallen out of the window last night. It was pulling itself with its arms. Its legs were being dragged motionlessly behind it. I didn't like the idea of going out there and killing it and it wasn't bothering anything right now.

February 7th

1826 hrs

Movement . . . John and I noticed it a few hours ago. From my angle, I couldn't tell if the admin building door had stayed secure with the zip ties. More of them were gathering on the west end of the fence. Went out to check the plane and make sure it was ready for flight if we needed it to be. I couldn't park the plane too close to the tower after our scouting trip to the city, because of the soft wet grass from a recent rain.

I had to park the plane a good two hundred yards from the tower so it was a trek to go and check on it. I snuck to the plane without incident. I didn't see the crawling ghoul anywhere around. This fenced area was huge and it could be anywhere. The fuel truck was about fifty yards further than the plane. I started walking toward it, and then I saw them. The angle I was standing before blocked my view of them. I counted ten inside the perimeter fence walking around the blind side of the admin building. They didn't see me, but they would see the truck if I tried to pull it to the aircraft to refuel it. My stomach ached at the thought of refueling the aircraft in the dark, but it had to be done.

2100 hrs

I grabbed the NVGs and spare fuel truck keys that John and I found a couple of days earlier, and went out in the dark to refuel the plane. Weapon ready, I slowly glided across the airfield to the fuel truck, this time taking a different angle so that I could see the admin building. No sign of them. Made it to the fuel truck and climbed up to the window and looked inside, (JIC). It was clear. Opened up the door, put it in neutral. I had never tried to push a truck this big, and now I know why. You can't. I was going to have to start the engine. I assume the creatures couldn't see in the dark, but I knew they would hear me.

Reluctantly, I took the key from my pocket and put it in the ignition . . . I hesitated and then cringing I pushed in the clutch, held the brake and turned the key. After turning it over twice, the engine came to life and I popped the clutch and shot over to the aircraft. On the way, I hit the pump controls inside the vehicle so they would be ready when I jumped out.

Parked the truck, jumped out and started walking toward the plane. I could make out something moving in the grass a hundred yards away. I adjusted the sensitivity on my goggles and saw it. It was the gimpy ghoul in the grass pulling itself toward the tower. I would have to take care of it on my way back.

Then came the blinding flash of John's flashlight through my NVGs from the tower. It was Morse code, to be sure.

B...E...H...I...N...D...

I swung around to see six of them working their way around the fuel truck. I had no choice. I readied my carbine and ran to the aircraft. I jumped up on the wing and started shooting at them. I took out two of them, and missed another.

I was careful not to shoot at the two that were in direct line of sight between the fuel truck and myself. I had two more to take down before I had to carefully handle the other two. Shot another in the head. Its forehead opened up like a spring flower.

The flash from my muzzle was really playing hell in my night vision. I had to adjust the intensifier; it was much darker through the lens as I took down the fourth ghoul with a head and neck shot. There were two more. The two (that were risky to shoot) closed in. They were at the plane. Trying to climb up on the wing. I shot one in the shoulder throwing it off. The other one almost grabbed my boot before I dispatched it with another headshot.

The last wounded ghoul got back on its feet and raised its

arms like a deranged Frankenstein as it came at me. I jumped off the wing opposite the monster and watched it as it started walking around the aircraft toward me. It was dark, and the thing just kept running into the wing and empennage of the aircraft. I carefully aimed, so as to avoid damage to the bird and let one shot ring out. The jaw tore away from the face, letting the orphaned tongue hang freely. Even in the limited color perception I had with the goggles, it was a disgusting sight. It slumped back and kept coming at me and let out a gurgling sound in its throat. I shot the bastard again, ending its miserable existence.

After dragging all the bodies by the legs, out of the way of the aircraft, I began to refuel it. It took almost ten minutes to top it off. During this time, I could now hear the moans of the undead carried on the wind. The gunfire excited them. It was a terrible sound. After getting the aircraft refueled, I made for the tower. No detours. Once again the gimp ghoul was nowhere to be seen. WTF? I'm safe inside for the night right now. The moans continue . . . another night with earplugs.

The thought of the night; I killed six of them . . . that leaves "gimpy" and another four inside the fence. Where are they?

February 8th

1822 hrs

Awoke this morning to a banging sound on the steel door downstairs. It sounded like more than one of them. John and I crept downstairs to check things out. From the sounds, there were multiple fists banging on the door. Low moans could be heard through the steel. I checked the lock to make sure it was solid. This was the only door in or out of the tower.

The only other way down was a two hundred foot drop from the balcony. John and I brought down a heavy desk to place in front of the door. I went up top and out on the observation deck. I couldn't see down because of the roof over the door area. Using my binoculars, I checked the west fence in the distance. There were more, but the fence was holding. I guessed that the creatures banging on the door were the leftovers from my battle earlier. I don't want to risk opening the door below. I don't know the best way to dispose of them.

February 9th

2142 hrs

The banging stopped last night, and the undead at the bottom of the stairs must have just given up, probably because they never saw us or heard us in here. John and I were still and quiet the whole day yesterday. There was no need to go outside today, as the plane was refueled and we still had power/running water in the tower.

I even got a chance at a shower in the bathroom one floor down. There was a deep sink and a garden hose. The floor panel was plastic and had a drain in the center and the whole room was just a janitor closet, so I rigged the hose up above my head and took a nice shower. Had to use a bar of soap for shampoo, but oh well, beggars can't be choosers, or so they say. I hadn't shaved in a few days. The razor felt good on my face. I felt like a new man after I had washed up. I did some laundry (in the sink with the bar soap) and hung it in the stairwell to dry. I told John about my little hose trick, but he wasn't interested. He just keeps getting worse and worse, grieving over his wife.

I do not know what my long range plans will be. The world is a different place now. The range on the turboprop aircraft is just over four hundred miles. That gives us some options. For a little while today, I actually thought about finding what was left of the military. The questions that they would ask me would be difficult to answer. "How did you survive on the base, son?" I almost feel guilty about not dying with my comrades. It reminds me of a twilight zone episode I saw before the shit hit the fan. It was an episode about a Navy submarine that sank with one survivor. The sailor felt guilty and kept seeing his dead bloated shipmates calling him to the deep.

Please don't let me dream tonight.

February 10th

2350 hrs

The west fence could fail. There are hundreds around the perimeter. The lights of the city have drawn them. I would hate to be shopping in downtown Corpus Christi right now. I have spent most of the day with the binoculars, studying their movements. I saw birds swooping down at some of them. One of the creatures had no arms, and two buzzards were taking advantage of this by perching themselves on the corpse's shoulders and pecking the flesh from its skull. The corpse just gnashed its teeth, snapping at them to no avail. Serves the bastard right.

John and I have tried to figure out what our next step will be, but the safety of the tower has lulled us into a semi-false sense of security. With the limited range on the aircraft, and some areas being radioactive (I'm guessing), it's tough to make a decision. I don't know how to fly a helicopter, so if we found an island, I would need a decent strip of semi-level land to take her down. It has been somewhere in the ballpark of a month since the dead walked. I see signs of decomposition in some of them, but some of them look as though they may have bought the farm recently.

I'm curious as to the effects of ambient radiation on the undead. I know for certain that they would be harmful to the touch, but what effect on the corpse itself? Would the radiation kill the bacteria that caused the corpse to naturally rot? I shudder to think that the bombs dropped could have done more damage than intended good. We are running out of food. We have perhaps a week left. I am sure there is food in some of the surrounding buildings, but I am not prepared at this time to risk my life to get it, as I am certain there are more of those creatures trapped in the confines.

I have been fighting off the shock of this for some time now, and I don't know how much longer it will be before I break down. I suppose it is the natural course of things and I just don't wish to be a basket case at the wrong time. John isn't any better. I played with Annabelle today, as she needed it. She is a good little pup. She can sense that both John and I are on edge, but she doesn't know how to make it better. John and I have decided that one of us needs to be up checking out the perimeter at all times. Going to get some rest and this is not to be confused for sleep. My shift is in four hours.

February 11th

1713 hrs

Using a variation of the square knot, I tied three lengths of one hundred-foot nylon line together to form a sort of escape line, if it were needed. Tying knots into the line every three feet (including the mating knots) caused the three hundred foot length to shorten some, but still allowed it to touch the ground when tied to the balcony and thrown over. I am almost certain these things cannot climb, but still, I pulled the escape rope up and left it neatly coiled outside the balcony door, tied to a sturdy exterior pipe.

The fence is still holding them out, but that is only because they have no evidence that food exists inside. I suppose if they were to see us, or figure out that we were here, they could knock the fence down with ease, making a bad day for John and me. I think we are too far from the west fence for them to see. Cleaned the weapons today, I also showed John how to operate the CAR-15. I also noticed a roof access on the tower. It was probably so that maintenance personnel could get up there and repair the numerous antennas and beacons. I checked it out and climbed up there. It was at least ten feet above the balcony.

I know it has been at least a month since any maintenance has been performed on any of the aircraft, so I went out today, and crept over to the aircraft and pulled out both the pilot and the passenger parachute to make sure they were in good working order. If something happened to the engine, at least John and I would have a choice. I never spotted the loose ghouls that were inside the fence (at least four plus the incapacitated "gimp" creature). Of course, I wasn't looking for them either. I took the parachutes back to the tower. After giving them a good visual inspection, I felt better about taking the plane (number 07) up again, when the need should arise. I keep looking west, making sure our life barrier holds.

February 12th

1913 hrs

There are dead birds on my side of the west fence. I could see them today with my binoculars. I counted six in all. They did not appear eaten; they just look as if they died there. They are on the ground, about four feet from the fence with the mass of the ghouls. I can't tell what kind of bird. They are black, so that rules out most birds of prey. Not a big deal I suppose, but I keep thinking about the black buzzards that were perched on the shoulders of the armless creature, pecking its flesh. Today was uneventful. The fence was still holding.

I am going out tonight to load the extra ammunition/supplies in the avionics bay of the aircraft. I will be especially quiet and leery of the unaccounted for dead that are lurking inside the perimeter. Only one thing drives these creatures, and that is living flesh. I have not seen them attempt to eat each other. Something must be drawing the inner perimeter creatures out of my view. Annabelle is sleeping. I wish I had the carefree thoughts of a dog right now. Ignorance is bliss.

2122 hrs

I'm shaking right now. I haven't been afraid of the dark since I was a child, however my fears were renewed tonight. I loaded the items into the bay of the aircraft. It was cloudy out and barely a moon, so it was pretty dark. It was then that my goggles went black. I had some batteries with me if this happened, but I didn't anticipate the goggles would die that quickly. I fumbled with them in the dark. I was well over a hundred yards from the tower. As I sat there in the dark trying to find where to insert the batteries, I kept hearing shuffling sounds. My mind was playing tricks on me.

The fear was mounting. I finally got the batteries inserted correctly and slammed the NVGs over my head and adjusted the intensifier. As soon as the grainy green image came in, I checked my perimeter. Nothing. This shit is getting to me. I ran back to the tower, up the stairs and sat there. John was looking at one of the charts we had found a few days before. Looking over his shoulder, I saw a place that he had circled. "Mustang Beach" was not very far from us at all.

February 13th

2013 hrs

It's dark outside, and very cold, especially up here in the tower. I suppose if we were to turn on the lights it would warm things up, but it would also excite the creatures on the other side of the west fence. I'm sure they would see it. I went up to the roof access at sundown, and marveled at the stars. There weren't any lights on inside of the perimeter, (John and I had taken care of this when the dead started massing on the west fence) and this made for a fine view of the Milky Way.

I think John is pulling out of his emotional low, and starting to recover. He actually joked around with me today. I didn't leave the confines of the tower today, but I do need to get those parachutes back to the aircraft so we have less to carry when we leave. I'm still sort of freaked out about last night, so I guess it can wait until later. It is still puzzling to me why the creatures are on the west end of the fence, and no other. I would love to have some real food. When monitoring the radios today, John heard a broadcast from an Air Force aircraft scouting the area. One key thing that John noted that disturbed me, the pilot had to turn back to base because he wanted to conserve his fuel. The pilot remarked about the limited supply back on the base. This tells me they are rationing jet fuel; therefore, they are confined to an area where it is not readily available. The government (or this part of it) is trapped just like we are.

An island off the coast of Texas is starting to sound better and better. The only problem is that supplies would be difficult to come by with just the two of us scavenging.

February 14th
1440 hrs

The fence is buckling inward and I don't know how much longer it will hold. It's today or nothing. Looking at the windsock, there is a strong wind blowing east to west toward the airstrip. We will take to the air as soon as

Tower

Situation is dire. My bleeding has stopped, but I'm still light headed from all the blood loss. It must have been right before I was writing my last entry yesterday when they broke through. I did not notice they were inside the perimeter until 1445, by then it was too late. John and I saw them. The fence was down in about a hundred-meter section and they were pouring into the airfield like runner ants.

We gathered the necessities (what we thought were needed anyway) and started out the door to get in the bird and leave. As we reached the bottom and opened the door, there were four of them there waiting on John and me. We slammed the door shut and pushed the desk in place in front of the entry that we had brought down days before.

We were fucking trapped like rats and those bastards could sense it. It wasn't long before the moans of hundreds could be heard below and the constant banging on the only exit door started. This tower was over two hundred feet high and only one way out. I went outside on the balcony, and my suspicions were confirmed.

There were literally three hundred of them congregated around the exterior door as well as the covered area of the tower. John muzzled Annabelle, because she was starting to go nuts. I grabbed the rope and looked below to see where it would hit when I threw it. No joy. Sadly, I pulled the rope back up on the balcony, as there was no way we were making it down that rope without a hundred of them seeing us and taking us out before we even touched the ground.

It was then that the situation worsened. The sound of bending, aching steel could be heard below. There were so many of them, the masses were pushing their way through. At that moment, I knew we were fucked. I looked at John and told him, "I'm not ready to die yet." He said, "Me neither." and we both rushed over to the door that led down the stairs and started throwing TVs, desks and chairs down the stairs. That would buy us a little time. We then shut the door . . . —It opened outward, *thank god*.

The upstairs door was not as sturdy as the bottom exterior door. Just as we got the door shut and the last remaining desk in front of it, we could hear the metal clanging of dress shoes on the stairs. John shoved Annabelle in his backpack and zipped her up to her neck. I motioned for John to get to the top of the ladder and wait for me to start passing up supplies.

John waited with Annabelle in his pack at the top rung. She could sense our fear and was whimpering. First, I passed him the two most important items of my plan . . . —The two parachutes that I never put back in the aircraft! Then I passed up a six-pack of water bottles, then the NVGs, then a few packs of MREs. Just for some odd novelty, I passed up my case with my small laptop. Lastly, all our weapons and much of our ammunition, although shooting every last round would still leave hundreds here to deal with.

They were at the upstairs door now. This door had a rectangular shaped vertical window, about six by ten inches. I could see one of them with its face pressed up to the shatterproof glass, sneering, trying to see what was inside. It started pounding and moaning when it saw me. The others soon followed suit. John climbed up onto the roof and I followed. It was windy like the day before. This was good news, maybe.

John took his pack (and his dog) off his shoulders and turned it around so it was being worn in the front of his body. I helped him put the parachute on and, using zip-ties, I strapped as much to him as I could without hindering too much movement. I quickly showed him the basics on how to get out of the parachute when he hit the ground.

I explained to him that it was very important that he unfasten the two inner thigh straps prior to the chest strap. He nodded that he got it, so I bent down and grabbed my chute. The broken glass sound erupted from below and I was sure they pushed the shatterproof glass through the doorframe. I hoped that these things could not climb ladders. Using the carabiners from my daypack, I secured the rifle to my chest d-ring through the carrying handle. My knife was strapped to my belt for easy access when I hit the ground.

I would be jumping first . . . at this moment came the familiar sound of bending steel, and the screeching sound of the wood desk being launched across the floor. There was no way to secure the top hatch from the outside. It was simple, if they could climb, they would get up here. I gave one last lesson to John . . . "Make sure you pull your risers to slow your descent." I described what they looked like to him.

I made John watch me as I crept to the edge of the roof. I could hear the sounds of them wondering below, trying to find their food. I could see the balcony door below me being pushed open, two, five, and now twelve creatures were wandering the balcony below. For some reason, they didn't look as rotted as I thought they should be. I was guessing that every bit of two-hundred walking dead were inside the tower at that moment.

John leaned over and saw them. He was white with fear. Not just the thought of being eaten to death . . . but the thought of jumping the tower, breaking both legs, and not being able to give yourself a fighting chance . . . I knew what he was thinking. I was thinking the same thing. At that moment the hatch on the roof access jumped up and slammed back down . . . Clang . . . clang . . . The creature's wedding ring was chiming on the hatch, making it rise a couple inches then slam back down, as the back of its left hand hit. I could see the white hand for a split second when the weight of the hatch pushed it back down. I almost fucking lost it.

I somehow grabbed John's attention through this and showed him how to pull the release d-ring for the drogue. The drogue is a small parachute that catches the wind and pulls the rest of the chute out. The drogue on this chute is spring powered. Pull the pin, and the drogue will shoot out, catching the wind, and deploy the rest of the chute. I checked the windsock on the far side of the field . . . good to go. Looked below. There were many, but most of them seemed to be in the tower. I pulled the pin and held on to the ledge, so I wouldn't fall off before it deployed.

The wind caught the main chute and literally yanked me off my feet. I could see the roof hatch swing completely open and heard it bash as it jack-knifed and hit the roof. John was right behind me. The creatures on the balcony saw John and I jump, and started almost screaming. I looked up as their outstretched hands reached for the dome of my chute.

There were windows every few feet that looked in/out of the stairwell. Damn . . . they were climbing over each other to get to the top. Many were in military uniforms. My estimate at two hundred was too low. From the way they were piled on top of each other in the stairwell, there were more than likely a thousand of them. I was slowly floating to the ground, it seemed like forever. Every window that I passed by on the way down was another snapshot, or Picasso if you will of dead faces and limbs crowded together . . . Then it was back to reality as I hit the ground. It wasn't a soft landing, but I didn't break anything. I immediately unlatched my chute and rolled out of it. I unsheathed my knife and waited for John to hit the ground. The creatures were closing in.

As soon as John hit, he was attempting to get out of the chute. Neither of us wanted the wind dragging us into a group of those things. I had to help him along by slicing through the nylon harness. I told John to grab one end of the chute. We then ran through a group of those things toward the aircraft.

John knew what my plan was. We wrapped at least ten of those things up in the damaged chute by running around them and tangling up the cut harness with the drogue. Luckily, we drifted fifty meters in the direction of the aircraft when we jumped. We ran as fast as we could. In all the excitement, the dog slipped out of John's pack onto the ground. John was ahead of me, and I scooped her up on my way. She was so scared that she was trying to climb on top of my head. I don't fucking blame her. I felt the warmth of urine seeping through my clothing. She pissed herself. *

We made it to the aircraft and I slung open the cockpit glass

*Come to think of it, it might have been me.

and threw my shit in the back seat. John and Annabelle jumped in the back and I told John to strap in. I immediately jumped in the bird and slid the cockpit closed and latched the lock. I remembered the startup sequence from the checklist, and out of habit started saying it aloud as I performed it . . .

"1 _ Clock started

2 _ Starter switch on

3 _ Battery above ten volts

4 _ Ignition light on

5 _ Fuel pressure light out

6 _ Oil pressure rising

7 _ N1 above 12 percent

8 — Condition lever to feather

9 — Thumbs up to the lineman."

I almost laughed at myself on this step. There was no lineman. Although I was sure the bastard was out there somewhere looking for us. I increased the condition lever to full bite and could feel the propeller catch air.

I couldn't have avoided what happened next. There were fifty of them closing in on us. All I could do was to attempt to get into take-off position. One of them near the nose walked toward the prop. I always wondered what it would sound like, now I knew; like a big vegetable processor. That corpse lost its whole left shoulder in the deal. I checked my prop RPM, it dipped a little but cycled back up to 2200 RPM. I didn't want to hit any more of them. Using the pedals, I weaved the nose in and out of corpses as I rolled into position, buzzing a few of them, but nothing big like the first one.

I checked my fuel pressure, good to go, everything was in the green. I pushed my power lever to max and I started my takeoff roll . . . 50 knots, the airspeed indicator kicked in . . . 65 knots, 70 knots . . .

I clipped one of them with my left wing, breaking its hip (at least) right before 80 knots. At 85 knots I pulled the stick back and we were airborne. John already had his helmet fastened; I grabbed mine from my lap and pulled it over my head. I checked the internal communications system with John. He was reading me but I could tell that he was in some sort of shock by the way he was talking and by the fact that his lips looked blue in the rear view mirror.

The worst part of this was that we had no real place to go. As we took off, I looked over at the tower. The roof was now full of them and they were walking off of the top of it like lemmings. I was trying to fly the plane and look at the chart at the same time. I was wobbling back and forth, and could hear John getting airsick on the speakers in my helmet. It was sort of funny, but I didn't want to laugh at him. I noticed a small abandoned airstrip called "Matagorda Island airfield" about 65 miles northeast of our position. I quickly marked it on my chart with a red ink pen. It looked like there were numerous islands there, and it wasn't too far from Corpus, so the power was probably still on.

We cruised northeast for about twenty minutes at 180 knots when I started having propeller trouble. The engine was fine, but the prop kept losing pitch angle thus not allowing it to grab as much air. In short, it kept feathering on me. I knew this was something to do with the corpse I chopped up earlier. I had no choice. I had to glide the plane in, because the prop pitch control was probably losing oil pressure. I feathered the prop with the condition lever and pulled the engine back to three hundred foot pounds of torque.

According to my chart, the strip was in sight but I couldn't see it. I descended to three thousand feet to get a good glide solution. Below me it looked like a tourist area, with numerous hotels lining the beach. Thank god it was February and not tourist season. At this point, I had to make a choice. I could either find another place to land, or say fuck it, and land in the street. Below, I could see a few of the creatures, but it was nothing like what we were running from. I was on borrowed time without a good propeller. I had to take her down. I pulled the stick back and left and pushed a little left rudder and glided into a 180-degree rendezvous with the road below. Nose down, gear down, and as soon as I was near the road, I flared my nose up and touched down with my main landing gear.

I hit the brakes and tried to steer my wings between the telephone poles. I still had a lot of fuel left and didn't want to be wearing flaming fuel because my wing decided to wrap itself around a poll. Along the way, I clipped one of those creatures with my right wing, doubling it over. It had hit its head so hard when it slammed its upper body into the wing that it died instantly, leaving a brown smudge of brain on the wing. I checked my speed, fifty knots . . . As I slowed to a halt, the immediate area was clear.

I signaled John to get out. I left the engine running so that the sound of the aircraft would muffle our escape. John and I jumped out, grabbed our shit and headed for a sign called "Matagorda Island Marina."

Now here we are . . .

I gashed my leg open on the sharp bumper of a wrecked car five minutes into the journey. It was a long hump, (a mile's worth of side streets, beach fronts, and backyards) but we are here. It is a decent sized marina with a large ferry, and a gift shop. Electricity is still on. Marina abandoned. Looks like the harbormaster took his own life. His bloated corpse is slumped over a desk in the front office, with what was left of his brain caked on a calendar marked January. The TV was still on, playing snow.

February 16th

1912 hrs

I am very weak today. If it were not for John, I would be dead. Annabelle is next to me sleeping. It is dark outside and I have been blacking out on and off most of the day. My leg is infected and I need some antibiotics. In the harbormaster's desk, we found some whiskey. This has served me most of the day as a disinfectant, as well as painkiller. Tomorrow, John will go out alone to find some medicine for my infection. We are in no trouble currently.

I could hear the sound of the aircraft engine still running yesterday for at least two hours before it died. No matter, it was junk now anyway, as I am sure there is no one left alive that knows how to fix it.

February 17th

2220 hrs

I'm feeling better today. We heard the sound of an engine in the distance that sounded like it could have been a dirt bike. John found a first-aid kit on the ferry near here. It didn't have any pill antibiotics, but it did have some of the topical kind. I have been keeping the wound clean and washing it a few times a day, and applying the medicine. It seems to be working. I'm just still very red and sore around the cut. Last night we heard the sounds of something in the darkness. Using the goggles, we tried to spot it, but it turned out it was only a raccoon looking for food. Tomorrow, I will try and walk so I don't get too stiff. John and I need to survey this area, as we are only safe here temporarily.

"Dark Knight"

There are sporadic gunshots in the wind. We picked up a distress call on the harbor radio from a family in the outskirts of Victoria, TX (50 miles from current location). The signal was faint and we tried to respond, however they could not hear us as they kept transmitting over and over as if we weren't there. I thought about it and decided that it would not be worth a fifty-mile trek through hostile territory to find a group of people that may be dead when I got there. Sad. I used to be more compassionate and chivalrous. I guess after seeing bad things happen to good people, you just don't want to be good. They are trapped in an attic with those things shuffling around below. I think I know who will be able to wait longer.

I guess they must have moved the essentials up to the attic when the "S.H.T.F." Something keeps eating at me, as if a shell of my former self were ordering me to do something. Or, maybe I do have a conscience left. Doubt it.

I am walking now, but not running. John and I unfastened the chain that held the floating ramp to the marina. We found some rope in the utility room of the marina office, and use it as part of our drawbridge mechanism. John and I thought of it today. When we are here, we simply pull the rope, and the floating ramp gets pulled away from the shore to the marina, making a hard time for any of those fuckers to get here. I hope they can't swim.

February 19th

1524 hrs

We are making good headway in securing the area. There are numerous small boats in the marina, and John and I have pulled the ones we think are worth a damn to our location. I want to check them all at once to avoid starting the engines at different times, making too much noise. This morning I saw a group of eight dead pass the street about fifty meters from the water's edge. The only thing that troubled me was that they were moving faster than the previous creatures we have encountered. By no means were they running or even jogging, but they definitely were *not* walking. My heart sank as I noticed the speed at which they moved.

I crossed the gangway to the ferry next to the marina office. It was a medium-sized ferry that could fit about twenty vehicles. I assume it was used to cross the channel to mainland Texas.

I climbed to the top deck and checked the bridge. I found a set of binoculars (left my others at the tower) and used them to try and spot the pack of dead. I looked up and down the beach, and checked the windows on the hotels. No signs of life. I counted five windows on the fifth and sixth floor in the nearest hotel (Hotel La Blanc) that did have occupants. Dead, rotting occupants that will never check out of their hotel.

These binoculars were built for sea service. They are large, heavy and have powerful magnification. They're not really suitable to carry around, but great for checking the area. Three of the monsters just stood there at the window staring out. One of them seemed as if it looked right at me. The two others looked like they were pacing the room. I wonder how they died.

My leg is much better now and I think I will be able to run on it if need be in a couple days. We are out of food today, so we are going to burgle the vending machines until I can run again. Then we will scavenge for food. I could only salvage 500 rounds for the CAR-15. John has a thousand for the semi-auto .22.

2223 hrs

Thirty minutes ago I heard a noise. I donned the night vision goggles on and expected to see another raccoon. Not the case this time. Four of them are standing at the waters edge looking out toward our location. They aren't making any noise. They are just standing there with arms swinging ominously at the waters edge. John and I are being as quiet as possible. I am conserving battery power by leaving the goggles off, but it seems every splash the water makes as it hits the marina pontoons, I imagine them swimming toward us.

February 20th

1854 hrs

I was up all night last night. The fog on the water made it impossible for me to see the shore after midnight. This morning when the sun came up and burned some of the fog away, I checked for them. I could hear some noise in the distance. It sounded like someone was knocking over tin cans. My leg is feeling much better. Today, we lived off of stale candy bars and soft drinks. Makes me think . . . There will probably never be another can of this made. Sort of depressing. I'm going to need a watch soon, as the battery in this one has been the same for over two years. I guess I will put that on the list of "must loot." Although, some would argue that stealing to stay alive is not looting. I say its just details. I'm not planning to raid a jewelry store but I won't turn down something that will keep me alive.

On a lighter note, John and I found a radio station still broadcasting music. Too bad it's automated and it keeps looping every twelve hours. Still good for morale and I'm glad it's still working. You can almost imagine it is live. It helps . . . a little.

February 21st

0800 hrs

We are in dire need of provisions. Plenty of water here at the marina in the drinking water dispenser, but we have been living off of caffeine and sugar. A detailed map of this area would be very helpful, although getting to it may prove fatal. Early this morning as the sun was rising through the fog, I could hear and see many of them walking the street in front of the ferry marina. For some reason they were moving together. Seemed like they were attracting themselves to the noise they were making. I couldn't see the whole group of them, but from the numbers I did see, I could estimate that there were hundreds.

John and I picked the best boat out of the few that we rounded up a few days ago. I checked the fuel tank and saw that it was 3/4 full. There was a fuel pump on the marina, so decided to see if it still worked. Went into the marina office, and checked for a pump switch. Number two pump switch was still on.

I went out to use pump number two to fill the boat up. No joy, the pump worked; however no fuel came forth. It must have been drained when the shit went down. I went back inside to flip pump number one back on line. Squeezed the nozzle and it pumped for a few seconds before any fuel came out. A nice rainbow of fuel was present on the surface of the water. In another time, that might have cost me a fine. A few seconds of pumping and the last 1/4 of fuel was added. I found a couple empty plastic gas cans in the marina, filled those and tied them into the boat.

John went back in and grabbed my rife and held it at the ready toward the shore while I worked. We still had no idea what capabilities the dead had when it came to water. Yesterday, while listening to the last radio music broadcasts of mankind, John and I found a metal key box next to a shelf in the administration office. All of the watercraft had a registration number stuck to the side of their hulls with reflective number tape, so finding the key was not a difficult task. I matched the number with the key marked 'Shamrock 220' and went back out to her to give it a shot.

The back end had drifted, facing the admin office door when I walked out. The boat's name was painted on the rear with a half-circle type banner. It was the *Bahama Mama*. I jumped on to the stern and walked over to the wheel and inserted the key. John was still sitting on the dock, eyes trained toward the strips of hotels and the street. I slid the throttle to the start position, and turned the key. On the second attempt it started with no problems and I let it run for about five minutes.

I sat there smiling at John at how lucky we had been. I turned the key to the 'off' position and just as the engine died down, we heard what it had been drowning out. A football stadium of hideous moans echoed throughout the buildings on the island. We could hear Annabelle's reaction from inside the marina. She was upset at the noise, and the hair on the back of my neck was standing up. Now that the engine worked without any doubt, it was time to plan a trip to gather supplies. Leaving in the morning.

February 22nd

0403 hrs

As the day went by yesterday, the shoreline was home to over fifty of those things, begging for our flesh. Something just isn't right about them. Their numbers have dwindled to roughly twenty. Bahama Mama and co. leaving for supplies.

Exodus of the
Bahama Mama

Using the night vision goggles, I prepped the boat for an early departure yesterday morning. It was around 0430 when I started loading candy bars, bottled water, ammunition, and extra fuel cans onto the boat. I brought a pry bar also, in case we had to strong-arm our way into a place. John was prepping our little man-made sanctuary for Annabelle. It would be dangerous to take her with us. She would be fine here in the confines of our little floating hideaway.

The twenty or so dead were still walking the shoreline, blind to the night, and hoping for a glimpse of prey. I found some plastic oars inside the maintenance shed and quietly put them in the boat (never know). John and I boarded the craft and I untied us. I reluctantly started the engine and checked the movement on the shoreline. Some of the creatures were flailing wildly and two of them were wading the water up to their knees. The fact that their fear of water was dwindling sent chills up my spine.

As we pulled out, I navigated west. I found a chart used for water navigation in the office at the marina. Too bad there wasn't a map of Matagorda Island in there also. I knew the general shape of the island, however, I had no idea of the details. I was now heading toward San Antonio bay. I was going slow, conserving fuel and watching out for any dangers that may appear in the light morning fog.

My choices were clear according to the sea chart. I would sail into San Antonio bay and choose either the west, or the east shore. To the west was the small (according to chart) coastal town of *Austwell*, and east was *Seadrift*. Neither John nor I were familiar with either. We both agreed on Seadrift. No particular reason. Perhaps in the back of my mind, I thought that because of its name, it would be a better suited docking point.

The sun was peaking up over the east horizon and was at our backs when Seadrift came into sight. There were numerous long docks, no doubt to provide berth for fishing vessels. I cut the engine and John and I started rowing toward the docks. Noise was a luxury we could not afford.

Using the binoculars taken from the large ferry, I scanned the coastline. They were here. I could see their pitiful frames walking aimlessly up and down the main street that ran the length of the bay. There weren't many, but enough to be trouble. The sign for the marina read, "Dockside Fishing Center." One of the boats berthed here held a deadly crew. John and I saw three of the creatures walking the deck of the fishing boat, only forty meters away. They saw us, and one of them lunged out at us falling off the boat, disappearing into the murky waters of the bay.

As we rowed closer to the dock, it appeared that there was a small grocery and bait store right off the pier. At arms length of the tie down, I secured the *Mama* to the dock. John and I carefully stepped onto the worn wooden planks of the pier. I grabbed the pry bar and stuck it under my belt. Every creak seemed like thunder. The sound of the dead walking on the other boat was much louder than we were, but it was still quiet. There were no sounds of nature and no engines; even the bay water splashing on the shore seemed muted.

The gangway to the boat containing the two remaining ghouls was still in place. They were a threat. I had John keep their attention. He waved his arms at them as I snuck over to the gangway (plank) linking the boat to the dock and quietly slid it into the water. The splash was louder than I expected, and they immediately turned toward me and let out the all too familiar moan. Crabs lined the deck of the fishing vessel with the two corpses. Dead fish could be seen in a pile on the stern.

The stink was incorrigible. The crabs were snapping at the pant legs of the dead. There were several crab carcasses littering the deck. Legs were pulled off and shells were cracked. Upon a closer look at the undead creatures, I could see that several of their teeth were missing or broken. The bastards were trying to eat the crabs.

John and I left the motley crew of ghouls and headed for the grocery store. Weapons ready, we approached the front door. No movement. Damn I was hungry. Just thinking about all of the food in there made it worse. In my right arm I had my rifle at the ready, in my left I tightly held the black steel pry bar. The little grocery store was no bigger than a tennis court. Hurricane shudders were in place prohibiting any view of the inside except through the glass front door. Two signs hung on the inside of the door. "Closed," and "Help Wanted." The *latter* was an understatement.

Walking up to the door, I grabbed the handle and pulled. No dice. It was going to have to be the hard way. Using the bar, I slid it between the door and the frame and began prying. I wasn't going to be surprised this time. I thought back to that Wal-Mart. Seemed like ages ago. I nervously watched the inside for movement, as I grunted and struggled with the locked door. John was becoming a good point man. He was scanning for movement, covering me. Finally after a few minutes of struggling with the door, I finally got it open.

The store was dark and it was very warm inside. I could smell rotten fruit. I turned the light on that was mounted on my weapon. I panned the area, listening for anything out of the ordinary. John and I each grabbed carts and made our way to the canned goods section. Quietly we filled our carts with anything that could be eaten and drunk, starting with non-perishables first. All the bread was moldy, but some of the cookies were still good. Of course, the canned goods were fine.

The refrigerator section was totally rotten. I panned my light through the glass and saw the yellow-looking gallon milk jugs, and molded cheese. Then something else caught my eye. There was movement in the freezer. I always knew there was walk space back there for the stock-boys to stock the cold goods. It appears that the stock-boy and another friend were still in there. The light excited them and I could see them pounding on the shelves full of milk. In one section, one of them was crawling through the shelf to the refrigerator door that led to us.

John and I decided that it was time to leave. We wheeled our carts back to the front and I checked the area for any signs of the enemy. I opened the front door and John wheeled out first. As I followed, I could see the refrigerator door open at the back of the store, and heard the sound of a body falling to the floor. I knew it was Mr. Stock-boy wanting to check and see if we were finding everything all right.

John and I hurriedly jogged back down toward the pier. The carts were making a lot of noise, and I didn't wish to wait around and see how things worked out. Quickly, we loaded the boat with the provisions. Behind us the front door to the grocery store was creeping open and I could see the pale figure of the creature that was in the refrigerator section. John and I jumped in the boat, and I kicked us away from the dock. We paddled as fast as we could, and stopped about ten meters out from where we were tied up.

It was time for a break. Using my knife, I opened up a can of cold beef stew and drank down the contents. John did the same. As we sat there drinking bottled water, our friend on the pier was giving us a warm bon voyage. The creature looked horrible, it was missing a right hand, and most of the jaw. It was wearing a long white apron with something written on it in blood. I pulled out my binoculars and in simple block letters it read:

"If you can read this, kill me!"

I smiled at this and thought to myself that I would have liked to have known this man when he was alive, as I appreciated his sense of humor. I slung my weapon to my shoulder and selected single shot. I then took aim, and shot stock-boy in the head. John gave me a "why did you do that?" look, and I just glanced at him and said, "Professional courtesy my friend, professional courtesy."

The trip back to our marina stronghold was uneventful. About a quarter mile from the pier, we cut the engines and quietly rowed to the dock. There weren't any of them on the shore, probably because they followed the sound of our engines away from the marina early this morning. We quietly unloaded most of the food and water. It was dinnertime for Annabelle. It's funny how she probably eats better now than she did before all of this.

February 24th

2047 hrs

John and I talked about family. I told him that I was worried about mine, and that I doubted they lived through this, even considering their location. John told me about his son and about how proud he was of him, and how he had gotten a scholarship to Purdue. He went on to tell me the antics of his recent family reunion and how his wife couldn't get along with his mother. John asked me why I joined the service. I told him my story of how I was a poor country boy from small town, USA that wanted to serve his country, and how I came up the hard way through the enlisted ranks.

(Not that it matters now what my rank is anyway.)

I'm sure somewhere deep underground in the northwest United States, rank still matters, but not here on this two-bit marina on some no name island. I went on to tell John why I didn't stay with my comrades at the base. I paused at this, questioning to myself whether or not I should have fought the good fight. I told John that sometimes I regret not going to the base with my fellow officers. The point of the matter is, I'm alive and they are not. I would rather choose *needle in a haystack over jackass in a fortress*. I expressed to him that I would have to live with my decision, but at least I'm alive to do it.

John looked at me and said, "You speak as if I am accusing you of desertion." I apologized and told him that it was a sensitive subject. I guess I am a deserter. Who is alive to tell? I suppose if things ever get back to normal, I will . . . No use thinking about that.

My heartstrings tugged at the thought of my parents being

boarded up in their attic, praying for help. My imagination could almost see their dirty clothes, matted hair and malnutrition-riddled frames. I had to compartmentalize this thought to keep from making a bad decision. Willingly attempting to save my parents who are hundreds of miles away would be suicide. I wonder how long it took for the devastation to reach the backwoods of Arkansas? It didn't take long from the time I saw it on the news to the time it was outside on my street, clawing at my wall.

It is a cold decision to make; however if I wish to live, I cannot let emotion tell me where to point my steps. Even in the best case, a minor lapse in judgment would mean death. If I chose to go to Arkansas to see if my parents still lived, every decision would have to be perfect, right down to where I chose to sleep at night, and where I chose to scavenge for supplies.

What went wrong? I don't know why it has taken me almost two months to really think about it, but what sick fuck would do something like this? I assume too much. Was man reaching the level of deity? Maybe it was something larger. I don't want to think about that right now, as I would only curse and scream, and if it was something bigger, I didn't want to take the chance of this higher force reprimanding me for being insubordinate. So for now, I guess we will have our little unspoken agreement. If you exist, lets just leave each other alone . . . I'll let you know when I'm ready.

I don't fear the reaper.

February 25th

1932 hrs

The coast was clear earlier today when I took Annabelle out to stretch her legs on the dock. I walked her up and down the wooden planks. I could tell she had put on a couple pounds and needed a little exercise. I kept her muzzle on to avoid any loud barking. The marina resembled a system of docks that would look like an "H" from the air. The floating marina office was attached to one side of the "H" and a single, floating ramp was the only thing that formerly connected this artificial island of wood, metal and foam to the real island.

I walked her around the perimeter of the dock. Yesterday, I took a long fishing pole from one of the boats and tried to touch the bottom from the point on the dock closest to the shore. I couldn't touch, so that meant that the water was at least nine feet deep in that area. For some reason I feared that they might be able to wade the water and just climb up here. I felt a little more assured after my depth finder test.

On our second walking lap around the marina, Annabelle started sniffing the wind, and the familiar scene of her hair standing up on her back became obvious. She sensed them. The wind was blowing from the shore, and we were downwind. I picked her up and took her inside. I went to the window facing the shoreline and waited. I told John what she had done while we were outside. John and I shared the window, and just kept watching.

The sounds came first and it reminded me of the sound of a distant street sweeper being carried by the wind. Then the mass of them came slowly stumbling and even walking by. There was no way to count them, and I knew that if they wanted, they could get to us here on the marina. When I saw them pass by our location, it reminded me of a big city marathon. All it would take would be the sheer number of them piling themselves up on the water. I was getting tired of running, but this is a big island, and I'm sure that we could never find enough weapons or ammunition to kill them all. If only we had a few more days back at the tower in Corpus to plan. John is picking up faint signals from the survivors trapped in the attic. That is another thing that is getting at me.

February 26th

0923 hrs

John and I were monitoring the radios this morning. It seems our attic survivors are still ok. We are still unable to raise them with our transmitter. The man's name is William Grisham, and he is making all of the broadcasts. From time to time, I have heard a female voice in the background, but I can't tell if it is a child or his wife. He says that they are not infected and have enough food and water to last a week, but the sounds of the corpses below are driving them mad.

He doesn't seem to think that they can make it out alive without help. Looking at the air chart that I still have, we could take the boat back to Seadrift, then find a car there and try to make it the rest of the way to Victoria, TX. I don't even know why I'm thinking this. The whole trip looks like about fifty miles. Ten of which are on the water. That means eighty miles of round trip danger. I can't ask John to go and actually, I would prefer that he stayed here. John is torn between doing the right thing and possibly losing his fellow survivor, or doing the wrong thing and losing his soul. My thoughts are happening in phases. I would hate to be in that position, but I was in that position and I did something about it. I chose to live.

2145 hrs

William has been broadcasting off and on all day. He sounds desperate. I can't stop listening because it is another human voice. His maddening ramblings are bringing my mind into a maze of darkness. I feel I must help. John and I have discussed it at length, and he will stay and hold down the fort with Annabelle. I almost feel like I am starting to get to know William. For some odd reason, he rambled on for about thirty minutes just talking about whatever was on his mind. I assume that shock may be setting in and he is using the radio as an emotional outlet. He spoke of his job, and how he was a chemist before all of this happened. I listened to his voice, and could almost hear his honesty and integrity about the fear of losing his family. I feel I *MUST* help. Tonight I will prepare and tomorrow I will go.

February 27th

0820 hrs

Leaving shortly. I will be taking the boat back to Seadrift, then the rest either by car, or on foot. This could take a few days. I found a CB radio on one of the boats here. It's a little heavy, and battery powered, but when I get within range of William's radio, I will use it to try and hail him. No use going the last twenty miles only to find William and family as one of them. I have nearly 500 rounds left from what I salvaged in my rush from the control tower, taking into account the one round used to shoot the stock boy in the head. With the radio, water, weapon, rounds, food, and other small miscellaneous gear, I am carrying over 70 lbs. This is why a car would be preferable.

My plan is to acquire a road atlas when I get to Seadrift, then "shadow" the roads all the way to Victoria (If I am on foot). I can't risk being seen by anything living or dead along the way. I will stay in contact with John as long as the handheld will transmit. I do not know its transmit range, but I am sure I could talk to him from Seadrift, as the signal will travel further over the water.

Last night I was outside looking at the stars when I saw bright green streak in the sky, similar to a shooting star. The green was probably the copper burning up inside a satellite that has long been forgotten. Only a matter of time before GPS fails, along with all other satellite based services.

Enough useless babble.

Time to cock the hammer.

1844 hrs

I paddled the boat out to about 1/4 of a mile distance from the marina, so as to not attract them to John. Had to gas up the boat last night. When I turned on the engine, I cruised west a bit to attract them away from the marina, just to give John a little more peace of mind. Didn't take long for me to reach Seadrift, as it is only about ten miles from the marina to mainland Texas. Once again, I shut the *Bahama Mama* down and did my best to paddle (with one oar) the rest of the way. When I reached the same marina John and I were at a few days before, I noticed the same two creatures on the fishing boat, and the re-dead stock boy face down on the dock. He was being picked apart by a group of birds.

Before approaching any of the docks, I tried the CB radio on the pre-selected channel that John and I agreed on. After the second attempt, I heard John's faint crackling voice asking me if everything was OK. I told him that everything was fine, and that his friends on the fishing boat were having crab this evening, and wondered if he would be attending. He laughed at this and I told him that I would get back to him as soon as I got back into range.

I knew that there was another creature inside the grocery store. I could see faint movement on the street about 1/4 of a mile north inland. I could see what looked like another set of marina docks further up the shoreline. It was too far to paddle without another oarsman. I had to start the engine. This excited the creatures on the fishing boat and it felt as if every set of eyes left in the world were staring at me . . . —Angry for the broken silence.

As I sped up the coastline, the creatures on the beach took notice of my boat and started following me up the waterline. I couldn't believe what I was seeing. These creatures were not the same, slow shambling creatures I was used to. Some of them seemed to move faster.

One of them appeared to be almost trotting, with its arms reaching out toward my boat. They were still very uncoordinated, and many of them were falling face down in the sand, only to get back up to pursue me. I decided to distance myself from the shoreline and approach the dock in a manner that would not attract this rag tag bunch to my position.

I took the boat a mile out into the center of the bay and approached the dock in a perpendicular direction. I tried to build up enough speed so that when I cut my engine, I could drift at least most of the way. Not being familiar with this dock, my weapon was at the ready as I inched closer. It was very similar to the east dock in many ways. I saw no dead in this area. There was a gas station in plain view about 300 meters from the marina. I shuddered when I thought of being on the roof of the last gas station back home. My fear started to grow as the view to the gas station became clear.

I finally cut the engine and drifted as far as I could without using the paddle. I eased into the marina, and tied the boat down. I checked the area for immediate danger, and then checked the fuel level to make sure I had enough to make it back to Matagorda Island. I turned the CB radio off, as I didn't want any calls breaking the precious silence I was trying to maintain. Shouldering my heavy pack I stepped up on the dock and began to walk toward the shore, taking extra precaution to watch my footing, and minimize noise.

I could see two vehicles parked in front of the gas station. One of the cars still had the fuel nozzle attached to it, as if the owner never got the chance to place it back on the pump. I could see that the other car, parked in front of the gas station, had the driver's side door open. I knew for sure that the dome light would have drained the battery long before I got here.

I made my way closer to the station, weapon ready. I knew that if I had to evade, I wouldn't be able to go for more than three miles without rest, as it was a chore to move with all the weight. As I approached the car near the pumps, the only sounds I could hear were the sounds of the water churning near the docks. I was at the pump.

I checked the gallons readout on the pump to see if the car had actually been filled up. No joy, it was digital and the power to the pumps was shut off. Quietly, I took the nozzle out of the car and placed it on the ground, then put the fuel cap back on. My best guess was that the car was a mid 80's model. The decals told me the car was a Buick Regal Grand National. It was black.

I went around to the driver's side door. The window was open, so I reached inside to check for keys. No keys. I made for the convenience store. The glass display windows and door were shattered, looted long ago. I wasn't there to loot; —I just needed a road atlas. I could see the map display on the same counter as the microwave, so I ducked through the broken glass and headed that way. My nose didn't warn me of any dead here. I scanned each aisle as I made for the maps. They were fresh out of road atlases, but I did find a laminated road map of Texas. Since I didn't plan on taking any interstate trips, this would do just fine.

It was now time to deal with the keyless Buick. Since this area seemed devoid of current danger, I decided it best to attempt to hot-wire the car, rather than attempt to find a working car in dangerous territory. I knew that I would be S.O.L. on a newer model car, but this old Buick would be easier. I found the "odds and ends" aisle and grabbed a small overpriced package of cheap speaker wire, then went to the front counter display cases and took an extremely cheap, poorly made, fake (convenience store) Swiss Army knife.

Leaving the store with my bounty, I checked the area once again and approached the Buick. As I passed the other vehicle parked with its doors open, I was startled by a sound from inside . . . A squirrel was making itself a nice home, complete with nest in the back seat. I opened the door to the Buick and popped the hood. I followed the plug wires to the coil wire. I took the speaker wire, stripped both ends with the shitty Swiss army knife and ran it from the positive end of the battery to the positive side of the coil. This would supply power to the dash. The car would be useless without this.

I had to locate the starter solenoid. It was logically found on the starter. Using the longer knife blade on the knife, I completed the connection between the starter solenoid and the positive battery lead. There was a spark. The engine cranked over, then came to life. I would hard wire it later. The noise would surely attract them, so I had to hurry.

I took off my pack and weapon, and sat them in the passenger seat. Using the flathead screwdriver part of the knife, I was able to push the steering wheel locking pin away from the wheel to unlock it. I then tightened the speaker wire so that it wouldn't come off during the drive. I closed the hood, got in and then rolled the driver's side window up fast enough to break the sound barrier and headed for the road. My lucky day, the poor bastard that owned the car actually filled the tank up before he presumably died. Looking at my map, my route was distinct.

I was on highway 185 northwest out of Seadrift, straight shot into Victoria. The road was far from being a major thoroughfare, so I had no trouble getting to the outskirts of Victoria in less than two hours. I was delayed by the occasional car parked sideways in the road, or an unusually large pack of creatures shambling across like sheep. As I approached the outskirts, I could tell that I was closer to a fallout area, as there was a light coat of ash on most horizontal surfaces, i.e. parked cars, houses and buildings. I am no expert on radiation, but I did see birds and small animals, so I took a chance in assuming it was semi-safe to at least transit the area.

Right now it's nearly 2030 hrs and I have been trying to hail the Grisham's on the radio for the past thirty minutes, No answer. This trip could have been a complete waste. Coming into town, I had to avoid being seen by a group of those monsters. I parked the car within short walking distance of the local Victoria, TX water tower. No sooner than I was three hundred yards away from my car, there were scores of them surrounding it. I have no idea how they can triangulate sounds like they do. A living person would be hard pressed to do this. My thoughts drifted to the structure of the ear, and how the parts must stiffen in death.

The sun will be setting soon, and I'm getting tired of writing. I am safely one hundred and fifty feet off the ground, on the tower with my pack. It is drizzling rain and I am miserable. I will continue to attempt contact with the survivors.

February 28th

0923 hrs

I found them. Not much time to write. I turned the radio on this morning at 0800 hrs, and walked around to the opposite side of the tower, just to make sure on reception. After three attempts, William's familiar voice answered up, "Thank god, we need help, where are you?" I exchanged information with him and told him that I have been picking up his transmission for a few days and that myself and another man named John were holed up at a marina on an island off the coast of Texas.

I asked him how things were and he said that his position was completely surrounded by the dead. I told him that I was broadcasting from the Victoria water tower and asked him where he was in reference to the tower. The directions he gave were simple, as he was only a couple miles from my location. Leaving now . . .

Left on Main. (Brown Ave.)
¼ mile. Right on Elm. Keep going.
I'll know the house when I see it.

1641 hrs

I have them. William is driving.

After speaking with William this morning, I departed the area to look for them. I hot-wired the car again (much more simple this time) and sped toward the directions that I jotted down. The house was not difficult to find, as it was the one swarming with at least a hundred undead. I could see William's face through the gaping hole where the attic vent once was. Even from this distance, I could see the defeat in his eyes. I don't know what came over me. Maybe I am still human inside after all. There just might be a conscience there. I radioed William to "hang tight." I slammed on my brakes, jumped out of the car and opened fire on the crowd of devils. A hundred sets of white eyes immediately turned my way, and I could swear, one hundred mouths opened in unison and called my name.

Of course, my fear was making my eyes see this, but they *were* coming after me. I jumped back in the car, slammed it in reverse and turned around. Just when the first of them reached the car and started to pound, I took off leading them away from William and his family.

I keyed the microphone and told William to get his family ready to get out onto the roof as near to the ledge as possible. I was going very slowly, so that they would give chase and stay with me. William told me over the CB that they were all following me and that the plan was working. The only ones left behind, were the ones I was lucky enough to put down with a random freak headshot when I opened fire.

Rounding the block, I waited until they were almost upon me until I hit the fucking gas and made for the Grisham house. I could see William, his wife, and a little girl on the roof. I drove the car up to the side of the house to lessen the distance they would have to jump. I got out and covered them as William jumped first and held his arms out for the others.

One of them came walking outside the shattered front door, and saw William's wife as she was sliding down the roof, legs hanging over. It made for her. I took aim and popped the bastard in the mouth. That didn't stop it. I was getting tired. One more round to the dome put it in its place.

I swung my upper body back around to the street like a tank turret. Still clear. They were all on the ground. William started to say thanks when I cut him off. The two girls were in the back. William got in and put his seatbelt on. I passed my rifle to William and sped off, back toward Seadrift. It is going to be too dark to take the boat back to Matagorda. I have no way to find it in the dark, as I left the NVGs with John. We are going to have to find a safe place to sleep in or near Seadrift tonight.

February 29th
0645 hrs

I could not get John on the radio last night or this morning. We ended up sleeping on the boat. I pulled her out a hundred meters from the marina and anchored her. We were safe, and I actually got some decent sleep. The Buick is parked right next to the dock. Not sure if I will ever need it again, but it is a good car. Leaving in a few minutes for the island with the new survivors. Have not had much time to chat with them, as they slept very deeply as soon as we were safely anchored. The little girl (Laura) whined in her sleep last night.

0900 hrs

No sign of John. No note written, nothing. No sign of struggle. Myself, William, Jan, and little Laura are safe within the confines of the marina. I am worried about John. He is much too conservative to do something like this. Annabelle was happy to see me, but she was especially happy to see Laura. The little girl smiled and was very happy to have a dog to play with. Maybe John took a boat out and will show soon . . .

Stand

There is still no sign of John. I feel like I need to look for him, but I have no idea where to start. What would make him leave with no notice? His weapon is gone and the drawbridge mechanism we rigged is drawn back. It is all very confusing. I am taking this down time to get to know the Grisham family a bit better. They do not know John, but can see the worry in my eyes that I am trying to hide.

March 3rd

0914 hrs

John was bloody, tired and defeated. He came back this morning and called out to me. I ran outside and pushed the marina draw-bridge over to him. He fainted at the shoreline and I had to carry him inside. John isn't a big man, only about 160 lbs. I slung him over my shoulder and walked over the drawbridge, and pulled the rope to slide it back my direction and attach it back to the marina wall. When I got him inside and put him on a makeshift bed, I noticed the photograph in his bloody hand.

   A bloodstained picture of a woman fell to the floor from his clutch. I knew in my heart who it was. It was his wife. He has been in and out of consciousness since his arrival early this morning. He has taken some water, and has attempted to drink some canned soup. Janet and I will continue to monitor him.

   William's wife, Jan was a registered nurse (quit her nursing job a couple years ago for medical school). She wasn't a doctor, but who is anymore?

Janet examined him head to toe, paying special attention to John's lacerations. None of them appeared to be bite marks. One of them looked like a small caliber bullet wound (entry and exit wound on his shoulder), while others looked like tumble injuries. John was in no shape to explain anything as he could barely take a drink of water/soup without vomiting and passing out. I am worried.

March 4th

2014 hrs

John finally snapped out of it. I told him how worried I was, and how I had no idea what happened to him. He then proceeded to tell me that he hit his breaking point during the loneliness of the past few days. While I was away, all he could think of was his wife and son, and how much he loved them. Jan was listening from the adjacent room, and I could tell she felt for him. John told me how he remembered leaving some items in the aircraft when we abandoned it, and he was missing the only picture he had of his wife. He told me that he could never ask me to risk my life over a picture, so instead of waiting on me to get back, he decided that he would attempt to get it on his own.

He made it to the ruined aircraft, and retrieved the small bag containing the photo, and immediately started heading back. He was soon besieged by many undead, and had to take refuge in a hotel. He managed to barricade the second floor of the five-floor hotel. He then proceeded to clear out any unsecured guests with his .22 rifle. After three days and nights of enduring the sounds of the trapped undead guests in their rooms, he decided to make an escape.

He went room to room (ensuring they were not occupied) and collected sheets from the vacant beds. Using square knots, he formed a long escape rope. Early on the morning of his escape, he found the right window to climb out of. The window he chose was on the third floor, and a large tree growing near the window obscured street view. He climbed down the sheets with his rifle slung over his shoulder. He dropped the non-breakable gear to the ground.

About the time he started climbing down, he felt one of the knots starting to slip on his sheet rope. It was too late to climb back up and check. He continued his descent. The knot gave way as he reached the 2nd floor level. He fell hard and fast through the tree branches and was cut up pretty well on the way down. When he hit the ground, his rifle discharged and the bullet entered the back of his shoulder and exited the front.

His next memory was of me carrying him back onto the dock.

March 5th

1230 hrs

Woke up this morning in a cold sweat around 0600. The Grisham family was still sleeping in the other room of the marina. John and I were crashed out on the two couches in the office. I know I had a terrible dream last night, but I just can't grasp what it was. I just remember running . . . fast. The first thing I saw when I woke up, were the small droplets of blood on the wall, left over from the harbor-master's suicide. John didn't wake up until 1130 or so.

Thankfully, the bullet wound and lacerations don't seem to be critically infected, just some small reddening around the edges of some of the cuts. Lucky for him, the round passed through his shoulder. He might have died of infection if one of us had to attempt to extract it on our own.

Medical supplies would be a nice luxury to have, especially since there is someone around that might be able to use them. Of course, a nice bunker with eight-foot thick steel walls, geothermal power, and unlimited food and water would be nice also. People in hell want ice water.

. . . Who am I kidding?

There is no more hell.

Hell is here.

I want ice water.

Quiet Time

1944 hrs

Laura and Annabelle played in the back room of the marina while Jan, John, William and myself talked about our experiences. William explained his situation in the attic, and how it came to that. John was lying on the couch with his makeshift sling (ironically made from a torn sheet).

I expressed the fact that we can't exist here on this island forever. We would never be safe from the hordes that are roaming the streets. What if a hurricane came and washed the marina away, or even worse, washed it up on the shore? A million things could go wrong. We only have limited fuel here for the boats. None of us know how to fix/operate the large ferry docked next to us. I asked William why he had to be a chemist and not a boat mechanic. He apparently has a decent sense of humor for a chemist.

I inquired to Jan as to how Laura was taking all of this. Jan expressed that she was unusually resilient to all of the horror she had witnessed in the past couple months. I heard Laura whine in her sleep again last night, but did not mention this to Jan, as I am sure she is no stranger to this.

It must be my military nature, but I feel like we are in the same situation as John and I were in at the tower. I feel like we need to make plans, and need to make them fast. I cannot foresee any danger here at the marina, as we have our own little man-made island, but again, John and I had a two hundred foot tower surrounded by a high chain link fence, and were under siege within minutes.

Maybe I am just paranoid.

We have our code words established for Laura when we see one or more of those things outside. We play *"quiet time."* This lets Laura know that it is not time to play and jump and giggle with

Annabelle. Today one of those things was shambling about, very near the shoreline where the floating walkway would be if it were connected to the shore. Its rotted body was having a difficult time raising its head, but it managed to look in my direction as I peered out the blinds at it. I know the thing is dumb and dead, but I still felt a calculating stare, as it kept looking over here. More came soon after. Some looked as if they died recently. These moved faster and more methodically than their rotted counterparts. I would definitely make it a point to avoid them with more zeal.

March 6th

0322 hrs

I woke up a half hour ago and cannot get back to sleep so I decided to check the shoreline with the night vision goggles. I see numerous figures walking around the area near the shoreline. I can hear a sound coming from the direction of the tall buildings. I can't quite figure out what it is. For some odd reason it sounds like a TV that is turned up too loud. This made me want to check our TV here, but I will wait until it is light outside so that the light from it cannot be seen on the shore. Why do they remain here? Do they sense us?

If I had a suppressed weapon, I would execute the lot of those miserable creatures right now.

1242 hrs

Brainstorming, brainstorming, brainstorming. I spent the whole morning thinking of possible safe areas. Of course, no place is truly safe. All of the heavily fortified buildings or prison facilities would be impenetrable, and useless without access. This island will not do. Maybe a smaller island, with less of an undead population. One would think that an island would be ideal in this situation but there is nowhere to run and the only supplies on the island are already here. Once we run out of the low hanging fruit-type supplies that are easily scavenged from nearby buildings, that will be it. William told me of his neighbor and how he was bitten. He swore it didn't take more than a few hours for him to succumb to the wound and turn. It only takes one of them. I read somewhere that even the best thieves concede to the fact they will get caught eventually, it's just the law of averages.

Basing my chances of survival on this premise, I too feel that my day will come. All I can do is attempt to survive. I have never had any children and I see the worried look in William and Jan's eyes when Laura asks to go outside. That *is* shit for an existence. I feel somewhat responsible for everyone. I know that if any of them succumb to the dead, I will feel great sorrow. There must be a group of people somewhere. The question is, do I want to make myself known? I moved the harbor radio near John's couch so that he could monitor it. He enjoys this, and it gives him something to do while he recovers.

I still have my stolen state map of Texas. There aren't many details given about Matagorda Island, but there is a hospital a couple miles south of our position. John's wounds do not seem to be getting any worse, so I'm not sure I will even need to find any medication, but I suppose it's nice to know it's there if I want to risk my ass.

No broadcast on the TV. I could have sworn I heard something like it in the distance this morning. One station has a high-pitched ringing sound, but only snow for the picture. The radio station is still playing, and I think I have almost memorized the order of the songs, and all the commercials. Just a constant loop until the power goes out or the tape/digital feed fails. I wonder what kind of rotting filth is trapped in that DJ booth right now?

We are fast approaching spring and I don't like the idea of being at the mercy of a hurricane if one were to pop up here. I hate to keep moving, but it seems to be the only thing that has kept me alive.

March 7th

2123 hrs

When John and I visited Seadrift on our food gathering expedition, we put all we could into two shopping carts and got the hell out of there. That amount would have lasted us awhile with just us. Now, we have three more mouths to feed. John wasn't yet able to handle himself out there, so that leaves William. I approached him about it today. I sort of feel guilty, considering he has a wife and child. I couldn't go out there alone and expect to survive. I needed someone to at least be the eyes behind me while I work. He looked at me and told me that I didn't even need to ask, and then he went on to tell me how grateful he was. I don't take compliments or tributes too well so I just thanked him and changed the subject.

After conducting an inventory of food and water, my best guess is that we have enough food to last a week. Just reading that sounds like great news, for a *complacent* person. I would prefer to have one month plus a week for backup. William only has very limited experience with firearms. This would have to change for him to be effective out there. After discussing with William what would have to be done in the coming days, he agreed to let me teach him how to operate John's .22 rifle.

We checked the outside for any lurking corpses. We saw only one shambling parallel to our position, pre-occupied with something on the ground. I loaded my rifle as well as John's .22 and enough rounds to do what we set out to do. I left my pistols behind for Jan, ready to shoot. I explained to her that she not leave them where Laura could get them, and the basics of how to hold and aim the weapon. I knew they would be safe while William and I were away, and we would only be gone for an hour.

William and I quietly stepped onto the boat and untied her. We rowed in unison for fifteen minutes so that we would be clear of the marina area. This time, instead of heading toward Seadrift (west), we headed up the coast toward the more populated area of Matagorda Island. No better way to practice than with real targets.

I could tell that William was nervous. I told him to relax, and that we were not going to set foot on shore today. This relieved some of his tension and made things seem more pleasant. Twenty yards from shore, and very near three large beachfront hotels was where we anchored the *Bahama Mama*. I hated to do this to William, but better he sweat in training than bleed in battle. I started making noise and whistling and screaming out to them. It wasn't long before the beach was teaming with dozens of them. Some of them waded knee deep in the water before stumbling backward to dry land.

It was then I started teaching William how to load and fix a jammed weapon. I figured that if he could load while being taunted by the dead, he could do it anywhere. He fumbled and dropped a few rounds on the deck of the boat, but overall he picked up quickly how to load the weapon and aim it. I took the weapon from him and replaced the loaded magazine with the spare unloaded I had hidden in my pocket (without him seeing). He was gazing nervously at the shoreline when I handed the cocked weapon back to him and told him to aim at the creature in the red shirt.

Dramatically, I explained to him the basics of aiming and how he needed a head shot to kill them. Ideally I told him I wanted the shot to hit on the top 1/3 of the cranium. I told him to breath, long deep breaths . . . Only when he was ready, should he squeeze, then only on the exhale . . .

I was testing him. Would he anticipate the small kick of the .22 and yank the weapon when he depressed the trigger? I told him to take the shot . . .

With both eyes open, like I told him, he gazed through the sights and squeezed the trigger. *CLICK* . . .

William jerked high and to the right, his mental reflexes telling him to do so. He then looked over at me, confused. I told him what I had done and why. Over the next few minutes I would take the weapon and randomly load a round to test him. Soon he didn't jerk the weapon at all. His first kill was a direct hit, entering the eye of the lucky corpse destroying the brain as the shell bounced around in the rotting skull.

I loaded ten rounds into the magazine and told him to go to town, killing the fully mobile creatures first. Soon the shoreline was littered with nearly twenty still corpses. In total, this little shooting lesson used up twenty rounds. We still had almost 800 .22 rounds.

We pretty much drew every corpse within a ten-mile radius to our position. No matter, better to draw them here than back to the marina. I pulled anchor and sped farther up the coastline leading them further away from the marina. After five minutes of this I flipped her around and headed away from the island to mask the sound of our return. When we were reasonably close, we cut the engines and paddled back to the stronghold. I feel a little better about taking William with me now that he is more confident in himself.

March 9th
2047 hrs

Yesterday and today were interesting. My humanity bucket hadn't been filled for a while, and it was getting dry and rusty. After the marital spat John and I witnessed today, I know that this plague cannot and will not destroy human nature. Since there was no television, and taking nice walks through the city was not encouraged, this was my entertainment most of the morning.

It wasn't my nostalgia that they were fighting about, it was theirs, but the pre-apocalypse nature of the fight moved me. It was a simple fight over laundry and housework, and who actually did it around the house before all of this. It felt so good to hear a normal conversation for once, and not once hearing about how we were going to avoid one of those things biting our asses off.

Food: Not critical yet, but a revised estimate of (5) days remaining.

Laura wants to go outside and play, "Like her friends at school get to do." I tried to explain to her, with my limited "small people" knowledge that it wouldn't be any fun to play outside right now, and that the people out there wouldn't be nice. She looked at me and rolled her eyes and said, "I know they are *dead,* you don't have to play." I was shocked at the little girl's candor and just sort of chuckled under my breath.

I wondered which parent she took the attitude from. Using my knife I carved a chess board into the table in the lounge area of the marina. I stole some fishing lures from the marina retail area and John and I are utilizing them (sans the hooks) as chess pieces. So far I have him three games to two.

I have a strange feeling that William and Jan have made amends for the silly argument, as I can hear no loud voices through the other end of the privacy curtain I put up for them a few days ago.

Enemy activity: Sporadic movement. Last night's full moon brought hundreds of them near us. Using NVGs, I studied them. They seemed to be more active. Could this be because of the full moon? I doubt it.

I gave my last few sets of foam earplugs to the Grishams. Laura was fascinated at how they returned to their original shape after you squeezed them. John still had his set in his pant pockets.

I had no earplugs left, so I took two 9mm rounds out of the ammo box and stuffed them in my ear. They were a good fit and really drowned out their moans last night.

March 10th

1222 hrs

The radio station stopped playing music today. For a brief moment I heard a human voice on the other end. It sounded like I heard the word "fortify" before the microphone cut out. John and I were playing chess again when it happened. Now, I can't even pull John away from the CB radio. He keeps trying to broadcast in the hopes that whoever stopped the music will hear and respond. The station is broadcasting out of Corpus, so I know for a fact they are overrun. I also know that the radio John is using won't reach that far. Whatever keeps his spirits up, I suppose.

William and I spoke about his chemistry skills. I asked him

if he could make anything useful, considering our current situation. He said that if he had the ingredients, he could make pretty much anything. With William being a chemist, and John being an engineer, I'm sure they can come up with something to help our current predicament.

> *Thought:* I wonder what historical sites were destroyed that Laura will never see. I remember visiting the Alamo last year. I wonder if anyone alive was holding their ground in the true last stand of the Alamo when the warhead hit.
>
> Maybe it answered a prayer . . .

March 12th

2145 hrs

⟶ *Food:* (2) days remaining.

⟶ *Water:* Still have pressure, however starting to taste funny. Will need purification tablets soon. If I develop any symptoms, i.e. diarrhea, I will have to find some purification tablets, or simply boil it.

William knows the time to leave is coming. Tomorrow we will have to head out for supplies or starve here. It is raining and the water is getting choppy, causing the marina to wobble just enough to induce discomfort. No signal on the formerly good radio station. I have been studying the map I procured last trip very closely. There are other options to scavenging. We could head northeast up the coast line and cherry pick, but run the risk of boat mechanical failure which would put us in a world of shit.

Another option is to go back to "old faithful" Seadrift.

Across San Antonio bay, on the western shoreline is another small town called Austwell. I figure we might as well check it out while we are gathering supplies, and food. I need extra batteries for the NVGs and some first aid supplies.

John is recovering nicely and almost has limited mobility of his arm. The lacerations are healing but without stitches, he will have to take it easy for a while. Jan used duct tape to dress the wounds and keep them closed. Yet another use for it. William promised Laura that he would bring her back something from our trip. I suppose it was customary when William went away on business, to bring his little girl something back. I will do my best to make sure that happens.

I really dread these outings, and wonder if there will ever be a time when I can walk freely again. I will continue making the shopping list tonight, and then, I will gas up the boat in the dark to avoid attention. I am going to try to be in the sack by midnight.

March 13th

0745 hrs

Ready to leave. The equipment is loaded onto the boat. It has stopped raining, and the water is not as choppy. Left my Walther P99 with John, and Jan. Not much firepower left behind for them, but I don't think they will need it. Our destination is Austwell, TX (Opposite side of San Antonio bay from Seadrift). Austwell is also a small dot on the map, hopefully indicating a small population of undead. This outing serves two purposes. One, to get William more comfortable with being among *them* so we can plan for a bigger picture. Secondly, to gather much needed supplies.

We now have six souls in our little marina island (including Annabelle), and with two people, I estimate we can only gather maybe a weeks worth of food at a time. This means that we are theoretically forced out into their world once a week, which in my opinion is one time too many. I need to step out of the box with my shopping. Yes, the junk food, soup cans, and other things we have been looting are great, but the lack of vitamins and exercise is catching up with me. My metabolism has slowed down from lack of being able to run.

Luck be with us.

2233 hrs

After leaving the marina and paddling out to "safe engine distance" we cranked it up and sped toward San Antonio bay. I could see birds in the air, and the smell of the open air was refreshing. Soon the Texas mainland was in plain view in front of us. Entering the bay was exactly like the two times before. After reaching the western shore, a few private docks could be seen. Up a small hill from each of them, stood a large house. I suppose the docks were for the owner's boats, although I could see none tied up.

We cut the engines and started our two-man rowing toward the shoreline. I sat and thought about how silly I would look to an onlooker if this had never happened. I closed my mind and continued to row, imagining that everything was normal.

It was a complete mess. Windows were shattered, rats, trash, newspapers, everything was blowing around the dock and street. There was a large parking lot in the asphalt area beyond the marina ramp. I could see five creatures surrounding a white compact car, and beating their rotting hands on the windows. I could not see inside of the car from this distance and angle. I assumed that there was definitely something in the car that the creatures were after, and an even further assumption would be that it was alive, whatever it was.

Quietly, we rowed to the tie-up point and docked the boat. I slung my empty pack on my back, put the pry bar in my belt, put some heavy plastic zip ties in my pocket and readied my weapon, then stepped into this new world. I didn't look behind me, but I could feel William's presence there. I could almost smell his fear. I was probably more afraid than he was. Scanning the area, we crept across the ramp to the shore, eyes trained on the small white Ford that was surrounded by the dead. As soon as I set foot on terra firma, I grabbed a fist-sized rock on the shore, threw it as hard as I could, about twenty meters beyond the car into the windshield of a large black truck. It sounded like someone beat a snare drum when the rock hit home. The things instantly stood erect and started walking toward the area beyond the car.

I told John to stay back and watch for them while I checked things out. I was almost on top of it. The car was an arms length away. I reached out to touch the hood, feeling its cold surface. I could see a figure with the seat down, lying in the driver's seat. It was an attractive woman that looked in her early twenties. The car windows were caked with dried rot, and puss from the creature's relentless pounding. Most of the windows were cracked in a spider web pattern.

I put my face up to the window to get a closer look at the woman. She looked dead. I could see signs of extreme dehydration in her face. Her lips were dry and flaky. The creatures that were gathered here, were now preoccupied elsewhere. I called William over. I asked him how long it took for one to turn (I remember him telling me he had witnessed this before). He said that he had seen a man die in the street, as he watched from the attic of his home, and he turned within the hour.

Nothing made sense. There was an open bottle of aspirin spilled out onto the passenger seat, and empty plastic water bottles strewn all over the car. She couldn't have been dead longer than a day. I suppose the question I was asking myself was, why didn't she turn like the others?

In the back seat, I could see numerous fast food beverage cups, filled with what looked like feces and urine. She had been trapped in this car for what looked like a few days.

Then there was movement. First her mouth gestured a weak yawn, and then her eyes started to flutter. I trained my weapon on her and told William to watch my back and keep a lookout in the immediate area. Expecting to see the familiar milky death orbs staring at me, I was surprised when she opened her eyes, and I could see the blue in her irises. She looked up at me in shock. To her, I was a strange man, wearing a mask, with a machine gun pointed at her. She looked behind her and around the car and with her lips only, said with no voice, *"I'm alive."*

I pulled off my mask and went to the door to open it. It was locked. She smiled and looked at me, and unlocked it. I took her arm and helped her out of the car. She stank worse than those things. Maybe it was the car. I had to support her as she walked. She was very weak and sore from being trapped in the car. Looking over my shoulder, I motioned William to follow me back to the boat.

After reaching the *Bahama Mama,* I sat her down, gave her some water and some canned beef (my lunch). I told her not to eat or drink anything too fast. I didn't have time to stay and chat. William had his instructions. He was to row the boat out twenty meters and drop anchor and wait for me. I was going shopping.

As I stepped back onto the dock, I could hear William rowing the boat away from me. I reached the parking lot again, and I could see more than five in the area. I stayed low and followed the shoreline toward the town. No sign of life anywhere. No dog, cat, nothing. I didn't even see any birds flying over this town. I was coming up on a group of buildings. I cut inland and walked toward what was the center of the small town of Austwell, Texas. After a few hundred meters of walking, I stepped through a clearing. I could see a Walgreen's and a gas station.

I doubted Walgreen's had any food, but I was certain they had medical supplies. I crept up to the front door, sticking to the wall. This door was different in the way that it actually had chains holding the doors shut from the inside. There would be no way for me to get in without busting the glass, and attracting them. I walked to the back of the store. There was a drive-up window for the pharmacy there. That side of the building faced the woods. There could be hundreds of them in there looking at me and I wouldn't know it. I couldn't feel them, but then again, I wonder if that sense still exists when it comes to their kind.

There was a steel exterior cargo shutter door, probably for new shipments. Tried to lift it up. Locked tight. I really need to get a book on lock picking from the local library. Pulled out the bar from my belt. I placed the bar under the shutter underneath the keyhole. After a few minutes of prying, cursing, and sweating, I finally broke the lock. I checked my surroundings, noticing that I had garnered some unwanted attention one block away and closing.

I attached my light to my carbine and twisted it on. It was dark in the cargo area as it was separate from the skylight lit main retail part of the store. I shined the light into the room. I could only see boxes, steel shelves and various other normal things. I jumped up into the loading bay. Just as I started to slide the shutter door down, two of them rounded the corner and caught sight of me. I slammed the garage door type shutter down and immediately thought of a way to secure it. I held the shutter down with the bottom of my boot just as the first creature started beating on the metal. They would attract more. The plastic zip ties in my pocket would do no good, as I had nothing on the ground to secure the door to. I glanced over to the corner of the room where I found a mop and some nylon string. Walking over to the corner, I kept my right foot along the lip of the door, and my left for balance. Grabbing the mop, I wedged it between the rollers that made the door slide up smoothly. Using the twine, I secured it in place. There was a heavy box on the shelf full of plastic bottles of mouthwash. I sat the box on the lip of the door where my foot was. This wouldn't work forever, but it would have to work for now.

After I was satisfied that the door would hold for at least a little while, I stepped into the pharmacy. Numerous pharmaceutical books lined the shelves. Picking up the *Physicians Desk Reference,* I scanned it for any possible useful information regarding medication. I would love to take this back to Jan, but it was a rather large book and would take up valuable backpack space.

There was another book listing numerous antibiotics. Using this book, I grabbed bags of pills left in the pick-up bin that would never be claimed. Basically anything with a "biotic" on the end of it found its home in the plastic zip lock bag in my pack. Jumping over the counter, I landed on the main floor and immediately pointed my weapon toward a blind spot of the store.

Looking up, I noticed that this store had convex observation mirrors, enabling an easy view of most of the area. I checked the mirrors, and cleared the store, row by row. The creatures were still steadily banging on the back shutter door. I hated this. I felt rushed. Tylenol, hydrogen peroxide, bandages, band-aids, I stuffed them all in the big zip lock freezer bag with the antibiotics. I saw some iodine on the shelf and remembered in Navy survival school that iodine worked as a water purifier. I tossed it in the pack. I was thirsty. I grabbed a warm bottle of water off the shelf and downed it. My pack was halfway full. I passed the candy bar section and grabbed a chocolate bar.

Opening it, I realized how long it had been since all of this started. The bar was long stale. No matter, I needed energy. On the toy aisle, I found a small teddy bear, and put it in the pack. After eating the candy, I started looking for my escape.

I was at the main entrance doors. The chain was a standard, heavy steel chain. I didn't want to walk in front of the doors, in case I had to use this way as a way out. There was no way I would get that heavy steel Master lock off without either shooting the hell out of it, or hitting it a hundred times with a fire axe. I grabbed some duct tape off the store shelf. Quietly, (not that it mattered over the sound of the creatures in the back slamming against the metal shutter) I taped up the bottom section of the glass door, making sure that I was not seen.

It took a few minutes but soon the whole section was covered. Then, using the fire extinguisher from behind the counter, I bashed it outward. It wasn't as loud as it could have been, but still too loud for me. Quickly, I headed back the way I came, through the wooded area toward the marina parking lot. I had been gone for over an hour. I ran through the woods. I was nearly sprinting. I could see the clearing ahead of me.

There were two of them in the woods in front of me. I juked them and kept running. When I hit the clearing, my heart stopped. There were so many of them. I skirted the parking lot, avoiding attention. I had no choice but to make myself known. I ran out toward the dock and I knew that they saw me. Their orchestrated moans bounced off the water and echoed from all directions nearly demoralizing me into the fetal position.

I was in flight mode. I called out to William. No sight of the boat. I kept running. —Still no boat. Looking back, I could see them all converging on the dock. No way out. I had ten feet of dock left and the things were twenty feet from my position. They were so hungry. They were rotted, putrid evil. In their frenzy, they knocked their fellow demons into the water . . . —just to be the first to eat my flesh. I turned and ran.

I dove into the water and started swimming away. I did the sidestroke for a full minute before I started treading water and looking back toward the dock. The dock was full of bodies, so full that many fell off from lack of standing room. There I was, treading water, alone. I kept imagining that there was something below the water tugging on my boots. I was terrified and accidentally swallowed some water down the wrong pipe and imagined how many of those things were rotting in the murky deep.

Then came the hum of an engine. I still had all my gear strapped to my body, but it is surprising how easy it is to float if you just blow some air into your clothing. I waved excitedly at the boat. It was William. He saw me.

The boat went to idle and drifted over to my position with the engine still running. I handed William my pack and my rifle from the water. I then pulled myself on board. William told me that the parking lot filled shortly after I left. He had no choice but to try and drive them away from the marina for my safety. I checked my backpack; only a little water seeped into the freezer bags. Not enough to hurt the contents.

We headed back to John, Jan, Laura, and Annabelle. I was wet, cold and without the food I set out to get. If the boat had not shown, I don't know where I would have ended up. I'm not sure how long I could have swam and would have undoubtedly been followed down the shoreline until I was too tired to swim any longer. Admitting defeat, my tired body would have been torn apart as I stumbled into the shallows . . . —Into open arms.

Ides of March

I spent yesterday and today fighting off a cold from my recent swimming adventure and also cleaning and drying my rifle. Only in a world like this could a common cold mean a death sentence. It's not bad, I just feel weaker than normal and a little fever. Jan advises against using any antibiotics unless in dire need, as she claims the body would get used to the medication and it would do no good in the future if really needed. Jan also tended to the new arrival, Tara. Tara had been trapped in that car for days. She was on the verge of dying from dehydration when William and I showed up. She was feeling better. Jan had made sure she stayed hydrated and in bed.

I caught her looking at me a few times today. She didn't catch me, but I did the same. She was attractive, and I am human. I overheard her conversation with Jan about how she got to the dock.

Trapped in her house in Austwell, she saw an opportunity for escape. She made it to the marina and was spotted by three of them while looking for a boat to escape in. She had no choice but to seek shelter in the nearest unlocked car she could find. Tara was a marketing major at a local junior college. She commented on how none of it mattered and figured that her marketing career was now over before it started. Both women laughed at this.

William and John took the boat out and caught ten fish yesterday. John was up to it and I figured some sun would do him good. Laura asked me how my trip to the store went. I told her it went fine, and that I was sorry I didn't find her anything to eat.

She said it was OK and that her daddy didn't bring her anything back from the trip anyway. I remembered the bear. I gave it to William so he could sun dry it before giving it to her, as it got wet when I jumped in the water to escape the creatures. I told Laura not to be sad and that he had a present for her and he was just waiting for the right time to give it to her. She smiled and walked off to investigate.

Raw fish isn't my favorite entrée, but millions of Japanese can't be wrong. Well, maybe there are a million of them left alive, I wouldn't know. Once again, my personal groundhog day is coming and I dread leaving again. We need a better life, and a better place to live.

March 17th

1833 hrs

Around the table we were, like knights of old, discussing our battle plans. Jan, Tara, John, William and myself discussed at length all possibilities for finding a new place to live. An island stronghold has a certain mystique and attraction, however we ruled this out due to the constant need to travel to the mainland and scavenge. Where would a defensible position exist that was not near a major city?

There was a large map of the United States on the wall in the gift shop. It had no detail, just rivers and state lines and capital cities. I pulled the map off the wall, and we all studied it at length. My own selfish reasons kicked in, and I suggested we take a boat along the coastline and cruise up the Mississippi river to find a suitable location (would be nearer to my parents). That was one option. William suggested we go by land to avoid the catastrophic effect of boat mechanical failure. John suggested sailing along the coast around southern Florida, and straight to the Bahamas.

Everyone smiled at that idea, but it goes back to having a limited supply of goods and the need to scavenge. We were safe for now, as all the noise our boat engine has been making on our fishing/scavenging trips has been fooling them to other parts of the island, but this wouldn't last forever. We needed a more permanent place to live.

We are all playing poker tonight as a morale booster. Lara, Annabelle, and "Tubby" the teddy bear have other plans, they are playing house.

Refulgence of Claudia

March 18th

2148 hrs

We have been living off of fish the past few days. I found a propane cooking plate on one of the larger boats in the marina, and finally had some cooked meat. We have different food now. I ventured out on the island today with William. We took the *Bahama Mama* out west along the island coast to find some food. According to my map, Matagorda Island is roughly 25 miles long and two to three miles wide. I thought about rigging a sound device up by remote as a distracter for these things, so as to draw them to a certain point on the island while William and I explore other parts. John is working on the idea.

William and I found something of interest today. We must have went ten miles west along the coast when something appeared inland behind some trees. It looked like some sort of tower. When we got closer, it became apparent that this was the island's lighthouse. It was a large black spire rising up roughly one hundred and fifty feet with a large glass lens room at the top. At the base of the lighthouse stood the keepers home I assume. This area seemed secluded, but I knew it wouldn't be longer than a couple hours before the sound of our engines would bring them to our general location.

We dropped anchor ten feet from dry land. I jumped out into the ankle high water. It was warm. This area was more rural than the marina area. The upside to this is, less living population = less dead population. The downside was that the trees were blocking my view to most of the area around the lighthouse.

William had gotten better with the .22 rifle the past few days. We were down to 700 .22 rounds for his weapon, and I only had

145

450 .223 rounds (a little target practice for me also). We crept up to the wooded area around the lighthouse. Something was making noise though. The closer we got to the structure, the louder the noise was. It was a constant, even interval banging noise, but still no visual sign of the undead. We were at the clearing. The lighthouse looked very old. I'm sure at one point its flat black paint was glossy, but years of salt air and rain have made their mark. The house attached to the bottom of the lighthouse seemed more modern. Three months worth of weeds and grass grew in the yard. The banging noise was obviously coming from the direction of the lighthouse.

We moved in. I kept signaling him to check our flank, as to avoid a possible rear assault. —Bang . . . Bang . . . Bang . . . The noise kept on, similar to the timing of a second hand on a clock. William and I walked the perimeter of the lighthouse/house. It was obvious the direction the noise was coming from. The basement access door on the backside of the house was shaking with every pound made below. I wasn't a hundred percent sure, but I knew what was down there.

I knew the door was secure (for some odd reason from the outside) and whatever was down there would stay down there until the door rotted of the hinges, or I let it out. We approached the front door to the house. It was not locked but the windows were boarded up, which for the life of me I couldn't figure out. I carefully turned the knob and flung the door open and both of us jumped back, aiming our weapons. We must have looked ridiculous.

The house smelled of rotting flesh. Not good. I almost wanted to say "fuck it" and just live off of fish for the rest of my life, but I was here, and we all needed food and supplies. The floor of this seaside dwelling was old and wooden. Every creek sounded like thunder. We were in the living room. I whispered to William, "Do you think there is a door to the basement inside the house?" He wasn't sure. I hoped there wasn't. On the floor I immediately noticed dried blood. It led to the hallway. Bloody handprints were apparent, and looked as if someone or something dragged itself into the hallway.

I went first, and William followed. Rounding the corner to the hall, I noticed that the blood trail curved into what I thought was a bedroom. I followed it. Heart pounding, sweating, scared, I was at the door where the trail led. The door was shut, and dried bloody handprints were all over the bottom half of it. I listened and reached for the knob. No sound. I quietly turned the knob and opened the door an inch, and rot hit my nostrils. I could see a pair of legs clothed in dirty jeans lying on the bed. I walked in. I saw what was left of a man, I think. His plaid shirt and denim were caked with blood, and his head from the nose up was gone. Maggots infested the open wounds, and I could see his skin move from the crawling larva underneath.

A twelve gauge hunting shotgun sat on his chest. Pulling the shotgun from his rotting grip, I noticed a yellow piece of paper with writing in black ink.

Feb. 12th

My dearest Claudia,

I love you so much. I know you are in heaven looking down, + you know the pain I am feeling. Even though I know that it is not you in the basement, still, I cannot bring myself to do it.

Please forgive me for not giving you peace.

I am a coward.

May God forgive me for what I am about to do.

I will always love you.

—Frank

I handed the note to William. Neither of us spoke for the next few minutes. The shotgun was a nice find, and so were the three boxes of shells on the dresser. We checked inside the dresser, in the sock drawer and found a .357 Smith and Wesson revolver with a box of fifty shells. Next was the kitchen. The canned goods, cooking oil and spices and anything else non-perishable were coming with us. There wasn't as much food as I expected to find. The incessant banging kept on relentlessly. Claudia wasn't giving up.

I remembered seeing a wheelbarrow around back near the basement door. I took it to the front and William and I filled it with our findings. I told William my thoughts about the basement, and that there may be more food and weapons down there. We agreed to open the door and take care of Claudia.

William volunteered to open the door and let me shoot. Carefully, he slid the "t-handle" lock up, out of the concrete sleeve, unlocking the door. The banging continued. She didn't know we were here, she just knew she was hungry and wanted out. I dreaded the thought of looking at her.

William grabbed the handle and was about to pull when I told him to wait. There was a safer way. I told William to find some rope or twine in the house. After a few minutes, he came back with a ball of knitting yarn from one of the spare bedrooms. I had him double it up and tie it to the handle and step back fifteen or so feet. I gave him the signal, and he yanked the doubled up yarn, pulling the door open.

There she was . . . rotted, putrid, evil. Her rotting milky eyes locked onto us and what was left of her lips curled back over her yellow, jagged teeth. Her hands were nothing more than bloody nubs from countless weeks of impact with the wooden cellar door. She lunged for us. Just as she reached the outside of the doorway, she tripped over the top step and tumbled face first into the ground. I took this opportunity to give her the peace that Frank could not. I shot the back of her head at point blank range, sending her back to her husband.

The cellar was dark and foreboding. I switched on the flashlight mounted on my rifle. The bright light filled the stairwell. Giving my eyes a moment to adjust, I thought about what other horrors could or would be lurking down here in the bowels of this old lighthouse. I stepped down into the darkness and found no creatures, living or dead. Claudia was it. I called William down to help. There were countless mason jars filled with green beans, yams, and other vegetables. There was also a considerable wine selection, and more canned goods.

It looked as if Frank and Claudia originally held up down here, as a bed, stove and refrigerator were in place and a Remington 7mm mag. hunting rifle with a scope sat barrel up, propped in the corner. On top of the refrigerator, were two boxes of 7mm shells. We took as much food as we could carry, along with the hunting rifle.

We filled our packs with the food, weapons and ammunition. The majority of the goods we found went in the wheelbarrow. I took off my pack and told William I would be back shortly. I walked toward the lighthouse. I wanted to go to the top to get a better view and see if we could expect any company. Round and round I went up the spiral staircase to the apex of the spire.

Reaching the top, I scanned the area. In the direction we came from, (east) I could see maybe twenty of those things milling about in a group headed our general direction. The sound of our boat and the gunshot were the catalysts.

I judged by their current rate of movement that we had plenty of time to leave. I ran back down the stairs and William and I took turns pushing the wheelbarrow back to the boat. We loaded up the *Mama* and headed back home. We got lucky today.

March 20th

1517 hrs

I just received a radio broadcast over the Citizen Band radio. The person claimed to be a congressman from the state of Louisiana, safe in a bunker a hundred miles north of New Orleans. His voice was rugged and tired. He went on to claim that he had many surviving soldiers of the Louisiana National Guard with him. The reason for his announcement was to warn any possible survivors of the threats posed by the radiation exposed undead. Apparently, New Orleans was destroyed in the strategic nuclear bombing campaign.

The congressman had sent out scouts equipped with dosimeters and Geiger counters to survey the damage to the city and the undead ranks. Out of the ten sent out, six returned. The scouts reported to the congressman that the radiation riddled undead showed little signs of decomposition and were faster and more coordinated than their non-irradiated counterparts. The radiation was somehow preserving them. One of the soldiers even claimed that they thought they heard one of the creatures speak a simple word. Of the four scouts that were killed two of them died from being overrun by a dozen radiated undead on the interstate outside of New Orleans. The other two died from radiation exposure because they unknowingly spent the night in a fire truck drenched with radiation as the other scouts slept safely in a concrete drainage pipe five feet underground.

The congressman claims to have limited high-frequency teletype communications with a base equipped with squadrons of prototype UAVs and warehouses full of high-ordnance military explosives.

According to the broadcast, EMP burst has rendered much of the non-shielded electronics around the devastated city useless. The scouts had no luck hotwiring cars or finding salvageable radio equipment. This is something that I will file into the back of my mind for future reference in the event my luck is bad enough to find myself inside the blast radius aftermath.

John tried to respond to the transmission, however our low power transmitter didn't have the juice to make it that far. Maybe on a low overcast, cloudy day . . . —But not today. Just another thing to worry about.

March 22nd

18 54 hrs

Tara is an interesting woman. I have to hand it to her for surviving. I can't begin to imagine her feelings of defeat as she sat in that compact car, and listened to them beat the glass for days. She told me that she spent one whole day attracting them to one side of the car, so that she could crack the window on the opposite side for a few precious seconds of cool air before they shambled back over. I haven't seen her break down and cry yet, but it is a natural thing, and I'm sure it will come.

Laura is in her own little world with Annabelle and her teddy bear. I have feelings of dread for the day that will come soon, the day we must move on. I somehow feel like I am responsible for everyone here. It would be too much to bear to lose any of them, however I know that sooner or later statistics will catch up with us. I have become decently good at chess and John and I are about fifty-fifty when we play.

William woke up last night at around 0200. I was awake looking at the map. He told me that he dreamed of our lighthouse trip and that the woman in the cellar, "Claudia" *didn't* trip in his dream. I thought about what he was getting at and just tried to put it out of my mind. I haven't seen any of them since our trip. We have been successful in confusing them with our boat/gunshot noise diversions.

No transmissions from Louisiana today or yesterday. We have been vigilant in having at least one person within earshot of the radio at all times. I have been in a slump since the lighthouse, so I decided to shave today for morale. Amazing how the feel of a good shave can make you feel more human.

I have been thinking about how many of them there are. I wonder just how outnumbered we are and just how much of the professional military was left. I remember the last U.S. census back in 2000 and how they claimed there were close to three hundred million people in the U.S. I have no way of knowing how many survivors there are, but I am certain that they outnumber us. I would say that the nuclear campaign cleared out a few million (including the living). I suppose I just don't have enough data for any kind of accurate estimate.

Drizzling rain dominates the visibility. Spring is coming and so are the storms.

March 23rd

1819 hrs

We received another transmission from Louisiana. This time, it was very garbled. The voice on the other end claims that all communications with NORAD have ceased. The theory they are posing is that it probably fell from the inside. They are trying to hack a video feed from their command center north of New Orleans, however attempts to do so have proven unsuccessful.

John is still drawing up some rough plans for a "distracter" to be used against the creatures. I also asked him to start thinking about a mobile way to charge dead batteries, as I feel that many of the car batteries on the mainland would be as dead as their owners. We are building the groundwork for escape and evasion. To where is not yet certain.

March 24th

2339 hrs

We have not been affected by radiation fallout. We should avoid the former major cities, as I'm sure deadly amounts of radiation will exist there as evident from the reports of the dead scouts. There is also the matter of the other information received a few days ago from Louisiana. I can hear them moaning. The wind is carrying it and it feels like they are right outside the window. I know this is not the case, but the thought of it is very disturbing. It is not a human moan. It sounds like a deep throaty sound, low and unnatural. I need to check the perimeter.

March 26th

2003 hrs

The creatures cannot swim, however they can "exist" in the water. It was clear outside today and the water was calm. We decided to go outside on the docks to get some sun. I brought my rifle in an attempt to make sure everyone was safe on our outing. Little

Laura was looking pale from lack of sun and I just felt guilty that she never got any outside time. I stood, facing the shore as the others took off their shoes and let their feet dangle over the edge of the dock, into the water.

As I scanned the shoreline, I saw no movement, other than the tormented creatures that were trapped in the hotel room across the street from our location. I checked back over my shoulder and they seemed to be enjoying themselves. They were being quiet, and conscious of the dangers that lurked in the urban area around us. I looked down into the water and noticed something dark moving about under the surface. The dark green seawater restricted my visibility.

I called John over, and told William to stay and watch the others, and to tell them to get their feet out of the water. On the wall of the marina was a round foam life preserver, similar to the ones seen on ships, and a lifeguard hook for grabbing people out of the water. I glanced at the hook and glanced at John. He brought it over to me as I continued to gaze into the green abyss. I saw it again. Something large was definitely moving under the surface.

I had John grab my belt and hold me solid as I dipped the long hook into the water. I felt it hit the object. After a few minutes of pulling and tugging, I finally snagged it. As I pulled the rotting thing up through the deep, I lamented over all the fish we had eaten in the weeks prior that had probably fed on this man's body. It was flailing and the mouth gaped and gnashed. As it opened its mouth in an attempt to take a bite out of me, I saw stagnant water pour out of the thing's throat and a low gurgle ensued.

It had no eyes, as they had surely been eaten by fish weeks before. This thing had been in the water a long time. I pulled it up onto the dock. As the torso cleared the water, it was apparent that the thing had no legs either. It was still dangerous so I decided to quietly dispatch it with a careful knife stab through the left eye socket. Using the hook bar, I held the head still as I carefully slid the knife home, neutralizing the pitiful fuck.

It would be a long time before I ever decided to take a leisurely swim in any body of water. I slid the dock bridge over to the land using the rope pulley. With the hook pole, I dragged the creature across the street as John covered me with his rifle. Laura saw the creature as I dragged the body away and started crying. I felt bad and hated the thing even more as I dragged the putrid mass across the ground. The corpse left a black stain on the concrete as the slimy torso grinded along the sun-baked pavement.

March 27th

1951 hrs

Wind is howling outside. The moans of the creatures seem to be getting louder as the days go by. There are a couple dozen outside the marina "patrolling" the shoreline. Every second they are out there I have to tell myself not to go outside and execute them. There will be 9mm rounds stuck in my ear again tonight, to block the maddening noise. Even in the darkness of the new nightfall, I can still make out the drag marks on the shore from the corpse I neutralized yesterday.

We have agreed it is time to move. We set a target date of one week. In the meantime, we will be gathering more supplies and thinking of a suitable location. I have come to realize that if you do not move, you die. Even then you do not die, you exist as them, which is worse.

Atlantis

We are in the boat. Early this morning at around 0200 hours, a glass cup that Laura had left on the bait counter the night before fell to the floor for no apparent reason. I immediately stood up on my feet, and felt as if I was drunk, and it became difficult to stand up. It felt I was walking up hill toward the broken glass on the floor. I flipped the light switch on, and called to John and William. They too felt disoriented and it finally dawned on me what was happening.

I had wondered what took *Murphy's Law* so long to happen. We were sinking. It stormed last night and rocked us around a bit. I suppose lack of maintenance, inspections, and the wrath of nature finally did the job. We woke the others up and I suggested to John and William that they start gathering supplies. I had no idea how long we had before the whole marina bait/gift shop went down. The imbalance of weight vs. buoyancy would eventually snap the lumber support and cause the whole building to sink.

I had no time to be quiet. I donned the NVGs and immediately began getting the *Mama* ready. The noise I was making, combined with the creaking, overstressed timber of the marina had drawn a crowd. Through the graininess of my optics, I could make out roughly twenty creatures. They were god-awful. I felt in my heart that if there was a hell, these things came from there and in my imagination I could feel their hot hellish breath all over me.

Even though I was almost sure they could not see in the dark, many of them were looking in my direction, attuned to the noise,

155

cocking their heads like a confused dog to its master. Most were in intermediate stages of decomposition, and I could not see their eyes through the goggles, only black circles, which added to their ominous horror.

Jan, Tara, John, William, and myself formed a human assembly line as we passed supplies hand over hand to the boat. Only half an hour had went by and already one of the corners dipped almost two feet into the water, causing the opposite corner to hang out of the water a foot or so. This meant the structure was getting over stressed.

I put the muzzle on Annabelle, and carried her and Laura to the boat and sat them down. The creatures were voicing their demented sounds toward us. I whispered to Laura not to worry and her job was to hold Annabelle, and not let her leave the boat. I handed her the teddy bear and pecked her on the cheek.

We loaded the boat down to an almost dangerous load bearing weight. It was the lowest I had seen her since we started using it. I helped Jan and Tara into the boat, and told William to stay while John and I made one last late check-out hotel room sweep of the place to make sure we didn't leave invaluable items. Satisfied with our sweep we boarded the boat and I fired the engine up. If it were not for Laura, I would have fragged a few of them that instant, if not only but to make myself feel better.

As we pulled away from the marina, I thought back to the places we were forced to take refuge in the past. They seemed to be getting less accommodating every time we move. We are now sitting one mile off the coast of Texas approximately, engine shut off, drifting to conserve fuel.

2144 hrs

Decided to cruise northeast up the Texas coast toward Galveston. Something is wrong with the engine. It keeps flooding. When I finally get the engine started again, it dies five minutes later. All hope is looking to be lost. By my approximations we have gone roughly 75 miles up the coast. We are running low on gas as I can see the level approaching the floor of the bladder tank. Still, that is not the problem with the boat. I assume it's something to do with the engine, and that means we are either rowing this tub at one knot per hour, or we are going to end up on foot.

It just can't get any better than this.

March 29th

0605 hrs

Oh yes it can. After rowing for four hours last night, we finally made it to a suitable anchor area away from any dead. After catching only two hours of sleep, we had no choice but to take our chances on foot. Tara had expressed to me that she needed to use the restroom, and that after the little problem we had with the creature under the water, she didn't really wish to hang her ass over the side. I guess I can understand. We can't stay on this small boat indefinitely. We paddled the boat near enough to shore for me to see the sandy bottom. I hopped out, ankle deep in salt water and pulled the boat further into the shore. William was covering me with the lighthouse keeper's shotgun. We unloaded as much as we could carry to the shore. We should be near Freeport, though I can't be sure.

Something seemed somehow perilous and foolish with the idea of trekking across mainland Texas with a little girl. I know she is not mine, but for some reason I feel very protective over her. As we sat on the shore I expressed to the men that we should move in a defensive posture, keeping the females (including Annabelle) in the middle and the males on the ends. We are leaving now and must leave some of the mason jars full of vegetables behind, along with some drinking water. We can't carry all the weight. As we leave the shore, I will take one look back at the *Bahama Mama* and say my mental good-bye, just as I would a high school car that I had owned for years.

1341 hrs

After five hours of marching northwest inland, we are taking a short lunch break. I feel so vulnerable compared to the safety of the marina. Enough of them could easily overpower us. Over the course of the past few hours, we have crossed numerous two-lane highways and some four-lane. We are in rough country. Some of it ranch. I guess our position to be somewhere in the vicinity of Sweeny, TX, but I cannot tell for certain and I refuse to ask the local population for help. The cacti grow freely everywhere. I supposed I never noticed it before, as I never made a point to just take off on foot across random ranch land.

We crossed one of the highways earlier this morning around 1030, there was a large six-car pileup about a hundred meters away from where we crossed, it looked like a fire truck was on the scene with the ladder extended into the air. I decided to check it out and see if anything was salvageable. Looking at the wreckage, I thought to myself that I really didn't want to risk driving on the highways due to all the pileups we may encounter along our route. I didn't want to be trapped and surrounded by them in anything short of a tank.

As I neared the wreck site, my mind started piecing together what happened. I motioned for the others to stay put. The enemy was nigh. On top of the mechanical extended fire truck ladder, a creature, hanging from a safety tether took notice of my presence. No telling how long it had been hanging there, like a wild animal in a steel trap. This undead public servant was probably a good man in his former life. The bright yellow fireman's clothing was still visible under all the dried blood. A United States flag was stitched on his left sleeve with the date "9-11-01" embroidered into the stars and stripes.

I wanted to send this thing away with one well aimed round, but I knew this was different. We didn't have the safety of the boat to our advantage. I would let it hang there. I walked around to the other side of the wreckage. I figure that this fireman was attacked and took refuge forty feet up, at the top of the ladder for no telling how long. There was a small bucket big enough for one man to sit in at the top. He probably turned into what he is now and inadvertently fell and was doomed to hang there the rest of his rotting existence, from his safety line. There were feces on the ground below the ladder suggesting he made his stand for probably a few days. My question was, his stand from what? Other than his misfortunate corpse, there was no sign of the undead for as far as

I could see to both sides of the wreckage. The bloody handprints at the base of the white mechanical ladder, coupled with the same prints all around the fire truck told a different story.

We continued on, —into the wasteland of the Texas plains, climbing barbed wire fences and negotiating heavy spring vegetation. We could be traveling for days, if not weeks before we potentially find anything worth holing up in.

2312 hrs

We are taking refuge inside a chain link razor-wire fence area for the night. We found it out of blind luck after fighting through cactus and heavy foliage for hours. The sign bolted to the outside of the fence stated the following:

> Warning:
> Controlled Area, US Government Property
> It is unlawful to enter this area without the permission of the installation commander. While on this installation, all personnel and the property under their control are subject to search. This area is patrolled by military working dog teams.

It was approaching nightfall when John ran into it. We had to take turns carrying Laura for the latter part of the day because her little legs were getting tired and she just couldn't keep up. The fenced area couldn't have been more than fifty feet by fifty feet. I hadn't the slightest idea what the government would want with this small area of land, or why such a big deal would be made for it.

I could see the panoramic view of the whole area and saw no sign of life or death besides our group. No building could be seen inside the fence as it was a flat grassy area similar to a regular yard. The crab grass had grown rather high and I suppose if someone were lying down, I would not be able to see them. We had no choice other than sleeping in a tree, and I wasn't much for that option. I grabbed the blankets out of the pack that Tara was carrying and folded them to a width of about three feet wide. I left the length the same.

The fence was around eight feet tall, so it took a couple tries, but I finally got the blankets over the razor wire, so that I could climb over without cutting myself to shreds. As I hit the ground, I pulled my weapon up to the ready and began checking the grass for any danger.

I walked around the inside of the fence, then toward the middle of the area. There was a large manhole type cover just sitting there on the ground. I bent down on one knee and noticed that there was no exterior handle, and if there were, I would definitely not be able to lift it, as there was four inches of steel showing above ground. There were very large hinges present on one side of this odd looking lid. I'm guessing that this lid/cover weighs more than all of us combined. I hear nothing but the sound of nature. The stars are very bright tonight, and the fence is secure. If it doesn't rain, it will be a nice night to sleep under the stars.

March 30th

1517 hrs

Our luck has changed. I woke up this morning to the sound of howling dogs in the distance. No way of knowing if they are wild or domesticated. Made me think of the sign we read on the fence yesterday. I was very curious why a thick steel manhole lid would be sitting inside a razor wire fence in the middle of nowhere, Texas. I told John that I wanted to take a look around outside the fence as on one side it seemed to be clear of trees and shrubs.

Once again, using the blanket technique, I climbed over the fence, with a fully recovered John in tow. John left the .22 with William and the girls and he took the shotgun, because the shotgun wouldn't be a good idea to use through the fence.

The fenced area we came from was about ten feet lower than the hill we were climbing to the clearing. As we topped the small hill, an expansive view unfolded in front of us. There was enough flat land here to land and take off with a small plane, and a fence, similar to the other was about three hundred meters ahead.

As we neared this second fenced in area, we noticed that it was much larger than the one we had spent the night in, and it harbored a small, shed sized brick building with a grey painted steel door and a series of antennas on the roof. When we made it to the fence, John and I noticed a helicopter-landing pad inside the perimeter. Also there was a large patch of blackened grass surrounding what looked like a very large square hole in the ground.

No sign of movement anywhere. We had a clear range of view in all directions. We could even barely make out the tops of the razor wire fence where William and the others were waiting. This was definitely not a base, but it was something. John and I went back for the blankets so that we could scale this new fence. We told William of our discovery and returned to the new area.

Before scaling the fence, I checked the gate just in case. It was locked solid with some sort of cipher locking device. The other area had a large chain and cut resistant padlock on it. I had a feeling that this area was a little more important than the other. We jumped the fence and began checking the perimeter. I walked toward the helicopter pad, keeping my eyes open for any sort of movement. The hole in the ground peaked my curiosity further so John and I decided to check it out. As we edged toward the chasm, I started realizing what this place was.

I had never seen one in real life, but this area might as well have a "Minuteman III" sign posted on the fence. I was standing where a strategic missile had recently launched. The ground was blackened around the gaping horizontal launch doors. I grabbed my flashlight from my pack and checked around the rim of the opening for some sort of access ladder. There was one about three feet below the lip of the thick steel doors that were retracted back sideways into the ground. John held my arm as I hung my leg over into the darkness of the vertical launch shaft. My weapon was slung over my shoulder as I started my descent down into the darkness.

The shaft seemed at least sixty feet deep as it took forever to descend. When I looked up, John seemed a million miles away. I didn't know if I was going crazy at the time, but I could swear I could hear the faint sound of music. I stood at the bottom of the shaft. Shining my light around, I could see dead squirrels that had fallen down the shaft and died from lack of food and water. Dirt and leaves also lined the floor. These doors have been open for a while. Some of the dead squirrels were all but rotted to the bone. I checked the bottom level of the shaft. I noticed an oval shaped door with a wheel in the center on the opposite end from where I was standing. I asked John if he could get down without my help, he didn't answer, but I could see his leg catch the first rung of the ladder as he began his climb down.

As John was on his way down, I grabbed the wheel and moved it counter clockwise (lefty loosy) to see if it would budge. To my surprise, it did. I suppose the three feet thick blast doors at the top of the shaft were good enough to keep intruders out, so they didn't bother locking the insignificant four inch thick oval hatch at the bottom, but why didn't they close the blast doors after launch?

John was now down with me. He stood behind me as I finished turning the wheel crank to unlock the access hatch. I turned it all the way left, and heard the sound of a metal clank as the bolts simultaneously released from the frame. I pulled the door outward and the hiss of air rushed in or out, I could not tell. I opened the door fully, bright light and the sound of music blasted out at John and I.

"It's the end of the world as we know it!" -REM

I guess the end of the world breeds cynicism. Pulling my weapon up to my chest, John and I made our way into the interior of this modern-day castle. I had no idea of the layout of the place. I took the lead as we headed toward the source of the music.

All the interior lights were on and we were walking slowly. The song ended . . . then it began playing again. It was in a constant loop. I had hoped different, because the music gave me a false sense of life. For all I knew the song could have been looping for months, now that I had heard it loop once.

We were closer to the music. It was blaring . . .

"Wire in a fire, represent the seven games in a government for hire and a combat site . . . "

Rounding the corner to where we thought the music was coming from; we came to an open door that I estimated to be a foot thick. It looked like a bank vault door. The music was coming from inside that room.

I could see computer panel lights flashing intermittently inside, and the smell of rot was pungent in the air. I gave John the look and I stepped in. Captain Baker was the first corpse to meet my gaze. Tied up in a steel chair, was an Air Force captain with the nametag "Baker" pinned above his right pocket.

He writhed and struggled with the bonds that held him firm. His skin was being torn off in places by the ropes. Another officer lay slumped over a command console with a Berretta 9mm in one hand and half his head missing.

I can only theorize to what happened. Baker had three gunshot wounds to the chest and a cracked skull. As the creature sat there writhing, I grabbed the sidearm out of the other officer's stiff rotting hand. Checking the magazine, I counted eleven rounds. Three for Baker and one for the no name tag "Major Tom" added to fifteen. I suppose Baker was infected, "Major Tom" tied him up, launched the missile, then shot Baker three times in the chest before taking his own life. Of course, it is all speculation and doesn't really matter at this point.

2326 hrs

John and I led the others to the silo, terminated Baker, and took him, along with "Major Tom" to an empty room for temporary storage. Power, food, shelter and water seem to be in abundance.

I have no way of knowing if the Internet backbone is still operational. I am currently utilizing this compound's computer system. Most of the secure consoles are still logged in, and many of the non-secure desktop computers are working. Need to figure out a way to get those blast doors shut. Will be looking for the "keys to the kingdom" in the following days.

Hotel 23

I searched the Baker and "Major Tom" corpses and found numerous personal items and a notepad. Of particular interest was Baker's notepad containing numerous passwords for the different systems in the facility, and a proximity card for entering certain doors.

This facility is powered by the local power grid along with four huge diesel generators. The local power has not gone out in this area. I have located some technical manuals in the desk drawers of the control room. They outline different emergency procedures and capacities for this facility. One of the manuals stated that if this facility is properly stocked, it would provide air, food, water, and shelter for one hundred people for 180 days.

One problem remains; figuring out how everything works, and where everything is. We have not explored the entire facility for fear that there may be more of the undead lurking in the catacombs of the outer reaching compartments. One thing worthy of mention is that all the manuals have the words, "Hotel 23" printed on the covers. A ceremonial wood plaque hangs over the main control console with the same words carved into it in English, and below that in Russian.

The facility galley has a large pantry full of canned food, and numerous items called "C" rations. I have never eaten one, but I have heard about them from some of the old timers I served with before all of this happened. There are also numerous cases of MREs lining the shelves in the back of the walk-in pantry.

John, while working with the computer control system, figured out how to operate the remote cameras outside the facility.

No luck on finding out how to shut the blast door. Found the main entrance and exit with John's security camera. Unfortunately, it is a quarter of a mile away down the access tunnel, and up an elevator. Worse still, the fact that a hundred undead can be seen on the closed circuit television milling about outside the doors.

April 2nd

2007 hrs

I have located a hand written schematic of the facility today. Some of the rooms don't match the schematic. I assume because some areas may have been added to the facility since it was drawn.

We plan to fully clear out the interior of the bunker by tomorrow. It stinks like rotten flesh and old fruit.

April 4th

1535 hrs

While rummaging through the living area of the silo yesterday, I found Capt. Baker's personal diary. It dates back two years to March. It pretty much outlines everything that happened here since the beginning. I have not read it in its entirety, however I plan to do so in the coming days.

Found this interesting:

Captain Baker, USAF   January 10th
"I have been ordered to alert status here at 'Hotel 23.'
We keep receiving startling communiqués from missile
command regarding our new coordinates for the
alternate target packages. Although the coordinates
are not in plain language, I have seen enough of them
to know that the data we are inputting will not point
the nukes overseas. We are confined to the silo on alert
status until further notice. Luckily, I thought to bring
almost a dozen books with me this time, unlike the last
drill we were running. My superiors seem to feel that
this epidemic may pose a real problem to our security.

We made an attempt to thoroughly clean the interior today. From time to time, I can hear a mechanical/electrical sound kick in from another area inside the bunker. I have a feeling it is some sort of air filtration system. We cleared most of the silo yesterday, all except the room marked, "environmental control." There is a heavy steel door with a cipher lock blocking access to the interior. The notepad taken from the officer a couple days ago had no useful codes for this particular door. John found a folder on the desktop of one of the launch control computers.

The non-classified computers are using Windows, however the secure tempest-resistant boxes are running some form of Linux that I have never seen. John has been using some sort of DOS like non-GUI (graphical user interface) to explore the computer. He has been able to bring up numerous color aerial photographs of the same area (unknown), only it seems like every time he accesses the folder with the photographs and selects the same filename, it shows a slightly different photo, i.e. different cloud placement, or some other minute detail.

Also on the list to access is a large seven-foot tall, thick steel safe marked ARMORY. Unfortunately there is a rather large padlock in place on the front of the safe, temporarily barring access. I haven't really gotten a chance to get to know Tara, but she did reveal just how curious of a person she really is. She did not like the idea of not being able to see what was in the safe, and searched the bunker for three hours, digging through boxes trying to find something that would be useful in cutting the lock. No joy.

On a side note, all of the toilets in this facility are similar to airplane latrines. Dry bowls. I suppose it conserves water. Which reminds me of the water supply here. We found a large rectangular tank in the diesel generator rooms marked "potable water." Using the butt of my rifle, I tapped the side of it until a hollow sound resonated through the chamber. It was over 3/4ths of the way full. The tank is roughly 20ft x 10ft x 5ft. I will do calculations in the coming days as to how much water we can and should be using.

A Picture Is Worth
a Thousand Words

April 6th

2144 hrs

It should have been obvious the reason the photos that John was pulling up on the secure UNIX computer were changing. They were near real time satellite imagery. John figured out what it was last night and also figured out how to zoom the photos down to what the computer indicates is .2-meter resolution. Using rough coordinates in the road atlas, we were able to see detailed photography of what was left of the San Antonio area.

It was difficult at first to interpret the overhead angle of the photos. Also, the color wasn't tweaked very well, making the photos look a little off. After numerous command line inputs, John zoomed down to a one thousand meter resolution and we were able to see a good section of what was left of downtown. The photo was a few minutes old according to the time stamp, due to the fact that the satellite was configured to automatically photograph a certain footprint at a certain time. John couldn't figure out how to get the bird to take a snapshot on demand.

Studying the photo, I could make out numerous destroyed buildings, and even some of those creatures that must have wandered back after the initial blast, attracted by the sound and light. I could also make out a group of them huddled around something. John zoomed in the best he could to the center of the group of corpses.

The group was fighting over the carcass of a large rat. I suppose a picture really is worth a thousand words. John and I plan to go city by city, entering coordinates and attempting to gather any information we can on what cities were destroyed and which ones still stand. This will take some time, but worth the peace of mind, or lack thereof.

Jan and William have settled into one of the larger compartments, with Laura. John told them it would be fine by him if Annabelle slept with Laura at night. John knew the dog helped Laura deal with our situation, as Annabelle was something familiar from a world long fucked.

Yesterday, Tara and I went topside to check the perimeter, as the camera near where we climbed in only covered the launch bay doors. Kind of ironic how John can figure out how to look at a dead man's wristwatch from a thousand miles away with a satellite, but can't seem to figure out how to get our back door closed. I have to give him credit as he has proven himself a good friend and a very adaptable person.

April 8th

2324 hrs

After a few days of figuring out coordinates with many failed attempts, we have come across cities on the satellite photos that are confirmed destroyed by either nukes, or more conventional MOABs.

I wanted to use the birds to see my home back in Arkansas, but they didn't seem to work above a certain longitude. San Antonio, New Orleans, San Diego, Los Angeles, Dallas, and Orlando and probably New York have been destroyed and we have confirmed that dead walk the ruined streets. This is a definite blow to the group's morale, including my own. John and I, using a larger resolution in order to see a more wide view of the cities, saw mass devastation. Not even one of the photos displayed any living human. Some of the groups we were seeing reminded me of old photos of the Woodstock crowds. There was no way to count, but I estimate there are millions of undead in highly radiated areas of ruined cities. There is no telling how many walk in unaffected areas of the United States. We are hopelessly outnumbered and worse, there seems to be no fragment of any government remaining.

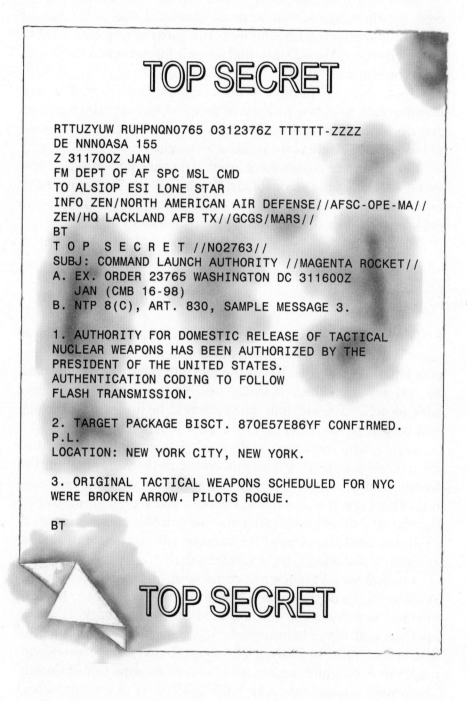

TOP SECRET

RTTUZYUW RUHPNQNO765 0312376Z TTTTTT-ZZZZ
DE NNNOASA 155
Z 311700Z JAN
FM DEPT OF AF SPC MSL CMD
TO ALSIOP ESI LONE STAR
INFO ZEN/NORTH AMERICAN AIR DEFENSE//AFSC-OPE-MA//
ZEN/HQ LACKLAND AFB TX//GCGS/MARS//
BT
T O P   S E C R E T //NO2763//
SUBJ: COMMAND LAUNCH AUTHORITY //MAGENTA ROCKET//
A. EX. ORDER 23765 WASHINGTON DC 311600Z
   JAN (CMB 16-98)
B. NTP 8(C), ART. 830, SAMPLE MESSAGE 3.

1. AUTHORITY FOR DOMESTIC RELEASE OF TACTICAL
NUCLEAR WEAPONS HAS BEEN AUTHORIZED BY THE
PRESIDENT OF THE UNITED STATES.
AUTHENTICATION CODING TO FOLLOW
FLASH TRANSMISSION.

2. TARGET PACKAGE BISCT. 870E57E86YF CONFIRMED.
P.L.
LOCATION: NEW YORK CITY, NEW YORK.

3. ORIGINAL TACTICAL WEAPONS SCHEDULED FOR NYC
WERE BROKEN ARROW. PILOTS ROGUE.

BT

TOP SECRET

John and I attempted to gather satellite intelligence on the more northern states, but were unsuccessful due to the fact of the limitations of the satellite footprint (area of effective satellite view). However, I was able to find some information on the fate of New York City.

Upon closer inspection of the command and control area, I found a black briefcase with a double spin lock set to the numbers 205 on both sides wedged between two consoles. The case was unlocked, and inside was a printed message.

I suppose the government used the space and missile command to take up the slack for the "rogue" pilots. They must have foreseen this coming as Baker commented on his new target packages well before the pilots decided to disobey orders.

April 11th

1233 hrs

Still no key to the small arms locker. I am debating on whether or not it is worth it to go out into an urban area to retrieve the necessary equipment needed to cut the lock off. A cutting torch would be optimal, but I doubt I would be able to procure one. It may have to be a hacksaw. Bolt cutters would be useless, as the lock bolt is so large, no cutters I have seen would get through it.

John found the access code needed to get into the environmental compartment. It was embedded in the file system in the facility control folders. As with any new area we were very cautious about going in. John held the door and waited for me to give the signal. I dreaded shooting anything in this compartment, as I did not want the ricochet to damage any vital systems inside. John slung the door open, it was very dark.

I pulled my NVGs down over my eyes, and switched them on. Walking in, I saw no danger. The room was very clean. Finding the light switch on the wall, I pulled the goggles back up above my eyes and flipped the switch. It took a few seconds for the fluorescent bulbs to kick in. The room touted a huge air cleansing system, of which I have no idea how to adjust or maintain. There were equipment racks holding all sorts of environmental monitoring gadgets. Right off the bat, I noticed two different varieties of gas masks, and also five Geiger counter devices sitting side by side in a neat row. The gas masks were without filters, as the filters were still sealed in the tins sitting next to the masks. I counted ten gas masks of both types, twenty in all.

On the floor there were several boxes that had "C.B.R. suit" stamped on the side. Using my knife, I carefully cut away the tape and found that each box contained ten olive drab chemical, biological, and radiological protective suits, sealed in plastic. Also in the box, was a set of specifications and instructions on how long and how much exposure a human can expect to take while wearing the suits.

It is clear that this facility was designed to endure a nuclear attack. I just don't understand why there were only two officers stationed here, and no other VIP survivors. Maybe the world fell apart too quickly, or this outpost wasn't even on the map. That brings up another important item. It was only yesterday when I found out where we were. It seemed like a long time ago when we left the *Bahama Mama,* and blindly ran into this place after what seemed like days of walking, taking turns carrying Laura and Annabelle. Using satellite imagery, John found our location. We estimated our general direction of travel from the shoreline, and used the atlas to enter in coordinates.

We first had to find the boat. We then adjusted our coordinates and resolution northwest in baby steps until we found the wreckage site where the fireman was hanging from the hydraulic ladder. After this, we kept walking the coordinates, painstakingly northwest again, until we came upon the facility.

It was easily seen, as the gaping hole of the launch bay was an obvious flag. John marked the exact coordinates on a piece of paper. Just to make sure we were looking at the right photo, I took a roll of toilet paper up topside, made sure the area was clear, and made a giant letter "X" with the toilet paper near the open launch bay doors.

After about fifteen minutes of waiting, John re-entered the coordinates and sure enough, the toilet paper "X" was immediately visible from the one hundred meter resolution we had entered. Keeping the same coordinates, we zoomed out to two hundred kilometers of resolution. Though we could not see our facility, we knew it was center screen, because that is how the program works.

We were able to determine using the atlas, and the photo, that we were near the small town of Nada, TX. The bad news was that we were also about sixty miles southwest of Houston. Houston was not destroyed in the nuclear campaign and remembering the photos we pulled up on the 8th, we knew it was crawling with the undead. Using the CCT cameras we can monitor undead movement at the main entrance, however using the satellite photos, we can attempt to monitor the big picture now that we have our exact coordinates.

"Knock, Knock"

I have not mentioned/documented much about the entertainment value of the facility. There is a lounge area, equipped with television, VCR and DVD player. Numerous DVDs line the inside of the wood case the TV is sitting on. After opening the case and checking the contents, I came across one of my old favorites, *Omega Man* on VHS. For some reason, I just cannot bring myself to watch it, sort of like watching a war movie while still on the battlefield.

I have taken to running the perimeter fence during the day. I check the CCT monitor prior to going outside, to make sure the crowd is still where I saw them last, hopelessly clawing at the thick steel door at the front of the facility. After almost fifty laps around the perimeter fence, I come in, and take a very short shower. I usually time myself so that I can conserve water. This reminds me of boot camp, and officer candidate school, where I had to put the shampoo in my hair before getting in the shower to save time in the shower. I have my time down to one minute.

The others don't seem to have the discipline, or the concept of conservation. I can't expect everyone to act like a machine I suppose. Perhaps that is my problem lately. I have been so shell-shocked that I have reverted to logic and emotionless response to deal with the situation at hand.

After checking the facility thoroughly a few days ago, we now have a suitable entrance to get in and out without having to climb the silo ladder every time. There were stairs that led up to where we thought was the shed-sized brick building with a grey painted steel door. Since this access door led to the surface near the launch bay doors, we thought it best and safer to use it.

Tara and I spent time together today. We are becoming friends. Under close supervision, she and I let Annabelle and Laura outside to play in the perimeter area. Yesterday afternoon John and I went outside. Using some twine and four wooden stakes taken from the maintenance compartment, we made a makeshift fence around the launch bay door area. I didn't want any of us accidentally falling in. Obviously, we still have not figured out the coding needed to operate the bay doors. John seems to know how to access the right area of the computer system, but he just doesn't want to make a mistake and open the main doors in front of the complex. Opening Pandora's Box would let hundreds of those demons inside, forcing us to quarantine a large part of the compound.

After watching Laura play outside with Annabelle, I forgot about the undead for a while. It wasn't until half an hour later, when the wind brought the moans of the dead to my attention did I remember the dire circumstances that brought is here to Hotel 23. I rushed them back into the facility just as the wind started carrying the smell of rot along with the symphony of horrible moans.

April 14th

2357 hrs

We experienced a blackout here for approximately two hours. The battery backups kicked in, providing some red battle lighting inside the complex. I suppose the power grid may finally be failing in this area. No way to determine. Power came back on at 2330. I am sure the system is automated, as I doubt any faithful electrical plant worker would be manning his/her post in times like these.

April 15th

1920 hrs

I am going out tonight to recon the area with NVGs. I will be avoiding the high undead population area of the front blast door. That area is a quarter of a mile away over a small hill. John will be watching with the remote cameras.

I told him that if there is any sign of trouble, I would lead them away from the complex and not to worry. It is not like they can see in the dark anyway. Perhaps I am becoming complacent, and I am underestimating them. I know that in large numbers they are lethal. On that matter, they are lethal in numbers of one.

Today I heard the strange mechanical sound four times. On one occasion I rushed to the environmental control room to see if that was the source. It wasn't. The sound is coming from somewhere in the bowels of this complex. It may be some sort of pump, or backup system, I cannot be sure. This is the first year I have ever been late on my taxes.

April 16th

1409 hrs

I patrolled the area last night. Before going out, I checked out the satellite photos in detail from the day before with John. The area is surrounded by two fences, and the main entrance is only accessible through an underground tunnel, or by walking up to it from outside the second fence. I also noticed that on the photos, there appeared to be a small group of bodies on the ground at the northeast side of the complex. I went up the stairs to the exterior access. I asked John to shut off the lights in my area to allow them to adjust to the dark before I went out. I waited twenty minutes for full night vision adjustment.

I slipped on the NVGs, tightened the straps and opened up the hatch. The cool night air smelled of spring honeysuckles. I stepped through the threshold into their world. After dogging the hatch behind me, I took the blanket from my shoulder and flung it over the fence in the same spot we originally climbed over.

I had the codes to the gate, but I didn't want to have to work the cipher lock during an adrenaline rush. The blanket was a safer means of traversing the fence in this situation. By now, the blanket had been cut up in many places and wouldn't be good for anything but a fire after a couple more uses. I left it slung over the razor wire as my boots hit the ground and I started walking counter clockwise around the perimeter.

I could see the eyes of numerous nocturnal animals in the area when I switched on the infrared on the NVGs. Rabbits and mice, and squirrels were thick in this area at night. This is something to keep in mind for future food possibilities. I rounded the first corner to the fence, and walked.

As I left the area I was familiar with, I stepped into part of the complex I had seen. There was a three hundred yard gap between our fence and the other fence I had never been to. Right where I stood, I estimated that John was eighty feet below. I could see the bright lights of the security cameras at the corner of our fence as they followed me. They also used infrared, so they were like beacons to my goggles. I approached fence number two after almost a minute of jogging. I edged up toward the northeast corner. The moans and the smell of the dead strengthened as I approached. I was now out of range of most of the facility cameras, sans the main access door.

I could now see the bodies piled up outside fence number two, and faintly in the distance I could also see the main mass of the dead relentlessly pounding on the main access door. I crouched down, and quietly approached the corpses. The nearer I got, the more it made sense. The fence had numerous breaks in it from what I assume was automatic weapons fire aimed from the inside out. The corpses on the ground fell victim to someone inside the fence firing through at them. The bodies on the ground had been there for a long time. Maggots and other insects covered their bare skin.

I scanned the interior of fence number two for the gunman that was responsible. I could see nothing inside the fence but tall grass. This fence must enclose something important, but I could not see any large steel hatches similar to the first fence we found.

I can't help thinking that whoever shot these ghouls retreated back into the darkness of the bunker for safety. We have explored the facility and found nothing else inside it, living or dead. My mind wandered to the intermittent mechanical sound.

I checked the fence where the damage was present, and found that though it was damaged; nothing bigger than a human arm could fit through it. There were dried blood stains and chunks of skin on the jagged edges of the damaged wire, indicating that some of them were in fact putting their arms through it, attempting to reach their executioner.

Quietly, I turned around and made my way back the way I came. Instead of going straight to fence number one, I crossed over between the two fences, taking a different route. I came out between the fences on the west side of the complex. Again I took notice of the long, level grassy strip. I noticed it when we first found this area. I could easily take off or land a small aircraft here. It wouldn't be a bad idea to try and find one just in case. After all, flying is *not* like riding a bike, it is a perishable skill. I jumped the fence, retrieved the blanket, entered the complex and commenced to tell the others what I saw.

April 19th

1211 hrs

I returned last night from a three-day trip to scavenge for supplies and needed equipment. I am injured and once again, nearly did not survive this outing. John faired somewhat better than I with only a scratched face. One of them, in all its flailing, scraped him. We were on foot most of the time.

Using the atlas and the air navigation chart I had from before, we were able to determine the location to the nearest airfield. According to our chart, a small private airstrip called Eagle Lake existed 20 miles NNE from Hotel 23. The night prior to our departure, John and I were able to pull up a satellite photo of the general area, and sure enough, two parallel concrete runways could be seen on the satellite visuals. A hangar and what appeared to be two small aircraft were parked near the small tower. As we zoomed out, the faint thread of I-10 could also be seen roughly eight miles north of the airfield. We knew transportation might be necessary to return safely, so we zoomed in on the strip of I-10 directly north of the airfield. Cars were haphazardly stopped all over the interstate. This was the main vein that ran between the ruins of San Antonio, and the city of Houston.

There were droves of undead on the interstate. John and I thought it highly unlikely that going to the interstate would be fruitful in any way. The cool morning air of April rushed into the hatch as we turned the locking crank. The flowers were blooming, and it looked like a beautiful day. John and I were loaded down with equipment. He entered the cipher lock code that unlocked the gate, linking us once again to a world where we were not welcome.

Sticking to the grassy and wooded areas, we made our way. As we neared the main entrance for the first time, we were able to see our door greeters in person, without the help of digital enhancement. John and I took turns with the binoculars as we watched from the distant bushes. Two words could probably sum them up; hungry, angry. I doubt anyone could fathom where their undying grudge toward the living originated. I didn't care to know either way.

I was repulsed as they clawed and pounded on the heavy steel blast doors, breaking fingernails and leaving a brown liquid behind with each scratch and thud. Some of them were clearly agitated and were shoving others out of the way so they too could get a chance at turning their arms into stumps.

Another startling fact worthy of mention was that one of them was using a rock as a bludgeon on the steel door. The rock was the size of a baseball, and the creature steadily and unrelentingly pounded away. I knew why we had never heard it before. The exterior blast door was just one of three doors that separated the outside world from our group inside Hotel 23. These creatures clearly retain some sort of primal sense about them.

John and I continued our northerly track toward Eagle Lake. Prior to leaving Hotel 23, we attempted to print out the satellite photo to bring with us as a visual reference. For some reason the security feature inside the control console would not allow printing operations that accessed the image intelligence (IMINT) folders. We were forced to draw notes and sketches on our existing atlas depicting landmarks of interest.

After contemplating the bludgeoning corpse for a few minutes, we continued our journey northward toward Eagle Lake. The terrain was rough and unforgiving as we dredged our way through, intermittently cutting our legs on nature's barbed wire. After an hour of hiking, careful to remain just out of sight of the two-lane road, we came upon a group of crosses erected in the center of a field. There were four crosses of varying height. There were three undead corpses bound to the crosses, as the fourth was dead. It appeared that the local avian life had picked a majority of this corpse's brain right out of its head.

Eerily, the other three corpses locked onto us simultaneously as we approached. Their snarling heads swiveled laboriously as they struggled to hold them up and follow our movements. One of them was not restrained as well as the other two and its legs flailed wildly in an attempt to free itself from the prison of crossed timber and restraints. John and I knew that if we shot them, it would without a doubt bring more to our position. The crosses swayed in their makeshift holes as the dead struggled for freedom.

We decided to leave the area and continue north. As we left this cursed field, I wondered what treacherous group of miscreants bothered to take the time and make the crosses, post them, and then crucify four dead on the cross. My mind then stumbled upon a very disturbing thought: *What if they weren't dead when they were crucified?*

I didn't reveal this to John, as there was no point to us both being terrified of nothing. As we approached the boundaries of the field, we climbed the barbwire fence, and headed out into the open plains of Texas.

I don't know if it was the prospect of flying again that forced me out here among them, or if it was just the need to see what was happening. I knew what was going on well enough. We were fucked, and there was nothing that could be said or done about it. Even a large spider is no match for an army of ants.

We headed toward the hangar for the simple reason that we needed some specific supplies, i.e. hacksaw for the weapons locker, and because, having an aircraft at Hotel 23 would be a very good escape vehicle. Another reason was that if we managed to clear out the undead in front of the blast doors, it would also be a good means by which to scout.

I thought back to the satellite photos of the airfield. Of course, they were taken from a straight down angle due to the fact that the camera was in space. I was decent at recognizing aircraft silhouettes, however, just being able to see the top view wing profile, I was not sure if I was looking at two Cessna 172s, or 152s. It didn't matter. The thought of being able to fly again gave me a positive feeling. John and I continued our journey to Eagle Lake airfield. It was 1900 hrs when we first smelled the aroma. It wasn't the rotting dead smell. It was the familiar smell of lake water being brought from the northern afternoon breeze. As we topped the next hill, a great watery expanse appeared before us.

According to the atlas, Eagle Lake was not a very big body of water. It seemed to welcome us, although after my experience on the docks, God only knew what was lurking in its dark depths. We were near the airfield, but John and I knew we needed to find a place to sleep before it got dark. There was a road on the other side of the lake. I took out my binoculars, and saw that a large steel greyhound bus was pulled over on the side of the road along with several other smaller cars.

I studied the bus for several minutes, making damn sure there was no movement, in or around it. I handed the binoculars to John and he did the same. We carefully edged our way around the shorter side of the lake that led to the road. The sun was getting dangerously low as we neared the two-lane highway. There were numerous cars strewn about, but no undead movement. I knew they were out there, I just couldn't see them. John and I held our weapons ready as we edged toward the Greyhound. No chances. I knelt down on my knee, weapon pointed outward and whispered to John to stand on my shoulder and look inside the bus to make sure.

After repeating this in six foot intervals all the way to the back of the bus, we were satisfied it was empty. We were edgy. I wasn't particularly looking forward to seeing another one of these rotting fuckers, but I knew it was going to happen sometime on this trip. I walked over to the door of the bus, and easily pulled it open. The locking bar wasn't set at the driver's seat, and the keys were still in it. I highly doubt that the battery still worked, but I didn't care, this was just our hotel for the night.

I stepped onto the bus, still careful. John followed. We shut the heavy steel/glass door, and pushed the locking bar in, making it impossible to open the door from the outside. The hair stood up on the back of my neck as my eyes caught a glimpse of something in the aisle on the back row. A human arm was lying across the walkway. It appeared in the advanced stages of decomposition.

John stayed back, making sure to keep an eye on the perimeter of the bus as I checked it out. Weapon trained, I approached the rear of the bus. At two-thirds the length of the bus, I saw that the arm was just that, only an arm. I put on my nomex gloves, and quietly opened a window and tossed the fleshy bony piece of shit out. It appeared that someone had wiped their ass all over the back seat, but it was only dried brown blood. I gave John the thumbs up and we proceeded to quietly set up camp in here (after I checked under every single seat twice).

I had two sets of AA batteries for the NVGs, but I was rationing them, and only using NVGs when absolutely necessary, so that night was spent in darkness sans the moonlight. John and I whispered to each other, talking most of the night about how we were going to handle the next day. The airfield was not marked on the road atlas. We were going to have to extrapolate the location of the airfield by the air navigation chart that I still had. The atlas and the air chart were in two totally different scales, so we knew it could take some time to find it exactly.

That night I went to sleep to the sound of rain on the steel roof. It wasn't until 0300 hrs when I was startled awake by lightening flash and thunder. I wiped my eyes, and regained consciousness as I peered out the semi-tinted windows of the bus. The lightening was becoming frequent, and I was glad that we were inside. Then another flash, and I could see the outline of a human roughly 20 meters away. This was one of those necessary times, so I quickly donned the NVGs. It wasn't a human; it was the lone corpse of a drifter that still wore a pack on his back. I could see his cheekbones jutting through his leathery skin as the thing shifted its weight back and forth. The backpack seemed to be of the type that not only fastened over the shoulders, but also with a chest strap to keep it steady while he walked. The creature's teeth were showing in an eternal grin as the water dripped from its lifeless body.

It couldn't see us. John was still asleep. I didn't bother to disturb him. It wasn't long before the drifter moved on, into the darkness of the Texas night to the next stop.

The next morning (17th), we quietly packed our things and started to head out. On the way out the door, I asked John to cover me as I tried to turn over the bus engine out of sheer curiosity. True it would make noise, but I just wanted to know if the battery still worked after all these months. I turned the key and held the starter switch. The bus made not one sound. It was dead like last night's drifter. John and I left the scene in search of the airfield.

After a couple of hours of searching, we found the runways. It wasn't that far off the main road. It looked exactly like the satellite photographs portrayed it, so I was nearly certain we had the right field. In the distance, I could make out the shape of two aircraft parked near the tower. Cautiously, we approached the airfield perimeter fence, making sure to stop and listen at regular intervals. This fence was not topped with razor wire. John and I easily climbed it and set foot inside. We could see for hundreds of yards. There was no movement anywhere. We felt confident about our safety for the time being.

This area seemed to be nearly devoid of all undead activity. I knew that I-10 was a few miles north of our position and the satellite photos indicated a large undead population there. Perhaps they drew each other to I-10 in a similar way that water drops seem to attract one another. It might have been the noise they were all making. It could have been my imagination, but every now and then I thought I could hear the wind carry their familiar macabre sound from far into the distance.

My main concern were the two aircraft, and if they were flyable. We edged closer and closer to the tower, eyes trained on the two birds, both parked close together. One of them was definitely a 172. The other was a 152, the slightly less powerful Cessna. I was no expert on how to repair them, but they seemed to look in decent shape from where we stood. Once again, I pulled out the binoculars to examine the perimeter from our vantage point. The hangars were closed and I heard no commotion from that direction. The tower's tinted windows were very intimidating, as I could not tell whether or not one of those things was frothing at the mouth at us from up there. It had to be done though, as we knew we were going to spend the night of the 17th inside the tower for protection.

Once again, John and I stepped up to the tower doors. John covered me as I carefully turned the steel handle opening the door. It was dark inside. I switched on the flashlight on my weapon and began clearing the stairwell. No sign of blood, no sign of struggle. The tower was abandoned.

As we neared the top of the tower, the feeling of dread soon left us. It was empty. Being inside the control tower brought back memories of our escape. That seemed like years ago. There was no power inside the tower, although I could see that an exterior light was on at the hangar. Must have been a tripped breaker. I never bothered to find out.

Our next order of business was to check the hangars, as more than likely the tools and materials we were after were inside. It was approaching 1400 hrs, and it was exceptionally hot that day. With complacency set in "heavy," John and I lackadaisically approached the first hangar. I signaled John to cover me and I slung the door open. It was then our lazy attitude almost killed us.

A rotted corpse in a white apron and undershirt came barreling out of the doorway with hedge trimming shears clamped in its left hand. It had no idea it was using them as a weapon as it charged John, seemingly oblivious to my presence. The thing stumbled quickly and fell onto John, gnashing its rotting teeth. The cutting shears cut John's cheek. I could hear the sound of some other movement inside the hangar. I kicked the creature off of John and spun around to the open doorway that was devoid of light. I thought John was fine, but apparently the fall had knocked him out. The thing that I had kicked off of John now had a new target in mind . . . me.

Again it charged in a slow stumble toward me. It was too late. By the time I reacted to the familiar gurgling sound it made, it had already inadvertently stabbed me in the ribs with the trimming shears. I spun around in red-hot anger. After kicking the thing in the chest, knocking it to the ground very near John, I trained my sights between the eyes and neutralized it. The brains looked like blue cauliflower right before the dust adhered to the sticky mess. The shears were still in the creature's hand, as I assume they had been for months and now will be forever.

I knelt down near John and slapped him in the face a few times. His blood was all over my hands. Although my wound was worse than his, he seemed to be bleeding more. I checked the shears. They seemed dry, other than our fresh blood. A sound from the hangar reminded me of the other danger we could be facing. I wasn't going to leave John knocked out.

I kept slapping him until he finally woke up. I helped him to his feet and told him to keep a look out. The light I had seen previously on the hangar was above the open door. Two large hangar doors were on both sides of the open doorway. I planned to enter the hangar and hit the door switch, bathing the inside with sunlight.

As I entered the doorway, I caught a glimpse of one of them. I had no choice but to take it out. My muzzle flash revealed more of them. The flash was bright and it temporarily burned the image of six other corpses into the back of my retina. I reached over for the switch and hit it. No joy. I tried the one below it and heard the rumble of the "garage door" sound.

I made for the door with my back to John, pointing the weapon ahead of me into the dying darkness of the hangar. Looking over my shoulder I could see that John was very light headed and leaning on his rifle. I yelled at him to get back with me. It was game time. I readied my rifle and waited for them to come. The first one made the roll call. I killed her with one shot. More soon followed, excited by their first sight of food in months. With outstretched arms, they gave chase. John was trying to shoot, but missed every shot. I finished most of them in one shot, however two of them I missed twice. The last creature fell four feet from where I stood.

There were eight expired undead at the bay doors and on the dirt in front of the hangar. I had killed them all. I checked my magazine and reloaded. John was regaining his composure, and the bleeding on his cheek had stopped. He nodded to me that he was OK, and that we needed to get these bodies out of sight, because the dead were not the only ones that could have heard those gunshots. We both knew what the other was thinking . . . the crosses.

We dragged the bodies inside a corner of the hangar, cutting shears and all. After looking around for a few minutes we found a blue tarp to disguise their demonic presence. I forgot about my wound until John stumbled across a first aid kit mounted next to a fire extinguisher.

Using my knife to break the seal, I commenced to taking out what I needed. I took out the iodine, the medical tape and the gauze. I unzipped my flight suit and pulled it to my waist. I could see the dark blood clearly through my dark green undershirt. I was afraid to pull up my shirt . . . Slowly, I slid the shirt up over my left rib cage, and saw that it wasn't that bad, but it definitely needed first aid. I shook the iodine, opened it and then liberally applied it to the wound. It was cold and stung a little. It didn't need stitches. The iodine turned my skin bright orange. I applied the gauze and tightly wound the tape around my rib cage until I was satisfied.

Checking the fence, John and I noticed that in the distance gathered a group of three undead. They were drawn to the sound of the gunfire. They were too far away to see us, but it was still an uneasy feeling knowing they were there and reacting to our audible presence.

After finding numerous supplies, i.e. hacksaw, wrenches, fuel siphon, spray lubricant and an old leather bomber jacket, we proceeded to look through the publications room of the hangar. Inside we found numerous Cessna checklists, some of them outdated but they would work in this situation. Also of importance was a maintenance manual covering the Cessna 172 and the 152. John and I took our bounty and headed toward the aircraft. Now there were four at the fence. We were at the aircraft and I immediately began to run the aircraft checklist to see if it was even operational.

It took me a few minutes to accomplish, however, after three attempts at engine start, the prop finally turned over and it sputtered to life. I got all the systems running and checked the fuel. I was sitting at half capacity, or two hours of airtime. I calculated that Hotel 23 was only about a twenty-minute flight, so fuel wasn't the issue. The undead quickly growing in numbers outside of the fence was. I shut down the engine and John and I proceeded back to the hangar to get a fuel can so that we could siphon fuel from the 152 to the 172. There were now ten at the fence. They were not trying to get in, but they were milling about, drawn to the noise of gunshots and aircraft engines.

John and I grabbed the can and proceeded to accomplish the tedious task of siphoning twenty-two gallons of fuel to top off the aircraft. After twenty gallons, the 152 was bone dry. Oh well. Doing quick math in my head, I knew we had roughly three hours and forty-five minutes of airtime before she glided out of the sky. We loaded up the back seat of the aircraft with our equipment. We also stuffed every nook and cranny of the avionics bay with everything we could fit. I also took some oil for the aircraft from the maintenance hangar, as you just never know.

As a final preparation, I took the battery out of the 152, and squeezed it into the pile of supplies in the back seat. We were running heavy, but I had experience with that and this time we had a real runway, not a dirt track. It was getting late. There were only thirteen of them at the fence, so I doubted that they would breach it. As we performed our final preparation on the aircraft, we heard faint automatic weapons fire in the distance. Upon hearing this sound, many of the creatures gave up at the fence and wondered off toward the new sound.

Who was it? John and I had no idea. Worst case, (and it probably was worst case) it was the crazy fuckers that crucified those poor bastards in that field a few miles north of Hotel 23. John and I prepped everything we could and retired to the control tower for a restless night of sleep.

I woke up the next morning to a shooting pain in my ribs. John's face looked much better, but my cut was getting infected. I cleaned it again, and applied clean dressing. It was 1000 hrs that morning before I felt like leaving the tower. There was no sign of undead at the fence now, and John and I did not hear any gunfire the night before. Now came the obvious problem. How the hell were we going to fly the plane back, land at the grass strip next to H23, get out of the aircraft and then climb the fence without getting eaten?

John and I thought on this for a few hours and narrowed down a night approach with night vision goggles as our best option. I expressed my concern that the loud noise of the engine would draw them to our position regardless of night or day. It was then that John asked, "Well, can you land it with the engine off?" I laughed at him, and told him that I didn't know and that I had never tried to land an aircraft with the engine cut except during flight training under controlled situations. I thought on this for a good while before agreeing that it might work.

John and I patiently waited for the night to come. It wasn't until 2050 hrs on the 18th of April, that we decided it was time to go home. That night, as we loaded up our bedrolls and random gear from the tower into the aircraft, we heard gunfire again. This time the weapons fire was closer, much closer. John and I could also hear something that sounded like vehicle engines between the gun bursts. We hopped in, locked our harnesses and I proceeded to get our asses home. I knew that we would easily be able to find H23 because of the security cameras. Using the NVGs I was able to see anything that shined in the infrared wavelength, just like it were a beacon.

We instructed William to make sure the cameras were on and infrared capable before they retired to bed each night. This was our failsafe, our breadcrumb trail that would lead us home. I taxied her to the runway, careful to skip the step that turns the landing lights on. No strobes, no lights, nothing to give away our position.

As I centered her nose wheel on the centerline of the runway, I could see grainy green images of numerous human figures on the other side of the fence. Neither John, nor I wanted to find out if they were friend or foe. I released the breaks, and at fifty knots indicated airspeed, I pulled her nose up and we were once again airborne. Using the air navigation chart, I began to point the nose of the aircraft in the direction of H23.

Just as we cleared the end of the runway, I could see automatic muzzle flash on the ground below. I had no idea if they were shooting at me, or if they were defending themselves. Thinking back to the crosses, I leaned toward the former.

It wasn't long until I could see the glow of the numerous security cameras in my NVGs. I made one circling pass to get my bearings, and then I climbed to 2,500 feet and began my circling approach. At 2,500 feet, I reluctantly cut my engine, and knew we were going to be on the ground whether we liked it or not. I didn't know how to air start this plane. This was a one-way ticket back to sea level. My right wing was parallel with the western fence (two western corner cameras). I kept checking my altimeter, and airspeed. Eighty knots, 1,500 feet.

I circled again, this time with a steeper angle of bank, because I was too high. I bled off some altitude and came around on final approach at six hundred feet. We were definitely falling faster than I was comfortable with. I could see H23 off my left wing. The NVGs were shit for depth perception, so I had to keep my eye on my altimeter. (I set it to sea level before I took off). Three hundred, two hundred, one hundred, 70 knots . . .

At ten feet, I flared the aircraft back to soften the landing. The prop was still windmilling as my main gear set down, followed too quickly by my front wheel. We slammed down hard, and loose shit flew everywhere inside the cockpit. I kept her straight as I slowly applied what was left of the hydraulic brakes to slow our speed.

Hydraulics don't work well with the engine off line. I could have cared less about the gear we left behind. All I had with me was my rifle, as I left the plane in the middle of the field and sprinted to the fence with John in tow behind.

We got to the fence and John entered the code. The mechanical clinking sound indicated that the cipher was unlocked. We entered the fence, shut it behind us, and finally, we were safer. I walked through the hatch last night into Tara's open arms and concerned eyes as she gazed at my bloody clothing. I spent most of this morning resting and getting medically tended to by Jan. She seemed to think that stitches were a good idea and abruptly re-opened my wound. She cleaned it up and proceeded to painfully stitch the laceration. I didn't argue. I simply took a few shots of Captain Baker's Captain Morgan to ease the pain.

April 21st

2118 hrs

We spent the day hiding the aircraft with brush and grass, and moving the supplies from the plane to H23. John is vigorously examining satellite photos to try and determine the identity of our ground to air attackers. Tara has stuck close to me since we got back. Tomorrow we will attempt to access the weapons locker with the hacksaw.

April 24th

2041 hrs

All is silent in the hotel. The infection around my rib area is receding. It is itching and feeling hot, without the familiar soreness of deep infection. Jan tells me that in a week, she will probably be cutting the stitches out for me. To bad for me, she used regular sewing thread. On the morning of the 22nd, William, John and I took turns sawing the huge lock off of the steel weapons locker. I sawed for ten minutes, the other two did the same.

We applied lubricant to the saw to keep it from burning up and breaking the tips of the saw blade. It took almost an hour to cut the lock. In my mind, I half expected a gaggle of corpses to come falling out of the locker when we opened the door. Of course, this was not the case. We were in luck. Inside this large locker was a cache of military grade small arms. There were five M-16s, and one of them was equipped with an M-203 grenade launcher. Not being a trained infantry soldier, I had some research to do long before I ever try to deploy the grenade launcher function.

Also inside our little pot of gold were two military modified Remington 870 shotguns, and four M-9 Berettas. As we started to take the weapons off of their racks and into the control room, I noticed another rifle, semi-hidden in the rear of the locker, behind the ammo cans. Reaching back into the locker to see what it was, I noticed that my hand was about to pull a Russian weapon out of a U.S. missile silo weapons locker. If it were not for the inscription on the weapon, I would have forever wondered what it was doing there in the first place.

In English, and some Russian the following was written:

> *For Colonel James Butler, USAF*
> *"Cold War 1945–1989"*
> *Dimitre Nikolaevich*

It didn't take much for me to have a decent guess at why this weapon was here. Although my Russian is rusty, and never was any good anyway, I still recognized "polkovnik" as Colonel. I knew also that "Voyna" meant war, and the cold war was considered officially over in 1989. This meant that "Khalodny" was probably Russian for cold. This Russian AK-47 was more than likely a gift of good will from one fallen superpower military man, to Colonel Butler. Of course I had no idea who Butler was, but it was probably a safe bet that he commanded this post sometime during the cold war and had encountered his Russian adversary prior to the fall of the USSR.

This made me wonder what Mr. Butler had sent comrade Nikolaevich in return. I guess I will never know the answer. This weapon looked in excellent shape. I decided to take it to my compartment as sort of a souvenir, a souvenir much more useful than a shot glass.

We are now well armed with at least one military grade weapon available per person. Unfortunately, the females have no idea how to operate any of these weapons, and this was something that needed to be fixed soon. John and I went out again to better hide the aircraft.

Now, you would have to be pretty much on top of it to find it. John is still busy figuring out all the various systems of this complex. There is still the intermittent mechanical sound coming from somewhere in the facility, and John and I are trying to isolate the source. After examining literally dozens of photos, we were unable to find any sign of our attacker(s) from the other night.

I half wondered if (he/she/they) would be good enough to locate us just by the general direction the aircraft was headed. I knew we would have been shot down that night if I had left the strobes and take-off lights on. A well-lighted target would have been easy to hit. The gunman was just aiming at the sound of the engine.

We are all taking turns monitoring the cameras at regular intervals, and John seems to think there may be a motion sensing function that the cameras are able to utilize with the right commands. For the time being, we have some weapons to clean.

April 26th

1954 hrs

Took some time, but finally cleaned all the weapons that needed it. I wouldn't mind getting some ammunition for the AK-47, as it requires a different caliber than its domestic comrade, the M-16. I spent the day yesterday teaching Tara and Jan how to load, aim, and adjust for wind with the rifles. I feel that those skills are in high demand these days.

In a fit of boredom, John and I took some satellite photographs of Houston. We were unable to locate any survivors. At one point, we thought we had a decent lead, as on the roof of one of the taller buildings we saw a hastily made banner that read simply, "HELP." It wasn't until John increased the magnification that we discovered that "HELP" had already arrived in the form of the undead. There were four of them on the roof, milling about, probably the same ones that constructed the makeshift banner.

We have also been studying the diesel generator manuals for this complex. There are large batteries that we had not noticed before in the back of the generator room, out of plain sight. Upon closer inspection, the battery gauges were in the red, not the green. John and I researched the meaning of the gauge being in the red, and found out that it meant the batteries had lost charge from neglect. We practiced the start up sequence, and then performed the real thing. It wasn't until the noise was so loud that John and I had to shout at each other before we realized the implications of our actions. We rushed to the control room and John immediately switched to the camera at the main access doors.

They were still there, and they didn't seem to react to the noise. John and I were a small distance from the generator room here in the control room. It wasn't loud, but you could definitely hear the steady hum of an engine. Satisfied that we did not unleash hell upon ourselves, we headed back to the generator room to monitor the battery gauges. They were steadily moving toward the green. It was only two hours before they were at full charge, and we shut down the generators. Main power is still holding, miraculously.

In the back of my mind, I keep feeling the ripple effect of

what that muzzle flash meant. Why would someone shoot at another human survivor, unless said survivor was trying to hurt them? I don't see what joy another human being would get out of killing a living person in a world like this. Since January, I had definitely done my share of killing however; I haven't had the choice of leveling my weapon on a living human. In light of recent events, this may certainly change.

Hotel 23 — Silo Doors

Amigos

It has been a very uneventful few days. I have been checking the security cameras at regular intervals for any sign of irregular undead movement. I feel that the ones at the front access door are not totally useless. They will tell me if anything living gets near them. I consider them sort of my back-up front door alarm. Considering the threat of possible living human aggressors, we spent some time over the past couple of days checking our physical security. We made sure to lock the hatch to the silo so that no one can climb down like we did, and get in. Still no joy on closing the silo doors. John seems to think that some sort of failsafe was in place to ensure that no one aborted a launch by simply shutting the doors.

Bits and pieces of the old world keep flooding my mind. I am not sure the fate of the friends I once knew. Their names are all but forgotten. I do miss them. One friend owned his own company, and was a successful businessman. He had a wife and kids. We were close. Part of my mind wants Craig to still be alive surviving with his family, however the other part of me just wishes his death were swift, as I feel those that died quickly were the lucky ones. My friend Mike was leaving for New York to attend a culinary arts school there.

Ironically, the bullet that killed him was released from Hotel 23. This facility was the backup for the rogue bombers. I suppose I would rather go in a hot flash, than be torn apart by the hands of over twelve million undead. Duncan was a professional lounger that didn't believe in working full time. I suppose he was the one that had it right. Instead of being a hamster on a wheel for his last days, he continued his mantra of just being Duncan.

April 30th

2010 hrs

Heard a loud "thud" coming from somewhere in the complex about an hour ago. After checking the inside of the complex, we could not find the source of the sound.

2342 hrs

I'm hearing strange thumping noises from inside the complex. John and I are headed to check the security cameras now.

Truth and Consequences

May 1st

1424 hrs

The loud thump that was heard last night kept playing back in my mind. The sound appeared to come from inside the complex, however after a good inside inspection we found nothing. This morning that changed. We started hearing intermittent tapping, bumping sounds, again coming from inside of the complex. We again checked the cameras just to make sure. We checked the perimeter. John sat there for a minute and suggested, "Why not check all of them just in case?" I agreed and we began flipping through the cameras inside the complex.

They all showed clear, until we reached the missile silo camera. The launch must have clouded up the lens, because it wasn't very clear at all. John tried to switch to night vision mode, but apparently this camera was not designed for that function.

We continued to watch. A large dark figure moved in front of the camera, blocking the view momentarily. Then more sounds coming from inside the complex. Whatever or whoever, was tapping, pounding on the silo walls. I decided to go topside and look down into the silo from above, avoiding the possibility of putting myself in a potentially compromising (deadly) position.

I grabbed my carbine and started climbing the steps of the alternate exit leading to the helicopter pad, and the large silo chasm. The cool May air rushed in as I opened the sealed door. I stepped out into the sunshine, allowing my eyes to adjust. The first thing that caught my eye was the gate. It wasn't closed. I walked up to the gate, and checked it for forced entry. Nothing seemed wrong, except that there was some dirt on the buttons themselves. For all I knew any of us could have pushed the buttons with dirty hands so I dismissed this and walked over to the gaping hole in the ground.

Fearing that the gusty wind could push me into the hole, I crouched down into a prone position and eased my head over the side. Looking down into the hole, I found the source of all the strange noise from the night before and this morning. At the bottom of the silo, stood a mangled Air Force officer with his arm showing numerous compound fractures sticking out from his rotted skin. The hideous creature took notice of the shadow I cast below and attempted to climb the ladder up to his meal.

I almost laughed at the creature as it attempted its ascent. I suppose the fall from up here broke its arm and dislocated its shoulder. It would put its foot up on the first rung and then fall backwards from lack of coordination.

This undead former officer was dressed in exactly the same uniform as the two that were here when we showed up. Coupled with this and the fact that something had to open the cipher lock, I assumed the worst. This could suggest that these creatures may retain more than primitive residual memories. This officer must have been stationed here and succumbed to his death months earlier, only to stumble here last night and somehow remember how to punch the five-digit code to get in.

Now came the task of disposal. I couldn't afford the full-on noise of my weapon being fired from up here. So I decided to climb down into the silo half way to shoot it. This wasn't something I was wild about, but I would rather do it this way, than draw the attention of the legions at the front of the complex.

I swung my legs over the edge and began my descent, weapon slung over my shoulder. At half way down, I held on with my left hand, and readied my weapon. The creature was rabid, and wanted nothing more than me to fall down and break my legs. I would be helpless as it devoured me. Thinking of this creature's spite towards me, I took aim and destroyed it.

I told John the news, and he definitely showed concern about the gate, and how the creature was probably the thing that opened it. I wanted to check its pockets, but I was in no mood to do it now. We would leave it there until tomorrow before we took it topside for disposal.

May 4th

2109 hrs

My mother would have turned fifty today. All hope is lost at the prospect of my family's survival. John and I changed the code on the exterior gate in the event we had another visitor. The day after our encounter with the "hole jumper," John and I decided to check his pockets. Absolutely nothing. He did however have something that caught my eye. On his left arm was a nice new-looking Omega wristwatch. No use letting it go to waste.

The hour hand of the watch was one hour behind mine, due to this thing being unable to set daylight savings time. Other than that, it was still running accurately. It was an automatic and the movement of the corpse kept it alive. It was a nice find.

I am going out to check the aircraft in the cover of darkness tonight. Played with Lara today. Took Annabelle for a walk also. I let them roam free while I repaired the weak barrier surrounding the launch doors. There was an open spot where the corpse tripped over it and fell.

The wind shifted and Annabelle could smell them. The hair on her back stood up like a hedgehog, and she started barking. I pointed at the dog, and signaled for Laura to pick her up. It was pretty funny seeing little Laura trying to hold Annabelle while she wiggled. Enough of their world for one day, I suppose. Back inside we went.

May 7th

2036 hrs

Although the sound of the evening rain cannot be heard from inside the complex, I know it is there, just like the moans of the dead outside. Thunder and lightning have dominated the sky for hours now. The CCT picture is crackling as the lightening bursts hit near the complex. I suppose no storm could be of harm to us under the ground, however, I bet a tornado could take down our perimeter fence.

In between interference, I can make out the undead horde outside. Many of them are being blown off their feet by the wind, or being knocked down by the ebbing tidal wave of the other undead. Digging through the lounge area yesterday, I found a book titled *Oryx and Crake* by Margaret Atwood. I spent most of the night last night, and most of the day today reading it. I suppose it sort of parallels my situation, in a weird sort of way. No need to go into it, I doubt anyone else will be reading it anyway. Sort of depressing I suppose. John and I have been hearing chatter on the HF radios. It is definitely not garbled, however it seems that the people/persons speaking are using some sort of brevity code. How optimistic of them to assume anyone gives a shit.

Tara and I worked out together this morning. Push-ups, sit-ups, side straddle hops . . . *"We won't stop 'till our freakin' heart stops."* That little line brings back memories of my Marine Corps drill instructor from officer candidate school. What a fucking hard ass. I bet the son of a bitch is still alive somewhere, making someone miserable at this very moment.

May 10th

1953 hrs

On the night of the 8th, something caused the undead at the front of the complex to move away for a few hours. Watching on the cameras outside the front complex, I could see their attention diverted. Their rotting heads swiveled around in that familiar expression of food for the taking. The hundreds in view of the camera faded into the night. What they were after, I do not know. William and I have a theory that it could be the same person or group of people that shot at me in the aircraft. It only makes sense that they would scout this area, considering its obvious value for sheltering.

More chatter on the HF band. I was able to make out the following words: *Band, offensive,* and *perimeter.* I am not certain the order they were spoken, or the context in which they were used, however they could mean many things. We have a few thousand rounds of ammunition from the weapons locker, but I don't think we could repel intruders if we were grossly outnumbered. If they breached the complex defenses, they could defeat us.

The girls have been learning how to aim the carbines, however I feel it necessary for them to get some actual live fire time with them to be at least semi proficient. It would be lunacy to do it anywhere near the complex, as it would only draw them to our position and they would see us flee back inside the fence. I will begin preparing for a daytime outing with Jan and Tara in order to make sure they can fire the assault rifles *when* the time comes.

I overheard Jan teaching Laura some basic mathematics. I suppose with no school around for her to attend, it is not a bad idea for Jan to keep Laura learning. Annabelle is getting fat from lack of exercise and lack of real dog food.

May 14th

2209 hrs

I took the girls on a little outing on the 11th. Hiked out about one mile around the complex so that we could see the main entry doors in the far distance. It was William, Jan, Tara, and myself. We took Jan and Tara out so that they could become more proficient with the M-16s that we had acquired from the weapons locker. Instead of wasting ammunition, we decided to aim for the undead at the complex for target practice. We eased inward toward the main entry area until we were about five hundred yards away, and within a clear field of vision.

I was spotting with binoculars while William kept a scan behind us. Jan and Tara were already loaded and carried extra magazines. It was now time for them to actually get to fire the weapons. They pulled back the charging handles, and I heard the clicks as they released, shoved the round into the chamber. They took aim. I plugged my ears with 9mm rounds, and pulled up the binoculars as they fired. With nothing really to aim at, they fired at center mass in the crowd. Through the binoculars, I could see some of them fall, while others had brown dust blowing off of them in places where the rounds hit. They weren't the only ones here for target practice, it was *MY* turn.

William, Jan, Tara and I waited as the massive formation of the undead began moving toward the location of the gunshots and away from Hotel 23. The girls continued to pick off the stragglers as I loaded the M-203 mounted to the M-16 I was carrying. I had never fired a grenade through one of these before, but I had carefully read the manual over and over the past few days.

A group of at least three hundred was making their way toward our location, with a straggler here and there around the formation. There were more than this behind that group that finally got the picture something was happening and they too started in our direction. The first group was about two hundred yards away when I fired the grenade. Not knowing the characteristics of the weapon, I overcompensated and fired between the group of three hundred, and the larger group behind them. I killed some from both groups. The girls were still firing, aiming for headshots. William was still checking our flank, trusting us to be his forward eyes.

I slid the second round into the launcher. This time my aim put the grenade into the center of the nearest group. The round exploded, and fragged at least fifty of them. The concussion knocked half of them on their ass. It was like watching dominos fall on themselves. Sure enough, many of them slowly lumbered back onto their feet. Now that I knew the capabilities of this weapon, and the girls had some real world experience with the M-16, it was time to head back. We disappeared into the tree line and circled back. Hidden by the foliage, we returned to the complex.

Trouble in Paradise

<u>*May 16th*</u>

1202 hrs

We are now under siege. This morning at around 0530 hours we heard a loud noise from above and within minutes started hearing those familiar thumping sounds, very similar to the sound heard when the lone undead Air Force officer fell into the open silo. I lost count of the thumps.

Must have been twenty, maybe thirty. John, Will and I went to the control room and reversed the surveillance recording to a spot on the hard drive just before the loud noise. On the screen we saw the source of the original noise. A tow truck, similar to the trucks that tow tractor-trailers, was chained to the cipher lock gate/chain link fence. I could tell the driver had put the hammer down due to the mud and grass they were throwing up behind the tires. The gate, and a ten foot section of fence instantly uprooted out of the ground leaving a fifteen foot open space in the fence. The tow truck was all but surrounded by undead as it sped off into the night. We could see them pouring into the perimeter, tripping over the destroyed fence section.

We switched back to normal monitoring mode, but it didn't do much good. I caught the last few seconds of seeing five men put potato sacks (or something like it) over the cameras. Why didn't they destroy the cameras? The only camera left is the main front access camera. I assume they either didn't see it, or the dense population of undead was too great in that section to deal with it. We hear intermittent sounds from topside, but really have no way of knowing what is being planned.

I theorize that if we were to open the silo access doors, we would have a small army of beaten and battered undead to contend with. I can hear the sounds of their muffled pounding even now. They want out of their cylindrical prison. That isn't entirely true. They really only want one thing.

Another thing that is on my mind was why didn't they just drive the huge tow truck right through the fence? It would have been safer than getting out and attaching a chain to both the fence and the truck. Unless . . . —They were trying to minimize damage to the compound. John is working the main camera. He can see vehicles moving behind the mass of undead. Just when they get into plain view, they turn off the beaten path toward the back of the complex where we are. John counted six vehicles in all, excluding the tow truck. The sun was just coming up. Right now, it is quiet. It is going to be a long day.

2018 hrs

I don't know why we didn't think of this before. They placed bags over the cameras to disable, not destroy them. John switched the camera view from normal to thermal. We were able to see any and all living human movement through the cloth bags as if they weren't even there. We have been panning the cameras back and forth, getting head counts on their numbers. Their orange and red glow can be seen swarming around numerous vehicles in their group. Multiple gunshots are apparent. As they fire, I can see the hot flash of their muzzles through the thermal cam. Their weapons don't look military. They look more like hunting rifles.

They keep moving, drawing the dead away from this area, then back again. I suppose they can't stay in one place due to the overwhelming number of undead in this area. They seem to be systematically herding them away, then back. Pretty ingenious. I suppose they have been surviving on the run since the beginning.

I bet they had been casing us for days, and they may have even been outside when we were testing our weapons. I don't hear any cutting tools or anything that would lead me to believe they were trying to force entry. The main camera in the front of the complex is still fully functional and shows an empty parking area on night vision mode.

These marauders have successfully cleared out our front door for us, but I have no idea if they are just waiting in the shadows to kill us at first opportunity. I placed my ear against the steel silo access door. I could hear them shuffling and moaning and beating the walls on the other side.

John's Deception

On the night of the seventeenth, they made their assault. We were watching on thermal cameras, and also on the unhindered front main camera when it happened. They brought crews of men to the launch bay pit where many undead had already fallen in. John's thermal cam had "whiteout" after a few minutes in the vicinity of the silo launch bay. After ten minutes went by, I used my gloved hand to feel the lower silo access door. The door was very thick and sturdy, but the heat from the fire on the other side was immense. They were burning out the undead in the pit. They wanted down below, and on the other side of the door I was standing at.

We had to formulate a plan. John told me that he saw on thermal, just before the whiteout occurred, four men carrying a large box toward the broken area of the chain link fence. It was probably some sort of cutting tool. Over the previous 24 hours (night of the sixteenth, to the seventeenth) I had observed them continuing to use the herding tactic to keep the undead manageable.

They had also brought a large eighteen-wheel gasoline tanker with their convoy. We saw this on the satellite image, before it became cloudy. I now estimated their numbers to be fifty men, and nearly twenty vehicles.

We monitored the citizen's band radio for any intelligence. We could definitely hear them communicating. The code they were using sounded very familiar. Much like the brevity code we were hearing on the radio a couple of weeks ago. It might as well have been Chinese. It didn't matter at this point. Judging by the thermal whiteout, the fire was still raging. I had to think of a way to get topside without detection, and then somehow disorient them to the point of surrender. It was going to take all of us to pull this off.

Here was the plan; I instructed Jan to make a radio call to the marauders at a certain time. The call was to inform them that this was an official government base and that there are more than a hundred soldiers based here, all well armed. If they did not pull out, the soldiers would be authorized to use deadly force. She was instructed to make the call on the marauder's frequency exactly forty-five minutes after we left the compound.

John and I remembered back to when we first came to Hotel 23. We slept in a small, enclosed chain link fenced area with a large manhole lid on the inside. In our days since the discovery of this place, John, Will and I found out that it was, in fact an escape scuttle, designed as a redundancy exit if the others were knocked out. It was quite a ways from the silo doors and main entrance and chances are it went unnoticed.

The girls armed themselves with the carbines, and the shot-guns. I instructed them on the proper use of the shotgun in a steel living area. If they aimed the shotgun down at the floor at approximately 45 degrees, the twelve gauge pellets would ricochet and destroy anything in front of them in the steel passage. I was taught this tactic in anti-terrorism training designed to repel ter-rorist boarders from U.S. naval vessels. They didn't even have to see their target when using this tactic.

I grabbed the M-16 with the M-203 launcher, all the ammo I would need, a blanket and my NVGs. John and William took M-16s and two M-9 pistols, and the binoculars. We headed for the emergency exit, approximately 1/3 of a mile down a dark access tunnel.

Some of the bulbs were burned out down here, and I con-stantly had to switch to night vision to lead John and Will to the hatch. John's hand stayed on my shoulder as I led them through the darkness. I could smell the fear in the air. We were all afraid.

No one wanted to kill another human being, but this was our survival at stake.

We could take no chances with those that wished us harm. We were at the hatch. Jan would be starting her watch countdown now. I checked the time. It was 2155 hours. At 2240 she would be making her radio call. We couldn't risk using the hydraulic motor to open the heavy hatch. Everything in this place had a backup it seemed. We cranked the hatch open exactly two feet with sixty-two revolutions of the manual crank handle. There was no moon and it was cloudy out that night. I could see the distant glow of the silo fire just over the hill near from the fence we were in.

Together we climbed over the razor wire fence, using the blanket I had brought from the complex. We were on the other side. There was no undead movement to either side of us at this side of the fence. We low crawled up the embankment to level our vantage point with the bandits. There they were. Using the binoculars, I started a head count on them. I counted forty-five in all. Many of the vehicles they were driving looked rather expensive. Many had Landrovers and full sized Hummers. They were all gathered around the fence near their vehicles and the large fuel truck used to re-supply them with dead dinosaurs.

At this point I was at a loss. We were grossly outnumbered and would easily lose in a firefight. All we could do was wait for Jan's radio message and hope they would pull out. It was 2215 . . . I could hear them talking faintly. I switched back on my NVGs to check the darker areas outside the burn of the silo fire. Funny, I could see the bags illuminated by the infrared beam of the camera inside them. The bags on the cameras looked like a green version of those old propane camp lights that used the cloth back and propane to generate light.

It was 2235. Minutes seemed like hours. In five minutes we would know what we were up against. The marauders were dressed in a mixture of blue jeans, and camouflage pants. Many of them looked fat and out of shape, their guts hanging over their pant line. It didn't matter, you don't have to be skinny to pull a trigger and hit your target.

Go time, 2240. I checked my watch and nodded to John and Will to remain very quiet. Nothing. No sign that they heard Jan's call. Then it came. I heard the group make the sound "Shhhh!" all in unison, signaling their fellow bandits to be quiet. Then . . . loud laughter from the group and one person shouting, *"FUCK YOU BITCH! YOU HAVE IT, WE WANT IT!"* Then came loud laughter, cursing and weapon's fire into the night sky.

I had to grab William's arm to keep him from standing up in anger. The flames were disappearing, and I could no longer see the tops of them as they sunk below the lip to the silo doors. Time was running out. Using the binoculars, I could see some sort of welding/cutting device being lugged inside the fence. These men wanted us dead.

It was a matter of survival of the fittest. I made the decision. Rather than wait for them to overpower us inside the complex, I decided to hit them while they were all close together. It is a decision that will haunt me forever. I told John and Will to get down as I loaded the M-16 mounted grenade launcher. I knew how far I was from the tanker. I adjusted the sights for my one hundred meter target. I sat there meditating for a moment, pondering on my decision. No more time to think. No more time to hesitate . . . I pulled the trigger.

The grenade whistled through the air toward the fuel tanker. It landed about two or three meters from the middle of the trailer and detonated, sending hundreds of steel shards into the metal skin holding the thousands of gallons of gasoline. Then came a huge explosion. I don't remember what happened after that.

My next memory was of John and William taking turns giving me CPR at the base of the razor wire fence. I later found out that the concussion of the blast knocked me off my feet and threw me backwards ten meters into the bottom section of the fence. They noted that I was lucky to hit a center section of the fence, and not the post, or the razor wire.

I have been in bed since that day, recovering from burns and a probable concussion, according to Jan. John and William carried me back to the command center and made the radio call out to the rest of the marauders. We assumed that some were out on "herding" duty. John broadcasted the following message on all available frequencies:

"For the rogue group that has recently carried out
hostilities against the government launch facility:
Be advised that four Apache helicopters were dispatched
to this area to neutralize all hostile forces in the vicinity.
Any further hostilities will result in
maximum retaliation to your faction."

John repeated this message for half an hour. As of right now, we have received no response to the warning. I only hope John's deception worked. We may have won the battle for Hotel 23 but if a similar force decided to attack right now, we would fall. Either way you look at it, after killing almost fifty living men, I have some serious issues to deal with. In a way I was happy to be knocked out to the point of near death, if only because I could not hear their last screams.

UNDEAD CONCENTRATION

FALLOUT AREAS
(UNCONFIRMED)

SITUATION: DAY 32

X:/NORAD/SCI/TALENT_KEYHOLE/fallout/UNDEAD

Day by Day Armageddon:
Beyond Exile

Aftermath

I started feeling physically better the day of the twenty-first. The attack from the raiders had really busted me up. I got out of bed, drank a gallon of water (over the course of a few hours) and stretched a bit. I asked John what it looked like topside. He didn't want to say much of anything so I followed him up to the control room to look for myself. The previous night John had rushed out in the darkness and pulled the bag off one of the cameras and dashed back inside. There were undead about and he didn't wish to be out for long amongst them.

More undead inhabit the area around where the fence was damaged. They are like water, flowing to the point of least resistance. My painful burns are healing, but they were not that awful to begin with. Just a few blisters on my face and other places. Our victory in the last encounter with the insurgents was largely due to chance. What if they hadn't been convoying cross-country with a fuel truck? We would have probably been executed, unable to overcome their numbers. Outnumbered not only by the undead but by those who wished us dead. I feared the insurgents nearly as much as the creatures. In theory they could at least outstrategize us by putting their heads together and brainstorming on ways to force us from this compound. We do not know how many tangos remain; however, I am sure they still dwarf our numbers.

...

On camera number three I could see the charred bodies of men walking about the wreckage of the diesel truck and trailer . . .

Men that I had killed.

That night we went outside and put them down. To avoid muzzle flash, I snuck up on them from behind in the darkness with NVGs, selected single fire on my carbine and popped them in the back of the head with the barrel almost touching the skull. After every depression of the trigger I saw them react to the noise and start moving toward the sound, blind in the darkness. They could still hear, even though many of them had nothing that resembled ears. I repeated this seventeen times before they were all laid to rest.

We noticed that three vehicles had not been harmed badly in the fuel blast from the other night. There was a Land Rover, a Jeep and a late model Ford Bronco a hundred yards from the charred grass zone. John and I approached with caution. Upon closer inspection I discovered that both of the Jeep's front tires were blown and the window glass was spiderwebbed and concave.

Fifty meters farther were the Land Rover and the Ford. As I approached the Land Rover, I noticed that it appeared to be in very good condition and had no previous owners inhabiting the interior. Bonus. John and I walked up to the door; I opened it and checked the interior more closely. It smelled like pine, probably from the tree hanging on the rearview mirror. We got in and carefully shut the doors just enough for the latch to catch. I reached down to the ignition and turned. It roared to life. I suppose I would leave the keys in it too in a world like this. I looked down at the flimsy plastic tag on the key. It read: Nelm's Land Rover of Texas.

I suppose the marauders had acquired this vehicle after everything collapsed. The gas tank was three-quarters of the way full and it had three thousand miles on the odometer. Not even broken in. I put the vehicle in gear and sped off back toward the perimeter fence of the compound. When we neared the raider-covered cameras we got out and took turns pulling the bags off them while the other covered.

The hole in the fence was about the same size as the length of the Land Rover. I didn't feel like doing any fence repair tonight so I brushed up on my parallel parking skills and maneuvered her in front of the fence gap to discourage any of our cold-blooded amigos from getting inside the perimeter.

John climbed out the passenger side; I climbed over the console and also climbed out the passenger side. I hit the lock in the door and slammed it shut, putting the key in my pocket. Who was I kidding? I'm still not leaving the keys in it.

1248

I woke up a couple of hours ago after another painful, sleepless night. My blisters are starting to pop, causing some respectable pain. I have a few blisters around my eyes where my skin was unprotected by my nomex gear. The lump on the back of my head is starting to shrink, and more recently I am noticeably sorer than I was right after my little incident with the tanker. This is a good sign. I am healing.

I have given up on the internet. It is down for the count. The websites that I had been checking to test things out are down, i.e., military bases in the four corners of the United States. No internet activity. It is probably safe to assume that if anyone is out there to log on to the net, it won't matter. The backbone is shot and it looks like all the IT guys are out to lunch for the next hundred years. The Land Rover has GPS navigation. I went out to check things over and it appears the GPS is only acquiring three satellites for purposes of position finding. I don't know how long those satellites will remain in orbit without ground control station support as well as the birds we are using to take photographs. We are fast approaching the Iron Age. I keep fighting off the mental urge of self-destructive behavior. I don't mean this in a "wrist-slitting" way; I suppose I'm just feeling the need to take more risks because I'm tired of being in this predicament . . . but so is everyone else, so I remain. Heading out in a bit with John to attempt to quietly repair the downed fence.

24 May

2344

John and I repaired the fence with the scrap metal and parts left over from the debris from the raider attack. We also retrieved the Ford Bronco. It had four full gas cans in the back. I filled the Land Rover up with one of the gas cans in the event we would be using it in the future. I don't know why I didn't think of this before but I had totally forgotten about the aircraft throughout all of this. I remembered just as John was pulling up in the Bronco. John and I went to the tree line to see if it had been tampered with or possibly damaged by stray fire. It was just as I left it. The foliage I had placed on the plane to hide it was withered and brown, making it stand out a little. John and I gathered more branches, improving the overall camouflage of the aircraft before we left it to its solitude.

The undead in this area have been scattered. The marauders neutralized many of them as they herded them back and forth around the compound. The cameras only show a few stragglers at the front blast door. The rock-bearing freak is still shambling about there and has been for over a month. It is banging on the blast door, marching to the beat of its own drum. The empty missile silo is a mess; John and I don't even want to bother with it. I don't know what is causing these things to get up and walk around after death and I don't wish to be shuffling around down there and accidentally cut myself on an infected jawbone. If I had a cement truck, I would fill up the fucking hole and just forget about it.

28 May

1851

We are still alive, but our scenario echoes of those that were in the hospital on life support before all of this happened. They were living on borrowed time, doomed to die. We are one and the same. Eventually the averages will catch me. It's the *when* that is the real clincher.

I wouldn't mind getting my hands on another fuel tanker (and not blowing it up) so that we would have fuel for any expeditions we may need to undertake. I could park it a safe distance from the compound, learning from the raiders' mistake. It would definitely be worth the risk to have an overabundant source of gasoline. I am not sure how much those tankers hold; however, I am sure one of them would supply enough fuel for our two vehicles here for an extended period. Finding one should not be that difficult, as we could cherry-pick one from the interstate up north a few miles.

2105

More *code* language on the radios. This time they are switching the frequency every minute to what I assume is a planned order. Good COMSEC.

31 May

0118

I cannot sleep. Tara and I talked for a few hours today. I feel like I have no more purpose, and I'm not alone in this. Many of us miss normal, we miss when punching a clock and doing a job was boring. At least before all of this happened I had a job and goals. My only goal now is to stay alive. The adults got together today in the recreation room and drank some rum and had a good old time. I almost forgot about our situation in my alcohol-induced euphoria. I needed the release. We have been eating the compound's packaged meals since our arrival here. I would like some variety in my diet but shopping is getting more dangerous by the day.

It has been Memorial Day for an hour and a half. Tara and I went outside yesterday to pick some wild Texas flowers as sort of a memorial to everyone we have lost. I personally don't think there are enough flowers in the world. It pains me to no end to think of my mother and father walking the hills of our land like those creatures. I'm almost tempted to go home, just to see for myself and put them to rest like a decent son should.

Laura's schooling is coming along. Jan asked me to teach Laura some world history since I enjoyed it in my former life as an officer. Laura's eyes grew wide when I told her the stories of how the United States came about and how men walked on the moon and such. She has never known a world without smart phones, HDTV or the internet and she's far too young to have ever seen *Schoolhouse Rock*. I'd give just about anything to be sitting in my living room on an early 1980s Saturday morning singing about being *just a bill, sittin' on Capitol Hill*. I feel a bit of guilt that she has no peers and that there is no little boy to pull her pigtails in school.

I really need my sleep as John and I have a little trip planned in the aircraft tomorrow. We are going out to find some fuel for the plane and do some reconnaissance. This time we won't be flying so low as to invite small-arms fire. I have my charts from our trip to Matagorda Island that cover this area's airports. I would also like to find some sort of synthetic camouflage netting to better disguise the aircraft.

Hobby

01 Jun

0140

John, William and I took off early yesterday morning toward the west. We snuck out to the aircraft just before the sun came up on the eastern horizon. We pushed it to the grassy strip where we would take off. In the distance, we could see some shambling stragglers moving about. It wasn't long before we were airborne. It was a last-minute decision to take Will. He insisted that he go. We were able to establish a communications link with Hotel 23 via the VHF radio on the Cessna. If the girls were to get into any trouble, we would be able to communicate with them. We were looking for a large airport outside a major urban center. Before forcing myself to go to sleep last night I picked out William P. Hobby Airport. It was just south of Houston, outside the center of the city.

It was not a long flight. En route we flew over numerous small towns, all with the same speckles of walking dead dominating the streets below. It wasn't forty-five minutes and already we were in sight of Hobby Airport. I thought it safe to lower my altitude, as I would be able to see any living human figures below trying to shoot at me from the open concrete. Approaching the large expanse of paved runway and taxi area I saw yet another symbol of death.

A Boeing 737 was on the tarmac with severe fuselage wrinkles indicating a hard crashed landing. It was the only large plane in the airport. There were other, smaller aircraft—executive jets and smaller props similar to the Cessna—but this was the last of the large passenger jets here at Hobby. We circled around once more

223

to make sure we had the proper assessment before we landed. I could see a fuel truck in the distance near one of the aircraft hangars. The hangar was large compared to the others and was most likely for Boeing aircraft just like the one that is forever disabled on the runway.

Our curiosity propelled us and we decided to land the plane near the large aircraft to see if anything of value might be inside. One advantage to this was that it was out in the open and not adjacent to any buildings that would leave us an easy mark for someone or some thing to sneak up on us. William would stay outside near the aircraft to keep watch as we found an entry point. All of the window shades were down on the 737. It wouldn't really matter since the windows were nearly fifteen feet off the ground anyway. The over-wing escape hatches were secure and we were not successful in getting them open as the fuselage ripple stresses had jammed them tight. That left the co-pilot's escape hatch on the starboard side of the cockpit glass.

I looked up, ten feet into the air on the right side of the cockpit, and saw how we were going to gain entrance to this aircraft. Using a grapple that Will and I had previously constructed from the rope and some metal left over from last month's tanker explosion, I was able to climb up to the window. First, I supported John's weight on my shoulders as he reached up to open the emergency access latch, releasing the airtight seal to the cockpit.

I almost dropped John when he carelessly fumbled the unattached piece of cockpit glass to the floor inside the plane. I cursed when I finally realized what he had done. I grunted under his weight on my shoulders and asked him if he had heard any reactions to our noise from the interior of the aircraft. He replied no, but also said that the smell coming from inside was beyond terrible and that the cockpit access door was closed. Using the pitot tubes jutting from the aluminum skin of the aircraft, John climbed back down off my shoulders and we made a decision.

This was enough for me. I wasn't going to risk my ass trying to squeeze through the tight emergency opening only to get it bitten off as I tried to regain my balance on the inside. This aircraft was a tomb and it was going to stay that way. I can only dream of the horrors that are waiting inside. Buckled passengers writhing to be set free from their belts, dead flight attendants carefully walking the aisles, still performing their duties even in the afterlife.

We returned to the aircraft to continue formulating our plan for getting the fuel and any other supplies we deemed necessary. The hangar was our goal. I doubted we were going to be able to move the fuel truck to where the aircraft rested so we all climbed back in and I started her up and taxied toward the hangar and the fuel supply. The closer we got, the more we knew the value of "ground truth" intelligence. We could see movement inside the airport through the aircraft windows. Dead, all of them. I gave them no more thought when I saw the horror spilling out of the open hangar that we were quickly closing on.

I stopped the aircraft and left the engine running as I jumped out, rifle in hand. John was out quick and Will followed, spilling out on my side. He started to walk past me when I reached my hand out, the way my mother used to reach out across my chest when our car was about to make a quick stop. He was fixated on the creatures and nearly walked himself into our aircraft's spinning propeller blades.

We fell back and began our task of killing them. There were roughly twenty that I could see. I could see shadows of movement dancing underneath the belly of the fuel truck. I screamed out over the engine for the men to kill the ones approaching the propeller first to avoid any aircraft damage. We needed the fuel and we needed to keep the engine running until we were safe from them. It was a Catch-22. I began firing and they followed suit. I killed five before number six refused to go down. Two shots to the head and it still came at me. I gave up on the head and shot its legs out from under it.

John and Will were making short work of the others as I picked off the remaining undead behind the fuel truck. We were clear for now. I checked the fuel truck to see if it was in working order. Using the butt of my rifle, I struck the tank. The sound that resonated indicated that there was fuel inside. One thing seemed odd. Why would a small prop aircraft fuel truck be parked in front of the Boeing hangar? I now began to think that I was not the only pilot that had visited this airfield since things went crazy. I wondered if this truck had been used recently/reused, or if I was just overthinking.

I climbed up to the driver's window and peered in before I opened it up. Nothing. Keys were inside and it appeared to be in decent condition. I turned over the ignition and it coughed to life on the first attempt. Either someone had been maintaining this vehicle or I was just especially lucky with the battery charge. I flipped the switches for the pumps and got out. Before shutting down the aircraft, I checked our perimeter to make sure we weren't about to be blitzed. As the prop spun down and the engine noise abated, the unnerving clicking sound of jewelry hitting the terminal glass a couple hundred yards away filled my ears and grabbed my attention. The undead almost seemed to protest our taking of the fuel. *They* could see us from the inside and *they* were thrashing the glass in protest. Watches, rings and bracelets sounded like loud rain on the tempered glass even from this distance.

I unplugged the fuel caps and walked over to the truck. When I opened the control box to flip the switch, a yellow piece of folded legal-sized paper fell out and started to drift downwind. I ran after the paper, caught it with my boot and unfolded it to read:

Davis family, Lake Charles airfield, Louisiana. 5/14

It was a family . . . survivors. It was brilliant of them to leave this note inside the exterior fuel pump control switchbox. Davis had shown himself to be an intellectual with this single gesture. He didn't overtly spray-paint the runway with his name and location; he left it in a place where another pilot could find it. Aircraft fuel is useless to automobiles, rendering an aircraft fuel truck the same. I took the note and put it in my pocket. Walking up to the aircraft, I could tell John and Will were edgy. I filled the aircraft tanks to the top as I watched them. Will's skin seemed to be getting lighter in color in anticipation of what I was going to say next.

Time to check out the hangar.

I don't know why they were afraid. The hangar doors were wide open and anything that wanted us could just walk out here and try. After all the gunfire, I was nearly certain that there were no more of those things inside this hangar. I was right.

As the three of us broke the threshold of the large rolling hangar doorway, I almost pissed my pants. Something swooped in out of the darkness and nearly hit me in the head. It seems that a family of swallows had a summer nest just above the entryway and the mother didn't like me near her young. I could hear them chirping above. Makes me wonder how many undead eyes she had poked out in the previous weeks. I steered clear of the nest and made my way back to the supplies. The hangar had numerous Plexiglas skylight openings. It was a nice sunny day. The smell of death was in the air, but the smell of rot had followed the undead outside the hangar to their demise at the hands of our small team. It wasn't long before we found the door to the large supply room.

Slowly, I opened the door with a long pole commonly used to clean out-of-reach aircraft windows. Nothing but the smell of mothballs rolled out to meet us. This room was clean. I was acclimated to the smell of the undead but I could surely tell when their smell was absent. The supply room could almost have been considered a mini warehouse. The shelves were lined with superfluous aircraft parts and equipment. This was the Boeing supply and maintenance hangar. However, I wasn't looking for jet engine parts, I was looking for survival radios and equipment. It was then that I came upon something that I couldn't leave home without. There were rows of black briefcase-looking devices labeled "Inmarsat." We had stumbled upon aviation portable satellite telephones. I had no idea if they were still operational. However, four of them on the right side of the shelf were still sealed in plastic. We took those four and moved them to the door. Continuing our loop around the supply locker we found numerous portable distress radios, inflatable life rafts and other things of that nature. We took the satellite phones and portable VHF maintenance radios and made our exit.

We were full on fuel, had four new satellite phones, some portable VHF radios and had also made a startling discovery that a family had headed out to an airstrip in Louisiana weeks ago. It was time to leave. We all loaded up the aircraft and began our journey home. This time I stayed above seven thousand feet until I was almost on top of Hotel 23. I didn't want to take the chance of any stray weapons fire shooting me down. As I approached the compound I called out over the radio to Jan and Tara, telling them, "Navy One is three down and locked for a full stop." I mused at the use of the presidential call sign, but no one got it. I bet Davis would get it. We landed and hid the aircraft once again. I entered the complex thinking of the Davis family and wondered if they ever made it to that airfield.

Tower of Charles

I have been arguing with our group over the past three days about whether I should attempt to find the Davis family at Lake Charles. I have checked my charts and it is not that far. Of course if this becomes a reality, I will calculate the exact distance and fuel required to make the journey. The others seem to think that the risk far outweighs the benefit of finding them. John is neutral but Jan, Tara and Will are adamant that this could swiftly develop into a suicide mission.

We were able to charge up the satellite phones but unfortunately, as previously determined, there is no one to call with them. They seem to work fine, though, when we use them to dial up the other phones. It didn't take long to figure them out. I just don't know how the billing works. I know the phones belong to the airlines and I know that no one is left to send a bill for the satellite usage; I am just worried that there may be some sort of automated system shutoff when the phones reach a certain number of minutes.

I wonder what they are doing at Lake Charles airfield right now. I wonder if they even knew their note would be found. I feel the need to establish communications with them, even if it means just dropping one of the satellite phones out of the aircraft door with a makeshift parachute. At least it would be something. We could communicate with them, get more information, more ideas.

08 Jun

0226

I am leaving this morning. John and the others are staying behind in the event I bring someone back. I don't want to terribly
overstress the aircraft. I hope they have stayed near the airfield at
Lake Charles. As I sit here and stare at the yellow piece of paper
that is almost a month old, I wonder if they still live or if they
were taken under siege as John and I that day at the tower. William almost begged to come with me but as I mentioned before,
I may be bringing back survivors. I have no way of knowing, so I
cannot take the chance on extra aircraft weight. I am bringing two
fully charged satellite phones and my usual load out of one pistol
with fifty 9mm rounds and carbine with a few hundred rounds. A
couple days of food and water will also make its home in the avionics bay of the aircraft. In this journal, I thought I would write
something pithy and creative in the event they would be my last
written words. Since I am neither pithy nor creative I shall borrow great words from a man long (really) dead:

"To the last I grapple with thee; from hell's heart I stab at
thee; for hate's sake I spit my last breath at thee."—Melville/Ahab

Off I go to the Pequod.

2201

One hundred and seventy miles as the crow flies, that was the
distance to Lake Charles. It wouldn't be a straight shot for me, as I
had decided to fly over Hobby airfield again to see if the fuel truck
would still be available in the event I needed it on the way back.
I had five hundred nautical miles before my aircraft would start
dropping out of the sky, very permanently.

As I buzzed the Hobby at two thousand feet, I could see the
fuel truck below just as we had left it. I could also see that one of
the terminal windows had shattered and numerous undead were
streaming in and out of this new opening, which spilled out onto
a rooftop roughly twenty feet above the concrete taxiway below.

I couldn't see any of them near the fuel truck area. However,
I knew that they had no fear of heights and would walk freely

off the roof if they thought they could make a meal by their efforts. Satisfied with what I saw, I headed northeast toward Lake Charles. The sun was up fully and shining right into my eyes as I leveled off at seven thousand feet. After thirty minutes I could see the remains of the city of Beaumont in the distance. I decided to go lower and possibly find survivors. According to my chart this was a medium-sized city.

Smoke and fire swirled about and inside the taller buildings. They looked like large matchsticks of varying height, each with its own unique shape of fire and smoke. This trip could have been avoided if the satellite photography system in the compound was working properly. We lost the Louisiana pass (satellite footprint) two weeks ago. I would have loved to have typed in the coordinates of Lake Charles and found my answer without ever having to leave.

Power was off in this area. All of the red anticollision beacons installed on the tall radio towers were out, compounding the fun. I was flying low and slow, scanning Beaumont's city streets and buildings that were not on fire. I strained my eyes best I could but saw no survivors. The only things out walking on this nice summer day are them . . . those that are not us.

After three passes over what I thought was the center section of the city, I was convinced that no survivors remained. At least none that had any way of signaling. Lake Charles airfield was roughly fifty miles east of Beaumont. At current rate of speed, I would be there in twenty-eight minutes. This turned out to be a very long wait. I was apprehensive about meeting new survivors. I had no idea what to expect. The note in my pocket clearly says "Davis family," but I still didn't know if this Davis fellow would turn out to be friend or foe. Hell, the note was dated for the fourteenth of last month, I had no guarantees they were even still vertical or at least living vertical.

It didn't take long before I could see the boot-shaped lake getting bigger off the nose of the aircraft. On the chart, this lake was just south and a little west from my destination. I had to find them. Having another pilot in the event anything happened to me would be useful to the others. At least having Davis around would be sort of an insurance policy. The sun was still high in the sky. It was almost two o'clock when I arrived in the area of the airfield. It took a little window shopping to pick it out over the clutter and smoke of the urban areas below. Lowering my nose, I slowed to seventy knots and began my descent. I could see numerous figures below near the runway.

From where I was it appeared that there were numerous survivors. I could see their brightly colored clothing even from this distance, unlike the soiled, worn clothing of the undead. It even seemed that they had people working, as I could see someone carrying signal cones—the cones that have a flashlight attached to them and are used to signal the flight deck to a parking spot.

I don't know what had caused me to see what I wanted, but I soon realized that I had been fooled. This airfield was overrun. A large section of fence was out on the eastern side of the airfield and the undead had overwhelmed the area. Leveling my nose, I attempted a pass at the tower in the event they had made a stand inside. Nothing. Nothing but them. They were everywhere, even inside the tower. As I neared the departure end of the runway I could see a small aircraft sitting below. The doors were open and there were bodies strewn all around the aircraft. I lost count of how many. Several of them were gathered around the propeller section of the aircraft as if they'd walked into it and were sliced up on the spot. I could also see numerous body parts, arms mostly, around the forward section of the aircraft.

My suspicions were confirmed as I began my climb out of the area. Practically the moment I had decided that it was time to leave and go back home, I spotted them. I could see two people waving frantically from the catwalk that surrounded the airfield's main water tank tower. Waving for their lives below were a young boy and a woman. I made another pass and rocked my wings to signal that I had seen them. There was a sleeping bag and some boxes sitting on the tower with them. It seemed unlikely that they had survived after being exposed to the elements for who knows how long, trapped on the tower. I was moving too fast to be able to get a good look at them, but slow enough to know that they were alive.

The tower was positioned off the airfield on the other side of the broken chain-link fence. I would have found them sooner by the masses of undead that were pawing on the pillars below if it were not for the bottom of the tower being shrouded in trees and smaller undergrowth. I could see the undead, relentlessly begging upward, when I flew nearly on top of the water tower.

Landing at the airfield was not an option. With the break in the fence the scores of undead gathered below the survivors would pour in and easily swarm me. They would be drawn to the noise of the engine. An even bigger problem would be taking off again without hitting one with catastrophic effect. I wanted to figure out a way to tell them I was coming back for them but with my adrenaline rushing at the prospect of dealing with the undead, I could not.

I brought the aircraft up and departed the airfield, searching for a suitable landing strip. I cruised east, flying as low as possible looking for anywhere within ten miles that I could set her down. According to my chart and the view from the cockpit, I was flying directly over Interstate Highway 10. I could see cars all over the highway in the eastbound lane. However, the westbound lane was relatively empty. I kept a mental note of how long and how fast I was flying so as to anticipate my hike back to the water tower.

As my mental calculations kept spinning in my head, I noticed yet another post-apocalyptic odyssey on the ground. A large section of I-10 was missing, along with an adjacent overpass. There was a green military vehicle parked near an explosion crater and numerous "Danger" signs posted around the area. I suppose that either the highway was intentionally blown in the days after the outbreak or the bridge collapsed and chronic erosion took the rest of the highway. Either way this was my opportunity and I had to commit. I commenced an emergency landing on the interstate. I remembered driving this very strip of highway two years before when I was transferred for military training and now I would be landing an aircraft on it.

It was clear. I could see some debris in the distance, but I would be well clear of it before it became an issue. I brought her down, but not without complications. I began to apply my brakes to slow my speed down the strip of road. One, two, then four of them shuffled out of the high, grassy median of the highway. Not as many as I would have thought. As I pressed the brakes a little harder, I felt a jolt in the pedals and the aircraft turned sharply to the right. I had lost one of my brakes. I had no choice but to apply opposite rudder to straighten the aircraft out and just ride it out until the aerodynamic drag stopped me.

Now, the debris that I thought would not be a factor suddenly became a big one. I tapped the good brake while applying opposite rudder to straighten my yaw, each time kissing the grass on the right side of the highway. I stopped barely short of the debris that would have resulted in a likely fatal crash. The obstruction and mess blocking my roll fifty meters in the distance was nothing more than another blast hole, a green army truck and collapsed overpass. I doubted that two overpasses would coincidentally collapse like that. They were likely a result of professional demolition. I barely had enough room to turn the aircraft around and get it set up for takeoff. That is, if I made it back. I shut the engine down, taking special care to keep an eye on the small numbers approaching as I readied my pack for the expedition.

I reached into the backseat of the aircraft and pulled out my carbine and magazines. I stuffed the extra magazines in my pack and put the other four "go-to" mags in easily accessible pockets. My sidearm was already at my side. I placed four bottles of water and two MRE packages in the pack also. I had no idea how long they had been surviving on the tower or if they had been without water for very long.

I shut the aircraft door and turned around, shock-startled by the snarling, decomposing face of one of the creatures. I struck it in the temple with the butt of my rifle and kicked it hard in the knee, bringing it to the ground. That one wasn't worth the bullet or the byproduct of the loud rifle report. It didn't move again as I walked away from the aircraft.

I walked perpendicular to the interstate into the woods. I would shadow the road from here, safer from their ever-searching, always vigilant gaze. I could see them through the trees intermittently as I passed. They seemed confused, knowing something of interest was near, but unsure how to benefit from it. It was hot and humid but I kept on; my soul had no choice. I finally made it to the point where the first demolitions had occurred. I hadn't noticed the undead soldier on my first flyover, as he was in my blind spot on the other side of the truck when I made the pass. It wasn't difficult to tell what happened to him. The back of his green coat was shut in the driver's-side door, prohibiting movement. His coat was zipped up to his chest and he was wearing a Kevlar helmet strapped to his chin. He was missing large chunks of flesh and muscle from his shoulder and neck. It was apparent that he had rushed out of the truck only to shut his coat in the door, inviting catastrophe. I suppose the Darwin award had a winner for this month.

No point in letting him see me, as he would only pound on the truck like a drum and invite more creatures. I needed to leave him just as he was. Part of me wanted to put him out of his misery, as he was a fellow military man. I quietly walked around to the passenger side of the large truck and had a look inside. Sitting in the seat was an M-9 pistol. The window was rolled up and the door was locked on my side. I only had my rifle and pistol and it wouldn't be a bad idea for the survivors to have a weapon for the rescue operation. I changed my mind and made the decision to kill the soldier as a trade for the pistol. I stepped down off the running board of the truck and walked to the rear. It was a transport truck with a canvas-covered wagon-type bed. I peered into the bed. I could see nothing of use in the back of the truck—just wooden crates full of God knows what. Probably explosives. That wasn't my field of expertise.

I picked up a large chunk of leftover interstate and tossed it on the concrete near the creature's feet to make it look the other way as I advanced. It worked. I quickly approached the thing and shoved the muzzle of my weapon underneath the helmet, getting around the Kevlar protecting its head. I squeezed off one round. The creature went limp and just hung there until I opened the door. I checked its pockets. Nothing of value. I took the M-9 and left the scene.

I didn't have much time to figure out a way to get them off the water tower. We needed to be out of here before sundown. Neutralizing the creatures was not an option. I had the advantage of a brain and firepower, but there were just too many of them. I needed another way. It seemed the only option was to run up to them and start screaming or shooting, drawing them from the tower, which was similar to the way I extracted the Grisham family. That was also too dangerous, as I did not have a working car to lead them away. More lack of planning. I had planned only to land at Lake Charles, make contact and possibly transport survivors to Hotel 23. I didn't plan for another ridiculous rescue effort.

The water tower was in view. I could see one of them on the catwalk. I tried to wave my arms and signal but there was no response. It almost made me second-guess myself. I wondered if I had gone through this trouble only to be saving two corpses. It was then that my efforts were reaffirmed. I could see a small male figure urinating off the edge of the railing onto the corpses below. Although I could not see the corpses through the undergrowth, I knew what the boy was doing. He was mischievously aiming for their heads.

I briefly chuckled to myself and got back to business. The water tower was only about ten meters from the airport perimeter fence. The top of the fence was not barbed and I could easily climb over it, so I jogged to a section out of view of the creatures and did just that. As soon as I hit the ground I started running toward the hangar. I saw a row of electric-powered luggage carts plugged into a charging bank behind the hangar. I slowly moved over to them. I had no idea how long the power had been out in this area so I didn't know if they would still operate. I unlatched one of them and pulled it out to the side of the hangar so that I could get a good look at it. I had drawn a curious corpse on the other side of the fence. It must have seen me jump over.

There were no keys for the small luggage cars, I suppose to avoid foreign object debris damage to the aircraft engines in the event the keys were dropped on the taxiway. I turned the switch to the on position, sat down and pressed the accelerator. The electric engine jolted over but the cart did not move. I tried another. There were several, all in a row behind the building. On the third cart, I was successful. It hummed to life and I immediately hopped on and drove toward the broken section of the fence near the water tower. I stopped on the center of the runway and got out, leaving the luggage cart on. I shouldered my rifle and began shooting at the base of the tower, taking down as many as I could before every undead eye in a two-mile radius looked my way.

I kept firing until the mass of them started pouring out of the opening in the fence, arms outstretched and wanting me. I waited until they were fifty meters distant before I got back into the cart and drove away, drawing the undead away from the tower. As I sped down the runway I reloaded my magazine. I couldn't tell but if I were to guess I would say there were at least two to three hundred of them behind me.

I was at the end of the runway. I got out and started shooting at them again. They were about three hundred yards away at this point. I had some time. I killed the ones near me that were already inside the airport perimeter first. Then I started selectively picking off the large crowd, aiming for the ones most distant first. That would buy me more time before they caught up to me when I made my transition back to the tower.

They were now at one hundred yards. There were so many flies buzzing around the mass it was sickening. I could easily hear the flies' collective buzz over their moans. I would have to say that the worst thing about them is their dried, decomposing faces. Their lips locked in a permanent snarl with bony hands reaching for purchase. It was time to roll. I jumped back in the cart and circled around the mass and put the accelerator to the floor. This thing had limitations on its speed for safety. I was only going ten or fifteen miles per hour at best. As I neared the tower I screamed for them to get ready. I couldn't tell if they heard me or not. The bulk of the creatures were almost one thousand yards away. We had time, but I still had to take care of the dozen or so that had remained at the base of the tower. The battery in the cart was beginning to show signs of drain.

I was at the break in the fence. The foliage was restricting my view and I had no way of knowing exactly what was hiding inside. I opened fire on what I thought was a head. I gave up on this tactic and carefully walked into the undergrowth under the tower. The ones that were left behind were probably deaf, as they were in advanced stages of decomposition. They probably didn't even hear my gunfire. Many of them had only one eye, or none at all. They were easy targets. It was not long before the base of the tower was secure. I called up to the survivors to get down as fast as they could.

I heard a woman's commanding voice say, "Danny, do as the man says."

Then the boy replied nervously, "Yes, Granny."

The boy went first. He was about twelve years old with brown hair and dark brown eyes with a light complexion. Then came the female. She looked to be in her late fifties or even early sixties. She had red curly hair and was slightly overweight. They were both on the ground holding what few belongings they had, looking to me for answers. My confidence seemed to drain along with the golf cart battery after seeing so many of the creatures. I mustered up what acting ability I had (Abraham Lincoln in kindergarten) and feigned confidence, telling them to follow me. Before we left I took a zip tie out of my pack and went over to the luggage cart.

They were closer now, about six hundred yards, and closing fast. I climbed into the luggage cart and put it into reverse. A loud warning beep sounded. I zip-tied the pedal down so that it would go until it hit something or the battery was completely depleted. I jumped out and rolled to avoid injury as the cart drove off, beeping loudly, in the direction of the undead mass. We headed back to the aircraft the same way I had come in, taking special care to remain undetected as we clumsily traipsed through the foliage parallel to Interstate 10. I could hear loud moans coming from behind us from the direction of the airport. We were upwind from them. No doubt they could somehow smell us, even though I admit I never bothered to examine one closely enough to see if it even breathed.

As we journeyed through the woods in the general direction of the aircraft, I handed the woman the M-9 that I had stolen from the army transport truck earlier. She told me that her name was Dean and that this was her grandson, Danny. I shook both of their hands and pulled out the yellow handwritten note that I had found hidden in the fuel truck at Hobby Airport.

The woman looked at the note. Her bloodshot eyes began to tear up and she stopped for a moment, looking into my eyes. She reached out her arms and hugged me while she cried. My first thought was that Mr. Davis was a close friend and family member of hers and that the note had somehow surfaced painful recent memories of his untimely demise.

"I know you are unhappy, but we have to keep moving. There are many of those creatures around. The golf cart won't fool them for long," I told her.

She insisted that she needed a minute or two to get her bearings. What could I say? If my mother ever found out I had disrespected my elder I'd get my ass kicked.

I asked the woman what had happened to Mr. Davis and his family.

She replied, "Danny and I are the Davis family. I left the note at Hobby Regional last month, right before we flew here."

Puzzled and feeling the ever-so-slight sting of sexism in the back of my mind, I humbly inquired who flew the plane.

She smiled and for a brief second looked a little younger and said, "I did. I am a certified pilot, or used to be, when being a certified pilot meant something."

Holding back my look of jackassery, I scanned the area for any threat and continued talking to the woman named Dean. Danny sat on the ground in front of her feet, his small head scanning all around for threats.

I felt peaceful as I spoke to this woman, almost as if she was the last grandmother left on the planet and I wanted to hear her stories.

. . . Now wasn't the time.

My main reason for stopping was to give them an emotional rest from what had just happened at the water tower. Although the woman was more than capable of handling herself, she was still an older woman and I felt that they had needed this brief break in the action. The woman called Dean showed obvious signs of malnutrition. Loose skin hung from her arms and legs as a testament to her love for her grandson. Danny didn't look great, either, but I could tell that food had been given up for his survival.

With guilt and a little sorrow in my voice, I made the suggestion that we keep moving and get to the aircraft as soon as possible. It would be very difficult to find the fuel truck at Hobby if we were forced to fly at night. As we walked, I tried to keep Dean's mind off today's events by quietly asking her why she learned to fly. She was eager and happy to talk about it. As she whispered, I kept glancing past her face into the breaks in the trees that intermittently revealed the interstate. From time to time during our move to the plane I saw them.

She quietly spoke as she walked of how she was a retired pilot, formerly of the New Orleans Fire Department, and how she missed flying and helping people in need. She also mentioned her age in the conversation, saying that she had retired ten years ago when she had turned fifty-five. I couldn't believe that the woman had survived as long in this, keeping this young boy alive. I was truly in awe and fully respected this woman's will to survive.

There were a few creatures up the interstate toward the airfield between the aircraft and our group. The moans of the dead were almost to the point of imagination at this distance. I told Dean how I had lost my left wheel brake in the landing and said that I hoped we wouldn't have to abort takeoff because there would be a nice, big, green army truck waiting for us at the end of this strip of interstate. She didn't seem to worry and never questioned where my piloting skills came from. She just seemed thankful to be alive. After arriving at the aircraft, I opened the door and almost caught myself shielding Danny's eyes from the corpse I had killed near the aircraft earlier. What was the point? The boy had probably pissed on more of the undead than I had ever seen.

After inspecting the aircraft and strapping in we started the takeoff checklist. Both Dean and I put on the internal communications headsets and she helped me run the checklist, as she had over two hundred hours in this particular model aircraft, much more than I had. The engine started with no problem. I gave the aircraft power and began my forward roll. There was no use testing the brakes. The area was clear; I kept my roll to fifty knots. A single corpse was approaching the concrete of the interstate from the grassy median separating I-10 east and west. I wasn't sure if I was going to make it.

I then felt the yoke controls of the aircraft being pulled back to me. Dean's voice over the internal communications said, "We can make this climb." I couldn't believe it. This climb was even steeper than the time John and I had to fly out of the dirt track back before San Antonio was rocked off the map by nukes. It was not the engines that pushed me back into my seat. It was gravity. We had missed the corpse and taken off nearly a thousand feet before I would have. I had to buck up and admit to myself she was better at flying this plane than I was.

As we passed the truck, crater and collapsed overpass, the airport once again came into sight. Out of pure curiosity I asked Dean to take us over the airfield. As we flew over I could see them huddled around the electric cart at the opposite end of the airfield. It was wedged into the fence and I assume was still beeping, because the corpses were quite interested in it, trying to rip it apart. Maybe it was the smell, maybe the noise, maybe both.

She asked where we were headed. I told her to fly us to her fuel truck. She did.

Curious how she came to be on top of the water tower, I began asking some questions now that we were safely in the air. They landed at Lake Charles on the night of May 14. She didn't go into detail, but her hands started to shake on the controls as she spoke of how she had to leave the aircraft running and both she and Danny had to run as fast as they could to the tower to avoid being eaten by the creatures. All they had on the tower was what they could carry in one trip. I asked why she just didn't escape in the aircraft. She answered my question with another by saying, "Didn't you see all the bodies lying around the aircraft near the propeller when you flew over?" I could see that she was uncomfortable talking about it.

She told of how she used her sleeping blanket to get water for the both of them. She had climbed up to the top of the tower from the catwalk on the side at day six, one day after they had run out of their rationed potable water. Somehow, she unscrewed the plug on the top of the tower that was commonly used to test the water inside the tank. Using the blanket, she dipped it down into the tank and was able to get it submerged approximately six inches into the tank without dropping it in. She and Danny had lived off "freshly squeezed Louisiana blanket water" for nearly a month while enduring the endless moans of the dead below. She cried again when she spoke of this.

Over Hobby, we were in need of fuel. We might have been able to make it back to Hotel 23 on fumes, but I didn't think it necessary to take the risk. I knew the fuel truck worked, I had used it recently and I knew it had plenty of fuel. The sun was approaching the western horizon as we circled Hobby to take a look. There were undead on the roof adjacent to the shattered terminal window and I did see a few of them on the ground below the roof. Some of them had rendered themselves immobile from the fall. Kinetics is a bitch.

I landed the aircraft and taxied it dangerously close to the fuel truck and told Dean to stay inside. She didn't like this idea and wanted to help, but I could see in her eyes that she knew I was right. She wasn't one hundred percent after starving, baking and freezing for a month on that tower, which is why, despite her high flight hours, I kept my hands on or near the controls the entire time she flew. She may have been a better stick, but she was worn down to the wire.

Leaving the engine running, as is my standard operating procedure for a situation like this, I made my way to the fuel truck. It wasn't long before I had the tanks full and the aircraft positioned to take off again. At the hold short line on the Hobby runway I realized that I hadn't checked in with Hotel 23 for nearly ten hours, nor did I have the headsets tuned to the VHF radio. Dean and I were talking on the way to Hobby and we were out of range of Hotel 23 anyway, so I'd switched the VHF off after taking off from the interstate to avoid the static. Dean was using the copilot's controls to get the aircraft airborne in the same manner that she had used them to give control inputs to avoid the corpse on last takeoff. I kept my hands on the pilot controls, shadowing her.

On a side note, as we were taking off and as I began to tune the radios to contact Hotel 23, I noticed a corpse hanging out of the large Boeing aircraft cockpit window that John, Will and I had attempted to explore weeks ago. It was obviously stuck at the waist and I could see its arms moving in a futile attempt to drop itself to the tarmac. All of the recent activity at this airfield must have excited the undead entombed in that large, multi-million-dollar sarcophagus.

I keyed the microphone: "H23, this is Navy One, over." John came back. He was borderline frantic. Using the proper radio discipline so as to not reveal any names or locations, he came back. "Navy One, this is H23, we have been trying to reach you for hours. It is not safe to land at H23 at this time." I asked John what was going on. I was instantly worried that the only enemy more dangerous than the dead was attacking again.

He came back and told me that there had been a recent influx of undead to the landing area and the area surrounding the back fence and that it would not be safe to land as there were currently over one hundred of them standing where I would be attempting to touch down. I asked him if there was any way he could clear it out, as I was coming back with "one plus two souls onboard." He replied that it would be too dark to do anything in twenty minutes. I agreed. It would be suicide to go out there at night and attempt to herd them out of the way, and even then there would be no guarantee that it would work. It would only take one of those things to hit the aircraft at eighty knots to cause terrible structural/engine damage and quick death to all onboard. We had to find somewhere to stay tonight, fast.

Eagle Lake airfield was out of the question for obvious reasons. I would not be willing to take a chance and land the aircraft in an unknown field. I had to find an airfield. I began scanning my chart for any possible candidates. On the chart was a very small airstrip called Stoval about fourteen miles southwest of H23. That would have to do. The sun would be down by the time we were there, so it was going to have to be another NVG landing.

This time I was not willing to cut the engines, as we had no guaranteed shelter to escape to if this went south on us. We had to take our chances with the engine noise. Not knowing how Dean would react, I asked Danny to reach into my bag and pull out the hard plastic green case. He did. Dean was at the controls. I began to explain to her what we had to do and that we basically had no choice in the matter. I asked her to cut the exterior collision lights and be prepared to give me control when it became too dark for her to see any detail on the ground. I pointed out the airfield we were heading for. She slightly altered heading and we made way.

I pulled the NVGs out of the case and strapped them on my head. I wanted to give my eyes plenty of time to adjust, just to make sure. I turned the intensity down so low that the goggles were acting more as a blindfold than a night vision aid. It was getting very dark outside. I asked Dean for the controls just as I adjusted the NVG intensifiers. The landscape below came alive in the familiar green color to which I had become so accustomed.

I began searching for the airfield. It wasn't there. I kept searching and searching, checking the chart. I was looking for an airstrip with a tower. It took twenty minutes before I realized that we had flown over it several times. This field was abandoned, and didn't have a tower. The strip was almost grown up to the point that the aircraft could nearly cut the grass with the prop as it landed. I could, however, still see the concrete and make out the strip. There was nothing in the area of this field except one lone hangar. I flew near it to see if any of the doors on it were open. It seemed secure. I brought the plane around for the landing. I had become acclimated to the depth perception problem I was having with the NVGs and made a better landing this time. I positioned the aircraft for tomorrow's takeoff, cut the engines and kept a vigilant watch.

They are sleeping right now. We landed at about 2100 hrs. I contacted John and told him our coordinates. He said that he and Will would take care of them in the Land Rover tomorrow and not to worry. He laughed and told me to make sure that I turned the radio on in the morning and said that he would be up monitoring his all night. I asked how Tara was doing. John said that she was sitting right next to him and that she said she misses me.

9 Jun

0218

I see movement in the distance at the outer perimeter of the airfield. Not sure what it is. The cabin doors are locked and I am sleepy but refuse to nod off. Dean is awake. I am not telling her what I see.

0354

The movement in the distance turned out to be a family of deer. I could tell they were living creatures by the mirrorlike reflection of their eyes caused by the effects of night vision. The undead do not share this comforting quality.

0622

The sun is up and the radios are on. I have already spoken to John and he will be giving me the go-ahead within the next hour. There is no movement in this area and the family of deer has moved out. Dean and Danny have already eaten much of the food that I have brought. Can't say that I blame them.

0740

Call made; John says it's clear. We are taking off shortly.

11 Jun

0940

We arrived at Hotel 23 on the morning of the ninth without incident. Jan stayed in touch via the VHF radios and relayed John and Will's position to us in the air as they herded the undead mob safely away from our landing spot. Before we touched down at H23, I told Dean not to expect much of our shelter and that there would now only be nine of us (including Annabelle). Danny was wearing a headset in the backseat. It was too big for him and I found it funny how it kept slipping off as he asked the question, "Who is Annabelle?" I told Danny that we had a puppy at Hotel 23 and that her name is Annabelle and she loves little boys. Danny began to tear up in happiness at the prospect of touching something truly good again and not having to look at the "ugly people," as he had been calling them.

I saved Laura as a surprise for him. I can't imagine the joy in his heart when he saw another child to play with, even though she was a *girl*. Although it only comes to me once in a great many years, a flash of memory, a familiar smell from an old cedar chest of keepsakes . . . I still remember what it was like being twelve.

Crude

We had a meeting today. All nine of us attended although Laura, Danny and Annabelle did not pay attention. They were quietly playing in the corner as we talked. Dean is looking much better. I caught her up on the recent events at Hotel 23 regarding the bandits and basically gave her a rundown on everyone here and how we came to find each other.

She had a few stories of survival herself regarding the months leading up to her imprisonment at the "Tower of Charles." She spoke of how she and little Danny had been in New Orleans and had heard the warning that the Big Easy would be a target and how they had taken off in her aircraft for the nearest safe zone. She never found it. They had spent months bouncing from airport to airport, scavenging food, water and fuel until their luck finally ran out.

Dean has become the resident grandmother around here, taking care of the kids and offering advice. She even approached me yesterday in private to tell me that she could see that Tara was fond of me. I had known this for a little while but have been too preoccupied with staying alive to do anything about it. She asked me what the purpose of survival was if I had no one to love and be loved by. I didn't really answer that. I was in no mood for emotion. We were still in some serious trouble and I felt like I have no time for love or romance.

I asked her if she had run across any survivors in her airport-hopping campaign. She told another grisly tale in which she and Danny attempted to rescue two survivors signaling to them from a field below. They were being flanked by hundreds of undead that they could not see over an adjacent hill. Dean had tried to warn them by flying over the area where the dead were advancing. However, it was too late. By the time they realized what was going on, the dead had topped the hill. The sheer number of them picked them clean like African driver ants.

Dean had felt guilty about that incident and often wondered if they were in that field solely to signal her and Danny. I tried to comfort her by saying that they were probably already there and that she had just flown over at the right time. Odds are, she probably did draw them out into the open to signal her, but what would be the point in presenting that gruesome thought?

I have gotten into a pretty good routine of exercise lately. The undead numbers have greatly declined around the complex since the raider attack. I have installed a pull-up bar in the control room. I constructed it out of scrap, using twine to secure it to the overhead beams.

John has been monitoring the radios and has had no sign of encrypted comms, or any chatter for that matter. Dean seems to think that we could be safe here as long as we keep aware of our surroundings. I informed her that there is more than one way in and out of the complex. I will be giving her a full tour of Hotel 23 in the coming days. She is no novice with firearms and I feel that she could handle herself if need be. She is a tough old bird, a product of old-fashioned upbringing. She lost her husband to natural causes years before the undead walked. She is no stranger to death, just a stranger to death walking.

17 Jun

2106

GPS is gone. I'm sure the satellites are still up there, but without ground station intervention to regularly recalibrate them they cannot transmit properly and I cannot get a receiver lock. The internal DVD/GPS navigation system in the Land Rover is useless. Because of the loss of GPS, I was eager to test the SATphones. They worked fine. John and I went topside with them and I dialed the number imprinted on a barcode on the side of the phone John was holding. It rang through and John did the same with the phone I was carrying. Although an excellent means of communication, they could not be considered reliable. The same goes for any communication that depends on complex third-party mechanisms. I have been sleeping in the environmental control room as I have given up my living quarters to Dean and Danny.

It is a little cooler in my new quarters. There are plenty of other compartments to choose from; I just like being somewhat close to everyone else. There is even a rather large compartment with lockers and folding cots. I am sure they are probably for civilian survivors that would encounter this place during and after a nuclear exchange. I just wish I had something useful and positive to accomplish, besides staying alive.

I pulled my wallet out of my personal belongings today and looked at my Armed Forces Identification Card. The man depicted on that card didn't look like me. Sure, it was my face, name and Social Security number, however . . . the eyes. They were different. The eyes in the photo didn't have the same gaze as those of the man I see in the mirror now. I will keep it. Keep it as a memento of what I once was; a cog in the wheel of something greater. It has been six months to the day since the first time I saw one of them eye-to-eye. They still have the same chilling effect. I am certain they always will.

20 Jun

2309

It is raining very hard right now. The weather is playing hell with the closed-circuit TV, causing static and loss of v-hold. The undead in this area are pretty spread out, but I can still make them out during an intense lightning flash. Still no joy on the radios. There is no one out there, or at least no one in our range. I have been flipping through the watchman's diary to pass the time during the storm. I sort of forgot about it due to the current events at Hotel 23.

I had gone to my old quarters last night to pick up the last of my personal effects when it resurfaced. Dean had packed my cardboard box for me and told me how nice I was for giving up my space for her and Danny. She told me that she had found my personal diary, but wouldn't dare take a peek. I explained to her that it wasn't mine and that it belonged to a person who was formerly posted here. I told her that I was keeping it for him. She understood and handed it to me, trying to figure out whether she had said something wrong.

I gave her a reassuring smile as I took the diary out of her hand, threw it into the box and started walking to my new quarters in the environmental control room. It wasn't until tonight that I reopened Captain Baker's personal log. January 10 was dog-eared, as I had remembered reading it before. I turned the page, and began reading January 11.

January 11

As suspected, according to the recently received message traffic, we will not be permitted to leave for quite some time. This facility will be more than adequate for extended habitability, but staying here underground really takes a mental toll on you. Unlike myself, he is married and I am not sure how long he will remain sane if this order to stay underground continues. He is constantly daydreaming and writing letters to his wife, letters that he cannot even mail until we are cleared topside by high command.

I have received official communications involving the situation in Asia. It is above the classification of this log and will not be included.

I know we will be secure down here no matter what and that is what is important to U.S. strategic deterrence.

The only other thing on this page was a freehand doodle of a missile flying through the air over what appears to be the United States.

23 Jun
2150

I have a splitting headache. Normally I force myself to drink enough water to remain hydrated, but today I just didn't get around to it. I have a dehydration headache and no matter how much water I drink at this point, it won't matter. It will just have to run its course. On the morning of the twenty-first, John, Will and I went out scouting. Instead of heading in the direction of the crucifixes, we went westerly, toward the small town of Hallettsville. We didn't take the Land Rover, as we wanted to remain quiet and avoid detection. For all we knew there were still bandits in the area.

We walked through fields and undeveloped farmland. It had been over six months since anyone was alive to maintain the land, so it wasn't a surprise when we stumbled upon them. We had jumped yet another fence into derelict farmland when we observed the sentinel symbols of United States greed and power. There was a large refinery field and the skeletal hulks of the large ground pumps were just sitting there, unmoving. Grass was overgrown all around them and it was obvious that they had been dead for months.

I suppose the bright side to the living population being annihilated is the fact that our oil reserves should last thousands of years longer. Of course, the downside is the fact that no one is alive who knows the art of refining the crude oil, hence making it as useless as a Hadron collider. John and I have long since discussed the need for technical manuals on everything from farming to medicine to things like refining crude. The information we require would be in countless abandoned libraries throughout the United States. However, getting to the information and getting it back to Hotel 23 could prove most fatal.

Passing the second large oil pump, I made yet another macabre discovery. I suppose when the world ended back in January the pumps were still running for a while. It looks like one of those bastards was crushed by the pendulum arm of the pump and its lower torso was caught in the machinery. I couldn't tell if it was still reanimated. I gave it no mind as I walked past. Obviously, birds had done their thing to this rotting monstrosity.

William had to force himself to look away from the creature as we passed. We kept on, seeing no signs of life. Our tactic was avoidance, as we had no suppressors or silent weapons to use. We would open fire only if our lives were in danger. We dodged three walking dead in the field before returning home. They were quite mobile, but still too slow to keep up. They would follow. However, I doubt they could ever make it over the many fences that separate our compound from this oil field. John and I have had further discussions about the need to gather some reference books, so we will be planning and executing this operation in the days to come.

Semper Fi

26 Jun

1853

During our normal monitoring of the parking lot area of the compound, we noticed movement on the road beyond it. It looked much like an eight-wheeled USMC light armor reconnaissance vehicle. There was only one. It was moving at a high rate of speed, headed northeast relative to the compound. I wish I could have recorded the image so that I could maybe enhance it and catch a better glimpse of the gunner. My only conclusion would be that this is a scout and he/she was sent as a forward observer only to return and report the situation to the person in charge. I could be totally wrong and this could just be a rogue unit, running and gunning in the LAV across the country. I don't know much about these vehicles and I have only seen one once. They are amphibious and capable of taking some serious small-arms fire.

This could be one of the last remnants of the Marine Corps in this area. Who knows if they are still loyal to the cause? If I were, I would not be writing this.

Dean and I took the children topside to play a few hours after the LAV sighting. I told her of my plan to take John into an urban outskirt area for the purpose of retrieving some vital technical manuals. She seemed to think it a good idea. However, she told me that she had already known my plan. Tara had told her about it after talking to John. Tara seemed to think it was a crazy plan. She hadn't mentioned her feelings about me, but it seems that she is able to talk to Dean about anything. Dean just warned me that she might be upset that I choose to leave the safety of the compound for something as trivial as books. After seeing the military vehicle go by earlier today, I am not certain what to do. I know we need specific medical manuals, as we have two children and an older lady at the compound. I am no doctor. Jan is the closest thing we have.

29 Jun

_1913_

It all began last night. It had started as simple radio garble. That night, it intensified. I could hear a frantic human voice, drowned out by automatic-weapons fire. Only bits and pieces were discernible. It stopped at nightfall. During John's watch that night, it began again. It was 2300. The weapons fire had lessened to a frequency and sound that reminded me of microwave popcorn in the waning phase of popping. The voice identified himself as Lance Corporal Ramirez of the 1st Battalion, 23rd Marines. He and his crew were broke dick and trapped inside their ride. He claimed to have six souls onboard. They had a mechanical malfunction and were stranded in a sea of undead. There was screaming in the background and I couldn't tell if someone had been injured or was just delirious. These Marines were most likely the same unit sighted yesterday speeding past our compound.

John called me into the control room at this point, and I made the decision to initiate communications with the Marines. I keyed the microphone and said in a calm cool voice:

"To the Marine unit transmitting a distress call . . . transmit your latitude and longitude, over."

After a few seconds of static, we received a reply:

"Unidentified station, we are in need of assistance and extraction. Please repeat your transmission . . . over."

I then repeated my request four times before the radio operator finally came back with the latitude and longitude of their position:

"Station calling, our position is believed to be N29-52, W097-02. Your transmissions are weak and nearly unreadable, two by five. We are out of crew-served weapon rounds and have closed the hatch on our vehicle. Situation is dire, please render assistance."

I really had no choice. I couldn't leave those Marines to die there. Those things couldn't get into the LAV, but the Marines couldn't get out either. I marked the position on the map and John, William and I began our hasty preparation. We left as soon as we could that night, to take advantage of the cover of darkness. I took one of the handheld shortwave HF radios, the M-16 with the M-203 launcher, my Glock and NVGs. I pointed out where we were going on the map and William suggested that we take one of the Geiger counters. I agreed. Before leaving, I asked John to help me cut the rank off of my shoulders. I couldn't risk these men finding out that I am or was military. We also grabbed several pillowcases in the event we had to bring them back here.

If I could land a plane at night with NVGs, I could definitely drive the Land Rover. The only problem that I found was the need to stick to the paved roads to avoid getting stuck. This vehicle was made for off-road use, but, unlike the LAV the Marines were trapped inside, it was not designed, if stuck, to repel hundreds of dead fists and bloody stumps.

We were out the door by 0030 hrs, and headed northwest to the rendezvous point. As I walked out of the compound, I reached over to my left shoulder and pulled off the Velcro American flag that I had worn on my uniform since the start of this. Once again, I couldn't risk being discovered and forced back to active duty for a futile cause or worse, sent to the brig. I made my bed when I decided to leave my unit and survive. I believe I'm the last one left. There was no way to defeat our foe. We had to wait them out. According to the chart, we had just over thirty miles of dangerous territory to cover.

Judging by the information they had given me, they were eight miles west of La Grange, Texas. Once again the map indicated this was a very small town. The Marines were less than a mile southwest of the Colorado River. The area they were in was technically deep inside the radiation zone and was also the closest I had been to a fallout area since rescuing the Grishams. I was apprehensive about this as I remembered transmissions from the Louisiana congressman last March. We could be going into the lion's mouth. We had lost the broadcast from Louisiana and I had often wondered what had happened there. Did the scouts that the congressman dispatched only draw a legion of radiated undead to their position?

We ran into no trouble until we arrived at I-10. Of course the interstate was a war zone, and tall grass had grown up between the east and westbound lanes. For all we knew there could have been an army of them behind the grass wall. All this projected a very surreal feeling, and made me realize how quickly things fall apart with no human intervention. Approaching the on ramp that would take us to 71 North we came upon a four-car pileup. There was no way to go around the wreckage, as a tall concrete wall had put the wreckage between a rock and a hard place. We were going to have to pull one of the cars out of the way with the Land Rover. We had removed the bulbs from the tail/brake lights a couple of weeks ago. With the headlights turned off, we would show no lights no matter how much I pressed the brakes. We also took the bulbs out of the blinker lights just in case one of us accidentally bumped the turn signal.

Of course . . . there was always human error. John and William got out of the vehicle to attach the chain to one of the wrecked cars. I could see through my NVGs that William was signaling me to back up. With the grainy green resolution I couldn't see beyond John and William into the darkness of the on ramp behind them. I shifted the transmission into reverse . . . instantly the light from the rear and side view mirrors induced whiteout in my goggles. In all our attention to detail, we had overlooked the bulb that illuminates when you put the vehicle in reverse. The light shone like a phoenix. Yanking the goggles off my head, I checked the mirrors again. Something was moving behind my friends.

I backed into position, quickly put the vehicle in neutral and put the parking brake on. I called out to John and William to drop the chain and get back in the vehicle. I was the only one who could see in the dark, so it was only logical that I be the one to face whatever it was that was moving in reaction to our light. While fumbling with the NVGs to get them back on, I could hear John and Will drop the chain. I heard their smacking footsteps and the sound of something more distant.

I stepped out of the vehicle and lightly shut the door, causing it to barely latch. Hoping for the familiar reflection of the living eyes of an animal through the NVGs, I stepped forward. Rounding the back of one of the wrecked vehicles was the corpse of some sort of builder or contractor. His leather tool belt still held a hammer in place. All the other tools must have fallen out. He wasn't badly decomposed. He could not see me and could not negotiate a path through the wreckage, so he just stood there, trying to sense where I was.

The former builder's hair wasn't long. He didn't have much facial hair. It was a common myth that when people die, their hair and nails continue to grow. This was not true. Upon death nothing grows . . .

Unless you count the undead hunger.

I wasn't sure, but judging by the tool belt, the short hair and the apparent clean shave, this man had been one of the first to go six months ago.

Aside from a large chunk of meat missing from his shoulder, he was very well preserved. As I got a closer look, I noticed some skin and hair stuck to the claw of his hammer. He likely had killed the creature that bit him with the tool now holstered on his belt. Since the creature was standing still and posed no immediate threat, I went back to the vehicle and grabbed the Geiger. I had spent some time reading the directions, as my recent new quarters was the environmental and equipment room of Hotel 23. I had learned all about the restrictions for the MCU-2P gasmask, as well as the limitations of the chemical, biological and radiological protective gear. I had even devoted a whole night to Geiger counter operations.

I turned the Geiger on and placed the ear bud in my ear. After giving it sufficient warm-up time, I used it on John. The Geiger indicated a normal RAD level. The static clicking sound in my ear was random. As I neared the vehicle wreckage the static picked up intensity. I was sure these vehicles had absorbed some radiation, being inside the zone. They were still within safe exposure levels, as long as I didn't sit in them for a prolonged period.

I reached over the wrecked hood of one of the cars to get a reading from the corpse. The sound in my ear sounded like that of an old dialup modem. This corpse was hot far beyond safe levels.

Looking down at the meter, I saw that it read 400R. I definitely did not want a hug from this one. As I pulled my hand back over the hood, the corpse must have caught the smell, as it walked violently forward into the car, shaking it on its shocks. It was jerking erratically, unlike any corpse that I have seen so far. It moved laterally to the car and then I caught a glimpse of its feet. The creature's boots were nearly worn away; it had likely been walking on them for months without pause. The soles were gone and its maimed feet were visible under nothing but strips of leather and dangling bootlaces wrapped around its ankle.

The corpse was visibly excited, possibly by my presence. It moved back and forth like one of those toy robots. It would bump into a section of wreckage and turn and try another spot. If it kept doing this, eventually it would make it around the wreckage. I couldn't afford contact with this creature, as it was soaked with radiation. Picking up the chain, I kept a close eye on the robot corpse. I attached the chain around the axle of the vehicle I intended to move. I silently moved back to the Land Rover and got in. I told John and Will that we had a *hot* one outside. I planned to pull the car out of the way, unhook the chain and leave without dealing with the corpse. I put the vehicle in gear and slowly pulled forward. I felt the tension on the chain and heard it pop taut. I gave it some more gas and felt the car give way. I kept going for at least fifty yards before getting out and executing my plan.

Once out, I trained my eyes on the place where the car used to be. The thing was approaching. It was trying to run, but obviously lacked the coordination to do so. It fell, got back up, and kept coming. It had no idea where it was going but as luck would have it, the thing was headed right for the Land Rover. I immediately unhooked the chain, opened the back door and tossed it in without looking. I heard William curse as the fifty-pound chain hit his feet. Just as I got back into the vehicle and locked the doors, I heard the corpse bounce off the back window. I floored the Land Rover and turned it around, speeding through the hole I had just made in the wreckage. In my rearview mirror I could see the corpse attempting to give chase as it clumsily half-jogged behind, homing in on the sound of the vehicle.

I can't lie to myself. I thought for a brief second about canceling this mission and heading home. What could the three of us do against an army of poisoned dead? We were closer now. Will attempted to make contact via the radio. He keyed the microphone and called out. We heard nothing, but this radio set wasn't as powerful as the one at Hotel 23. They could still be alive. After imagining what it would be like to be them, I pushed the thought of mission abort out of my mind.

Only minutes after Will first tried the radio, they came back. Again, the lance corporal identified himself as well as his unit. I pulled the vehicle over and grabbed the radio from Will. I asked the corporal if he had an update to his coordinates and if he had any small arms inside the LAV. He replied that they were still at the previous position and they were all armed and had small-arms ammunition. However, there was no way to fire outside the vehicle accurately without the top hatch open. He also commented that they were out of ammo for the crew-served weapon and that was the reason they had to close the hatch. I asked how many undead were at his position. After a pause (it seemed he didn't want to tell me), he informed me that he was a Marine and couldn't count that high. I asked him, *"Hundreds,* Corporal?"

He replied, "Yes, sir."

Both John and William cursed loudly and shook their heads in apprehension of what was about to go down. It was about to get real.

We only needed I-10 for two miles. We exited north on 71 and sped toward the Marines. The only tactic we could possibly use is the one that I had executed with the Grishams and one that I had seen performed by the raiders. I had to try to herd them away from the broken-down vehicle. Maintaining radio contact, I tried to make some small talk to keep their minds off of the immediate surroundings. The corporal informed me that they had left the highway for the river because the sheer number of dead on the highway was overpowering them. Their vehicle experienced mechanical failure near the river. They were going to attempt to cross the river and escape the undead using the amphibious capability of the LAV. Initially it wasn't the corporal's beacon light that enabled me to find them, it was the overwhelming moans of the dead.

I told the men that I would attempt to lead the mass of them away with the noise of our vehicle and the horn. We established a rally point and I told the Marines to escape the LAV and evade to Highway 71 at the same spot they initially left the highway. They agreed. After saying a little prayer in my head, I asked John and Will if they were ready. Giving them no time to reply, I hit the gas and sped toward the moat of undead that surrounded the stranded Marines.

The ground was littered with corpses, victims of the LAV's crew-served weapon barrage. I was maybe one hundred meters from the moat when I rolled down my window and opened fire. John and Will were on reloading duty. The flash suppressor was helping keep my goggles relevant, but it was almost more advantageous to just use the muzzle flash without the gogs to see my targets as I was firing very rapidly at the dead.

I must have killed twenty of them before I had to relocate the vehicle another hundred yards down track. Will handed me a fresh magazine and I popped out the empty, handed it to John and quickly slapped another in the receiver. The dead were advancing quickly, as they were very attracted to my rifle muzzle flash and loud report. Like the undead builder we had avoided earlier, many of these corpses were coming at us in jerky, erratic movements. The way they approached was reminiscent of a line of police searching for a body. Ironically, the dead bodies were now searching for me.

I kept shooting them, kept moving the vehicle. John and Will kept reloading. After moving the vehicle for the fourth time and opening fire again, I could see movement on top of the LAV. I stopped firing for a moment to allow my eyes to adjust. The Marines were taking their opportunity for escape. Exactly as planned, they were moving as a squad toward the pick-up point. I emptied my sixth magazine on the mob and then handed the very hot weapon to Will. I honked my horn and led the dead just a little farther away from the Marines before speeding back for the pick-up. The six Marines were in a defensive posture, weapons aimed outward into the darkness. They were in uniform, including flak jackets and Kevlar helmets.

I rolled down the window and told them to get in. Out of

courtesy, I closed my eyes and turned on the dome light so they could see us. They jumped in the Land Rover. Three of them had to sit in the very back, but I'm sure they didn't mind. We sped off toward I-10 and then back toward the Hotel. Every Marine in the vehicle sincerely thanked each of us for their lives.

While driving back, I asked John to check them with the Geiger to see if they were fine. The meter indicated that they were giving off some ambient radiation from the mass of the dead, but it was insignificant. We really had no way to tell how much they had absorbed without their wearing dosimeters. We could only measure how many RADs they were now giving off.

Just before reaching the point where we had had to pull the car wreckage out of the way, I stopped the vehicle. I looked back and asked who was in charge. The lance corporal sounded off that he was in command of the others.

I commented that he was a pretty low rank to be in charge on a remote reconnaissance mission like this. He was coy in his remark: "Wait until you meet our commanding officer."

One of the others elbowed him to shut up. This was the moment I picked to lay down the law.

I stated, "Lance Corporal, I can take you to a safe place with water, food and a place to sleep, but you have to follow my rules. You will not be prisoners and you can leave when you want."

I could see him nod in the rearview in acknowledgment that he was ready to listen.

I said, "You are going to have to surrender your firearms and submit to wearing a hood over your head until we get inside our home and can sort things out."

Reluctantly, the Marine gave the order for the others to comply. John confiscated all the weapons and placed them in the front with us. William checked them for pistols. I told William to let them keep their knives. With six Marines wearing pillowcases over their heads, I sped off. Passing the point of the wreckage I saw no sign of the radioactive builder corpse.

It didn't take long to return to Hotel 23. As I approached the compound, the infrared lamps on the cameras shined brightly in our direction. The girls were watching us. We parked the vehicle and led the Marines through the fence and down the stairs into the large berthing area. I told them that they could take their hoods off. We took the magazines out of their weapons and gave the M-16s back to them, bolts locked to the rear. I told them that they could have their mags back when they decided to leave. It was late and I showed them where the cots and extra blankets were stored. I informed them that they were safe in an underground bunker and that they could sleep tight tonight and we would talk things over when they woke up.

Early this morning the lance corporal appeared at my door wanting to talk. He was reluctant to tell me where his unit was located, but he did say that there weren't many of them left. I told him that he was welcome to use our radios to contact his commanding officer. However, I would not allow them to know where this compound was located. I suggested to him that he should stay another day and get his thoughts straight and some food and water in him before making the decision to leave. I don't know the names of the other Marines, sans the last names embroidered on their uniform tapes. They are playing cards in the berthing area right now. I overheard one of them commenting on how nice this place is compared to base camp. I wonder just what is left of the military. Part of me wants to tell these men who I am.

01 Jul

_2224_

Corporal Ramirez and the five other U.S. Marines departed this morning. I sat and talked with the men for a few hours last night. They were all young men. Ramirez, Williams, Bourbonnais, Collins, Akers and Mull were their names. I didn't bother with first names, as I did not see the point. When asked about their commanding officer and base location, they declined to comment. Ramirez brought up the point that we didn't want them knowing the location of our stronghold, either. I agreed, as it was only fair.

I asked Ramirez about the government and if there was any form of it left. He told me that the last official government orders from the top were received in early February. Ramirez didn't think there was any formal civilian government left. He had heard rumors about the president's underground haven being infected from the inside. That would explain the First Lady's final transmission after the president's death.

I asked how a large unit like his could survive this long aboveground. The lance corporal just smirked and said, "We are Marines, we just do." I was trying to get a bead on the size of his force by the wording of that question. He knew it. He was young, but he was intelligent. At around 1030 this morning, the Marines, John and I departed in two vehicles. We put the hoods over the men and led them to the Land Rover. John followed in the Bronco. We drove in circles and did our best to deceive our passengers. I was almost certain that they were honest men, but I had no idea what type of commanding officer they had.

It didn't take long to get to the point that we agreed we would take them to, a point from which they knew they could find their way back home. When we arrived at the drop-off point, we took the pillowcases off their heads and gave them back their magazines. John left the Bronco running. We said our good-byes to the men and they all piled into the Bronco.

One of the youngest Marines rolled his window down and said, "Thanks for the hospitality, *sir*."

It was the way he emphasized the *sir*. I felt that he knew something. Perhaps it was just my paranoia and guilt kicking in. Following the young Marine's example, the others followed suit, and I could have sworn that Ramirez saluted me before stomping on the gas and heading off into the void of the undead badlands.

Klieg Light

It has been busy here at Hotel 23. The day after the Marines departed, we started picking up chatter on the UHF band. Then on the morning of the third we picked up a convoy of LAVs and Humvees going in the same direction Ramirez was headed days earlier, before we rescued them.

I don't know what to make of it except that they may have attempted to go and retrieve their abandoned vehicle, as it is quite valuable and irreplaceable in a world like this. On more than one occasion I had thought of attempting to retrieve it myself. This idea was shot down, as the vehicle weighs literally tons and it would have been impossible to fight my way in with the Land Rover, attach the chain and crawl in low gear back to the compound. The Marines could do it. From the looks of the military convoy, they had plenty of torque-abundant vehicles to make this happen.

The radios are still busy but the transmissions are not voice. It sounds like an old dial-up modem trying to connect. I am almost positive they are using encryption on the radio. I would, if I had it.

We keep seeing part of the previous convoy passing in front of the complex as if searching the area. I hope the Marines made it back to their base. One of two things can be deduced from what we are seeing. Either they are searching for their Marines or they are searching for us.

07 Jul
2038

Just received a radio transmission from the military. They are calling out to the civilians in the underground compound that rescued the Marines. At least we know they made it back. They say that the commanding officer requests a meeting with the man wearing green coveralls. We have not answered this transmission and I bet that they are just randomly transmitting every few miles to see if we will pick it up. I am very apprehensive about the intentions of the Marines, due to their understandably cryptic answers when I probed for information. I really don't know what we are up against here, but I am certain that sooner or later they will think to check the chain-link fence area that they have passed by so many times . . . Hotel 23.

11 Jul
2121

The military is still in this general area. From the information we have gathered from radio chatter on nonsecure lines, it is safe to assume that they have put up a forward camp in this vicinity to find us. They have recorded a message and have it playing on most frequencies, including the distress frequency. We all had a meeting a couple of days ago and decided it was best to stay out of the military's path and eyes. They could easily find us, and I am sure they could eventually get into the compound using the same tactic as the civilian marauders. They would simply blast their way in using high order explosives (in lieu of cutting torches).

The undead are slowly building numbers at the front blast doors again. A week ago there were only ten or fifteen. Now, scores of them cluster around the heavy steel doors around the front of the complex. We have been leaving off the IR mode of night vision at night to reduce the chances of the Marines' seeing our infrared camera beam on their own night vision devices. This has forced us to monitor living activity via thermal mode. This was the only thing that allowed us to see the small group of Marines pass within four hundred yards of our complex last night. They are getting closer, but for some reason have not stumbled upon the field of chain-link fence and open silo door that marked Hotel 23. Something in the back of my mind tells me that perhaps they know what this place is and that they could be just casing the area to determine weak spots to exploit.

Normally John only monitors a few HF channels at night. He cycles through them on a random schedule so that he can possibly catch a transmission that he normally would not. Last night, he did. It was severely garbled, but John swears he heard the words "Andrews Air Force Base." Andrews is very near D.C. I had assumed that D.C. had been nuked along with New York.

I don't know how much longer we will be able to hold out before the military finds us. I suppose they might give up, but I find that prospect unlikely. Another haunting thought is that they refuse to mention the commanding officer's name and rank in their recorded transmissions. Perhaps he wishes to be anonymous, as I do.

Siege

We have been discovered by what is left of the Marines in this area. Fifteen military vehicles are parked nearby and shots are again being fired outside Hotel 23 directed at the undead. They have made no attempts to disable our cameras, so we have been watching them carefully. Of the fifteen vehicles, six are LAVs. There are some military Hummers and even a four-wheeled ATV. I didn't count the ATV or the olive-drab dirt bike as part of the fifteen. They all appear to be in Marine issue digital camouflage, which tells me that some order still might exist within the unit. The radio has been playing the same loop. I cannot get an accurate head count on them, as the dead are amongst them attempting to converge.

The creatures that the Marines are dealing with outside are not the same as the one I had to avoid when on my last rescue mission. I have a feeling that if I were faced with an overwhelming army of the radiated dead, I would eventually fall to either their slightly faster mobility or their extreme radiation. The small numbers outside at this moment should not be a problem for the men dealing with them.

We can escape now (via the alternate exit) and leave Hotel 23 forever, never knowing if the military outside are our allies, or we can stay and fight or maybe attempt communication. We still maintain our radio silence and do not plan to break it unless absolutely necessary.

They are making no attempts to gain entry at this time and have made no gestures toward the cameras. The sun will be down in roughly two hours and if they plan to gain forced entry, I feel they will do it in the dead of night.

One thing is absolute . . . defeating foolish raiders with a lucky cheap shot is one thing, but going head to head with a couple of dozen well-armed U.S. Marines is quite another.

17 Jul

2236

Negotiations at first were civil, then turned to threats that in turn led to violence. They began with radio transmissions directed "at the ones in the bunker." Then came the explosives. They set the explosives but did not detonate them. They wanted to get in without resistance. After seeing block after block of explosives being carted down into the silo hole, I had no choice but to break radio silence with the Marines.

I keyed the microphone and said (to the best of my recollection):

"To the men trying to take this facility by force, please cease hostile actions or we will be forced to retaliate."

I thought for sure I would hear laughter on the radio, but they were professional.

"No one wants hostilities, we just want the complex. It is U.S. government property, and we have rightful claim to such properties, in accordance with applicable federal laws and executive orders. We ask that you allow us to gain access and no one will be harmed."

That was the moment when I wanted to laugh at *them* on the radio. We were at a standoff. I had to speak to the person in command of this unit. I requested to do so and was met with evasive wording and lip service.

"The commanding officer is at headquarters and will not be present."

I asked for the person speaking to identify himself. He refused.

I asked, "On what real authority do you claim this compound?"

He replied, "On the authority of the chief of Naval Operations."

"Don't you mean the Commandant of the Marine Corps?"

At first there was silence, and then the tinny voice came back and said, "The commandant is missing in action. It is our best guess he is with his fellow cadre of the chairman of the Joint Chiefs at some *secure* location, along with most of the nation's leadership . . . dead."

"So you are under naval operational control at this time?"

"We are the Marine Corps, Department of the Navy." There was audible laughter at this point.

I didn't see any point in hiding that we were the ones who had saved Ramirez and his men.

These Marines probably knew that we were the same people, so I asked, "What about Ramirez and the other men that we saved from the disabled LAV?"

"They are fine and one of them is with us now. Ramirez is back at base camp on perimeter defense duty but wanted to pass something along face-to-face."

With as much sternness as I could muster on the radio, I yelled into the mic, "Let me speak to a commissioned officer now, Marine!"

"I can't do that."

"Why not?"

"We don't have any . . . er, I mean we don't have any *here*."

The Marine had slipped. I began to wonder who exactly was in command of these men. More banter went on until I finally convinced the Marine on the radio to put me on with the senior noncom present. Gunnery Sergeant Handley answered the call.

The Gunny bellowed, "Now listen down there, we need the complex as a forward command center, as there's still a little bit a' hope. A plan is being formed for the remnants of the U.S. military to attempt reclamation of the United States from the creatures."

I asked him how often they had communicated with the Chief of Naval Operations (CNO).

"We got regular but sunspotty HF comms with his carrier and they're still flyin' very maintenance-limited sorties off the boat doing airborne reconnaissance on the mainland in an attempt to give accurate intelligence to what's left of the men on the ground.

Hell, they've even dropped some iron a time or two for us when things got real bad."

I asked him, "So, I suppose much of the Navy has survived the plague?"

He replied, "A lotta ships turned into floatin' caskets in the beginnin'. Of the ten carriers in active service at the start a' all this, only four were not infested and overrun by the dead. You might also wanna know that there is a ballistic missile submarine that has been under for seven months. They're livin' off powdered eggs 'n' dried fruits 'n' meat. That boat is the last normal piece of the lifecycle. . . . People can still die in peace there and not come back."

I asked the gunnery sergeant what he meant by that.

He said, "The boomer sub was under before all of this happened, so somehow they're unaffected by whatever is causin' the dead to rise. They radioed in on the very low frequency band that they had suffered one natural death in the month of February but the corpse didn't rise. After a twenty-four-hour observation, their doc put the corpse in the freezer and had it restrained with riggin' web. The thing has been there since, motionless. Of course, they will have to surface sooner or later or they'll run outta food, but for now they are the last unaffected humans known to exist. All the other boomers and fast attack subs didn't hit the right time gate to avoid exposure. I guess we all have some form of this plague dormant inside us . . . waitin' on the day our heart stops beatin'. The whole thing's fucked up as a football bat."

Then came a chilling silence, interrupted only by the random report of 5.56 rounds being fired at the creatures.

"Sir, we don't wanna blow a big hole in your clubhouse and then take it from ya. Isn't there some sort of peaceful agreement we can come to? There are civilians at our compound that are happy to be there."

I replied, "We won't be happy there, Gunny, we aren't cattle. We have been surviving on the run since the beginning and much of it was before we found this place."

"That is impressive, but it doesn't change the fact that this complex falls under military jurisdiction."

"Gunny, you still haven't given me proof that you all aren't some rogue group of military survivors with no government leadership backing your actions."

"Sir, government guidance and hesitation are what brought us into the shithouse and to the point of extinction."

"Yes, Gunny, you may have a point. However, we found this place and we don't want to live under any iron fists, even if they belong to the U.S. military."

He just replied with a "very well" and then came more radio silence. This was the night of the sixteenth. Two hours after the last radio call they detonated their first charge in the silo. It had no effect save for a barely visible crack in the eight-inch-thick window glass of the blast door. Then another detonation, and another. The already damaged camera in the silo was disabled at this point, not even returning any variance of visible signal. The explosions were having no effect.

Thinking of this, I wondered if the civilian marauders had even had a chance at getting in with their cutting tools before I killed them. The alloy and fiberglass embedded concrete that made up Hotel 23 was very strong. I suppose it would need to be to withstand a nuclear blast. I felt an ever-so-slight sting of guilt at the possibly needless killing of the civilian raiders. Perhaps they would have given up when their torches turned out to be ineffective. Maybe I didn't have to see them as walking, burnt men. Rationalization tells me that they deserved it . . .

Every synapse a ping of pain.

I snapped out of this thought at the sound of another explosion. I felt a slight pressure change. This change caused me to pinch my nose, close my mouth and blow to equalize the pressure between my ears. The explosion did not damage the structure of the complex, but it did vibrate the alloy enough to induce a quick change in pressure inside. Jan and Tara were very upset at the thought of being captured and taken to a military-controlled camp. For all they knew at this moment, they would be used as breeding vessels; I would never let that happen. The explosions weren't making anything better. Laura was crying and Annabelle yelped in fear and stuck her tail between her legs every time another went off. After thirty minutes of this, the explosions ceased. They must have been fresh out of plastique.

The radio once again crackled.

"Had 'nuff yet? Why not just open the doors and come out peacefully? You will not be harmed."

I asked the gunnery sergeant to give us until sunrise to pack our things before we opened the door. He bought it.

I gathered the adults and we began brainstorming on what cards we could possibly play in this scenario. Options were limited. We could go on the run again and try to find another defensible location, but nothing would compare to Hotel 23. It would take us years to build anything as durable and safe.

Jan suggested we take off in the aircraft. I explained to them that the Cessna could not possibly hold us all, let alone our gear, and that that option was out. Besides, the aircraft was not in excellent condition; the brake on one side was out. It was midnight and we had six good hours to come up with something. I turned to John, who would normally have an "outside the box" answer to give me. He claimed that there was no logical answer.

I was not sure that they knew the alternate exit existed, but there were vehicles parked in that area near the fence. They probably knew about it. The front door was a decent option, but there was a growing group of undead there, still banging on the door. The other option was to trust the Marines. If they kept their word, they would simply let us go after they seized the compound.

I had no desire to be on the run again with an older lady, two small children and a dog. We would be dead before the month ended at the claws and maws of those things. I just didn't know what to do. I sat in my living quarters pondering on any possible solution to our conundrum. If only I had possessed some sort of leverage.

I hadn't put my belongings away since I let Dean have my other living area. A small box of what I had was still sitting in the corner of the room, waiting for the day I got tired of looking at it. Now it seemed that day would never come. I stared at the box for a few minutes, thinking of how we were going to transport all of our gear with us cross-country and survive. Walking over to the box I began to inventory its contents. Two extra flight suits, gloves, kneeboard for flying, Glock 17 handgun, three small family pictures, six boxes of 9mm ammunition and my Velcro name patch with, of course, my name, rank and wings embroidered into the fabric. I hadn't worn this patch since civilization fell. What was the need? Finally, I pulled my wallet out of the box . . .

Looking inside my wallet, I found numerous cards. I was an NRA member back when it existed. It wasn't that long ago. I also had a card for what seemed like every video rental chain. Would I be exempt from the late fees if society ever rebuilt itself? I am sure the server that housed my felonious late fees data would long be rusted by the time the power grid was restored. If ever.

Then came something that changed everything. Last month I had remembered looking at my military identification card with a feeling of nostalgia. It was two years until it expired. I stood there looking at it, running my thumb across the microchip embedded in the front. My data was on that chip, along with the data that was embedded in the barcode on the right side of the card. Again there was my photo. A clean-shaven, naive version of myself who would have never thought the dead would walk.

If these men were still U.S. Marines, following the Uniform Code of Military Justice, then I was still a commissioned officer and still their superior. If anyone still followed the rank structure of the military, it would be a Marine. In all my limited encounters with the Marine enlisted men in my military past, they had always stood up to address me when I spoke to them. The gunnery sergeant had said himself that there was no officer available topside and that he was the senior man present.

He was lying and didn't know it.

I was, in theory, the senior man present.

As I stood there with my back to the door, staring at the card in my hands, I saw Dean reach over and take the ID card and look at it. She carefully examined the military ID and looked at me.

She said, "Looks a lot like you, sailor."

I smiled back at her and said, "Yes, it used to be me."

She replied, "It's still you, it's just that you lost your military bearing and it looks like you need to shave!"

I thought for a moment that she could be right. I had done some bad things since January, but that didn't change the fact that there were military units still active and I was still a military officer. My unit was destroyed, probably with no survivors. I knew this; I had flown over my base and seen it with my own eyes. The base had been overrun, then later nuked. Game over. For all I knew, I was the only one left.

I called the group together and discussed what I planned to do. They all gasped at the thought but eventually agreed that it was the only real way to handle the situation.

It was 0500 hrs this morning before I woke up and switched on the lights. I took my shower kit and began the laborious task of getting myself together. As I passed my old quarters, the door swung open and Dean stepped out with a pair of scissors from the control center office.

"Can't have you going topside without a haircut."

I laughed and made sure my towel wouldn't fall off in front of her.

"I suppose not, Dean."

She had cut Danny's hair when he needed it, and she made sure to tell me that he had never complained. My hair had grown long and far out of military regulation in the past months. I had shaved it off three months ago, but I had not touched it since and it was rather long. It was unlike me to let it get this way. The end of the civilized world was a decent excuse, I thought, but Dean wouldn't have it. Like a master barber, she restored my head to unwritten aviation officer regulations (just a little longer than that of the enlisted men).

As I finished up in the shower and hacked my thick stubble off, I looked in the mirror. I looked presentable for what I was about to do. I had no dress uniform or officer's sword, but I would make do. With my towel wrapped around me I walked my way back to my quarters. Outside my door were my boots, shined to perfection with a note in child's writing: "I hope you like I shined my dad's boots before—Danny."

He must have come in and retrieved them while I slept. I leave the door open so that I can hear if anything is going on in the walkway. I must be losing my edge, or he must be a very quiet kid.

I thought back to when I had seen Danny urinating on the undead at the tower. What a funny sight.

I put on my clean flight suit, with rank on my shoulders and name patch on my chest. I pulled my garrison cap out of the leg pocket where it had been for six months and put it on my head. I walked out of my quarters in uniform, prepared to meet the Marines. It was 0550 hrs and I could see on the cameras that the sun was coming up, making the clouds to the east shine with an ominous orange tint.

I keyed the radio. "Gunny, are you there? . . . over . . ."

After a short pause, a tired, haggard and perturbed voice came back, "Yes, I am here, and I have been here all damn night."

"Good, now clear your men away from the silo opening, I am coming up."

"We'll be waiting on you at the top . . . out."

Armed only with a sidearm, I went to the access hatch that led directly into the silo. John and Will covered me with their weapons. It took three of us to spin the wheel and open the hatch, as all the heat and explosions had expanded and contracted the alloy. As soon as the hatch opened, a flood of light shone down from above and dust billowed in. John and Will quickly dogged the hatch. I hadn't seen the inside of the silo close up for quite a while. There were bits of burnt bone and clothing all over the bottom. Lots of teeth were scattered on the deck. There must have been quite a few creatures down here when the marauders started burning them. The walls were blackened from all the explosives that had been detonated during the past twenty-four hours.

The men at the top could not yet see me, as I was near the bulkhead at the bottom. With cold anticipation I stepped into the light and began climbing up the ladder to the top. The ladder was covered in ash. I kept climbing. The sound of "Holy shit!" signified that I had been sighted. I kept climbing until I reached the top. The gloved hand of a USMC gunnery sergeant reached out to help me over the lip of the silo doors. I stood there and looked him in the eye. He squared off in front of me and rendered a sharp salute. I returned it with the same bearing and he dropped his. He immediately led me to his tent and a handful of staff sergeants followed.

"Sir, we had no idea, I . . .

"No need for that, Gunny, you didn't know I was an officer and I wasn't going to tell you until I had to."

A question-and-answer session followed, and I told him my story from day one. I left out the part about my XO ordering me to report to the base shelter. I told him that I was probably the last surviving member of my squadron and that I had been surviving and picking up others when I could. It was then that he ordered the staff sergeants to leave the tent.

He leaned in close to me and with a very quiet and nervous whisper said, "Sir, I have not seen an officer for months. All of our ground-pounder brass was ordered to an undisclosed location months ago and we have not seen nor communicated with them since. Basically, they left us to die in the open out here. I have been tellin' the men that the commanding officer was alive and issuing orders directly to me via secure radio. It is not really lying, considerin' I have been receiving orders from an Admiral Goettleman, onboard the flagship USS *George Washington*. They are starting to doubt my word. I had to keep the men's morale up. How would they fight or even work as a team knowing their unit's superior officers left them in the open to die and were probably dead themselves?"

We both sat there. I pondered what this implied. My concentration was broken intermittently by gunfire as the men fended off the undead.

"What are you telling me, Gunny?"

"Sir, I'm telling you that you are the first officer I have seen in a long time, and we need you, if only as a mouthpiece leader for the men. Leader or not, I just need you to play the part or this whole thing is going to unravel quick-like and blow up in everyone's face."

"Gunny, in that case, this place, Hotel 23, will be *my* command. You will need to stay and send most of your men back, along with your most trusted staff sergeant." He agreed. I told him that I would address the men while he decided who stayed and who didn't.

Over the next half hour, I stood on an ammunition crate and

watched the faces of the young patriots who looked on and listened.

"I am the commanding officer of this stronghold, and I need a few good men."

This was met with aggressive applause.

"About six and a half months ago, something really rocked our world. Now no one really knows what it was that happened, but it doesn't really matter what it is."

I didn't think I sounded that great, but the men disagreed with their whistles and clapping.

"The way I see it, we may run out of rounds, but we still have sharp sticks! It may take a long time, but we won't give up. We're going to save as many as we can and we are going to put the hurt on those *things*.

"I want you men to never forget that you are in the United States military. I don't want to hear any talk of there not being a United States. That is nonsense. Our Constitution may be sitting there in D.C. just fine or it may be burned up, but that doesn't mean it's dead like those things out there. We will still support and defend till the end."

This was met with cheers and claps and also led to a crowd of men gathering around the Gunny, volunteering to stay here at Hotel 23. The sun was now rising over the tree line on this summer morning. My simple address was over and I could already see a visible boost in their morale. The compound was buzzing with purpose.

The Gunny said, "One more thing, sir. Ramirez wanted me to give you this."

He handed me a fixed-blade knife with a heavy-duty leather sheath. The sheath had a small pocket containing a sharpening stone. I pulled the knife from the sheath and noticed that it was a very high-quality combat knife with a black micarta handle. The knife appeared to be stainless steel and had the words "Randall Made Orlando FL" stamped into the blade near the handle on one side. I laughed as I thought to myself, "They don't make 'em like this anymore." Hell they don't make anything anymore.

After all was said and done, three LAVs and a covered supply truck stayed here along with twenty-two men, including the Gunny. We were topside when the staff sergeant and his convoy left for base camp with the news that they had found an officer to help with the cause. Two military radios, loaded with crypto key-mat code from KYK-13s (small cryptographic storage units), were taken down into the compound and set up in the command center. The Marines quickly set up their berthing below.

Most of the afternoon was spent returning Hotel 23 to an operational military combined operations center.

C4I

18 Jul

1605

We have established communications with the USS *George Washington*. The acting Chief of Naval Operations is currently away from the carrier on one of the small boys planning with one of his commodores. I am certain there will be more to come in the following days. I'm told they are sending someone out to reprogram my common access card (CAC) chip on my military identification card in the next anticipated supply run, but I'm not sure what good that will do or why it matters to me here.

22 Jul

1720

I have opened a Pandora's box. I now have more responsibility than I know what to do with. The twenty-two new Marines have been busy militarizing the perimeter and standing security watches. I now have a full-time radio operator with direct links to the carrier strike group. Message traffic has been heavy with updates to the status of the Gulf and eastern coastlines. Even daily threat assessments are being received indicating large undead swarm movements in some areas. I was curious about how the carrier was getting food for the three thousand plus skeleton crew they were running. One of the young Marines told me that they had units of Navy strike teams stationed onboard supply vessels and they used these teams to infiltrate and exfiltrate, via zodiac boats, the government coastal supply centers to identify good targets so that the larger cargo choppers can get in and airlift the food.

I listened to the battle group radios for a few hours today, monitoring Navy and Air Force aviation communications, in particular voice traffic from a U-2 reconnaissance aircraft flying over the eastern seaboard. I was curious to know how they were able to keep the DRAGON LADY airborne with the hefty maintenance and long airfield requirements.

Apparently the U.S. Army didn't fare very well, and according to a report received day before last, they have suffered a loss of over 70 percent of ground troops in CONUS. There just wasn't enough room for them on the ships. The sailors and Marines took priority and the U.S. Army units were left to defend themselves inland. They were given advance warning of the nuclear strike, but many of them were overcome by the radiated undead that were pouring out of the radiation zones after the strike.

Some of the voice communications I was monitoring indicated that there were still search teams out surveying the ground for military survivors. One particular communiqué received was from a surveillance aircraft flying over the Virginias, in search of a lost tank convoy. Apparently the convoy met its demise after one of the lead tanks crushed an overpass under its massive weight. The structure of the ill-repaired overpass gave way and took four tanks with it. The convoy was being pursued by thousands of "hot" undead, and it only took a couple of hours before the swarm caught up with them. Three tanks were disabled in the fall from the overpass and their occupants were left to die in metal tombs with countless bodies pounding on the heavy armor and squirming over the turrets and tracks like maggots over roadkill.

The remaining tanks scattered to the winds and got the hell out. Location unknown.

The crew in the back of the aircraft commented on the radio that the occupants of the disabled tanks might already be exposed to high levels of radiation due to the sheer number of dead below. The aircraft sensors indicated that the horde was emitting deadly amounts at ground level. After surveying the situation, the aircraft headed back to base, reporting that they were on *bingo* (emergency) fuel.

One thing is for sure, the number of new inhabitants here will force us out soon to find a water tanker to fill Hotel 23's tanks back up to maximum capacity. Hitting the tank with my rifle today revealed that the level is down to the bottom eighth. We are already rationing water and have set up numerous rain catches around the compound to help fill the critical need.

A technician showed up at the command center after flying in today to reprogram my identification card. There is a chip embedded in the card. The technician inserted my card into a reader/writer connected to a laptop and instructed me to enter a pin number at least six digits long. I thought of a number that I knew I'd never forget and entered it into the terminal. The technician informed me that I would have full control over all sensitive systems at the compound by using my card and pin at the computer terminals in the command center. He warned that I am the only person that would have this access until I was relieved. I asked him why this mattered and he stated that he didn't know but that his instructions from headquarters were to give the ranking officer at the compound this access. The only way to designate another person would be for my card to be used in the command center to give permission for the transfer of authority to another officer designated by higher authority. If my card or pin number were to be lost or destroyed it would take ninety days to reprogram another, as the system has a time-lock fail-safe to avoid the unauthorized transfer of power.

The technician said nonchalantly as he walked out the door, "Too bad you are empty, this authorization would have given you nuke launch authority. Although *I* wouldn't want it."

26 Jul

1422

I cannot be certain that having men topside standing watch is a good idea. The men are firing fifty rounds per twenty-four-hour period and I feel this may be a cycle of waste and danger. Last night I ordered them inside to see if not having them up there would lessen the undead activity in the area. It seemed to work better. This morning, there were ten undead at the fence. Killing ten is better than shooting fifty. The men are using bayonets to dispatch the undead at the fence, then dragging them near the tree line fifty yards off using ATVs and webbing that they wrap around the corpses' chests so that they avoid any chance of getting scraped inadvertently by the inanimate body.

Communication from the aircraft carrier has been sporadic, as our ground unit is an insignificant speck compared to what the rest of the military is dealing with. Andrews and D.C. apparently were not hit (according to message traffic), and there is currently a team of scouts on the ground surveying what it would need to retake the District of Columbia. Another option discussed is moving the capital out west, but little is known about that region of the country. Communication with the other Marines is constant and steady, with the noncommissioned officer in charge checking in every hour on the hour.

I have made it clear to the Gunny that having the other men and civilians closer to our position may not be a bad idea. I tried to connect to the internet backbone again today. Down. This would have been an excellent means of long-range communications with other countries and units, since our main enemy cannot read or use a computer.

The water supply is getting dangerously low and a team is being assembled and briefed for deployment tomorrow in the A.M. I will be accompanying.

30 Jul
1934

Our small unit left in search of water on the morning of the twenty-seventh. John was the temporary appointed civilian leader holding down the law at Hotel 23. He promised he would take care of our folks while we went looking for the H_2O. Our path took us north, lateral to the radiation zone outskirts. We took three LAVs and thirteen men. Our goal was simple; we were headed toward the interstate to find a water truck or any truck that could hold water. Hotel 23's tanks were nearly dry and it was going to take ten thousand gallons to fill the reservoir up to capacity. I was informed of the location of the original Marine base camp days ago. Our journey took us within forty miles of their location. Forty miles equaled eighty miles round trip, so a visit was out of the question for now.

After an hour of pulling wreckage out of the way and dodging pileups, our LAV convoy finally made it to what remained of Interstate 100. This stopped being fun before it started. I hate doing this with the white-hot intensity of a thousand suns. I could see a group of them walking about, weaving in and around the abandoned cars. They were four hundred yards off, and if I imagined and concentrated, I could make myself believe for a few minutes that they were not dead. Soon our scent (could they really smell?) would be carried on the wind to them and they would start the slow but determined march toward the living.

It seemed like a balancing act. I sometimes think of the living and the dead as chromosomes, only the dead are the dominant chromosomes. No matter what, all you get in this world are brown-eyed babies. They are dominant if numbers dictate. In this day and time they seem to do just that.

Dean really wanted to come along with us. She could probably handle herself, but I quickly made up another important task for her to accomplish so I didn't have to tell her it wasn't a good idea. Tara and I are probably considered an item now. I suppose I knew it was coming. That is in itself another story. Perhaps I will write about it someday. Jan, Will, John and Tara are showing the Marines at Hotel 23 the basic operation of the facility as well as the escape routes in the event of the worst-case scenario.

I was thinking of Tara as we closed on the interstate . . . I was two hundred yards out when I saw a surrounded vehicle. Reminded me of her. I truly thought she was dead back at the dock that day we found her. We advanced closer and I had to see what was in the car. I could tell the window was cracked on the side visible to our convoy by the undead arms that were reaching in, only to be stopped at the elbow by the partially opened window.

One LAV ran interference and drew the group away from the car so that we could have a look inside. Of course, it worked. The radiation measurement equipment onboard indicated that this area was nearly free of radiation. Some residual radiation remained and would for hundreds of years if no cleanup was done. We were closer to the car now. The men covered us as myself and two other Marines jumped off the vehicle and headed for the car.

I was pleased to find a mother bird and her chirping babies safely nestled in the backseat of the vehicle. I was sure that those creatures were making it extremely difficult for the mother to leave and find food, but she seemed to be doing all right. I thought of rolling the windows up just a little more to make it more difficult for the creatures but much to my disappointment the windows were electric and the battery long dead. Looked like I was leaving this one up to *unnatural* selection.

We radioed the herding LAV to rally with us one mile east of original position. The highway was thick with undead, but a strange sense of security came with riding in these capable vehicles. We had plenty of weapons and ammunition, as it would be dangerous not to. We searched east along the interstate until we were perilously close to the outskirts of Houston. Houston was not hit in the offensive months ago and it most assuredly had an abundance of undead at its core. We had found numerous eighteen-wheeler trucks with fuel trailers probably full of gasoline. It was too bad we couldn't drink fuel. Reminded me of the real world, before all of this, when a bottle of water was much more expensive than its equivalent in gas. Either way, we did find a truck that held a lot of water and it made me feel a little ignorant for not thinking of it before.

I don't know why we didn't just seek out a small-town fire department rather than risking our asses on the interstate. I didn't let on I was thinking this in front of the men, but it would have been much safer the other way. Sitting in front of us was a nice (dirty) fire truck marked "San Felipe Fire Dept." It was a large truck, but not the largest I had seen. We attempted to start the truck. No joy. It turned out to be a difficult task to turn the vehicle around and get it hooked up to one of the LAVs, a task that has aged me a few years.

Continued soon//

• • •

The fire truck was a tomb. Inside were two dead firemen, who actually were dead and not moving. I was not close enough yet to know how they took their own lives and avoided reanimation, but it seemed they succeeded. The interstate was thick with them but they were not the ultra-deadly variety of undead that would have been found nearer the radiated zone west of this position. The only other option besides towing the vehicle would be to attempt to trickle-charge the battery from the equipment onboard the LAVs. First we needed to quietly clear out the immediate danger in the area. From my perch on the crew-served weapon of number two LAV, I counted thirty-eight undead. I radioed Gunny and he claimed to count thirty-nine.

When we left Hotel 23 the Marines had regular M-4 and M-16 carbines not unlike what the Hotel armory held when we first opened it months before. I knew that this was not a unit composed of all original members.

The Gunny had relayed to me in the first days of their arrival that the unit was made up of surviving Marines of several units that followed radio signals and ended up in Texas. Of course, not all of them found the surviving military cell in this way, as many times when the core of the unit went out to find supplies they found survivors. Many times the survivors were military or former military. This explained the weapons that the Marines in LAV number one pulled out of the vehicle. Four Marines that I had previously remembered having dive bubbles and jump wings on their chest pulled out suppressed H&K MP5s. I would have loved to have even one of these weapons in the first months of the end of the world.

I held my fist up in the sign to hold fire while I radioed the Gunny. I asked him how many suppressed weapons the unit had. He told me that the recon Marines had raided their local armory before they had bugged out and took all the suppressed weapons that they could, likely in preparation for a quiet guerilla campaign.

I radioed LAV number one (point) and gave the men permission to fire suppressed rounds at the undead surrounding the fire truck. I hadn't even finished my radio call when I started hearing the eerie sounds of the action of suppressed submachine guns.

One by one the undead fell. Many times the Marines missed. During the shooting the Gunny read my thoughts and informed me that these suppressed 9mm weapons were not nearly as accurate as the M-16 but they *were* quiet and didn't draw unwanted attention.

The sound was very nearly the same as if you were to pull the charging handle on a regular M-16 quickly, in succession. A barely audible popping sound was heard. It took four minutes to clear the area around the fire truck. We parked the LAVs around the truck, and we all got out. The Marines had restowed the suppressed weapons, as firing them too much would render the suppression ineffective in the long term (according to them). Eight men set up a defensive perimeter in the LAV gaps. I approached the fire truck and reached up to open the door. It was locked. Same story, the pus marks of dead arms were present on the doors of both sides, indicating that the dead firemen inside had held out in the abandoned truck until they had apparently taken their own lives.

Using a large wrench taken from one of the vehicle's tool bags and some hundred-mile-an-hour duct tape, I quietly broke the glass so that I could open the driver's-side door. I reached in to unfasten the door lock and was grabbed on the wrist by one of the firemen. I tried my best to pull my hand back through the broken opening. The thing almost had his mouth on my wrist when a Marine opened fire and shattered the creature's head. Both of us had thought the firemen were dead. The loud noise must have awoken the creature from some sort of undead hibernation.

The passenger-side fireman inside really was dead, as most of his upper body and head were gone, probably rotting in the other creature's throat and stomach. After opening the door and pulling the driver's-side ghoul to the ground, I nudged the passenger with the barrel of my rifle. No movement. He still clutched a blood-stained axe.

The advantage of having a unit of variously skilled and capable military men became apparent when I realized that I knew nothing of large-engine vehicles. One of the Marine mechanics went to work, popping the engine compartment, checking the salvage potential. Low on oil, dead battery and no fuel was the prognosis. The fuel was no problem. We used some of our LAV reserves to partly fill the tank. The oil would have to wait as neither I nor the mechanic knew what oil we needed without taking the time to read the manual. That was not an option now, as I could hear the perimeter guards shooting a small group of dead that had been drawn here by the sound of the fireman's execution.

The last thing to handle was the battery charge. The Marine was not certain of the battery's condition, sitting out in the elements unchecked for six months. We attempted to charge the battery. A waiting game began. It would take thirty minutes to charge the large battery enough to turn the stagnant engine over. In the meantime, we all stood defensive duty, sans the mech working on the fire truck. He was also charged with setting up the towing chains needed in the event the battery would not charge. Shot after shot. There was a virtually unlimited supply of undead. The city was in view on the horizon, smoke still spiraling up to the sky from fires left unopposed. I wondered which one this fire truck was meant for. Probably one long burned out. Another shot . . . then another . . .

They were coming . . . thicker, heavier . . . faster. Just ten more minutes . . . The sound was droning ever louder. Moans on the wind and intermittent sounds of metal banging or falling in the distance, those things tripping over road debris. Looking back over my shoulder I could see the mech attaching the chains to the underbelly of the rig. He didn't run the other end to the waiting LAV. He simply wrapped the length of chain around the hooks that were welded to the front bumper of the fire truck. Then came the sound of the engine sputtering and turning over. It worked. The engine turned and brought a new noise variable to the problem. Looking back, I saw smoke rise from the exhaust pipes; the huge red behemoth was waking up, waking up to a world very different from what it had known before.

The mechanic was grinning. I shot him an approving look and told the men to return to their vehicles. I sprinted to LAV number two, waving the men past me, and then I jumped in, screaming, *"Last man!"*

I could not be sure about the mechanical reliability of the fire truck. I radioed the mechanic to take the third position in the convoy. LAV one, two (I was in two), then the fire truck and last, LAV three made up the formation. I didn't want the large truck to break down, entombing another poor soul. I know the truck was probably fine and had just run out of fuel sitting in gridlock on the interstate. The poor firemen were surrounded with no way out. The rest is pure speculation.

We were on the move, headed for H23. Along our route, the Gunny and I took note of the numerous fuel tanker rigs by marking them on our maps. We would eventually need a lot of diesel fuel. That would be for another day. I don't think the power drain is affected by the recent population boost back home. The generators only run a few hours per day to power the batteries for the lighting, air, water circulation and limited cooking that is done. We have been surviving on MREs and limited dried goods since the beginning and they are getting old, but I know these Marines have probably eaten them longer in *normal* peacetime conditions.

We made it to the same point at which we first encountered the interstate. The sun was getting low, and that was a catalyst for something bad to happen. It did. The fire truck died. I sent two men from my LAV to attach the chain to our towing point. This vehicle had no problem in the torque department. I was sure one of the younger Marines probably knew every nut and bolt of this machine, but I only knew one thing . . . It was tough.

The large steel chain jerked and popped every time the tension did not balance the weight of the massive emergency vehicle towed behind. I felt our vehicle surge and the independent gearing kick in, dispersing the traction to the wheel that needed it. The undead were here in force. I could not count to five without hearing our vehicle impact one of them with a commanding *THUD*.

Looking through the thick armored glass window I observed them bouncing off the vehicle, some of them thrown nearly twenty feet into the overgrown ditches along the road. We were only half an hour out from H23 when I radioed the mech, asking him to check the water gauge on the truck. The mech couldn't read the gauge, as the water control panel had no power. I hoped that the truck at least had enough water to last us until we could repair the truck and find another water source. I was certain that the compound's water would run out any time, if it hadn't already.

Using the night vision capability of the LAV, I was able to pick up H23's camera beacons. We were on course and tracking. We made it back home with the truck in tow. The fire truck had a five-thousand-gallon capacity, and was one-quarter full. This would be enough to last us until we could find another water source. With the medical kits we have at H23 as well as the kits the Marines have, we should be able to purify the water using iodine. It would be wise to kick in a few suburban doors and grab some household bleach at some point.

Messages are constantly coming in from headquarters, most of them only for our information and not calling for action. I have had to send in one status report concerning Austin, Texas. The brass on the carrier needed the data to update their all-important status boards. I have a feeling we could soon be sent into a radiated area for the same type of *status* information. I suppose I will cross that bridge when it falls out from under me.

Cutter

I was inside Hotel 23. Trapped. The dead Marines outside were pounding on the door to the environmental control room. Sliding the steel peephole to the side, I could see her . . . Tara was there, bloody, dead, wanting. John was behind her pawing at the door. I couldn't remember how I had gotten here; I only knew that I *was* here. Surrounding the familiar faces were the Marines. Many of them were riddled with fatal bullet holes. My radio operator was there also. He still had his headset strapped to his head . . . then . . . he talked. The dead radioman talked! He said . . . "Sir, wake up . . . I have some important information for you."

I am not certain of the nature of the message that arrived last night while I was sleeping. I woke up to the sound of the radioman tapping on my door. The message stated that we were to deploy to the coastline to help out a wrecked Coast Guard cutter. They were in no immediate danger and were anchored off the coast of Texas, only eighty miles up the coast from where the *Bahama Mama* probably still rested on the shore. After I had read the message and discussed its contents with the Gunny, we decided it would be best to leave tonight.

Shaken from the dream, I told Tara what I had seen in my vision. She was more than a friend and I felt I could tell her anything. Also, Dean was a rock. Her wisdom helped me deal with the demons that racked my soul more often than not these days.

The feeling was similar to coming off a long vacation to find that work had piled up in my absence. As I write this, my third in command is charting our course overland to rendezvous with the cutter that is dead in the water. In any other situation we would have departed already, but since the men onboard were relatively safe, we were taking the time in planning and provisioning to ensure a safer trip.

I would like to keep this excursion to a maximum of forty-eight hours. There is still much that needs to be done with merging the two camps. Hotel 23 cannot accommodate all the people, but I feel that with the right heavy equipment and some concrete dividers taken from the interstate, we could form a large wall around the perimeter outside the chain link fence. It could take months to gather the needed barriers but it might be worth it.

On another note, Danny hurt himself today playing with Laura outside. They were chasing Annabelle and Danny tripped in a small hole in the ground, spraining his left ankle. They are getting to go topside more these days, but the Marines are under strict orders to ensure their safety whenever they are aboveground. I have already packed my equipment into LAV number two. I have affectionately (and secretly) named this LAV "bumble bee tuna." I don't know why, it just fits for some odd reason.

It is very hot outside today and we will be bringing some extra water along with us in order to stay hydrated and alive. I know our water situation is not as good as it should be and neither is our fuel situation. This is a problem that will need to be resolved between official duties. In a way, I am happy that Hotel 23 is a small drop in the strategic command bucket. I am taking the same Marines with me on this mission. I didn't notice any huge screw-ups from any of them on the last mission, so I don't see the need to fix something that isn't broken on a mission with such short notice. Perhaps I will mix them up on the next mission, if there is one.

11 Aug

2228

The departure from Hotel 23 was uneventful. It was very humid outside and it felt as if we were entering a sauna when we opened the hatch leading topside from the compound. The vehicles were already fueled up and ready for departure.

The roads were in severe need of maintenance that would never be given. The concrete was cracked and I hadn't seen roads this bad since my overseas duty in Asia.

We continued east to the coastline until we came across what used to be a major roadway. Now it more closely resembled a field with wrecked cars lined up pointing east. It wasn't what I was used to seeing. The rusting hulks were the only indication of the direction and curve of the road.

We crept along beside the wrecks in the general direction of the road, making sure to keep a safe distance from them to avoid any problems. The undead were not intelligent and this was not a known radiation zone, but the rolling hills of Texas could hide them easily in the troughs between here and our destination.

Another thing in the back of my mind was the difference in the big picture. In the old world, there were only a handful of animals that could deliver a fatal bite, such as some breeds of snake. Now the pendulum of deadly creatures to vulnerable humans has swung toward cataclysm. At least with a deadly viper one might have a possibility of survival. From the stories I am hearing from the Marines, these creatures that haunt the world have no antidote. The Gunny claims to have seen hundreds of men, strong men, who succumbed within thirty-six hours of being bitten or scratched. There is even a documented case of a few victims' being infected by the accidental transfusion of saliva to open wounds.

Something still haunts me about them. Where do they get their energy? They seem to have unlimited supplies of energy in death. I secretly hope that someone or some think-tank is working to assess the strengths and weaknesses of these things, which most likely outnumber us by millions in the U.S. and billions abroad. These were among the thoughts swimming around in my mind during our mission to rescue the cutter *Reliance,* dead in the water. We were quite a few miles from our destination when we saw the first group of them in our NVGs.

I carefully outlined the unit's rules of engagement (ROE). They knew to only use force against them when absolutely necessary. The loud engines of our LAVs triggered the undead to jerk on their axis and move toward us as we passed. They were conditioned and knew that any loud noise most definitely meant food.

I just glared at them from the gunner's turret, then stared ahead into the night. The goggles were good, but one could see only so far with them, unlike the naked eye in daylight. It was sort of like having a huge green torch that lit up the night out to nearly eight hundred yards.

It was the same thing, corpse after corpse, wandering in the areas around their respective demises. Traveling with eight-wheeled vehicles had its advantages. We were fine trekking off-road until we came to bridges or overpasses. Approaching these structures meant that we would have to either pull the clogged arteries of the highway free from the vehicles that blocked them, or descend into the depths of the riverbeds. Sometimes it wasn't a riverbed that the overpass was hiding, it was an interchange, or a smaller highway that ran underneath. That is what we happened on the night of our trip to the cutter.

LAV number one radioed back two hundred yards before reaching the decision point. They also knew never to stop. They idled forward as the radioman's crackled voice came through: "Sir, we are approaching an overpass, the road is congested, what do you want to do?"

I asked, "What types of vehicles are clogging the pass?"

He replied, "Sir, I see a couple eighteen-wheelers."

I had no choice but to order the men down into the embankment that lead to the perpendicular road below. I told the men to take it diagonally as they descended, and to stop for nothing. As much as I hated to think about it, these machines were still in need of depot-level maintenance (professional civilian maintenance), and on more than one occasion they have been known to sputter and die when coming to an abrupt stop.

Just as LAV number one disappeared fifty meters ahead of me into the abyss below, the radio keyed up, and then only static.

I keyed the microphone, asking for the station calling to repeat.

LAV one came back, "Sir, you might want to step on it and get around this. There is a school bus full of those things and there are quite a few of them around it."

I gave thanks for the warning and asked the sergeant to keep me updated. We were almost on the crest of the hill and in view of them.

The radio again crackled. "Sir, we got active Geiger . . ."

I sat there for a minute, stunned. We were farther away from radiated zones than Hotel 23. Why were we getting Geiger readings this far out?

As the nose of LAV two (mine) tipped over the ridge and began heading down the ravine to rendezvous with the highway, I saw the school bus. It was nothing special at first, until I took a second look.

The bus was ready for battle. Its windows had chicken wire and chain-link welded to the sides and a makeshift snowplow attached to the front. Our Geiger was now going off as we neared the big yellow bus. The bus was giving off high amounts of radiation. There were numerous undead occupants. On a more disturbing note, I could see nearly a dozen corpses on top of the bus, permanently dead.

I could not even begin to speculate on this one. The bus was hot, but the undead surrounding it were not nearly at the same level. The Geiger counter indicated the bus was giving off radiation levels that would make it deadly for prolonged exposure. Some of the occupants of the bus appeared to have very traumatic wounds, but some of them looked unscathed. They were very excited at the sound of our vehicles cruising by. The last sight I had of the bus was the second-to-last window on the right side. A young boy was hanging out of the window by his right leg. Nothing but bone was left on his left leg. His face was full of lesions and blisters. He didn't appear to be dead, or undead.

Maintaining radio contact, we eventually skirted the wreckage and eluded the undead as we began climbing the hill to return to our easterly course. Something about the bus disturbed me. I wondered if the bus had been filled with survivors attempting to reach a safer area. They obviously came from a radiated zone and knew that to stay meant death.

I wondered how those on the roof of the bus had taken themselves out. I didn't see any guns there with them. It was a few hours before I could think of anything else. We went on, all through the night, towing, skirting, avoiding. The only other complete stop we made was when we arrived at a fuel tanker that was at a safe distance from any bottleneck of pileups and traffic jams.

Since we didn't have any time to figure the vehicle out, or to try to bring it back to life, one of the men simply attached a cloth-wrapped chain to the valve of the vehicle and yanked it from the tank. Diesel began to flow onto the ground. We all knew that diesel was not very volatile, and posed no real threat as long as we were smart about handling it. Using one of the k-bars, we cut one of the rubber hoses from the side of the tanker and taped it to the broken valve with hundred-mile-per-hour tape. It wasn't pretty, or watertight, but it did the job. We filled the vehicles and the exterior fuel tanks with the fuel. One of the mechanics tested the fuel and claimed that it was still okay, but it probably wouldn't be in a year or so, without treatment.

We stuffed the broken valve with cloth that we cut from the seats of the vehicle, a large 120-ounce drink cup and a piece of rope.

It dripped a little, but it would take ages to leak dry. We marked it on our charts as a possible refuel point if needed on the way back. The prospect of having a known fueling point made me feel a little better, but with the shoddy maintenance on the vehicles, coupled with questionable fuel quality, any positive feelings were diminished.

As the sun came up, we arrived at Richwood, Texas. The sign indicating the name and population was partially obscured by graffiti crossing it out. I could smell the salt air. We were not far from the Gulf. We had been attempting to contact the cutter via radio all night. No joy. The men were tired and movement during the day was risky. We were in an industrial area and it didn't take long to find a fenced-in factory in which to play hide and sleep.

The factory was called PLP, and judging from the equipment sitting outside the main building, they had something to do with industrial piping. One of the Marines knocked the lock off with an axe that was strapped down to the exterior of LAV three. We drove through, shut the gate and reattached the chain using tape and spare tent stakes. We parked the LAVs around back and set up a watch rotation as well as defensive perimeters using the stacks of pipes that littered the exterior.

We got very little sleep that day, because of the incessant banging from inside the factory. The undead workers knew we were out here and wanted to be also. By the time we woke up and cleared the heavy stacked pipes out of our way, we had an audience at the fence near our area. Not many, but enough. One is too many. Another random thought . . . how many humans could one of them infect if victims walked in a line, allowing the creature to bite everyone? Unlimited? Fifty?

We sent four men to distract the undead audience so that the rest of us could open the gates and exfiltrate the factory. The sun was hanging low. It was thirteen hours since we had stopped. We needed the extra time to allow full sleep rotation. We could have saved four hours by just letting everyone sleep at the same time, but that would have been foolhardy. We were out of the area quickly and on our way to the coastline. It had been a bit since I had seen the ocean. The familiar smell brought back memories, like the smell of old cologne found in the back of a medicine cabinet.

Once again, we tried to establish communication with the cutter. Our HF radios could easily reach Hotel 23 if tuned properly and should have been able to reach the cutter even more easily. The only thing I could think of was signal bounce, a phenomenon well known to radio operators. Being too close or too far from the intended recipient of a transmission could put the signal in a position to bounce over the receiving radio antennas. There was overcast, and sometimes this was a factor in a signal bounce problem.

We checked in with John and the rest of the Hotel originals. I told them of the school bus and the fuel truck and factory. I asked John if Tara was in the room and he said that she wasn't. I then told him to tell her not to worry and not to mention the school bus to her. The main purpose of my call was to get an accurate position for the cutter. John said he would have the radioman send out a message and would get back to me within the hour.

As we idled along toward the ocean, her green color came into view. The vast expanse of the Gulf lay before us. Her palette of color had been long missed. Judging by the reactions of the men, they too missed the view of open waters. Approaching the marina, John came back over the radio and relayed the response from the carrier. Carrier intelligence had received the last Link-11 datalink update thirty minutes prior. The cutter was at 28-50.0N 095-16.4W. According to our charts, this put the ship four miles off the coast.

We were close enough to the marina to see the details. Only small sailboats remained there. This area reminded me of Seadrift. Why wouldn't it? It was not far from there. I wondered if the pickled onions were still sitting on the deck of the *Mama*. She wasn't far from here either.

We were going to need a while to plan this amphibious rescue mission, so we pulled our three-vehicle convoy into the parking lot of the Fair Winds marina. I radioed John again and asked him to get a message to HQ requesting updates if the cutter's position drifted more than half a mile. He told me to be careful and he would see me in a couple of days.

With the lack of communication between our convoy and the cutter, I wondered if this was in fact a rescue mission or a salvage mission. I was startled from this thought by the sound of carbine fire. I cursed under my breath and wondered which man had broken the ROE. I picked up the microphone and keyed out, asking who had fired and why. The senior man on LAV three came back asking me to turn the scope directly to six o'clock and see what was approaching.

I complied and saw probably fifty of them pouring out of the urban area a quarter mile from our position. Fifty was better than five thousand on any day, so I wasn't too worried. The sergeant wasn't shooting at the undead fifteen hundred feet away; he was shooting at the ones pounding on his back doorstep! I don't know why, but the group of four corpses behind LAV three looked familiar. I couldn't place them. I had seen thousands of these things since they first walked, and I was probably just being paranoid.

I signaled the men to prepare the vehicles for amphibious travel. These Marine LAVs were just as seaworthy as most small boats. They were large, heavy and slow, but they could move in the water. They have two small screws in the back, boosting the vehicles to speeds approaching ten knots. We opened up on the ones in our area and the chain of them that popped up between the water and us. Our path was clear and our vehicles ready so we barreled into the Gulf of Mexico, undead hordes behind in pursuit.

The water that splashed up onto my face was warm. Water began to spill into the troop compartment, and I shot a worried glance over to the Gunny. He smiled and told me not to worry, that if it weren't leaking *he* would be the one worried. I trusted the man and popped my head back topside to observe the activity on the shore. I told the other LAVs to cut to idle and form a line one hundred yards from the marina. The inside of my vehicle had two inches of water, but it showed no sign of sinking.

I climbed out onto the top and just watched them gather on the shoreline like ants. It was then that the radio beeped again with another voice message incoming. It was the familiar sound of crypto syncing up. It sort of sounds like an old computer modem, until the voice comes into recognition. John came back and told us he had a position update on the cutter. Even though we had only requested updates in the event of a drift greater than a quarter mile, HQ felt that the news of the cutter's not moving at all would also be valuable. I had to agree. The ship had no significant movement since the last time an automated update was sent from the antenna on the mast of the ship.

The moans from the dead carried well over the water and into my microphone. I heard Tara's voice and a struggle for the microphone back at the compound. She came on and asked if everything was all right. I explained our current situation and informed her that we were in no immediate danger. I asked her to put John back on and she reluctantly did. I told John that we were about to head out into the open water in search of the ship. Fog was beginning to roll in. The light of the moon, as well as the cold of the night, magnified the fear that every man felt.

We left the gaggle of undead at the shoreline and headed for the coordinates given to us by the carrier battle group. As we slowly advanced, the moans were drowned out and we forgot about our enemy for the time being. I tried not to think about the undead that were lurking on the ocean floor or floating with neutral buoyancy just below the surface. I wished them the worst, as those were the ones I feared most.

The LAV's onboard optic was much better than my goggles, so I scurried back in the hole and deployed the sensors. I could still see the shoreline. The undead were still there. Again, like ants they swarmed. I swung the viewer back around toward the front of the vehicle. My feet were wet from the salt water that had leaked or splashed into the compartment.

We were now one mile off the coast and I could see a small shining object on the horizon. It almost looked like a candle. When we reached the two-mile marker, the radio came alive again with a position report. John claimed that the Coast Guard cutter had again remained stationary since the last update. That was fine by me. The less hunting for it in the open water the better.

I grabbed a strobe light from one of the survival kits and clipped it on the cargo net topside. I wanted to do everything I could to get indications that the crew was alive before attempting to board. I still could not see the silhouette of the cutter. We were now at the three-mile distance from the shoreline. The source of the candlelight became apparent. The light was the flame from an offshore oil platform. At her base was the cutter. It appeared to be moored on the southeast support column of the rig. There was no sign of life from this distance.

As we approached the rig, I could hear living human voices in the distance. They appeared to be yelling. I was nearly certain that our strobes could be seen from their vantage point on the vessel. As I got closer, I began to realize that the voices were not coming from the ship, but from the platform. I listened and went back inside to use the LAV optics. I could see the green outline of men on the platform waving their arms. We were now close enough to make out what they were saying. They were telling us not to board the ship.

It was overrun.

I wondered how a mechanical malfunction had turned out to be an infestation onboard this warship. The Gunny and I were the first to touch the ladder of the oil platform. On my way up, I could make out figures on the boat. It was a long climb to the top, even longer than the ladder in the missile silo of Hotel 23. As I reached the top rung, I was helped to my feet by one of the crew. I counted roughly thirty men on the platform. They all appeared to be in good health.

I asked who was in charge, and one of the men replied, "LTJG Barnes, sir."

I asked to speak with the LT, but the men quickly informed me that he had sealed himself inside a compartment on the vessel and had no way out. I had a feeling that my next question had been anticipated, as, when I asked them how the hell those rotting shitbags could take over a warship, they started to explain the situation piece by piece.

I was talking to a petty officer. He was one of the ship's information systems technicians, who ran the ship's automated systems and networks. He seemed to have it together. The petty officer explained that they had run aground near the offshore rig. The updated charts they would normally have onboard were not available and they were not sure how deep the water was in this area. It wasn't bad, but they ended up damaging their screw while getting themselves off the sandbar. The boat could be operated but that would cause too much stress on the engine and shaft because the screw was not functioning at 100 percent efficiency.

There would be no time like the night for us to retake the vessel. I knew for a fact these things could not see in the dark any better than the average living person.

Despite the petty officer's explanation of how they came to be nearly dead in the water, the question remained about the undead and why they were present on the cutter in sufficient numbers to cause the crew to abandon the vessel. I ordered him to explain this. He was hesitant at first, but I explained to him who I was and under what authority I operated.

After lowering his head so that his eyes were hidden below his ballcap, he said: "Word came down from the top to get and transport specimens of *them* for research on the flattop [carrier]."

Insane . . . really? Would the people in charge actually want these things onboard their command ship, no matter how critical the research? Bringing them onto a cutter was one thing, but onboard the acting U.S. military command ship?

I know that the carrier had a full onboard medical staff and decent equipment for research, but this research could be done somewhere else, anywhere else, away from the military's leadership. We were getting thin on active-duty military personnel or so I estimated.

"Why the Gulf of Mexico?" I asked.

He replied, "Because command wanted the radiated ones."

I nearly slugged the man right where he stood for agreeing to follow those orders, but I restrained myself, and he went on to tell me that many smaller ships had been dispatched with extraction teams to the radiation zones of destroyed cities to find specimens for study. I agreed in my mind with the intentions, but not the means or storage of these things. Why did they need them from different areas? This man did not know the answer to that and I was betting the only people who did were on that aircraft carrier. I asked the man how many radiated corpses were onboard; he told me that they had acquired five of them from the New Orleans hot zone.

I asked him how only five of those creatures could effectively mission-kill the cutter. He stared off into the night and sat there for a minute, not knowing what to say. I snapped my fingers in front of his face, pulling him out of his trancelike state. He then began telling me what I had feared and suspected.

"These aren't the same as the others, sir. They don't decay like the others, they are stronger, faster, and some say more intelligent. I don't get it. The radiation does something to them, preserves them. The doctors on the carrier think the radiation is some type of catalyst for preserving motor function and regrowing dead cells. Oddly, the regenerated cells are still dead. They don't understand it, no one does. They won't admit it, but I know they made a mistake when they dropped the nukes.

"The creatures on the ship broke out of their restraining straps and killed the three men guarding them. Those men turned and it was all we could do to secure the bridge and get the ship moored alongside this oil platform before we were eaten."

He estimated that the ship housed nearly fifteen undead now.

It was time to act, I supposed. I told the man that I was sorry and that the carrier would not be acquiring their specimens from this ship. We were going to kill them all.

We lost a Marine in the assault. All in all it took forty-five minutes to secure the ship. It was dark and it would have been suicide for our whole squad to board. I took the Gunny and a seasoned staff sergeant with me. He would have had it no other way. I have recently been informed that he had a spouse back at the original Marine base camp. I can say that he fought valiantly and probably saved both the Gunny and me.

We carefully boarded the ship by jumping over the mooring lines onto the weather deck. Staff Sergeant "Mac" had the only suppressed weapon in the group. We left the others at home in the event they needed the weapons to defend themselves.

I was not familiar with the weapon's handling, so I left it to the Marine. I would have loved to take more than three, but unfortunately we only had three sets of night vision goggles. Mac wasted the two creatures on the weather deck. Those two were part of the original crew. We piled them on the forecastle and proceeded to secure the ship. Using the ship's 21MC bitch box we were able to establish communications with six surviving crewmembers holed up in the galley. I could hear the sound of the undead in the background through the speakers, relentlessly striking the steel rolldown galley shutter.

This partition was the only thing keeping the culinary specialists and the ship's senior officer from being eaten.

They proceeded to tell us that they had taken down one of the radiated undead with a fire extinguisher and a fire axe. One of the men who had downed the thing was vomiting and weak, probably from exposure. The sailors wore radiation suits inside the New Orleans zone to acquire the specimens, which were no doubt very radioactive and dangerous to be near. The lieutenant told me that the other two were outside the galley partition pounding on the bulkheads. He seemed to think that much of the undead crew was there with them but wasn't sure if all of them were present on the other side. We crept through the passageway, down the steep ladders. The galley was in the center of the ship, deep below the waterline. As we approached the main deck, Mac whispered that he was going to destroy one of the bright passageway lights so we could continue to have the upper hand. He shot it out, and this change in atmosphere triggered one of those things to move into the open in front of his weapon.

Mac took it out with two shots. The first shot hit the creature's left shoulder and did nothing but spatter black, putrid blood on the wall behind. The second shot hit the creature right on the nose, and I suppose just enough of the brain was scrambled to do the job, as it moved no more.

We dragged it to the corner of the passageway and used zip cuffs to bind its arms and legs just to be sure. We kept lurking through the darkness. Every sound was thunder and every blinking LED seemed like storm lightning. The ship had the familiar smell of mothballs and a tinge of death. We came to a hatch. It was a large steel door used to keep water from flooding adjoining compartments in the event of an attack or emergency. There was a small circle of thick glass no bigger than the diameter of a coffee can on the door where a peephole would be. I looked through and could see the ship's emergency lighting was on. An eerie red glow filled the small room beyond. I cranked the handle on the door, trying to be as quiet as possible, moving a centimeter at a time. We all winced when the hatch creaked from lack of maintenance. I stopped moving the handle and checked the hole again. I saw movement in the compartment beyond. A loud thud rang through our compartment as something very strong hit the hatch. It nearly opened from the pressure, but fortunately I hadn't fully slid the handle to the open position.

The creature on the other side obscured the red lighting behind. Its face was pressed against the thick glass and it was banging its head in a futile attempt to get to us. Every fiber in my body was telling me to leave and not open the thick steel door. We could still turn back and survive. There were men down there and I knew that every hour they stayed in proximity to the radiated creatures meant they were an hour closer to their death. I told the sergeant that I would slam the latch open, then he would pull the rip cord that I had attached to the door, yanking it open.

As there was no use in being quiet about it anymore, I used no care in forcing the handle to the open position. I slammed it home and Mac yanked the cord. The door flung open and the creature came through. Luckily for us the creature was not accustomed to shipboard life and promptly tripped over the knee knocker, landing flat on its face. Expecting this thing to take its time getting up, I readied my weapon for careful aim. I did not get what I expected. This creature was on its feet fast. This was one of the preserved dead from the New Orleans zone. It lurched toward me and my goggles seemed to crackle like a late-night hometown TV channel that had just finished the national anthem. The last thing I saw was its bony claw reach out before intense light blinded me and I heard the action of Mac's suppressed H&K.

I felt the air move and heard a loud thud as something hit the steel deck. I pulled off my NVGs. As my eyes adjusted to the bright light, I saw Mac's Surefire torch lighting up the compartment. Using two mops from a nearby bucket, Mac and I pushed the creature into a corner and tried as best we could to stack heavy objects on top to incapacitate it like the other creature we had dispatched—again, "just in case." We could not zip cuff the thing, as the radiation was likely at a deadly level. We took no time getting out of this area and through the next. Anywhere this creature had been was probably unsafe. I know it was my imagination, similar to the feeling of your head itching when someone mentions lice, but I could almost feel the heat of radiation on my face and neck.

The next compartment was clear. Only one more steel door separated us from the galley area. We were now facing two problems. First, our NVGs were "snowing out" due to some sort of electromagnetic or radiological interference, and second, the heavy steel door was in fact cracked open slightly. The only real barrier that separated us from the bulk of the undead in the galley was a long, dark corridor and a half-open steel door. I could see their shadows moving through the crack beyond the door. From where we were watching, the door was roughly ten meters away.

The only thing we could do was bust in there and shoot them. No special tactic, no smart way to handle it. I hated this and wished for a better method. We approached the door. I stopped Gunny and Mac and we checked our weapons. No safety, and no inhibitions. We had eighty-seven rounds ready to go between us. More, if we needed to reload, but we all knew if it came to that we were going to die anyway.

We checked our clothing and tried to cover as much skin as possible. As near as I could figure, there were at least ten in there, and at least one of the *special* type. This hatch opened outward, away from us and toward them. I gave the signal and the Gunny kicked it fully open. It slammed against the bulkhead and locked into place. Inside this room were eleven undead corpses. They were all banging on the metal partition and didn't notice us at first until I took a preemptive shot. I killed three before the rest took notice. I had hoped that one of them was the New Orleans creature. We began to shoot, three-round bursts. Limbs, jaws, shoulders and teeth were flying everywhere. I was careful not to aim in the direction of the partition, in case one of the sailors stood near. We were down to three when I heard a loud scream from over my right shoulder. It was Mac. He was bleeding from his face, and one of the creatures was standing behind him attempting to bite him.

I looked again . . . it was the same creature we had shot two compartments back. The one we didn't touch, but tried to incapacitate. It hadn't died. I emptied the rest of my magazine into the creature's head. It fell, most of its head missing. I was almost overrun by the last of them when Gunny took care of them for me as I tended to Mac.

The bite wasn't bad. It was actually not his face, but his ear. The creature had bitten part of his ear off. Mac was breathing heavily and going into what I would have described as shock. I asked Gunny to look after him as I went to check for survivors in the galley. This was no time to screw around. The ship wasn't safe and would need a scrub-down before it could ever be used in a normal capacity again. I rapped on the steel shutter, asking if anyone was alive. I heard a series of mechanical clicking sounds and the door next to the shutter opened up and they started pouring out . . . living. One of them looked pretty bad. It was the one who had the hand-to-hand altercation with one of the New Orleans creatures.

The ship's OIC was present, and I informed him of the situation. He knew it and hated to admit it, but he had no choice but to abandon this ship and hold out on the rig until we could get support from carrier HQ. We got the hell off the ship, with Mac and the sick sailor being first priority. Mac was a dead man. The other man had not been bitten and only needed decontamination treatment. I wasn't certain whether it was too late. On the way out, I stopped off in the one of the ship's heads and ripped the soap dispenser off the wall. I took a roll of paper towels as well. We were finally topside. It was still dark outside. It was only 0300 hrs. Mac and the sailor were in no shape to climb to the platform where the other survivors waited. We rigged a makeshift harness and pulled them up one at a time. I never really knew this Marine, but that doesn't change my sadness. As the acting commander it was my duty to travel to the camp where his wife lived and tell her the news. Although I had no flag to present, it didn't change the need to fulfill my obligation to Mac, as he is and always will be a United States Marine.

Gunny shot Mac in the back of the head two hours after we returned to the rig. He had already passed out from the infection and was not far from turning.

This mission ended the next day, with radio contact being established with the carrier battle group. I relayed a message to command through the radio operator at Hotel 23 and informed them of the situation and location of survivors here. Using salt water from the Gulf and the soap and towels, we attempted to decontaminate Petty Officer Tompost. We left the men with every bit of our food and water and departed the oil rig after making sure a rescue was en route. We also left the sailors a functional radio in the event help didn't show. The only thing we had going for us were a few full cans of diesel and a spot to refuel on our charts. It was a two-day trip back. I brought Mac back home wrapped in canvas strapped to the exterior of LAV number two. I made sure he wouldn't return, but his wife didn't deserve to have his body thrown into the Gulf. He deserved a proper burial.

19 Aug

2350

Day before last I made my trip to the Marine base camp. This is one of the many reasons that I wish I were not the senior man present at the facility. I took four men, including the Gunny, and one LAV. Correction, there were five men. Mac was with us in a pine box, covered by an American flag. The flag wasn't easy to come by, as it took forty rounds of ammunition and ten years of my life terrified away from me to get it. It was the least I could do. Tara asked to come with me to comfort the widow. I told her that it wasn't a good idea, of course. Besides, this world is so full of death and doom. Mrs. Mac wasn't the only one to lose someone, but I still felt for her. There weren't many pre-existing relation-ships left here in the apocalypse.

I didn't have a formal uniform and the nearest uniform shop was out of business. I knew it really didn't matter. It was a solemn moment when I handed the widow her tattered one-sided flag. I didn't know what to expect. I had never had the honor of doing this. In the movies, the widow always hugs the guy who gives her the flag and they both have a somber moment. All I got was a cold stare and a feeling of hatred. Who am I to blame her? If I can somehow be an outlet for her emotions, then it's fine by me. I do know that I feel bad about what happened. He was a good man.

RIP Staff Sergeant Mac.

Exodus

RTTUZYUW RUHPNQR0234 TTTT-UUUU

ZNY TTTT

1734Z 22 AUG

FM: CDR NADA MISSILE FAC

TO: USS GEORGE WASHINGTON //CNO//

BT

S E C R E T N//002028U

SUBJ://SITREP RELIANCE

RMKS://IAW CMD DIRECTIVES ISSUED
BY RECIPIENT, UNIT DISPATCHED TO
RESCUE OF RELIANCE ON PRE-DET
COORD. CUTTER FOUND OVERRUN BY
UNDEAD W/ 03 RADIATED. ALL UNDEAD
DESTROYED, SHIP SCUTTLED, RESCUE
AUTHORITY CONTACTED. RECOMMEND
RAD UNDEAD NOT BE HELD ON ANY
NAVAL VESSEL DUE TO INAD. FACILITIES.
THIS UNIT DOES NOT ADVISE RAD DEAD
BE HOUSED ONBOARD FLAGSHIP. PLEASE
QSL THIS MESSAGE AND ADVISE.

BT

AR

#N0234

22 Aug

HQ has not responded to my recent communiqué. I have released a radio message preparing the other camp for evacuation. This comes after a thirty-six-hour swell of undead near that area. It will take them two days to transit to this location with women and children. Here at Hotel 23 we are busy finding supplies to expand our safe boundary so that we can house the extra occupants. There is no way we can accommodate them all inside the facility; it simply wasn't built for so many. The other camp has lost eight people since I ordered a contingent to be stationed here. I cannot help but think animosity may exist. Apparently one of the civilian males was allowed to hunt for deer last week and returned with nothing to show for it but a bite from one of the creatures. The man hid the bite for fear of quarantine or summary execution. He turned in his sleep three days later and took the lives of two other civilians—three if you count the young girl who was executed because she was bitten and getting sick. They didn't shoot her like an animal. They gave her a morphine overdose, and after her heart stopped they immediately drilled a small hole in her head above her left ear to destroy any chance of reanimation.

When this type of thing happens, I lose sleep. I know that millions have died in a much worse manner than this over the past months, but it always hurts to see a young child get taken by this sickness. I don't really even know if that is what it is. Some seem to think so.

While monitoring the daily message traffic coming off the archaic dot matrix printer, I saw a message I had been expecting. The ballistic missile submarine that had been submerged since before the plague was forced to surface yesterday. That was the last sanctuary of real death.

The last known place on the planet where men could die in peace . . . until it surfaced.

The man who had died of natural causes and had been stored in the freezer came back after only two hours of exposure. Luckily, they had it strapped to a crate of low-grade beef. The ship's cook discovered it when he went down to the freezer to retrieve the last of the ship's food stores. The cook nearly had a heart attack when he walked by the corpse and noticed its head tracking him across the reefer, gnashing its teeth.

The submarine intends to follow the battle group until it can acquire enough food to stay submerged for a useful amount of time. Its mission now, instead of blowing up large foreign cities, is to scout coastal areas and discourage piracy on the high seas. The status messages that are sent weekly state that most of the nuclear ships won't need to be refueled for twenty-plus years. After that, all bets are off. I doubt there will be enough qualified people to refuel them even in one hundred years.

I'm sending all our LAVs out tomorrow to meet the other survivors at the halfway point and to escort them the rest of the way here. From that point it will take every man, woman and child to expand our safe boundaries. We will have no choice but to make perilous trips to the surrounding interstates to retrieve concrete barriers so that we may better fortify our compound.

Tara and I have been spending more time together than ever since my return from the Gulf. Dean has been dubbed the official teacher of this compound. Of course there are only two children to teach, but soon there will be more. Annabelle is allowed to attend class, on the stipulation she does not bark and disrupt the instruction. I sat in on one of the classes last night. Laura is becoming pretty decent at her multiplication tables. Danny is a little better due to age. She is learning her sevens and Danny is up to division and fractions.

Jan is still the resident nurse and helps out a lot when some of the men come back with bumps, scratches and bruises. John and I have not had much time together lately. I remember in the beginning he was all I had. I suppose I will never forget that. Sometimes when I daydream, I can see John on his roof with his thermos and large rubber yoga band. I can only see it in black and white in my mind, as if it happened ages ago.

I wonder what the response will be from the carrier now that they know we had to destroy the creatures to save the rest of the crew.

05 Sep

2036

Sixty percent. That is the number of survivors we have here from the other Marine outpost. Many are civilians. It was a constant battle to get them here. The chain-link fence surrounding the silo area is packed with makeshift tents and survivors. Hotel 23 is very much over capacity for the interior to handle. After their arrival ten days ago, an accurate muster was taken. We came up with 113 souls. The Marines sent to rendezvous with the other camp at the halfway point met extreme opposition. The convoy was moving slowly to accommodate the civilians who were on foot. Many rode scavenged bicycles to keep up with the armored vehicles in the front and rear of the convoy. The women and children were first to be allowed to ride. The bulk of the casualties came from attacks perpendicular to the formation line.

The undead came out of the thick underbrush and picked off many men with only scrapes and bites. Most men held on and kept contributing to the security of the convoy despite the death sentence dealt to them by the bites. Others simply walked off into the underbrush and committed suicide. The convoy was low on ammunition by the time it pulled into Hotel 23. They were in constant firefights the whole way, pushing back the surge of cold hands reaching over the railings of the vehicles. The convoy did its best to distract the dead away from Hotel 23 before circling back to the compound. The tactic seemed to work, but I have noticed a steady increase in activity since the others arrived. I have been forced to order squads of "fence men" to the chain-link perimeter to kill them. In large numbers, they could buckle the fence. This is the main reason I have organized a team of individuals for missions to the interstate. That gridlocked infinity of concrete barriers holds the key to our temporary survival. We needed the hundreds of concrete barriers present there to reinforce our boundaries to hold the new survivors safely within the fence line.

The most difficult part was getting the equipment needed to transport the barriers. We needed flatbed tractor-trailers and forklifts. Only a few men in the compound were former fork-lift operators. We were able to acquire four propane-powered forklifts from a lumberyard near the interstate. We have also scavenged and repaired two flatbed tractor-trailers to transport the barriers. Only two truckloads of barriers have arrived since the operation started. The progress is slow but steady. I estimate the fence would hold up to five deep. Any more ghouls than that would force the fence to cave inward, and our new citizens would surely perish. I have given up my living space to the women and children. I have only permitted women who have volunteered to remain topside. Tara insisted that she stay with me. I am okay with this because I cannot let the other women volunteers stay here and discriminate against her.

Last week I transmitted a formal request for a helicopter equipped with antipersonnel weapons and a pilot to be trans-ferred to the compound to help police the perimeter against a large influx of undead. I overjustified the need to ensure that our request be met. We needed some form of air power for both se-curity and reconnaissance in this area. Fixed-wing would be out of the question and more trouble than it's worth due to main-tenance and the requirement for five thousand feet of runway. We'll see what happens.

Dragonfly

1837

This morning I received a message indicating authorization of a rotary-wing aircraft, one pilot and one maintenance person to be transferred to Hotel 23. The message did not state what model, but it did state the aircraft was due for arrival tomorrow morning. This aircraft will not only strengthen our perimeter defenses, but will also make it easier to scout for essential supplies. Depending on the range of the aircraft, I plan to fly northward to scout non-radiated cities. I will post a notice in the common area both above and below ground for people to list items of which they are in dire need.

Certain medical prescriptions, eyeglasses or possibly female products come to mind. I'm excited to take to the air again. I have not flown in ages and the Cessna parked at the edge of the field is probably not safe to operate. I know one of the gear brakes is not functioning properly and the engine needs a detailed check-up that it most likely will never receive.

I almost feel as if I'm putting the cart miles before the horse by thinking of ways to use the helicopter. It isn't even here.

John and I played a nice game of chess today in the control room. Dean has a respectable-size class of young men and women now. Including the original two, she now has fourteen students. Annabelle does not fancy all the new children in Dean's class. Dean will have to break up the time spent by age groups as I have noticed that ABCs are a little too elementary for some of the older kids. I stepped in today and heard Mozart flowing through the air.

The children were listening attentively. Who would have

thought? A year ago, the whole room would have been moaning in protest. Considering the terrors these children have witnessed, the beauty of the music was actually making them smile. I thought back to the last time I had listened to Mozart . . . but didn't hang on to the thought long.

Secure space is at a premium inside the compound and Jan has her medical tent set up topside. Only the really sick or injured get to stay down below within the safe steel sanctuary. Not a bad system. Lately, the only thing she has had to deal with is minor cuts and abrasions. I have a standing order to be notified of all injuries reported to the resident medic. I have tasked the *originals* with the duty of drafting a book of rules for Hotel 23. Of course the Uniform Code of Military Justice will be followed, but I feel a need for this compound to have its own bylaws that the people should follow. Seems silly, the need for rules these days. I almost feel like I am rebuilding a government within the compound. Of course any regulation created and imposed will be based strictly on the Constitution of the United States.

08 Sep
1800

Today one MH-60R Seahawk helicopter, along with the allocated personnel, arrived. The pilot, a retired Navy commander by the name of Thomas Baham, was the pilot in command. His maintenance person, an active-duty Navy petty officer, was to be the noncom in charge of keeping the aircraft airworthy until more parts and personnel could be flown in.

My first action was to inquire about the condition of the aircraft, as I planned to execute some airborne recon in the coming weeks. CDR (ret.) Baham was a volunteer. He willingly gave up his safer job with the carrier battle group to relocate to southeastern Texas and work with us at Hotel 23. Although an older man in his late fifties, he still had the fire and drive in his eyes. I had secretly wished he were active duty, and thus would be lawfully in command of Hotel 23 as the senior officer. The Seahawk was a rather large helicopter. The petty officer told me that the range was 380 miles. On the way to the compound they flew by numerous abandoned military airfields that they suspected had at least some JP-5, a common military aircraft fuel.

This type of fuel had its advantages, as it didn't spoil nearly as rapidly as conventional gasoline. It would still be usable if found inside a fuel truck. I had a message drafted to HQ the moment the chopper reported. Although I did thank them for the aircraft, I also requested more parts and personnel to maintain it. Tomorrow I would like to head out with Baham and the flight engineer to survey the surrounding area for useful intelligence.

11 Sep

2354

Today marks another anniversary of the day I thought it couldn't get any worse. I suppose times like these make me wish I were back in that time, when the world had no idea what terror was. Undead movement is still growing in the surrounding areas. I feel that there is virtually no chance of survivors in any major city at this point. Of course, the ones that were nuked would be void of survivors. My reasoning is simple. The undead seem to be fanning out away from major areas into mass mobile formations. I am sure the cities that are still intact have a concentration of undead, but they have probably been out of food for a couple of months. This could have prompted them to leave their native areas and search for prey. I could be totally wrong in this theory. Baham has conveyed that the aircraft is ready for recon missions. We have discussed the areas that would be good candidates for survey. Ruling out any areas that have been bombed, we have decided to head north by northeast. Our destination will be Texarkana. This is the safest area to survey while avoiding the undead and radiated cities. According to the charts, Texarkana was not a high-population area and the nearest nuked city to that destination is Dallas, Texas. This gives us roughly 120 miles of safe distance.

Unfortunately, due to the distance, we will need to find fuel. It's 240 nautical miles one way from here to Texarkana.

15 Sep

2219

The aircraft performed well in today's scouting mission. We did not make the long journey north to Texarkana; however, we did find a suitable area to refuel the helicopter. We went north to Shreveport, Louisiana. We had nothing to guide our way sans the inertial navigation system (INS). The INS is a self-contained gyroscopic navigation device that does not rely on any outside information for aircraft navigation. As long as you give the INS a good latitude and longitude before you take off, the INS will keep an accurate gyroscopic position the entire flight. Since the GPS satellites have long failed, it would have been nearly impossible to find Barksdale AFB in Shreveport without the INS. We would have run out of fuel long before we reached our destination. We only had forty-five minutes of fuel left when we were over the base.

The fence was damaged in some areas, but still held. The undead were heavy on the northern side of the base perimeter fence. As we neared the aircraft parking spots, I could see numerous B-52 bombers parked in neat rows outside the hangars. Some of the planes still had bombs sitting on carts underneath. I was not certain, but I had a feeling the bombs that were sitting under those aircraft were not conventional. The pilots just never got the chance to take off and accomplish their assigned bombing package. The aircraft are useless in our current situation. They would require too much fuel and maintenance to be of any survival value. I suppose if we had a qualified or suicidal pilot to fly the bomber we could remove the extra payloads and fly it overseas, but it would be a one-way trip, as I was certain that it would require professional maintenance after such a long flight. I did feel a sting of patriotism as I gazed upon their decadence. I wondered if any of them had flown over the Hanoi Hilton, giving at least some comfort to the guests. We were hovering over a forgotten piece of United States diplomacy. Now the BUFFs were a decaying museum exhibit.

We counted twenty-seven corpses inside the airfield perimeter. There were two fuel trucks, one marked JP-5 and the other marked JP-8, sitting on the median between the runway and taxiway. Since we were on a skeleton crew to conserve fuel we only had the pilot, the flight engineer, the Gunny and myself on board. The Gunny and I had to cover the flight engineer (FE) while he fueled the helicopter. This was an operation that would require the aircraft to remain running. This is not a normal procedure, but no chances can be taken. As we fueled the chopper, a dozen undead approached, attracted to the sound of the rotors spinning.

That sound was extremely loud, and the Gunny and I had to rely solely on sight to detect and eliminate them. I stood aft, a safe distance from the tail rotor, and the Gunny held the forward position. Our shots could barely be heard over the turbine engines and the swinging blades. I was wearing my helmet with the visor down. The helmet served multiple purposes onboard the aircraft and off. It helped shield my ears from the harmful decibels that pierced the immediate area and saved my eyes from flying FOD. Using my weapon, I was able to neutralize most of the undead with only single shots. None of them moved with the same quickness as their radiated counterparts. The Gunny was using the MP5 SD. I hated that weapon for its accuracy and lack of stopping/piercing power, but it was useful because of the silence factor. The only other advantage it had was the ability to interchange ammunition with the Gunny's M-9 pistol.

As I dispatched the last of the undead approaching my end of the aircraft, I moved forward to help out with the increasing numbers there. I had a better killing range with my weapon; I used this advantage to destroy the walkers that were one hundred yards out and closing on our position. The engineer gave us the thumbs-up, indicating that he had successfully refueled the aircraft. I wondered how he got the fuel truck started and later found out that he had carried a portable starter to the truck. He had faced this same situation before and had been prepared.

After the engineer was safely back in the helicopter, I plugged my helmet back into the aircraft's communications system and informed the pilot that the Gunny and I were going to scout the immediate area for any useful items or information. I asked him to keep it hot until we got back for dustoff. The pilot keyed the microphone and told me he and the flight engineer could handle security while we were gone and that they would take off and circle the airfield until bingo fuel if we were not back within one hour.

I secured the side door and waved good-bye as the Gunny and I set out for one of the larger buildings nearest to our position. There were no external markings. It was just another bland government building, lacking any detail that would give away purpose. As we neared the structure, we knew it would be suicide to explore. In nearly all of the windows the shades had been yanked down from the wall, exposing the occupants inside. Some of the windows were spiderwebbed with abuse from the punishment they had received in the past months. There were too many undead inside the building to count.

Since noise wasn't a factor, I readied my weapon and took a potshot at one of them on the top floor. It was banging on the window with both fists until my shot cut through the window. I missed the creature, and it looked at the new hole in the window with the curiousness of a cat looking at a laser pointer. I scoffed at this and the Gunny and I began our return to the chopper. As we turned, I could see and hear the FE taking shots at an approaching group of undead with the side-mounted machine gun. Great for close encounters.

The ride back was uneventful, but any time I could spend in the air was fine by me. I even got some stick time in the copilot's seat. It would take a lot more than this to make me semiproficient at maneuvering this aircraft, as it was the hardest thing I'd ever flown. I looked like an idiot as I tried to hover the beast. Baham had to take over every time.

25 Sep

_1900_

It finally happened. I won't cheapen the experience by putting it into writing. Last night was a good night, and I feel more human already. Part of me would like to think I cared about her the moment I found her trapped in the broken-down car that day, surrounded by the creatures. Despite her less-than-glamorous living arrangement in the car, she was pretty even then.

29 Sep

_2239_

The time has been set. Tomorrow morning, I will set out with the Gunny, engineer and CDR (ret.) Baham in the chopper in the direction of Shreveport again. We have decided to survey the area around Barksdale AFB, since the base had an ample supply of helicopter fuel. Texarkana would not be the goal of our expedition this time. John had begged to go with me, as he really wanted to get out of the compound for a couple of days. I had assured him that I really needed him manning the control center and for the basic organization of the civilians. He was not a military man, but the men respected him and appreciated him for his knowledge of the base systems. After dinner he insisted that I memorize a series of code words so that I could transmit my location in the clear using letter and number association.

Annabelle is enjoying herself with all the new children in the compound. The Gunny and I are leaving military command to one of the most senior staff sergeants and civilian leadership to John. There are rules governing who has what authority in the compound and the military men know too well that, constitutionally, their job is still to protect civilians, not run roughshod over them just because they have firepower.

There is also a team of men working on the new perimeter. Trucks come and go daily with new concrete dividers from I-10. Casualties have been zero since the operation officially started. The men have a system for vehicle formation and a certain path that minimizes the undead attraction back to Hotel 23. Most of these men had at least one tour in Iraq or Afghanistan under their belts, but they were the first to admit that convoy operations currently are much more dangerous than they were during the war. The Gunny still insists on the H&K, and I still insist on American metal. We will be traveling light to conserve fuel and are taking a three-day food supply.

Icarus

30 Sep

Time/Location: Unknown

Situation bad . . . surviving twenty-four hours ~~not likely~~ not looking up. Must keep record. The trip going as planned until aft
Fading in and out of consc. Head swollen, ear bleeding. Bloody
hands.

30 Sep

Making a point to document in the event that I don't make it out.
Will write more when better . . . Important.

~~Water should have grabbed more water more ar~~

We were overhead Shreveport and decided to take it farther
north since we had the fuel and a known fuel source. I was not
watching instruments, as Baham was doing the driving. A light
came on on the master caution panel. It was the chip light. Baham
recycled the light to see if it was simply a short in the panel. It illuminated once again, indicating that there were pieces of metal
detected in the aircraft oil reservoir. The normal procedure would
be to land the aircraft immediately, but none of us wished to land
in the known hostile territory below.

It was not long until we lost useful power to the rotors and
Baham began autorotating down to the ground. The altimeter
was spinning as if we were coming in for approach. The Gunny
and the petty officer were strapped in side by side in the rear of
the aircraft. I was strapped in the copilot's seat. The last thing I

325

remembered was an earsplitting noise and the sound of metal tearing and water and dust flying upward over the chopper and across my face.

I don't know how long I was out. I was dreaming . . . it was a nice place. I was with Tara, but not at the compound. I was back in time, in the living world. It felt very real. Then came the light taps on my shoulder . . . then the pulling of my sleeve. Someone was waking me up from this feeling of tranquility. I started to feel my head. Intense pain shot through my temples. Every time my heart beat, I felt the blood surge through my head in spikes of pain. My vision was blurry. I was back in the helicopter, away from my fantasy.

Still blurry . . . I looked to my left in the pilot's seat. I could see Baham looking at me, shaking my shoulder with his right hand, saying something. Why was he pulling on me? I looked back over my shoulder and saw Gunny and the engineer reaching out, as if trying to help me. I seemed to be looking at them through a pool of water. The pain spiked again and my eyes slowly came into focus.

I looked over at Baham. Fear shot through my body as I looked at his chest. A piece of the helicopter's rotor blade was sticking through his breastplate. He wasn't dying . . . he was dead. His taps, nudges and what I thought was him talking were not attempts to wake me, but attempts to kill. He was still stuck in his harness and unable to reach me. I sat there stunned for a moment before looking back over my shoulders at the Gunny and flight engineer. I was the only living person on this helicopter. Reaching up to my forehead, I felt a sting. A piece of rotor shrapnel had pierced my flight helmet and was stuck in my head. I didn't know how deep. I just knew that I was still alive and had cognitive function.

I reached down for my carbine so that I could take out the rest of the crew and safely exfiltrate this tomb. When I tried to yank the carbine up to my shoulder, I saw that the barrel had been bent at almost a ninety-degree angle and was caught inside the flight controls at my feet. Cursing, I threw the weapon on the deck and looked around the chopper for anything I could use. The Gunny's MP5 was on the floor behind my seat.

I took out my knife and used it to snag the sling to bring the weapon close enough so that I could grab it. Charging the weapon, I first aimed at Baham. His snarling teeth and sagging old skin were enhanced by his current health status. He didn't know me anymore; neither did the men in the back. I was going to save the Gunny for last.

I pulled the weapon up and Baham began slapping the suppressor around, as if somehow he knew what was coming. I wasted him. One second later I shot the engineer in the head. His arms went from Frankenstein to limp as if he had never been reanimated. I said some words for all of them and then paid final respects to the Gunny by shooting him in the forehead. I hoped he would have done the same for me. Looking out the window, I could tell that we had been here for at least a couple of hours, as the sun was already nearly at its apex in the day sky. We were in the middle of some sort of waist-deep small pond. A tinge of guilt stabbed me in the heart when I realized Baham had probably thought our best chance of survival was to put it down here. I had paid him back by quick-acting lead poisoning.

It was a good place to crash-land as the portside door was off its rail, exposing the aircraft to the outside world. There were numerous undead curiously circling the pond, somehow repelled by the water. I carefully surveyed the 360-degree area and noticed a gap in them. I grabbed my gear and whatever else I could carry. As I walked to the door to escape the wreck, I ripped the Velcro flag off my left shoulder and slapped it in the Gunny's dead hand.

I made for the door. As I stepped off the chopper, I sank waist deep into the water. This made it difficult to quickly move to the open area for my escape. I was nearly swimming to the shore of the small pond. I made it to dry land and began running. I blacked out shortly after and woke up about four hours ago. I am sitting in a high school football stadium announcer's box at the top of the *home* side . . . I think. It is nightfall and I am hungry and dehydrated. I had to perform minor surgery on myself an hour ago by removing the metal shard from my head with the needlenose on my multitool. Using the mirror from my camouflage paint kit, I stitched myself up with the sewing kit in my bag. The shard went more than an eighth of an inch into my head, above my left temple. I do not know at this time if this injury is life threatening. I have limited food and water but I am conserving as much as possible to prolong survival. This could be the end. I hear footsteps on the metal bleachers below.

01 Oct

Time: Unknown

It's coming back to me in flashes. I vaguely remember fighting three of them. They must have seen me make for the top of the bleachers and followed. When I woke up, I was flat on my back lying in a pool of blood and broken glass in the center of the floor of the press box. As I tried to lift my head up and check the door, I noticed the shatterproof glass. From the looks of it I shot through the glass to kill the things but missed, as the bullet holes are accompanied by larger holes. The edges of the larger holes in the broken glass hold pieces of skin and clothing, indicating they tried to reach inside. There is also a diagonal line of bullet holes starting from the doorknob and trailing down to the bottom left part of the door. After checking my weapon, I figured that I had shot between fifteen and twenty rounds.

Forcing myself to my feet, I stumbled over to the door. Looking through the broken glass, I saw four dead bodies strewn on the bleachers. In the distance I could see another two beyond the goalpost, milling about in search of prey. My memory is still spotty but I remember shooting at least one of them at point-blank range right through the glass, killing it instantly.

02 Oct

Approx. 1600

Woke up this morning to the sound of a dog howling. It could have been a wolf, but with the lack of living humans in North America, I'm certain all the domestic dogs are becoming feral. I'm curious if they would remember me as a living man or attack me on sight as they do the undead. I have seen a canine's resentment of them. Reminds me of how some dogs despise uniforms. Annabelle dislikes the creatures, and the hackles on her back stand up the instant she smells one of them drawing near. I have dried blood all over my face and I continue to inhabit this crow's nest above an overgrown football field. The only evidence that remains that it was ever a playing field is the goalposts and the bleachers on either side.

I am beat up and sore. The crash may have injured me seriously. My kidney area is extremely tender and I find it difficult to stand for very long. In the packs I grabbed from the helicopter, I salvaged three hundred 9mm rounds, five MREs and a collapsed roll of rigging tape. I'm somewhat encouraged by the fact that I had the forethought to grab my pack with my multitool, two gallons of water and NVGs along with other survival odds and ends.

I will try to keep myself to one quart of water per day. If I don't overexert myself, I feel I may have enough water to get healthy enough to move. I also have the equipment that was strapped to my vest under the harness when we crashed (pistol, survival knife, flares, compass). The stitches in my head are very uncomfortable and I wish that I had had something better than sewing thread. A bottle of vodka or any hard alcohol would really help. I have a handheld PRC-90 survival radio that I have been using to try to communicate with Hotel 23 on frequencies 2828 and 243. No joy. Either I am out of range or the radio isn't operating properly. John knew our intended flight path but even if every Marine were dispatched with all vehicles and weapons they wouldn't make it as far north as my location. There are simply too many undead between us. I don't think I'll be making it back at this point.

03 Oct

Approx. 1900

It is time to begin formulating a plan. I'm down to 1.5 gallons of water and the number of undead in and around the field seems to be increasing. I find it difficult to think with the pain I'm experiencing. I keep telling myself to bring it back to basics. I need food, water and shelter. In today's day and age, that isn't enough.

As of this very minute, I can see six of the creatures from my vantage point. They don't seem to know I'm here, and not one of them has made an attempt at the bleachers. With the range and accuracy of the MP-5, I dare not make any attempts to take them out, especially by the grainy green picture provided by my goggles. The pain in my head is driving me mad. I've thought on a couple of occasions of just leaving the box, going down to the field and killing them all from behind with my knife. Then the pain subsides and I go back to reality and realize what a shit plan that is. When I urinate, I can see small amounts of blood. I figured this out when I accidentally pissed all over my hands today. I must have really socked my kidney when the helicopter autorotated to the ground.

First off, I need to figure out exactly where I am. After I do that, I need to figure out where I can go to get some better gear and try to communicate with Hotel 23. At this point I'm positive they know the aircraft is down. I will rest and recover until I get down to half a gallon of water. I have decided that at that point staying could mean death. It's getting cold here at night, especially when you're only wearing two layers of clothing and have a door with as much unintended ventilation as mine. Damn myself for getting so used to being around others.

My watch is busted, only showing the day under the dead hour and minute hands. I suppose I can just kill one of those things and take its watch. I need to know the exact time of day so that I can monitor sunrise and sunset. It's been about nine months since a watch battery has been manufactured. I'm sure they have a decent shelf life, so I might as well get a digital watch with a timer and chronometer while I can still use one. It's a shame I have to think of shit like this in my condition.

04 Oct

Approx. 0200

Another one of those things found its way up the bleachers at around midnight. I slid on my NVGs, trying to make sure when I turned them on that no green light would spill out around my eyes. I watched the corpse for five minutes as it stood there in front of the door at the top of the bleachers . . . then the batteries on my NVGs slowly started to fade out. I didn't have any more AA batteries in my pack so I was forced to sit there in terror as the thing slid its hand in and around the broken glass.

Every piece of glass that hit the floor sounded like thunder to me. I came very close to turning on my flashlight but kept the urge at bay, knowing that it would attract more of them. It reminded me of the scene from a dinosaur movie when the girl just couldn't bring herself to turn the flashlight off to avoid being eaten by a Tyrannosaur. The only difference was, I was the scared girl who couldn't turn the light on.

Now my species was becoming extinct.

After about thirty minutes of mental torture, the thing slipped and fell backward down the steps and hasn't come back up since. I thought the sound of its falling would bring more, but so far this hasn't happened. I should really pick up some batteries the next time I go shopping. For now, I have a tiny red LED light that I keep attached to my flight suit zipper. Writing this down in red light doesn't seem to affect my night vision and the red light does not attract them. It is such a low-power LED that the creatures have not reacted to it as I sit here writing this.

Approx. 0600

The sun is peeking up above the trees. The glow of the morning is lighting up the area and revealing the undead milling about below around where the fifty-yard line should be. The windsocks on the goalposts are floating on the morning breeze. I didn't get to sleep until about three hours ago and even then I woke up to every sound, every expansion and contraction of the bleachers heated by the morning sun.

This press box is starting to smell very bad. The bucket in the corner is filling up fast and the smell is starting to really fuck me up. I've noticed that the blood in my urine went away. My kidney area is still sore but not as bad as two days ago. I miss home. Was it the smoldering and burning San Antonio? Was it Arkansas? Was it Hotel 23? This is all cloudy to me right now. I just want to go home . . . somewhere happy, somewhere devoid of death and destruction. I wish that I could have good dreams, because that is the only way I can escape this.

Caller

Water is all but gone. I maybe have the bottom eighth of a gallon left. When the chopper went down, we were headed north from Shreveport. I don't know my exact location but after careful consideration I have decided to head southwest back in the general direction of Hotel 23. I need clean water to cleanse my head injury. Pus is seeping out of the open wound and I have to squeeze it every few hours to relieve the pressure. It's also very hot around the laceration. At least I know my body is fighting the infection. I would normally move at night, but my water situation has forced me out into the dead world again. There are about a dozen creatures below and I know they will see or hear me when I leave the press box, as I'm not about to attempt to climb down behind the bleachers and risk a broken leg.

I've been thinking a little more about writing down what has been going on. I think I might ditch this for the time being as I am busy trying to get back, and writing in this situation could prove unhealthy (fatal). I must confess that I tried to stop but it didn't last long. I write when I can and it makes me feel better. It may be sporadic or it may reflect my boredom at times but I stay more sane putting all this shit on paper.

As I write this, I'm trying to remember all my bank pin numbers and email password from before. I've had an account at my credit union for over ten years with the same pin and I can't remember it! I had to really concentrate to remember my email password, the same one I used every day for years until the shit hit the fan.

pin: ~~4601~~ ~~4897~~ ~~4609~~

e-mail pword: n@s@1Radi@t0r

I've packed my go bag, loaded the MP5 and put all the frequently needed items at the top of my bag for speed and convenience. Using a collapsed roll of rigging tape, I taped my knife sheath and survival knife to the left shoulder strap of my pack with the handle down. I want easy and quick access to it if I need to get personal with one of those things. I've rested enough that I think I can make it somewhere and maybe with luck hole up for a bit. I'm going to leave in one hour.

Late PM

I went to battle at the football field today. I stepped down out of the press box after gulping down the last bit of water. My pack was full and tight against my body, making my lower back hurt a bit. The first contestant on "The Headshot is Right" was a young male wearing one sneaker and a fucked-up green 7-UP T-shirt. He saw me come out of the box and immediately stumbled up the stairs. I still wasn't sure of myself with this weapon so I let him get pretty close before the action chambered back and the top of his head flipped open like a cookie jar lid. He fell backward, making the bone in his leg snap louder than the bullet that ended him. More witnessed what I had done and came for me.

Again I had to deal with the talented tenth, a very different talented tenth than W. E. B. Du Bois. In my recent travels and travails, I've noticed that about one in ten of these things is either smarter, faster or both than their compatriots. I picked her out immediately. She was more aware and came at me with more coordination than the rest. She stood upright and walked briskly to me, while the others just stumbled. I gave her no quarter and shot her in the neck and head. She went down just as easily as the others, but she probably came from a hot zone. She wasn't as radiated as the horrendous creature on the Coast Guard cutter, but I knew the odd effect radiation had on them. It kept them on a more level playing field with the living—me.

I didn't take care of all of them at the field. I just killed enough of them to keep the threat at a manageable level. My plan was to kill the ones I needed to, fall back to the far side of the field and circle around and retreat. I killed four and kept an eye on the other eight. I tried to get a good look at their wrists because I would be willing to make two passes if on the second pass I could pick up a watch from one of them. I couldn't get a good look and quite frankly I was a little scared to linger on that field.

I made one pass and evacuated the area, heading southwest by compass until I came upon a sign that said "Oil City 10 mi." I was at an intersection of the rural road and a two-lane highway. I walked a ten-yard offset to the road to avoid being seen by anything. In my experience in this world I've noticed the most lethal enemies are not the dead. From my vantage point at the crossroads I could see an old roadblock set up on the southbound side of the highway and a forty-car pileup on the northbound side. A small creek trickled from a drainage pipe near the road. I decided that my need of water temporarily outweighed my need to remain invisible, so I ventured over to the sound of the water.

As I approached the barrel-sized drain, I could swear I saw movement near the distant roadblock. I stood there for a full minute, just to make sure. Whatever it was, it didn't move again. I bent down and drank water until the sound of something caught my attention. I picked up my head so fast I hit the back of it on the top of the drain, temporarily causing me to see stars. I shook it off and kept listening. I made out the sound of an engine, cycling in a rhythmic pitch. It wasn't unlike an electric lawn mower. I tried to look in the direction I thought it was coming from, but I couldn't see it no matter how much I strained my eyes. The sound vanished as quickly as it had come. I sat for a while thinking of what it could be. Motorcycle? No. It didn't seem like that at all. It was something familiar.

I drank until I couldn't anymore, filled up the water reservoir in my pack and moved on, keeping the thirty-foot offset. I saw all sorts of things that a man should never see along the way. Rotting corpses were strewn in and around the roadblock. They seemed to lie in a bed of expended brass, as if an army had attempted to dispatch a horde of them here months ago. There were dead men standing on the highway in a hibernating daze, presumably with nothing to motivate them. I suppose they conserve energy that way. In the distance I could see a pack of dogs running across a field. I was downwind, so I'm pretty sure they didn't know I was near. There were no signs of human life whatsoever.

The sun was getting lower in the sky and it was time for me to find some shelter for the evening so that I could attempt to relax my nerves and collect some thoughts. It must have been two or three miles from the intersection that I noticed a house sitting behind a tree line in the distance. I carefully approached, watching all sides and looking over my shoulder much more than I needed to. It was very quiet, and I was still shaken up from the day's events. My kidney was full of water, and I had to pee. I thought back to playing hide and seek as a child, having to pee at all the wrong times. The house was an old 1950s era two-story. The paint was peeling off it seemingly before my eyes.

I sat and watched it for a very long time. I took notice of the burned-out late-model Chevy sitting a few meters to the side of the house. There were bullet holes in the hood and carriage. The first-floor windows of the home were boarded over, and old human remains were on the ground below the windows. I listened and watched until the fading light forced me to make a decision. The house seemed abandoned. I walked around it, looking for possible entry points. Even the front and back doors were boarded over. The only way in was to climb onto the roof and go in the unboarded upstairs windows.

I mustered all the courage I had and pulled my sore body up the porch pillar and onto the overhang leading to an upstairs window. I never would have made it had I not done pull-ups with the Marines every day back home. I sat up there admiring the view and listened to my surroundings. It was dark behind the window, so dark that I would not want to be in there for anything. The window was raised about six inches, giving airflow to a part of the thin white curtain. It blew in the breeze, or perhaps it was my breathing that was causing the curtain to flutter. I held off for what seemed like hours. I didn't want to go in. I debated sleeping outside but quickly ruled that out due to fear that I would roll off the roof and into the waiting arms of the dead. The sun's light was filtered red through the atmosphere as it said its good-bye with my spirits on the western horizon. I reached into my pack and grabbed my flashlight.

I held my arm out to the window and it felt almost electric as I touched it. I tried to pull it up with one hand, but it had been in that position so long that it wouldn't give. Using both my arms as well as my legs, I was able to get it high enough so that I could crawl in. I parted the curtain and twisted the tail cap on my light. The room appeared as normal as a room in an abandoned home could appear. The door was shut, the bed was made but there were bird droppings and leaves all over the floor.

I poked my head farther into the window to make sure it was clear all around. I was satisfied, so I crawled in. The first thing on my mind was the door and whether it was locked. I slowly walked over to the door, feeling the wood floor creak under my weight. After every sound I made, I stopped in my tracks and listened for any reaction in the hall or downstairs. I heard none. I reached up and checked the lock on the bedroom door—it was already locked from the inside. I then quietly checked the closet and under the bed and everywhere else bogeymen dwell. There was a burned candle and half a box of matches on the dresser.

I debated whether I should light the candle to conserve my flashlight batteries. After some thought, I closed the curtain on the bedroom windows and quietly hung extra blankets from the closet over them. I lit the candle and warmed my hands over its flame. My eyes eventually adjusted to the candlelight and I began to drift off into something . . . not sleep, but something.

I wasn't sure how long I had nodded off, but the sound of thunder startled me awake. I looked down at the candle and noticed that it had not burned down that much. I walked over to the window and pulled the blanket aside, looking out into the field. The lightning struck, revealing a human silhouette off in the distance. I had no idea of the creature's status or intent. I kept gazing out into the void—waiting for the lightning strikes to reveal the night. Eventually the shape went away, and I wondered if I had ever seen it in the first place.

It is still raining now and I've decided to use the bed. No noise has come from the other side of the door but I'll be sleeping with my weapon again tonight and probably every night for the rest of my life.

06 Oct

I awoke this morning to nothing but the sound of the wind outside. I needed to eat. I have three MREs left from the crash. I've only eaten bits and pieces of them since then. I think today is a good day to force more food into my system. My head feels a little better. The stitches itch but I'm trying not to touch. As I look out the window into the distance I can see no sign of the undead. It's dreary outside and it looks like it might storm again.

I started to stretch my body out and get ready for the day when I remembered the most important thing in my life right now—the downstairs portion of this house. I let my mind slip for a second, for the first time in a long time. I forgot where I was. It seemed like I had been in this room for days, but it had only been one night. My mind relayed to my subconscious that the home was safe, that it was mine. Of course this was not the situation. There could very well be a dozen of them down there, standing in a dormant trance, unaware of my presence. They seem to go into some sort of strange hibernation when there is no food or stimulus near. I could imagine a whole family of them standing downstairs in a daze, waiting for the first sign of life to wake them into hunter-killer mode.

I tried not to ponder exploring the house until I had eaten some sponge cake from my pack. After eating, I gulped down some water and started thinking of excuses not to go downstairs and look around. I knew that I had to, because there were things in this house that could keep me alive. It wasn't until the sun had crept through the clouds and was high in the sky that I decided to move on to the bottom floor.

I checked my weapon over and rigged my LED light to the suppressor of the MP5 using the duct tape I had in my pack. I pulled the slide of my Glock back a quarter-inch to make sure I could see brass in the hole. No part of my body was exposed as

I reached out with my left hand to unlock the door. It was stuck, probably from being in one position for months. I had to force it open, making a loud clicking sound. I placed my hand on the door, securing it as I listened. If the noise brought them, I would lock it and head for the hills.

I waited for at least five minutes, thinking I heard everything from the undead to a lawn mower to a foghorn. I released my hand from the door and reached down to turn the knob, presumably the first time it had been turned in ages. Twisting the knob, I readied my right hand to kill whatever stood in my way. The taped suppressor of my weapon was the first part of me to make it through the door. The blue tint of LED light lit up the upstairs common area as I panned my weapon around.

I kept wondering whether I had actually checked my magazine or if I had just imagined it. Pushing that thought out of my head, I advanced. I looked back at the bedroom door I had just walked through. There were old bloodstains on the door, as if something had beaten on it until it lost interest. These things know.

Swinging back around, I noticed something odd. There were white spots on the wall where pictures would have been. It's as if the owners of the house made sure to take the pictures with them. I can think of a few hundred more important things than pictures to take. There were dead flies all over the floor, as common as dust. The upstairs floor was covered in layers of both, with no footprints to indicate recent activity. If there was something dead or alive in this house, it had never bothered to wander around up here. This was when I found out why. As I crept to the stairs, almost stepping down, I stopped and looked down at my feet. There were only two steps before they disappeared. Someone had taken them out. Below were the bodies of six undead, all shot through the head. It was starting to make sense. Whoever owned this place had probably taken out the stairs and bugged out to the second floor. They had most likely shot the ghouls and retreated out the bedroom window. That's the best I could figure. That still didn't explain the bloodstains on the door I had come from or how the things got into the house, but I hadn't checked the whole upstairs yet.

I steered clear of the area of the floor near the damaged staircase and slowly made my way to the two closed doors at the other end of the hall. The floor creaked as I walked, but I ignored the sound. I didn't sense anything was here. The first door I came to was an upstairs bathroom. If the power had been on, it would have looked like any bathroom did before the dead came back. Everything was neatly in place, with dust-covered towels draped over the shower rod and a new bar of soap sitting in the soap holder near the sink. I swiped it up and zipped it in my leg pocket. I went over to the toilet and looked around. Nothing out of the ordinary but a weird little plaster mold in the shape of a toilet seat sitting on top of the toilet tank that read: "If you sprinkle when you tinkle, be a sweetie and wipe the seatie!"

For some reason I thought that was funny and sat there laughing for a couple of minutes. Before walking out of the bathroom, I checked under the sink and found a plastic container full of various medications. I took a tube full of expired triple antibiotic and a roll of toilet paper and moved on to door number two.

I readied my weapon as I opened the door. It was pitch black inside, with heavy curtains over the windows. I panned my light around the room, revealing its disheveled condition. The bed's mattress was flipped over and dirty clothes and trash littered the floor. Small rat droppings were spread all over the room, adding to the room's "old book" smell. I was letting my imagination go wild before I went into these rooms, half expecting to see something horrible and demented. I was certainly happy not to find an old lady swinging by her neck from a light fixture in a failed attempt to kill herself properly . . . swinging by her purple neck, screeching out in a witch's voice, "Be a sweetie and wipe the seatie!" Not today, thank goodness.

The downstairs remained unexplored, but I didn't like the idea of climbing down there only to get my ass bitten off by a crafty ghoul. I doubt any of them are crafty, but I've seen them do increasingly weird things since they started reanimating. I suppose that alone is weird.

After careful consideration, I decided to take the small hand mirror from the upstairs bathroom and use the rigging tape to attach it to a broom handle from the upstairs closet so that I could get a better view of the downstairs without having to risk my own ass. I was at the top of the destroyed stairs on my stomach for twenty minutes looking around with the broom mirror before I decided it might be safe enough to go down. The only thing that was out of the ordinary were the dead bodies on the floor below and an open door that looked like it could lead down into some sort of basement. I was so paranoid of falling down into the bodies below that I tied my leg to the sturdy upstairs railing while I investigated. I'd hate to have found myself with a broken leg and facedown on a pile of corpses with more pouring out of the open door and no quick way back upstairs. I untied my leg and used the same dirty sheets to fashion a makeshift rope for my descent. Feeling more frightened than I had on my first day of school, I quickly shimmied down and bolted over to shut the open door.

Approaching the door, I noticed that there were definitely stairs leading down into the dark abyss. I didn't care if those stairs led to a cache of M-16s and a year's worth of food, I wasn't going down there, not after what I've been through. I shut the door and scooted a large couch in front of it as quietly as I could. After I was certain that the basement door was secure, I began methodically clearing the bottom floor of any perceived threats. Closet by closet, nook by cranny, I made sure that none of those things were down there with me. I checked everywhere, making sure that not even a severed upper torso could be hiding in wait for me under a table, or in a downstairs shower.

Satisfied that the house was clear enough, I began searching for items that I needed. I went through the drawers in the kitchen, finding waterproof matches and three packs of AA batteries. My NVGs were again serviceable. Further investigation revealed an old box with two large rattraps inside. I took these traps, as I felt they were easily large enough to take a small rabbit or a squirrel when my ready reserve food ran out. In reality, I should have been hunting to preserve my nonperishables, and I may begin to do so as soon as I feel a little stronger.

In a downstairs closet, I found a black and gray hiking pack with "Arc'teryx Bora 95" embroidered on it in gold letters. The pack was clearly of higher quality and more comfortable than the one I was using and looked like it could hold twice as much. I walked over to the bashed staircase, careful not to touch the bodies on the floor. After reaching up to shove the pack onto the second floor, I continued my investigation.

I walked around the lower level of the house, checking out the boarded-over windows and reinforced door. Propped up next to one of the windows to the left of the door was a long mop handle with an ice pick bound to the end. The pick was attached with skill, the twine holding it in place showing intricate knots that formed a pattern, holding the pick very securely to the end. Brown, dried blood covered the metallic end of this homemade spear. It wouldn't be good for hunting an animal, but if you hit one of those things in the eye, or the tender part of the rotting skull, you could bring it down without a shot, saving valuable resources. I took the makeshift weapon and placed it on the kitchen counter. When I went back into the main area where I had made my descent, I heard a creaking sound. I stood still and it happened again. My main fear was that it was coming from the basement area. I walked over to the boarded-up door to take a look outside so that I could make sure I had a clear escape out the front door.

As I brought my eye level to the peephole the outline of a dead man projected into my pupil. I was terrified for a moment, just gazing at it, unable to look away. Its skeletal face was no more than a foot from me on the other side of the door. I wanted badly to shoot the thing through the peephole, but I would probably have missed and complicated things with the noise it would make splintering the wood. I couldn't take my eye off this train wreck. The face was rotted, the milky eyes bugged out and the lips were gone. The thing seemed to stare at me through the door. It didn't move a millimeter the whole time I watched. The creature must have been over six feet tall. Standing on my tiptoes, I tried to look down at an object in the creature's rotten grip. I couldn't quite make out what it was. I waited at the door, only pausing my peek to blink so that my eyes wouldn't dry up. It didn't budge.

My choices were limited . . .

I could either sneak back upstairs (by climbing the sheet) and call it a day or dispatch the creature once and for all at that moment. I chose to quietly look around the house for more supplies that could be of use before going back upstairs. Moving like a cat, I went back into the kitchen to check the cupboard. I caused a slight creak in the floor as I crossed the kitchen's threshold. I paused for a few minutes, listening—creak . . . creak . . . was the sound from just outside the front door. I dismissed the threat, half imagining the creature cocking its head from side to side, trying to decide if it had made the noise or if it was made by some tasty morsel on the inside . . .

Checking the shelves in the cupboard, I found six cans of chili no meat, two cans of vegetable beef stew and various other foods in advanced stages of decomposition. I shoved the cans into my pack and looked under the sink for anything of use. Under the sink sat an old rattrap identical to the two that I had taken earlier. Only the skeletal remains and shriveled tail of the long-ago-tricked rat were present. Satisfied with my find, I grabbed the mop handle with the ice pick and crept back to the improvised rope ladder, fighting back the unnatural urge to peek through the peephole again.

Using the mop handle, I carefully raised my pack to the second floor so that it would be easier for me to climb up. The pack was overfilled and too heavy so I wobbled a bit trying to keep it balanced. A can of chili fell out and hit the floor, making a sound so loud that it might as well have been artillery fire. I cringed as I shoved the pack up onto the second floor next to the larger empty pack. As I bent down to pick up the can of food, a loud banging sound erupted from the front door. The thing must have been hitting the door with something, as it sounded harder and louder than a bare hand. I shoved the can into one of the pockets in my vest and nearly jumped to the second floor.

I lay there on the top floor, using my pack as a pillow and looking at the ceiling as the monster kept the time for me by door whacks. Relentlessly it kept on . . . I heard the door splinter some and decided to use the mirror to watch the door. I jumped and shook a little every time the creature hit the door, making the mirror shake in my grip. A very small beam of sunlight was poking through a hole in the door about two feet above the knob. Blunt objects don't cause damage like that. The door was boarded in three places and I remember it being boarded on the outside as well.

I retreated into the bedroom I had previously comman-
deered and locked myself in as the sun dipped to the horizon. It
would be dark soon. Using my multitool, I opened a can of chili
and pulled out my brown plastic MRE spoon. I sat there counting the thumps downstairs as the sun set. It took me 353 thumps
to finish my chili.

Night Run

From the sounds below, I can tell that the thing is all but inside. I heard a board hit the floor about half an hour ago. Of course I don't have any idea what half an hour is anymore. In the fear that it may draw more of its own, I've decided to use the night as cover and escape from this place. I spent the evening stuffing the new pack I scavenged from downstairs. I've rearranged everything so that the most needed items will be on top or in a compartment near one of the zippers. There is a lot of extra room in my bag so I'm grabbing a green wool blanket from the closet.

I checked the batteries that I acquired from downstairs. They don't expire for six more years. I put them in the NVGs and turned them on. The green light shining from the optics onto my palm indicated that they were working fine. No use looking through them with the candlelight shining. I also tried my hand-held radio again. I didn't hear anything but static. My mind was playing tricks on me as I thought I heard voices on the other end. I transmitted my situation in the blind, but was vague on my location. Maybe when I get farther south I'll use the memorized codes that John insisted I learn. My stitches are itching again so I tried the antibiotic ointment. I hope it will help fight off any infection. In a few more days, I'll be cutting the stitches out.

It's time to blow out the candle.

07 Oct

Early AM

I'm not certain why these things are the way that they are or why they are different . . .

More aggressive and persistent.

When I departed the house last night, I did so from the same window I entered. I made the bed, mostly because it made me feel better to do so but also because it postponed my inevitable departure. After making the bed, I doused the light and put on my NVGs. As I adjusted them my fears became reality when I saw that the noise the creature made downstairs had drawn a dozen more undead to the area. That was just what I could count from one window. By my estimation, there were probably nearly thirty around the house.

As I made my way out onto the roof I could hear the sounds of them moving through tall grass and tripping over branches trying to locate the noise in the dark. Old habits die hard, and I knew I had twenty-nine rounds of ammo in each of my magazines, even though it didn't matter with this weapon. I carefully moved to the edge and looked down. There were two below. Leaning over the edge I popped both of them, missing the head of one. The one I hit fell into the other, giving me another chance. I shot number two and started climbing down the side of the house the same way I had come up. Moving to my best evasion route, I killed three more. Each trigger pull illuminated the surrounding area with a green flash. The NVGs were magnifying the flash from the tip of the suppressor.

I was much too tired to sprint. I walked at a near jog, simply dodging them. I looked back toward the house as I neared the road. One of those things seemed to be nearly running in my direction. For a moment, I thought that it could actually see me in the dark. My fears subsided when it moved off to the side and stopped. It seemingly sniffed the air and slowly turned its head from side to side as if trying to sense me. It held an object of some sort in hand. My gut told me that it was the same creature I had seen through the peephole.

I started to move away from it and turned to the road. I had no idea where I was going. I traveled south for miles along an old paved highway, stepping over cracks so as not to break my mother's back. The signs indicated that I was closing in on Oil City. This road might even take me into Shreveport, a city that I dared not enter. I needed a place to sleep tonight. I walked until I could almost see a bit of light on the horizon, meaning that the sun would be up soon. I could make out a school bus up ahead on the road.

My best guess was that it was about 0430. The cold was getting to me and I needed at least a couple of hours of sleep to face the coming day. I kept heading toward the bus, careful to scan my surroundings. The area seemed clear but there were a lot of unknowns. A few derelict cars and trucks littered the side of the road on the way to the bus. Rotted skeletons were strewn about near the vehicles, picked clean by the dead and the birds.

Approaching the bus, I was happy to see that the door was open, telling me that at least nothing was trapped inside and too dumb to let itself out. Carefully maneuvering to the front, I climbed the bumper and stepped up onto the hood. The bus was slippery from the morning dew. From the hood I looked into the front window down the rows of seats. It was empty. I climbed onto the roof of the bus to get a better 360-degree view of the area. There was no movement except for two small rabbits in the ditch.

I thought about shooting them but it was too dark to risk even that slight noise. I took the wool blanket out of my pack and left the pack on the roof of the bus. I climbed back down the hood and entered the bus door. Throwing the blanket onto the bus driver's seat, I knelt and pointed my SMG under the seats. I could see nothing but an old paper lunch sack. I reached over and closed the bus door with the manual crank lever as slowly as I could, making sure to minimize the noise it made. Sadly, this isn't the first time I've slept in a bus.

With my pack safely on the roof, I could escape out any of the windows and retrieve it if I needed to make a quick departure. If I had kept my pack inside I might not have been able to fit it through the window, losing all my food and supplies if I had to run. I cut strips of vinyl from one of the seats on the bus and very sloppily braided it into a rope. I used this to tie the door handle in place to make sure that nothing could get in to see me without making a lot of noise. Time for sleep, if anyone would call it that.

Late AM

It's about midmorning now and I'm sitting in the fourth seat back on the right side of the bus. I've slept a needed four hours, or so I think. My pack is still on the roof. There is no movement around me and I'll probably climb up, get my things and leave as soon as I'm sure it's safe. The more I think of Hotel 23, the more important it becomes for me to get back there to my family. Even though the thought of my parents' being alive is still inside my head, I know that most likely they are dead. My home is no bunker, and just like every other home built in the United States in the past fifty years, my parents' home was not built to outlast a siege. I wonder how many people might still live if they "made 'em like they used to."

PM,
Still the 7th

As I geared up to get my stuff off the top of the bus this morning, I was confronted with a very grim surprise. The bastard from the house had somehow followed me. I was on the hood of the bus, about to climb to the roof, when I heard the sound of steel on steel. The sound startled me so much I nearly fell off the hood and flat on my back. I jumped forward into the bus window, causing it to crack. Looking over my shoulder I knew instantly that it was the creature, the same apparition that stared at me through the peephole at the old house. How could this dumb thing know anything about following me? An even better question was how did this thing know how to swing a hatchet?

I jumped onto the roof of the bus and just watched the thing work with amazement. It was actually trying to climb up there with me. I wasn't making the same mistake this time. This member of the undead talented tenth had to go. I flipped the indicator on my weapon and blasted the creature in the face, dropping it instantly. The thing made a lot of noise before I killed it, so it was time for me to depart.

Before leaving I checked the creature for anything valuable, and lo and behold it was wearing a beat-up plastic G-Shock wristwatch. I grabbed the watch and looked at the display before stuffing it in my pack along with the hatchet. The digital display read 10-7 and 12:23 P.M.

I kept making my way south and west, passing scene upon scene of decay. How long had it been since I had seen the first of them? I walked and imagined how it would feel to talk to someone again. The feeling of loneliness was setting in. From all my experiences with survival, this was the most serious of all emotions. It is different with everyone, but for me, the emotion attached to being lonely is fear.

I kept pushing the thought of the dead out of my consciousness, but I could not control what I was about to think. The "daymare" brought me to an open field that I was crossing to the wooded area beyond. As if in a scene from a war movie, as I approached the middle of the field an army of radiated dead appeared at the crest of the hill. They immediately ran for me. Right before I could see the rot of their eyes, I snapped out of it and kept walking. There was no sound. Only the slight breath of wind on my face let me know that I was back to this reality.

Caddo Lake

Yesterday I walked until I came upon a lake. The signs leading up to it read "Caddo Lake Boat Landing Ah." The last letters of "Ahead" had been shot off the sign by a shotgun long ago. It was about 1400 when I came to the lake, so I had to start making preparations for somewhere safe to hole up tonight. I carefully approached the boat dock, thinking back to Matagorda Island and how that situation had ended up. Many boats were still docked, and there were a few that had succumbed to the deep and pulled part of a dock down into the water with them. There were two sailboats of decent size docked and still afloat, but one of them did not look serviceable, because the owner had left the sails on deck to endure months of wind and weather. The other twenty-footer most likely had the sails stowed and would probably work. I could see a working anchor and a chain propped up on the rails of the forecastle with a hand-cranked winch.

I was only a hundred feet away from the boat, close enough that I could stand there and observe my surroundings. With the food and water I had on hand, I could pirate the boat, sail it out into the lake and get some real sleep tonight.

My goal was to move south and west back in the direction of Hotel 23. If the lake were shaped to my advantage, I could cover a lot of ground with the safety of water around me. Edging closer to the vessel, I saw no threats near. I wasn't taking any chances, though, and approached the vessel scanning every direction. That dirty fuck with the hatchet got one over on me and I could have been dead or dying right now if my luck had run out on the hood of that yellow bus.

In a moment of nervousness I chambered my weapon again to

make sure I had one in the hole and a 9mm round dropped to the ground. I picked it up and put it in my pocket. I was getting closer to the vessel . . .

Did I chamber my weapon?

I asked myself again. Pushing back the fear and anxiety, I kept moving. I was out in the open, within view of anyone or anything. I was at the boat. She looked derelict, with the nylon lines on the deck covered in mildew and bird crap. The curtains to the be-lowdecks were closed, allowing me no view of the interior.

I again checked my surroundings and jumped across to the starboard catwalk. Edging to the stern I could see remnants of bloody barefoot prints leading all the way back to the stern. I kept moving aft, making sure to point the dangerous end of my weapon at any blind spot. I followed the prints as they trailed off the stern into the water.

My next task was to make sure that there were no surprises waiting in the cabin below. I twisted on my weapon light and flipped open the door. No smell. Kept walking farther, into the bowels of the sailboat, bending over so as to not hit my head on the fixtures that littered the ceiling. Aside from the familiar *old* smell, the boat was abandoned. I began to inspect the sails, an-chor and all the rigging to make sure that she would be safe for my transit across the Caddo.

The sails had some mold, but they were still workable. The motor would probably never work again and I doubted I would even attempt it. It was pulled back and out of the way so it wouldn't matter to me either way. All that really mattered were the sails, anchor and rudder. I checked the pantry of the vessel—nothing but old and rotted beef jerky, two bottles of cloudy water and a pack of bar soap. I checked a small storage locker holding a small CO_2 inflatable lifeboat. Sitting in some storage netting attached to the bulkhead inside the locker was a set of Steiner Marine binoculars. These will really come in handy when I make landfall and when I need to scout ahead on my way south.

After taking one more look out the porthole to make sure nothing was about, I commenced to rig the sails to head out into the lake for some rest and relaxation. Barring being at the sum-mit of Mount Everest or at the International Space Station (poor bastards), this was the safest rest I could hope for in this day and time. It had been a while since I had taken my sailing lessons, but I still remembered how to swing the boom and raise and lower the sails. The wind was blowing to my advantage, which was the second lucky thing to happen to me in the past forty-eight hours. I'm sure I am due for something else.

Kicking the dock from the bow, I started my travels south and slightly west out of the small inlet toward the expanse of the lake. The sails caught the light wind and pulled me at a speedy three knots toward my destination. This was a happy time for me. I forced my current situation out of my head and imagined I was sailing on Beaver Lake back home before all of this happened. I thought of being home on leave and visiting my family, and of my grandmother's brown beans.

I could see no sign of the undead on the shore but I was a decent clip away from land. I was careful to remain in the center of the small channel as it opened up to the lake. As I approached the mouth of the inlet, I locked the wheel and ran up to lower the sails. I wanted to be far enough away from land to feel safe, but I still wanted to be close enough to swim easily ashore if something were to go wrong with my little floating sanctuary.

The sun was getting low in the sky as the boat drifted to my self-assigned safe zone. I dropped anchor and estimated that the lake was about sixty feet deep. I unpacked all my gear and hung up the wet stuff to dry out. I scavenged the boat once more, checking out the head and galley. There was no usable food but there was a tin mop bucket and an old grill top that had been cleaned before it was stowed long ago. In the head, I found a stack of magazines. I kept some to use as toilet paper when the good stuff ran out.

I had about an hour or so of daylight left so I took the mop bucket and dipped it over the side to get some water. I then took a bar of soap and the grill top and used them as a washing machine to clean up all my dirty gear. Not as good as Maytag but better than nothing. My undergarments and socks were starting to smell pretty bad and I am getting a light rash under my armpits and around my crotch. I spent the rest of my daylight washing and wringing my clothing dry. I used some nylon cord that I found in a trunk at the stern to improvise a drying line below the guardrail in case the wind blew my stuff off the line.

Just as the sun dipped down below the tree line I secured myself belowdecks in the stateroom, wearing only the green wool blanket that I had acquired from the old farmhouse, hoping that I didn't get into a naked gunfight. For the first time in a while I feel safe to sleep and let my guard down so I will do just that.

09 Oct

I slept in until 0830. A light eastern wind kept the boat pointing into the breeze. My head was scratchy around the makeshift stitches. I knew it was time to remove them. Using the mirror from the boat's head and the same needle I had used to stitch my head, I began to remove them one by one. I stopped about five minutes into the procedure and thought it might be a good idea to boil some water to clean the area every few seconds, but changed my mind, realizing that it would be dangerous to make a fire on a boat in the middle of a lake with all my gear spread out. I had visions of a burning beacon signaling the dead and any band of miscreants within twenty miles. After about ten minutes I was done and cleaned up the wound as best I could, rubbing in a small amount of expired triple antibiotic.

My clothing had dried by noon, and I could see that some clouds were forming on the western horizon. Looked like it could possibly rain. I brought my dry clothes down into the cabin, folded them as best I could and repacked them in the order I thought I might need them. Before getting dressed for the day I again dipped the bucket into the lake water and tried to take a modified sponge bath, using one of my clean socks as a washrag. It wasn't a hot shower, but it sure as hell felt better than being dirty. I dried off with the wool blanket and had started to get dressed when I heard them in the distance. The wind carried their cries to my sanctuary and once again reminded me that this was not a camping trip or a pleasure hike down the Appalachian Trail. This was a death game.

I could not tell how far away they were but it didn't matter. Using my new binoculars I scanned the shoreline of the lake.

Something was moving along the shore northwest of my position. From this distance it could have been a deer. I went belowdecks just as it started to rain to check and recheck my gear. There was some motor oil in the sink area so I tried to make good use of it by oiling some critical parts of my weapons. I figured that if it's good enough for an engine it's good enough for a weapon. The guns have seen some use in the past days so I figured that it couldn't hurt.

As I wiped the SMG down, I once again heard a faint buzzing sound. It reminded me of a few days ago at the watering hole. It seemed mechanical in nature. I had enough daylight to sit and think inside the boat and formulate my plan. I knew that Hotel 23 was south/southwest from my position. Just a WAG (wild ass guess) at the distance would be two hundred miles. My general heading in true, not magnetic should be 220 to 230 degrees. At two hundred miles, traveling on foot most of the way, at ten miles per day, I should be in the neighborhood of Hotel 23 in roughly a month. For anyone who finds this, that is/was my plan. I will follow a general heading from Caddo Lake to Nada, Texas until I reach the facility. My first priority is to knock a gas station and grab a road atlas or maybe check for one in abandoned vehicles along the way.

After gaining access to an atlas, I can formulate a better route, going around towns and cities instead of blindly stumbling into them. I'll hunt for food to replace my perishables and try to travel at night when possible. Supply priorities are: water, food, medical supplies, batteries and ammunition. Funny how priorities shift. In the beginning ammunition would have been my first priority.

1623

Sound has strange quality on this lake, like some strange parabolic antenna attracting the sounds of the dead to the mast of this sailboat. I can hear the moans and rasps of them. Terrible things. Thinking of this I pulled out my survival radio and gave it a shot—nothing. Once again I grabbed my binoculars and scanned the distance. I could see them everywhere I could see the shore. They swarmed the shoreline like seagulls. I'm noting any change in trend in their movement at the shore.

western group   50+

moving north

Sooner rather than later, I'm going to have to make landfall and continue my journey south. I'm not looking forward to making a two-hundred-mile walkabout across dead-infested territory with over sixty pounds of gear. Every now and again I think about this and it still shocks me down to my DNA that this is happening. The suicide rate must have skyrocketed in the past few months among survivors, because not a day goes by that I don't think of ending it here and now. There are no red days on the calendar anymore. I have no days I can rest and let down my guard. Even on this boat I dream of them somehow getting onboard and taking me out. Looks like tonight will be a can of chili, and with my gear safely centralized, some boiled lake water for dinner. All I can do is sit here and enjoy the coming sunset and try to ignore the ominous bellows in the distance.

10 Oct

0630

I feel well rested and recovered enough to start heading south and west on the water. My intention is to triple-check my gear and raise sails for shore. Loneliness is magnified by the solitude of the lake. I remember staying in a hostel in Brisbane, Australia, a couple of years ago. Not wanting my things stolen, I chose a single and stayed there for three days nursing a hangover for the first two. Somehow, in some detached way, that time of solitude in Brisbane reminds me of how I feel now. Maybe it is the fact that I am traveling alone and the only other things that matter to me are my pack and weapons.

2200

After fooling with the sails for an hour or so, I pulled anchor and made very slowly southwest. I know these things can see my sail; I just did not know how the sight of it cruising across the lake would affect their decision to follow. My plan was to run the boat aground to save time. I could not afford the time it would take to properly moor the vessel and tie her up securely. This would be a one-way trip, as after the boat was run aground it would take another motor-powered vessel to pull her back to the lake. Using the binocs I scanned the shoreline for any indications and warning of the dead reacting to my presence.

I tied off a knotted line to the bow so that I would have an easy deboarding when the time came. In between boom swings of the sail, I positioned my three MP5 9mm magazines where I could reach them, with the fourth full at twenty-nine rounds in the weapon chambered. Make no mistake—this was not Normandy beach in the forties but was Caddo beach with potentially more ghouls than German soldiers and one man to push back their numbers.

I wished the vessel had a speed slower than five knots—I wanted to approach more conservatively. After two hours of steering the bow port and starboard, I could finally get a good look at the beachhead that I would be assaulting. On first count I observed a dozen dead at the shore with icy gazes locking to my center mass. Using the compartmentalization techniques that I had learned in the military, I made a poor attempt at pushing the thought of getting torn apart out of my gray matter.

Knowing that this vessel had a draft of at least six feet, I anticipated a respectably violent impact when the sails pushed the vessel and keel into the rocky shore. Nearing land, I tied off the boom and lay flat on my back with my feet braced on the forward railing. Lying on the deck I tried to push the mental image of the dead out of my thoughts by looking up at the mast and clouds in the sky above. Then came the impact . . .

The vessel leaned violently to port while the bow turned starboard and I could hear everything on the shelves below fall and crash to the deck.

Regaining my footing, I shouldered my heavy pack and readied my submachine gun. I estimated that there were twenty of them closing my position with the potential of thousands if I didn't move fast. Aiming as best I could with the short-barreled MP5, I took out five of them so that I would have the time to carefully climb down the knotted rope to the shore. I was down to about nineteen rounds in this magazine as I only had a 50 percent head hit ratio past twenty yards with the SMG. I knew my Glock was loaded and ready as backup as I hit the water at the bottom of the rope. I carefully scanned for any open spots in the group of ten or so that remained and once again played offense as I threaded the needle and ran through them as best I could.

Those ten would turn to a hundred if I didn't lose them, so I decided to run down the shoreline in plain view as fast as I could, prompting them to follow. It was about a mile before jogging became nearly impossible with the pack. I turned ninety degrees right, into the tree line out of my pursuers' sight and then started the system of *walk twenty paces then jog twenty paces* for about an hour. I had successfully lost the dead and was marginally safe in the open plains of what I believed to be Texas. Until I find a reliable map of the area, my plan is to head west until I reach a two-lane highway running north-south and shadow it south until I hit the interstate that runs east-west into Dallas. Of course I will not be visiting Dallas—ever. I will simply shadow the interstate highway system going in the general direction of Hotel 23 using roadway lateral navigation.

As I walked west with the sun at my back I started to feel more energized despite the painful blisters on my feet. What I wouldn't give for some moleskin in my gear. I might try rigging tape. By the late afternoon, I had found a deserted two-lane highway and approached cautiously from the east. I had depleted my water supply down to half the Camelbak bladder so I thought it best to stop at the nearest small bridge over a creek to fill up. It took a mile of paralleling the road before I spotted a steel drainage tube running underneath the road from the field in which I was walking.

The Steiner binocs had already earned their weight in my pack for helping me to find the water supply. As I approached the drain carefully from the northwest, I spotted half a dozen dead cattle— what was left of them. In virtually all of the cattle carcasses the legs were removed and strewn about the field, indicating that they had likely been taken down by the dead. I would have believed that feral dogs or coyotes had done the job if I hadn't seen a long-dead corpse with a hoof mark through its head and a mouth full of cowhide covered in white hair. The beast must have knocked one of them down and taken a lucky step. No matter. The dead had probably swarmed the cattle like Amazonian piranha. I could almost imagine the event in my head, remote-viewing back to the beginning months.

Leaving the field, I moved to the water supply and could hear the trickle of the water as it fell from the drainage pipe under the highway. The pipe was about the diameter of a fifty-five-gallon steel drum. I pulled out the water bladder and had begun to fill it when I heard a shuffling sound inside the pipe. Looking into the darkness I could make out the human shape of what I believed to be one of those things. Using my flashlight I discovered the partially decomposed body of a creature lodged among drainage debris and unable to get out.

The creature's head was caught in such a position that it could not see me. It did, however, know I was there. I poured out my contaminated water and dried the inside of the plastic water bladder as best I could with a clean set of spare skivvies. Leaving the poor bastard to rot in his steel cylinder tomb, I kept moving, looking for water. Now that I had been forced to give up my entire water supply, I felt even thirstier. I continued to shadow the two-lane highway south. Using my binocs I saw that I was following the direction of Highway 59. I took a few minutes to scratch this down in my journal. I continued to keep a lookout for any of those green signs that gave the mileage to the next city.

HWY 59

The sun was starting to go down by this point so I decided, despite my thirst, that it was best to use the remaining hour of useful light to find a safe place to hole up for the evening. There were houses in the vicinity of the road but I didn't have time to break and enter and properly sweep a house before sunset. I kept moving and scouting with my binocs until I discovered a suitable location to sleep—the top of a relatively easy-to-access roof. I stopped in a field and checked my pack to make sure everything was in place before bolting across the road to the target house. I put the wool blanket I had on the top of my pack for easy reach and extra 9mm ammunition in the zipper pouch on the lid of the pack. I then dropped the magazines from my MP5 and Glock to make sure they were at capacity—fifteen plus one on the Glock and twenty-nine plus one on the MP5. Weapons hot, with the MP5 set to single shot and my pack rearranged, I made for the house of choice, a two-story home on the outskirts of a small neighborhood.

The sun was getting low and the temperature was falling as I sprinted as fast as I could to the fence line. I threw my pack over the three-wire barbed-wire fence and climbed over, being careful not to cut myself. After lifting the pack back on I checked the road in both directions. There was undead movement in the distance on both sides of the road. I crossed the road slowly and deliberately, using the cover of an old car, long abandoned. Standing on the other side of the road, I knelt and scouted ahead with the binocs in the fading light. It seemed relatively clear so I double-timed it to the house. I chose this house because of the ladder that I had spotted four hundred yards earlier. It was leaning against the guardrail of the front porch.

I made it to the house and positioned the ladder so that I could easily climb to the roof and sleep there tonight. Before climbing up, I surveyed the outside of the home, noticing that the front door had been splintered in from the outside and bullet holes peppered the front of the house and the wooden pillars of the porch. Another site of a last stand gone wrong. The whole perimeter of the home was covered in what I call gore marks, places the dead had pummeled for days in an attempt to enter.

Makeshift board barricades were nailed up on the downstairs windows but most of the boards were ripped from the window frames and *all* the windows were busted from the outside. This house would be a terrible choice in which to sleep tonight, but a fairly decent choice to sleep on. Satisfied that this place was condemned and that it was not worth investigating its interior, I carefully climbed the ladder to the roof. Once on the roof of the first-story overhang, I pulled the ladder up with me and then climbed to the second story. I didn't want to take a chance of one of those things breaking through the second-story window and attacking me in my sleep. After making it to the roof of the house I pulled the ladder up with me.

I had a pretty good vantage point with enough light to spare to set up camp on the roof. I pulled out my blanket and strapped my pack to one of the roof exhaust pipes. Using the pack waist strap, I attached the secured pack to my arm so I wouldn't roll off the house in my sleep. I was able to use part of my pack as sort of a pillow. What with being fully clothed, with a thick wool blanket, it is not that bad up here. Good night.

Chain Gang

I awoke this morning to the feeling of cold rain on my face. I glanced at my watch, which indicated 0520, and I could tell my core temperature was falling quickly by the annoying chatter of my teeth. I was dog thirsty and fought through the cold to reach into my bag and pull out an old plastic MRE pouch from days ago. Wrapping the wool blanket around my cold body and tangling my foot into my pack strap, I leaned over the edge of the roof and hung the MRE pouch over the edge where the water was steadily streaming down to the first-story ledge below.

After I filled up I drank the shingle-flavored water until the pouch was empty and then I filled it again. Fighting the chill that nearly shook me off the roof, I kept gathering water until my water bladder was full. I repacked my gear (sans the wool blanket), leaving the bladder drinking tube accessible to the outside of the pack and started to think about moving again. There were no dead in sight from my view on the roof. Using my knife, I cut a slit in the center of the wool blanket so that I could fit my head through and use it as a poncho. It was wool and wet so there was no use packing it away. At least wool keeps its heat even when wet.

I then attempted to position the ladder for my descent to the first-floor overhang of the house. As I lowered the ladder my grip slipped a little and the other end hit the overhang with a loud bang. I put the ladder where I wanted and then put on my pack and started my descent. The rain seemed to be getting worse as I climbed down. When I reached the bottom of the ladder I nearly jumped off the roof in fright, as one of those creatures had its face pressed against the second-story window in response to the noise I had made when dropping the ladder.

I saw it and it saw me. Quickly, I positioned the ladder on the ground so that I could start climbing down. The thing was beating on the window in an attempt to break out and get to me. From the sounds, it did not seem that it had enough strength to break through. I didn't want to think about why, but the visions and memories in my mind when I reached the bottom of the ladder were not of an adult corpse—it was a child.

I left the ladder where it stood and made my way to the road that I had used to find this overnight sleeping arrangement. The rain was making me miserable, and I wanted nothing more than to build a fire somewhere and hang my clothes to dry. I thought back to central heat and air and remembered how dependent we were on electric power to survive as a society. I'll bet we lost thousands of elderly over the summer just because of the heat waves. It had been a bit since I tried my radio so I decided to give it a go and xmit out on the preset distress frequency. After going out three times with no response, I switched the radio into beacon pulse mode and decided to leave it on for a few minutes. The rain continued as I shadowed the road, which I remembered from the day before as Highway 59 South.

As the rain lessened in intensity, I could hear the familiar hum of a distant engine. I had heard this sound on more than one occasion since my helicopter crash miles and lakes behind. Part of me thought it was due to my head injury and the infection that I had endured. I rubbed the area where my stitches had been days before. The soreness and sensitivity were virtually gone. I continued to follow the direction of the road for what seemed like miles. It started to warm up around 0800, and the rain decreased to a light drizzle. The haze was thick and there were patches of fog, largely due to the moisture, combined with the heat of the rising sun. My feet were sinking deep into the mud as I kept my distance from the seemingly empty Highway 59.

After a few hundred yards I had to turn ninety degrees and head to the highway, as I realized that the mud was not related to the rain. I was walking into what appeared to be a swamp. The road started to elevate and just as a patch of fog blew by I could see for an instant that a section of the highway a quarter mile down the road was up on short stilts to raise it above the marsh. It seemed to go on forever that way into the distance. I didn't fancy disease, and I knew that swamp bacteria or hypothermia from walking waist deep in cold mud could kill me just as easily as any of those things. Adding to my fear were the various open wounds I had on my body from being banged up from the crash and on the run from those things. My wounds were scabbed over, but that was nothing that a few hours of submersion in swamp water couldn't fix.

Having no choice, I had to take the road as it departed from ground level and continued into the haze and fog south over the swamp. Visibility was poor and I could see only maybe a hundred yards in front or snapshots of the distance during random breaks in the fog. I walked for twenty minutes and there was no sign of dry land on either side of my position. There it was again . . . the sound of an engine somewhere in the distance, or perhaps over my head. I wasn't sure of the source. My concentration was broken by a metallic sound up ahead. It sounded like chains being pulled across concrete. I tried to listen and separate the sounds of the chains from the mechanical buzzing sounds but could not.

Both sounds became insignificant when I heard one of those things trip over an old bumper that lay rusting on the bridge. It was coming from the same direction I had just walked. I walked over to it and shot it in the back of the head with the SMG. As I looked up beyond the corpse into the distance from where I had come, I noticed more shadowy figures in the fog. It seemed I had some undead stalkers closing on my position. They were still a couple of minutes out. I turned around and continued in the direction of the metallic sounds at a better pace.

Leaving the stalkers behind me, I started my jog ten paces, walk ten paces regimen. Then came the sound of metal on concrete again. I slowed, knowing that the undead behind me were perhaps ten minutes from my position. I had passed abandoned cars up to this point but none of them were occupied and they all showed signs of the *gore marks,* like those on the house I had slept on last night. I crept farther. The sound of metal got louder and drove me mad.

It was almost as if the mechanical sound abated to allow for the metallic sound to increase its intensity in a cruel game to send me over the edge. The lack of visibility made it even more torturous. I knew the sound up ahead of me had to be within a few hundred yards, but with the highway up on stilts and the barriers up on either side, the sound could be coming from much farther off.

I tried to drive the thought of the creatures behind me out of my head, impossible as that was, and kept moving forward, squinting as if that would help me see through the fog. The noise was very loud at this point and I could hear the sounds of undead activity up ahead. I now had a choice to make: either turn around and deal with the stalkers behind me or push ahead and deal with the noisy dead in front. The other option was to jump into the cold swamp and hope that the other side was near, and also hope that there were no undead in the swamp waters to greet me as I made my way to land. Since going north was not my objective and getting my ass bitten off was out of the question, I chose to press south on Highway 59 toward the metallic sounds.

The fog remained thick but I could see far enough ahead to know what I had gotten into. I estimated that the stalkers on my tail should be about five to seven minutes behind me, judging from the pace I had used to get here. As I moved forward I could see at least thirty undead dressed in bright orange jumpsuits. On the back of the jumpsuits were reflective letters that said COUNTY. Leg shackles and chains bound most of the creatures.

They consisted of units of three to five inmates per chain gang. It looked like only a few were immobilized. One of them was chained to what was left of a shriveled human leg. It walked around and tugged the leg behind. The things could not see me and I used this five minutes before the others behind caught up to figure out how to get past them. Only around thirty were visible. As I thought of ingenious ways to evade them by jumping on cars or running past, one of the first stalkers appeared from the fog behind me. I shot it in the face, decided that thinking was a dead man's game right now and pushed forward.

As I made my way to the chain gangs, I picked the left side to attempt a breach. The right side seemed to have more of the unhindered variety. My tactic was simple: to shoot the ghouls on both ends of the gang, leaving the middle creatures trapped by the literally dead weight. In all I had to shoot five creatures to accomplish my goal. I used a whole magazine.

I'm not sure whether it was the lack of visibility, or knowing that I was surrounded, or the fact that there were large undead inmates in orange jumpsuits and chains coming at me that made me so nervous. I was freaking out and practically praying and spraying my way out. I had to stuff one of the empty mags in my leg pocket and rack another one as I made my way past the bulk of the gang.

Even though three of the five-man chain gang teams were hindered in movement, they still continued to pursue as the unhindered teams marched past them toward me. The sound of the chains scraping across Highway 59 scared the living shit out of me as I ran from these things. They were not the only threat out there. I passed fifty other undead as I escaped the chain gang. The pack was heavier than ever as I returned to my jog ten, walk ten pattern. Up ahead the fog was beginning to clear . . .

I kept on. Looking back into my new circle of visibility I could see nearly a hundred of them in pursuit less than a quarter of a mile behind. I was starting the undead snowball effect. They were making enough noise to start a chain reaction . . . each pack of wolves howling at the next.

The sound of metal and undead approached as I heard the buzzing again. I couldn't hold this pace forever, and I didn't think that losing a hundred undead could be easily accomplished in one day. As I neared the end of the stilted section of Highway 59 and looked back, I could see much more than a hundred.

I glanced down at my watch; it read 0950. I had been evading for hours. Just as I looked up from my watch I witnessed a huge explosion in the mass of the undead and instinctively cupped my ears and sat down on the ground. Just as my ass hit concrete the overwhelming sound of the explosion hit me like a punch to the chest, rolling me over. I got to my feet and noticed that the explosion had done overwhelming damage to the group that pursued. I didn't question where the explosion came from or why I had encountered a fucking dead chain gang, I just accepted it and got the hell out of it. After a short lunch break sitting under an old propped-up car hood out of the rain, I intend to continue south shadowing the highway again, pending swamps, random high-order explosions or undead chain gangs.

2148

Tonight I have found respite in an old refinery field with sections of high chain-link fence squares spread throughout the area. The oil pumps have long since stopped movement. Most of them are grown over with weeds and are home to nesting birds. The small fenced area was securely locked with a hardened chain and pad-lock so I was forced to climb over. After throwing my bag over the fence I draped my wool blanket over a section that I thought wouldn't be damaged by my climbing it.

There was no barbed wire at the top, but it was half habit and half safety to have the blanket there to protect against sharp edges. I could not afford to take the chance of getting an infec-tion—there was no place to receive a tetanus shot. After getting inside the perimeter I carefully and slowly walked around the fence looking for holes that wild dogs or undead could squeeze through. Satisfied that there were none, I picked one of the refin-ery pumps to camp near for the night. It stopped raining down on me around 1500 today, giving me a chance to dry out somewhat before reaching the campsite.

I had some wet gear, so I decided to lay it out to dry on the horizontal metal pipes of the rig. It had been a little cold out-side because of the recent rain, but not as bad as it is right now. My thoughts were on today's events and the mysterious explo-sion that had occurred. I also thought of chain gangs and how I seemed to remember that they were outlawed years before this all went down. I guess when society is failing and you don't have enough police to guard the inmates, chaining them together makes sense. Poor bastards. I can't imagine the horror of it. One of them gets infected and the others are left to fight it, or even worse, four are infected and one is left to fight. No wonder they all eventually turned.

I wondered if the undead child in the house was still bang-ing on that upstairs window trying to get at me, as if I were still within reach. As truly gruesome as the thoughts of the chain gang and child were, the explosion . . . Was it an old weight sensor charge left on the overpass?

In any case I didn't know what to think. As the sun was setting I searched the area for anything of value and found nothing but an old stripped-out Phillips screwdriver half buried in the polluted ground at my feet. I set one of the large rattraps along the fence in an attempt to conserve my nonperishables. With the rest of my remaining daylight I inventoried my ammunition and counted 210 rounds of 9mm. The chain gang fight had depleted thirty rounds of my supplies.

I walked the perimeter once more, careful to avoid the trap, just as the sun dipped below the horizon. There was movement on Highway 59 off in the distance, probably what was left of the group that was tailing me on the swampy overpass. I felt relatively safe here and didn't think that any of them knew where I was. Even so I will still sleep with one eye open and my finger on the trigger and the safety between my ears. Before racking out tonight I intend to slip the NVGs over my head and sleep with them. If I need to investigate something, I won't have to fumble with them and I can just switch them on as needed throughout the night.

Boots

Hours before fully awakening to rain on my face—again—I fell into a daydream phase of consciousness. It was getting cold and my bones had a chill to them that I had not felt since survival school in Rangeley, Maine. My mind wondered back to the POW camp and the stress inoculation.

The cold also made me think of Rudyard Kipling. In my tiny cell they played Kipling's "Boots" poem over and over and over again. The narrator, speaking with a thick Russian accent, said, over and over: *Foot-foot-foot-foot-sloggin' over Africa—Boots-boots-boots-boots-movin' up an' down again.*

After hearing that poem for hours and hours, I had memorized it in detail. Even now I can hear the raspy Russian voice saying it over and over again in an infinite loop in between training sessions. I woke up in the cold rain reciting "Boots" to myself over and over again.

Using the rain dripping off the oil pump, I refilled my water, drank, then refilled it again. I repeated this until I could no longer drink without thinking of vomiting. After a short while, I walked over to where I had set the trap to check on it, as well as to urinate. The trap was empty, indicating that I had to eat some of my valuable nonperishable food. Just as the rain began to subside I decided to build a small fire to heat a can of chili that I had been carrying in my pack for miles.

Using the hatchet, I gathered some dead wood from the other side of the fence and chopped it to a manageable size. I then dug a hole in the ground a safe distance from the oil pump and built a fire using the driest wood I had. I doubt that making a fire will ever be difficult, because of all the things that people have left lying around. Using my multitool I cut some holes in the top of the chili can so that I could hang the can over the fire to heat it. As the chili heated I surveyed the area with my binocs. There was no movement on the highway in the distance or on the other three sides of the fence.

I reached for my survival radio to hail anyone that I could. Since the crash, I have made every effort to conserve its battery power. As I pulled it out to select 282.8 on the handset I noticed that I had inadvertently left the radio in beacon mode from the day before. The battery was dead and I had no spares. I pulled the battery out of the device. The battery appears to be a proprietary type and I doubt I could ever find a replacement. I copied the output voltage and battery type to my journal and threw the battery over the fence to save weight in my pack. Anyone who has gone any distance with a pack knows that every ounce must be justified.

I intend to keep the radio in the event I can rig up power to it in the future. I am now cut off from anyone who could have been monitoring the survival frequencies.

After my morning flashback to survival school I started thinking about the big picture of survival. I knew that some remnants of the U.S. government remained. Aircraft carriers, possibly refugee tank convoys, remote military airstrips as well as Hotel 23. There must be someone out here who can help me get back. Communications with the aircraft carrier had been interrupted before my helicopter crash. Couple that with the stupid idea of researching the radiated dead and bringing them back to the flagship, one might consider that even the carrier could be overrun.

Overhead satellites are likely useless and spinning out of orbit. I know that the GPS satellites have failed already. I have not seen a living person since the crash and I have covered quite a few miles. If the patch of land that I traversed is representative of the rest of my journey, I will be in for serious tribulations. Even if only one percent of the population has survived, I figure I would have seen someone by now. Today I intend to leave a signal indicating my intended direction.

I'll make a large arrow on the ground using rocks or whatever I have available to signal any surviving airborne assets my direction of travel. The only problem with this is that the aircrew that discovers the signal may decide that it is old news. Either way, I'll take any chance I can get for rescue from this war zone.

The explosion that rocked the overpass is persistently on my mind. At the time I just wrote it off as good luck, but the more I think of what happened the more I realize that the odds of an explosion of old ordnance with that timing is unlikely. The buzzing noise I kept hearing was also present just after the explosion.

There have been some deer running about in the area. Chances are slim that they could elude the dead for any prolonged period. I plan to take one so that I can make my nonperishable food last longer while evading and making my way back south to Hotel 23. The rain has stopped but there is still overcast in the sky today. I am wearing my wool blanket poncho for warmth and I will continue my route south today along 59.

There are a few items that I need to find before I get too far south. I need a road atlas so that I do not find myself critically off track on my trip. Iodine tablets or another way to purify water is also a good idea. Regarding my current route, I have no idea if this road runs right into a medium-sized city or interstate exchange. I have had to reposition my gear so that my binocs are easy to grab. Before heading out in an hour or so, I'll wipe down my weapon with the oil and old rag I salvaged from the sailboat. That seems like forever ago.

There's no discharge in the war! RK—

Deer Hunters

After leaving this morning, I had my gear positioned and straps on my pack adjusted for a long march south. I noticed that my clothes fit rather loosely compared to just a couple of weeks earlier. I know that I feel constantly hungry because of all the walking I am doing. Thank goodness this area of the United States is relatively flat. I think I might have perished if I had had to traverse the Rocky Mountains with so few provisions. After an hour of slowly moving south I saw a buck with my binocs a hundred yards in the distance.

My hunger took over as I went down on one knee and quietly set the pack down next to an old stump that would be easy to find. I stalked the deer in front of me, keeping close to the tree line to avoid detection. One hundred yards would be a near-impossible kill shot with my 9mm submachine gun; I would need to get inside twenty yards to make the shot count. The buck did not detect my presence as I closed on him. I took another look at him with my binocs from fifty yards to make sure he would be a healthy mark. I tried to check him over to verify that he had not been injured by the creatures. I could see no bite marks and he seemed to be relatively healthy. His muscles flexed as he walked and grazed. He did not appear too skinny or too old. I could not count the number of points on his rack because of the foliage around him. I looked back to make sure that I wasn't spotted by the undead and to make sure I could still see my pack next to the old stump. I had stalked closer, to within about one hundred feet, when the ears of the buck perked up, sensing that something was not right.

Perhaps it was the smell of a living human or maybe I was not walking as quietly as I intended.

I pulled the weapon up and aimed it at the buck. Using my thumb I checked to make sure the weapon was in single shot, as I didn't deem it necessary to waste ammunition on my mark. It was now or never, as I had a premonition that within a few seconds the animal would get spooked and run away.

I squeezed off two rounds and hit the mark in the neck and behind the head. The animal fell on its side, then got up and started to run. I tracked the animal, cursing half to myself and half out loud over how stupid I was to be so greedy and reckless. I hated killing animals unless absolutely necessary for food, and now I might have killed this animal for no reason, losing it forever. I tracked the blood for what seemed like an hour, carefully gauging my distance from my gear and from the highway to be sure I would not get lost.

The blood drops trailed down into a small valley and behind a finger of terrain. I carelessly ran down and around the finger, thinking only of my growling stomach, and came out of the shrubbery right into a baker's dozen of undead feeding on my mark. They were on their knees over the buck and scratching and biting at the hide of the animal. One of them had already pulled the skin back from where the bullet penetrated. Guilt and anger fell over me as I saw them devour the animal. The poor beast's eyes were open and as I looked through the corpses that were all around it, I felt that the animal was looking at me and thinking, "So this is why you took me?"

I was only ten feet away from the things. I decided to start walking backward to get out of this little valley. One of the creatures looked in my direction with buck blood and flesh dripping from its rotting jaw. It then put its arms out to reach for me. It moaned and then two others looked up and did the same. I turned to run back to my gear and followed the blood trail. I opened the distance between the pursuing dead and myself. I noticed as I ran a dramatically skinny house cat jump from a tree near the buck. It scurried off into the field nearby.

Seeing those things reminded me how close to death I was again. I had thought that I would be desensitized to them after so much exposure. Each one is a Picasso of terror that reminds me that I will be at war until they all rot into the ground whence we all came.

I checked behind me every five seconds and just ran, still cursing under my breath at how stupid I was for even attempting to shoot this animal at that distance with the weapon I had. The *buzzing* had once again returned by the time I was close enough to see the stump where I had cached my gear. I looked all around and concentrated on where the sound could be coming from. The sky was too overcast for me to see anything above the tops of the trees. In a solemn state of concentration I began to hear the snap of twigs in the trees off in the distance. The deer hunters were in pursuit of something new. I grabbed my gear and readjusted the pack straps. I was thankful to be alive but felt deep guilt for sentencing another living thing to be eaten by those fucking abominations. It was almost as if I had scored a goal for the other team. The deer was put on this earth for living things to eat in need, not to be poached by the likes of them.

I evaded the creatures by carefully crossing the highway and following the other side. This side did not provide the same amount of cover as the other, as it consisted mostly of a large field for the next few miles, with sparse cover every few hundred yards. I decided to cross back over when the first safe opportunity presented itself.

The rest of my day was spent walking slowly south and attempting to keep my mind off the food in my pack that I needed to conserve. It drizzled most of the day and was generally miserable, but I suspect that in times like these a sunny day would be just as miserable. I had heard the *buzzing* three times total today at random moments and decided to start mentally noting the times of day and duration of the sound.

As I looked at my watch, gauging how much daylight I had left, I began to formulate my strategy for a secure sleeping area. By 1500 I was able to see the outline of a town in the distance. This prompted me to start looking at the highway for signs indicating what I would be walking into. I decided that if the population sign read more than thirty thousand, I'd make no attempt to get near it. After all, I needed some food, a road atlas and maybe some ammunition, but not at the cost of dealing with half a million of those things. Even though all it takes is one of them to do you in, a bite is exponentially easier to evade when dealing with a smaller population. This is not a science, but it makes me feel better to draw my line in the sand.

It would be getting dark in a couple hours. I was getting a little uneasy. Sleeping on the ground was not going to happen in a million years. If I did not find shelter before dark, I was going to stay up all night and keep moving. Originally, following the crash, I had thought that I would limit my movement only to night, but the lack of batteries for my NVGs and the idea of sleeping during the day when those things can see had changed my mind. I know they can't see in the dark, as was evident the other night when I departed the top story of the farmhouse. They responded to sound but could not see me.

My choices were lessening by the minute so I looked to the highway for a place to hang my automatic weapon. There were a few options. There was a Winnebago, but I ruled that out because there would be no escape in the event the RV was surrounded. The next option I came to was a UPS truck turned on its side. Once again I felt that this was too small to use since it could also be easily surrounded. The next option I came to was a large semi-truck that had a long feed trailer on the back.

Using my binoculars, I scanned the truck for any sign of death. The windows were rolled up on the tractor-trailer. The truck was high enough off the ground that those things could not climb up on the hood and the rig had a sleeper cabin behind the driver. The words "Boaz Trucking, Inc." were painted on the driver's door. Two of the tires were flat on my side. The rig was leaning a little because of this. I thought it best not to rush into this and just keep an eye on the area to make sure there was no danger. I listened and watched for half an hour before I dropped my pack and headed for the rig. When my foot touched the asphalt I could see clearly in both directions up and down the road.

An ambulance sat derelict in the distance to the north, and to the south I could see a green sign that I thought could indicate the miles to the next town. I made for the running boards to step up to the cab. On the driver's side I noticed the door was locked, but the other side was not. There was no sign of any danger inside the cab. I jumped down and ran around to the other side and opened the door. The old truck smell of fast-food bags stuffed under the seat, and a sun-baked dashboard told me that no one had been in this rig for a very long time.

I climbed inside and looked in the sleeper behind the front seats. The bed was not made but was serviceable. Inside this truck everything seemed normal, other than the faded fast-food bags sitting on the dashboard. I climbed out of the truck, satisfied that it was safe, and went to retrieve my pack. By the time I got back to the truck it was getting too dark to try to read the sign up ahead so I decided it was best to prepare for the night. I placed my pack on the driver's seat and pulled the privacy curtains so that I could not be spotted easily. With the doors locked, I started to inspect the cab for anything of value. I found a disposable lighter and a can of Vienna sausages along with a nice ink pen and a Sharpie marker. I devoured the canned meat. In order to conserve my flashlight batteries, I intend to check the rest of the vehicle over when the sun rises in the morning. The doors are locked and the windows, I suspect, will never come down again.

13 Oct

_0822_

I slept well last night despite hearing something outside before falling asleep. I was so exhausted. I thought that I would attempt to remain still and quiet and in doing so, I fell hard into deep sleep and didn't wake up until about 0630. The light was shining into the cab through the curtains. I kept them closed as I slid my boots on and laced them up and splashed some water on my face. I climbed over to the passenger seat and peeked past the curtains into the area outside. I thought I could see something moving around far to the south. I reached over and grabbed my binocs and checked it out. There was a single corpse in the distance wandering about the abandoned cars. I could see no sign of any closer threat. Cracking the curtains to let more light in, I began a more thorough search of the cab.

The glove compartment revealed nothing but an insurance card that had expired six months ago and a picture of a man and his family standing in front of the Alamo. My mind drifted back to San Antonio and the fate of the Alamo. The area was nuked and is now a wasteland of radiated undead. I wouldn't go back there even with a thousand AC-130 gunships over my head. The back of the picture was dated December of last year. I looked at the picture and wished that I could go back to that time. I would give many things to have one day of normalcy from before all this happened. Behind the family were others laughing and carrying on. They were oblivious to what the world would be like just thirty days after the tourist photographer depressed the shutter release.

Dead Drop

There is so much information to write and process I do not know where to even begin. After leaving the rig this morning, I kept trekking south and checked the sign that I had discovered the day before. I didn't need to get that close, as the binocs once again saved me some time and energy. The sign read "Marshall 6 mi." I had heard of the town of Marshall, Texas, somewhere before and decided that if I had heard of it then it must be too large to attempt a scavenging operation. As I headed back to my standard highway offset I heard the buzz again. The sky was clear, so I immediately pulled the binocs up to survey the sky above. No joy. I kept walking south and east, offsetting further and further, so that I could go around Marshall instead of through its center. This was going to add some extra miles to my trip. After about an hour the loudest sound I had heard since the explosion commenced.

In the distance I heard the unmistakable noise of the sound decoys. I remember the distinct tone because they were deployed at the start of the undead infestation to draw the things to the nuclear target packages. My mind immediately wandered to the worst-case scenario as I thought to myself, Am I about to glow in the dark?

Obviously this was not the case, or I would not be alive to write this now. The sound was not deafening, because it came from so far away from where I stood. It seemed to come from the east, far in the distance. It was not nearly as loud as the decoy I heard when they dropped the nukes, which leads me to assume that the device was deployed a considerable distance further than the first one I had encountered.

Nervous and confused, I kept my pace south and east until I heard the unmistakable sound of aircraft engines approaching. Looking to the eastern sky I saw the shape of an aircraft flying very low directly to my position. I immediately reached for my pencil flares and launcher but before I could screw the launcher onto the flare to fire, the aircraft pulled up and began a steep climb, shrinking quickly back into the big empty sky. I nearly cried until I was almost killed by a huge pallet falling to the earth attached to a large green parachute. The drop landed twenty feet from where I stood and threw wads of dirt and grass into my face. The chute went horizontal and I quickly ran over to the drop and gathered up the chute before it pulled whatever all this shit was across the field. After disconnecting the chute I haphazardly folded it and placed a big rock on top. This drop was wrapped in very thick layers of plastic wrap and measured about four by four by three feet.

I pulled out my Randall knife and started to cut away the plastic wrap. Spray-painted on some of the plastic layers were the letters "OGA load-out 2b." After removing the plastic, I clicked open the carabiners and pulled off the webbing that held the items in place. On a plastic pallet were numerous hard plastic Pelican cases of various sizes. There was a bright yellow case on top of the others labeled simply with the number 01. I checked the perimeter, reached for the case and flipped the latches open. Opening the lid, the first thing I noticed was a cellular phone. I could tell that this was no normal phone simply by looking at the large antenna folded down the side. The word on the front of the phone read "Iridium." I pulled the phone out of the case and hit the menu button. It came to life, indicated a full charge and gave a notice that stated, "Acquiring Lock." I set the phone aside and inspected the yellow case in more detail. On the lid of the case was a chart that seemed to indicate Iridium satellite orbital paths for this region dated for this month with 80 percent of the satellites out of service. According to the chart, only two hours of satellite coverage per day were available.

The hours were from 1200 to 1400 daily with an error of plus or minus seventeen minutes depending on atmospheric conditions. There was an asterisk that warned that the availability would shift to the right two minutes and twelve seconds per year with the current satellite configuration. Sitting in the foam below where the phone was fitted was a small solar charger. As I reached for the next case to examine the contents the phone began to ring . . .

I sat in shock for a few seconds before I hit talk and said hello as the noise faded into solid connection from a digital modem shrill. A slow and mechanical voice emanated from the speaker: "This is a remote six recording. Please monitor text screen."

I followed the onscreen text, as instructed.

6 minutes of satellite coverage remaining.
Officer-in-charge reported missing FM Nada launch facility
via radio twelve days ago. Since that time this station utilized
remaining overhead imagery capability & Global Hawk & Reaper
UCAVs to direction find location. Search aborted until distress
radio beacon detected. Beacon remained active sufficient time
to refine position for Reaper UCAV coverage. Remote Six is one
of *garbled* teen facili *garbled* mission as a command and
control node for *garbled* . . . gov *garbled.* Maintenance
garbled dation has mission impacted airborne opera
garbled on most of air breather aircraft.

Out of the sixty *garbled* Iridium satellites orbiting
garbled resources and computing power to maintain the
orbital paths and data compression algorithms for 2 hr/day
coverage.

3 minutes of satellite coverage remaining.
Vast surplus of experimental Reaper UCAV aircraft *garbled*
support systems we have resources to provide dedicated
overhead coverage for 12 hr/day. Remote Six UCAVs are
equipped w/ two 500 lb LGB *garbled* replenished daily w/
full EO/IR optical turret. In C-130 drop you will find device that
commands Reaper LGB munitions as well as low-drain beacon.
Instructions are included with equipment. To designate target
you will *garbled* be inside the Reaper operating time gate, in

close prox. to the Reaper and must keep target LAS *garbled*
ten seconds. Lasing attempt at less than ten seconds will result
in nonrelease. Deploy low-drain beacon on outside of clothing to
ensure escort. Aircraft will remain angels 10 *garbled* avoid
audible undead detection.

01 minute of satellite coverage remaining.

Utilize text pad on handset to answer the following
question(s):

Do you hear a high pitch sound?

I responded yes.

The SATphone screen went blank. The sound decoy in the distance seemed to get softer until I could barely make out a sound. The sound decoy now seemed to emanate sound all around me . . . just barely audible.

The text screen asked again:

Do you hear a high *static* sound?

Yes.

The sound faded from my detection and the text screen once again asked:

Do you hear a high pitch sound?

I responded no.

Please repeat text.

No.

The text screen immediately scrolled with:

Project Hurricane variable noise suppression activated
on three dimensions. All infected vari *garbled* will flow away
from center eye. You have twen *garbled* hours of variable
suppression battery life remaining. Iridium satellite coverage
degradation immin

Apparently the device that was used to attract the undead to nuclear demise was also designed to make a safe radius by drawing the undead away from the quiet center safe area. Aptly named Project Hurricane, no doubt due to the serene nature of the eye of an actual hurricane when compared to the turbulent hurricane wall. The voice on the phone in the beginning before the data went to text sounded as if it was mechanical, but there is no way this whole operation could have been automated. John must have immediately reported the helicopter missing the instant we were overdue for return.

Many months ago, radios at Hotel 23 intercepted transmissions from a person claiming to be a congressman from the state of Louisiana. Aside from his grim report on the effects of radiation on the undead, he mentioned that he was in limited high-frequency radio communication with a government base equipped with prototype UAVs and a surplus of explosives.

There were numerous boxes on the drop that I needed to inventory and inspect before sunset.

The first case was small and had the symbol for laser engraved on the lid. I unfastened the clasp and opened the case to find a rectangular black device with common pic rail equipment mounts on the bottom. Packed with the device was a one-page sheet of instructions printed on plastic paper and a box of CR123 lithium batteries. The instructions stated what the SATphone comms had referenced. Also inside was a small folder with documents, including a satellite hybrid map of Texas with strange numbered markings indicating various locations. I took a quick second to check the laser device compatibility on the MP5 with no success.

There was a small hex wrench included to adjust the laser beam, but the instructions stated that the device was precalibrated for accuracy within five feet if mounted on the T6 pic rail. Even if I decided to attempt adjustment I would only have about five seconds at a time to do so before a five-hundred-pound LGB detonation wasted something. A very small clear plastic beacon device was pinned to the lid of the case with instructions on how to wear it. The device appeared very similar to the avalanche beacon reflector that I had on my ski jacket, which would have helped rescue personnel find me if a ski trip had gone bad. The Reaper beacon battery life was advertised at six months and the stated purpose was Reaper escort tracking and escort self-destruct avoidance. No boom-boom when accidentally lasing your foot as you trekked cross-country.

On the back of the instructions was a basic capabilities and limitations brief on the Reaper. The satellite text stated that I would have twelve hours of coverage per day during daylight hours. The coverage did not match the advertised endurance of the Reaper, leading me to believe that Remote Six could be more than just a few klicks away. According to the instructions my Reaper would be with me overhead until 1800 tonight and again at 0600 in the morning.

The next case held an M-4 assault rifle with a red dot optic and Surefire LED weapon light with five-hundred rounds of .223 ammunition and five magazines. There was a mount for the laser designator on the side of the weapon opposite the LED light. In the foam below the rifle was a Glock 19 with 250 rounds of 9mm ammunition and three magazines and a screw-on can (suppressor). Two frag grenades were also enclosed in the weapons case. This is the case that was to be a cause for decision on what to leave and what to take.

The next case held vacuum-sealed dried food. There were twenty packets of food with three meal servings in each of varied types. Enclosed with the food was a plastic bottle with one hundred water purification tablets.

I arranged the new food on the ground and the new weapons adjacent to them. Two cases remained. The next case contained a small bottle of gasoline treatment that was marked "experimental" with explicit directions on the back that stated: "1/4 bottle per ten gallons. Wait one hour prior to internal combustion. Exceeding dosage could result in unstable and dangerous combustible liquid." The case also contained a hand siphon pump that was portable enough to think about taking. It seemed the purpose of this part of the drop was to enable me to find and exploit an alternative means of transportation.

The last case contained a compression bag holding a mummy sleeping bag with no brand marking and a very odd camouflage pattern. Digital, but without right angles on the digital print. The bag had a Gore-Tex marking as well as a tag with an NSN number that stated that it was rated for zero degrees C and waterproof. The bag had snaps instead of a zipper to keep it closed. A canvas pistol holster was sewn flat into the outside of the bag at hip level where one would wear a pistol naturally. This bag was designed to go from sleep to fight in a hurry.

Checking my surroundings to make sure that there were no undead about, I took off my pack and proceeded to unload everything to one side. Now came the time to prioritize items, from items that I absolutely needed to items that were just nice to have. The sun had begun to wane on the horizon when I hit the timer on my watch, setting it to go off in two hours.

Keeping the MP5 was now nearly pointless, with the M-4 as an option and suppressed Glock as the backup. I can't discard the MP5 until I field test the M-4, but I cannot take two rifles cross-country on foot for any extended distance with all the gear I have acquired. I have room to keep my old G-17 as a backup, but the G-19 is the logical choice to wear on my person since it's smaller and has night sights and a detachable can. The magazines from the 17 fit the 19—an added benefit.

The mummy bag is definitely coming with me, replacing the heavy wool blanket that I had modified to wear as a poncho by cutting a hole in its middle and wearing it Villa style. Five hundred rounds of .223 is heavy. I'll think about shooting some tomorrow while I still have the alleged Project Hurricane suppression active. I'll do the shooting right before departure in the morning just to be safe. I had 210 rounds of 9mm left over from the helicopter salvage. Combining this with the 250 rounds from the drop brings the 9mm round count to 460 for the pistols.

I'll be shooting some rounds through the 19 in the morning as well, to ensure its reliability, even though I'll be keeping the 17 as a backup due to its great cost/benefit in weight on my pack. Grenades are a given value, as are the water purification tabs and the dried food. I'll need some new socks very soon and will use the old socks to hold the grenades to ensure the pin does not accidentally get pulled as I transit south.

1610

Sunset Approaching

Working List
* = new gear

Weapons
~~MP5 9mm (4 mags)~~
G-17 9mm (2 mags)
210 9mm rds (combine with new ammo)
*M-4 .223 (5 mags) w/ laser designator, LED light and aim-
point
*500 rds of .223
*G-19 9mm (3 mags) plus suppressor
*250 rds of 9mm (460 total)
*2 frag grenades

Survival Gear
Trekking pack
Combat knife
NVGs w/ spare batteries
Water bladder (100 oz)
Flares/compass
~~Green wool blanket~~
Binoculars
~~PRC-90-2 radio (no batt)~~
Waterproof matches
1 Bic lighter
2 large rattraps
3 packs of AA (NVGs)
1 tube triple antibiotic
1 roll of TP
Hatchet
Digital watch
*Satellite phone w/ solar charger
*Topographical map of Texas
*100 water purification tablets
*Mummy sleeping bag

*Experimental fuel treatment (small bottle)
Heed warning on treatment!
*Small gasoline siphon

Stores
2 MREs
3 cans of chili *heavy, eat first
2 cans veg. beef stew *heavy eat first
100 oz water
*20 (3 meals each of dried food)

I've decided it's best to ditch the PRC-90 radio due to not having functioning batteries and the extra weight. The wool blanket and, tentatively, the MP5 are also on the list to discard. I intend to put the weapon and magazine in a safe place and mark it on my new map. I've repacked my gear. The ammunition is the heaviest part of the pack, pushing the overall net weight a few pounds heavier than the original weight. Not having the MP5, wool blanket and radio has offset the increase slightly, but noticeably.

There is a residence not far from my position and now that the gear is packed, I'm moving to a position to sweep it to determine habitability for the evening. The only things I'm leaving behind are the wool blanket, the nearly useless PRC-90 radio and half a parachute. I cut some of the paracord and chute in the event I needed it for shelter. Getting tougher to find military-grade cord these days.

The plan is to sling the M-4 and give the proven (albeit mediocre) MP5 one last patrol before she's cached away and reduced to nothing more than a cryptic mark on a treasure map.

2145

The sun had a little sky left when I shouldered my pack and left the drop. I could tell the pack was a little heavier, as the extra rifle I was carrying accentuated the weight. I walked south and west to the dwelling I had scouted with the binocs earlier. It was a two-story house with the windows still intact. They were not boarded over but they were too high off the ground for someone or some thing to climb into them easily. The sill of the window was about my head height. Curtains were open on some windows and closed on others. It seemed very typical and nonthreatening. I walked the full 360 around the home, checking for any signs of struggle or *gore marks* indicating any previous undead encounter here.

There was no car in the garage. The grass was of course grown up pretty high and the only disturbance in the growth looked like small rabbit trails. I walked up to the front porch and set my gear down. I leaned the M-4 against the wall and made sure the MP5 was fully loaded as I reached out to check the screen door. The screen door was locked, so I pulled out my knife and cut the screen so that I could reach in and flip the switch to unlock the door. As I reached inside and began to unlock the door, something in the window near the door moved. I instantly jerked my hand out of the screen, scratching it as I ran back off the porch and holding back a scream . . .

It was only a curtain that had shifted in the wind, nothing more.

I sat on the porch, concentrating and trying to listen for any reason to force myself to sleep on the roof tonight instead of inside where it would be warmer. There were no sounds from inside the house and no movement outside besides the tall grass in the wind around the house. The sun projected the red-orange glow of the approaching sunset as I made my second attempt. I never knew it would take this much courage every time I did this, every time I needed a place to sleep or reorganize or think.

I walked right up to the flimsy screen door and slid my hand into the screen to open the first barrier to my entry. It took some force to pull the screen door. Some dust and dirt fell on my head as it pulled free, giving me access to the main entry. I reached down to grab the brass doorknob, feeling its cold metal in my hand. I let my hand grasp it for a good while and wondered which way to turn it. Of course, a year ago I would have known this, but the simple, civilized and familiar things get more foreign as time goes on. I slowly turned the knob to the right, and the door swung open with a push from my boot. The room was abandoned, long derelict. No sign of anything for months. It looks as if the people that once lived here left before the outbreak/plague/locusts or whatever.

I kept clearing the bottom level and opening every curtain I saw so that the house could hide no devilry in the shadows. After clearing the bottom level I made my way up what I thought would be the creakiest stairway on planet Earth. I was right. After getting to the top I knew the home was clear, because there was no reaction to the noise I had made on the way up. It didn't matter. I had almost been killed many times before today because I had underestimated the low-gear lethality of those things. I nervously cleared the top floor with the same thoroughness and fear I preserved inside from months before. As I moved from room to room, my mind drifted into darkness and daymares of what I would do if I were to become infected tonight. My first thought was of suicide and how I'd end it with a bullet to my brain. Perhaps I would leave an ominous but witty message, like the young stock boy I had killed what seemed like years ago. How long ago was it?

Snapping out of my morbid thoughts, I kept going room by room, checking in closets and under bathroom sinks to make sure.

What if one of them was under the bed? What if it was a little child?

I had to stop myself. Did I check under all the beds? Obsessive-compulsive, are we? I swept the upstairs again and did the same downstairs before bringing my gear inside and closing and locking every door and window in the house. I noticed four different decorative candles placed in various locations in the living and dining room areas. I brought them upstairs with my gear and picked what I thought was the master bedroom as a base of sleep operations. There were no sheets on the bed and no dead little children under it.

I lit two of the larger decorative candles and placed them on the empty chest of drawers at the foot of the bed. I put my gear near the window that I would use to make my escape if things were to go badly for me tonight. I also shut and locked the bedroom door and pushed another chest of drawers in front of it to buy me some time. I checked the window to ensure that it would open in my second of need. At this point it was dark enough that I could use the NVGs to do a quick 180-degree scan out the window for any sign of them. There were none.

Sitting in the darkness listening to the house creak in the night wind, I began to think of today's events in more detail, and this only brought more confusion.

Why didn't the C-130 cargo plane pick me up at a nearby airfield or cleared strip of land?

Who are Remote Six?

Instead of counting sheep, I count unanswered questions before I drift into a deep sleep, guarded by the flickering light of fortunate candles . . .

Candles used against odds for their intended purpose.

Thread the Needle

I slept solidly last night, with no interruptions. I dreamt of the noise barrage beacons, or perhaps it was the wind shifting just enough for my subconscious brain to actually hear them. The sun is rising in the eastern sky and I have had plenty of time to inspect some of the other documentation that dropped with the gear as well as have a go at some target practice with the M-4 and G19. Enclosed in the documentation is a map of the predicted hurricane noise suppression target set. The three units were deployed to Shreveport, Louisiana, Longview, Texas, and Texarkana, Texas/Arkansas, and they were set to varying intensities, judging by the SATphone transmission.

I'm currently a few miles north of Marshall, meaning that I'll need to split the distance between Longview and Shreveport in half to attain maximum threat avoidance. The noise suppression modeling on the map indicates areas of suppression, with red circles surrounding the target areas that show danger zones. There is a green safe corridor area that depicts a recommended path south between danger areas. The circles are not perfectly round where the suppression devices are located, possibly due to terrain and other factors that limit transmission of sound. This map was obviously modeled via computer. Also of interest are the orange overlay areas over Dallas and New Orleans, with the international symbol for radiation displayed on them. The areas cover a significant radius around the cities, trailing eastward at the small end like a teardrop. Looks like the orange shows the boundary for radiation fallout with winds factored.

The Texarkana noise suppression zone is at least 30 percent larger than the other two for reasons unknown. The recommended evasion path takes me skirting southeast of Marshall, across Highway 80 and twenty more miles south by southeast. The safer green area ends fifteen miles east of Carthage. I do not know what will happen when the batteries run out on the beacons in the three cities. The last time these devices were deployed they were blown to bits by nuclear warheads, taking many of the living as well as the dead with them. My best guess is that when the batteries run out the dead will simply start spreading out again in search of food. I can make fifteen miles in a day at best with this gear on my back. I'll run out of noise cover in about twelve hours, judging from the garbled SATphone transmission.

Also included in the documentation are the estimated infection and casualty rates for North America. Calculations estimate infection and/or casualty rates to be at around 99 percent. The last census I remember had the U.S. population at over three hundred million people. Using some basic math for threat analysis, I think I am outnumbered by more than 297 million undead. That number is undoubtedly growing daily. The undead can afford to make mistakes, they can afford to fall off a cliff or get hit by lightning or get shot in the chest. The living do not have this luxury. Any mistake on the part of the living results in us getting closer to 100 percent infection. My numbers do not include the countless undead I have exterminated or the millions that were instantly disintegrated in the nuclear blasts early this year.

A large folded topographical map of eastern Texas is also included in the documentation. The map is made out of waterproof material and contains illustrations of the common edible plants for the region as well as water-gathering techniques. GPS is gone. This map, coupled with a road atlas that I intend to scavenge, will help me find my way south, back home.

After examining the documents once more I went outside to check the perimeter so that I could test-fire the new weapons. The area was clear, so I locked and loaded and commenced a very short torture test of the M-4. I looked through the optic and immediately noticed how intuitive it was for aiming. I wasn't going to be hammering nails with this, but it was easily accurate enough for a head shot. I was hitting golf-ball-sized rocks fifty yards out with no difficulty, shattering them into dust. After shooting forty rounds through the carbine I broke her down to check the components, then put her back together and shot ten more rounds to make sure everything was running as it should. I was now down to 450 rounds of .223, which made the load a little lighter in the pack.

Before checking the laser designator, I made sure to clip the beacon to my vest over my left shoulder. I then flipped the designator on and hit the pressure switch on the side of the hand guard. As soon as I depressed the switch, I heard a beeping tone that increased in frequency the longer I held it down. I quickly released the switch after counting to three Mississippi. I wanted to make sure the thing worked, not drop a bomb near my position. Satisfied with the M-4, I moved on to the Glock and shot thirty rounds with no difficulty. The last ten rounds I used the suppressor to judge how it affected the accuracy of the weapon. No concerns were noted, sans the time it takes to screw on the suppressor. I am not certain I have what it takes to do this quickly at this time and will need practice. The threads seem fine and one must get it right in the beginning to attach the suppressor correctly.

I found some plastic shopping bags under the sink in the kitchen. Saying good-bye to the MP5, I wrapped her up with the empty magazines in plastic bags with a fresh coat of motor oil from the old rag I had salvaged. I checked the refrigerator in the kitchen, but it had been cleaned out a long time ago. It didn't even stink and had not one bite of old food inside. I yanked out the shelves of the fridge and put them in the pantry. After placing the weapon in the fridge barrel up, I marked it on my map and wrote a note that simply said: "Kilroy was here. Check the fridge."

I left the note on the kitchen table weighted down with a candle I had used the night before.

Rearranging the equipment in my bag, I was reminded of the Iridium satellite phone so I decided to turn it on and give it a shot despite the known time gate. I sat and watched it for five minutes as it attempted to search for a satellite lock. No joy. I set the alarm on my watch to remind me of the gate. I want to ensure that I remember to have the phone switched on with clear view of the sky thirty minutes before the comm window.

I plan to leave in a few minutes and shoot the hurricane path between Longview and Shreveport, but not before I eat two cans of food to lessen the weight of this pack. A can of chili and a can of beef stew should give me some energy for the grueling hump I have ahead of me.

1300

The weight of my pack is really taking some getting used to. I estimate that I have covered about six or seven miles since this morning, moving at an average of one and a half miles per hour. I have consumed about half my water, motivated by the fact that the weight is taken off my shoulders and put into my stomach. I have not seen movement since I left the drop zone. Not a bird. The wind is light and variable, causing the lack of *anything* to be even more disturbing. I know that the noise beacons are either dead or very near depletion, causing who knows what kind of result. Every now and again I get frightened and raise my rifle to a phantom target that turns out to be nothing. The last nothing was a shirt left hanging on a long-abandoned backyard clothesline. I thought for sure it was one of them.

Chernobyl . . . I remember something significant from before all of this. I remember reading a news article on Chernobyl and reading an explorer's account of how quiet and spooky it was to her. She carried a radiation measurement device with her and explored the dead city. People had actually booked tours there to see it for themselves. Many requested to leave before the tour's completion due to the quiet. Now most of the continent is dead and will stay that way.

There's no discharge in the war!

I stopped an hour ago to wait on the Iridium comms but there were no texts. I tried to call in to Remote Six by scanning received calls and using the callback function . . . busy tone. I am sitting on top of an old armored car in a ditch with a corpse inside, in the driver's seat. Almost nothing left but bones and a uniform now . . . must have killed himself early. I scan the 360 from here but see nothing around me.

I am feeling sick from the two cans of food eaten earlier this morning and wishing I had already found a safe place to hole up for the rest of the day and night. I plan to keep moving for another two hours before finding a hideout. Sleeping in a vehicle, like the corpse in the seat below me, is not an option. The gore marks around this truck tell me that. This poor bastard was probably surrounded for days and maybe weeks before he gave up and killed himself. My map is folded to the area I am in. The map was not printed recently and is therefore not a completely accurate representation of the region, but it is far better than nothing.

Storm clouds are gathering on the western horizon and chances are that it will be a wet night if I end up sleeping under the stars this evening. I feel like I may be catching a cold and I just hope that's as serious as it gets.

2134

Someone is following. After I left my rest area this afternoon the SATphone rang. The time was approximately 1355 and I almost missed the call. The phone was tucked under the top portion of my pack with the antenna sticking out the right side. By the time I took off the heavy pack and unfastened the pack buckles the phone had rung three times. I hit Talk and listened for the familiar sound of digital sequencing as the satellite text data was compressed for downlink.

. . . SITREP follows:

Project Hurricane: Successful. Evasion route acceptably clear southwest w/ light undead density.

Reaper: Remains FMC w/ two LGBs on rails for
deployment.
Threats: Unidentified armed male trails from north. Thirty
undead w/ two hot located ten mile radius current location via
Reaper sensors . . .

The phone lost synchronization immediately after the last word and I quickly brought out my binoculars and began to scan the area behind me to the north. I saw no sign of an unidentified man following. The phone gave me no chance to ask any questions or direct the text communication. Something isn't right about this relationship between myself and the unit on the other side of the phone. Perhaps there is a problem with the satellite network only enabling remote relay or something of that nature. There must be a data link from the Reaper overhead to a control area where the aircraft is piloted and the screens are monitored. "Thirty undead with two hot." This can only mean one thing—Dallas, Texas. I have seen what these types of undead can do and I will double my efforts to evade contact with any of those things now that I know that there are two of the radioactive creatures in my area.

It is raining right now and I am taking shelter in a farm tractor cab left abandoned in a large field surrounded by a damaged cattle fence. The rear axle of the beast is fouled with meters of barbed wire wrapped around it as a result of running over the fence. Another relic from months ago. Every now and again if I squint my eyes just right I can see something out there. Just enough to scare me into leaving my shelter and running as fast as I can in the dark through the Texas night.

My mind keeps playing tricks on me, making me think I see glowing and radiated undead in the distance—moving quickly. It is cold in here and I have my legs bundled into the mummy bag. It seems to be working well. The tractor is John Deere green. Just like the color I see through my electronic relics every few minutes when paranoia takes over and I must look.

I wonder if the man that might be following feels the same fear. Tomorrow I continue south through the temporary safe area back to my home.

15 Oct

0800

Woke up to the sun peeking over the horizon right into my face and pondered once again the message delivered during yesterday's phone call. Today will be a day of looking over my shoulder as I travel south and west, keeping my foot back just in case. If the situation report from the SATphone proves true, I may be in for some trouble in the near future. The mummy bag that was dropped will be draped around my civilian pack to lessen my visibility to any person who may be following. This man is on foot. Finding a car and getting it running using solar charger, fuel treatment and hand siphon may become my best option for evading the follower. The only drawback to this plan is that using the charger on a car battery would take the entire day for one start attempt, never mind the probability of a hotwire attempt. I'll need to find a car with the keys in it, which most likely means the previous owner will be too.

0900

I have dug a hole in the overgrown farm soil, using the end of one of my large rattraps. Gathering some small firewood I managed to make a semismokeless fire using a sideways stovepipe technique with shrubs and leaves to diffuse the smoke. I heated up a can of chili today and consumed a quarter of my water stores. I know that having less food is never good, but every time I look at my pack I get anxious to eat any and all of the canned food and then the MREs so that all that is left is the dried food. The limit of my anxiousness to get rid of heavy gear ends with ammunition. I will preserve it to the maximum extent in the event I'm forced to defend myself from the dangers that are ever present around me and far in front. It was probably not the best idea to make a fire, in light of recent events, but I need the morale boost of warm food before I depart.

16 Oct

2143

This is evasion. Avoiding the undead follows a set formula. Stay low, quiet, and plan your movements ahead of time. These rules are invalid when evading a human tracker. Staying low and quiet only gives a pursuer time to follow your tracks and catch you if he is following a different set of rules. Careful balance between the two methodologies is all that has kept me out of my alleged pursuer's immediate line of sight. I have received no calls from Remote Six in the past thirty-plus hours. I know now that the fact that there is overhead satellite coverage does not mean that this organization will use it. Despite not seeing my follower, I have the feeling that someone is watching me and I cannot decide if this is paranoia or if I am actually sensing the eyes of a stranger watching from a distance. I have no one to share a night watch. I attempted to remain awake during the long night I have just spent sleeping in the grassy loft of a farmer's barn. Every creak from the wood or flutter from a nocturnal bird's wings brought me to my feet gazing about by the green glow of my relics and looking at the red dot glowing through my optic as I frantically tried to acquire a target that was not there. I never knew fear until tomorrow. I write this because I thought I knew fear the day before, but every day fear takes a new and more voluminous meaning. I had a friend in the military who took a different path in the service than I did. "The only easy day was yesterday" was not his personal motto, but he often referred to it, and it applies more than ever in these times.

My back is sore and I am suffering from fatigue. After last night's torturous experience in the barn, I awoke to the sight of one of them standing in the field facing the loft window where I stood. Pulling out my binocs I watched it look right at me and lurch toward the barn. The thing was one of the originals. It had been dead for a long time and its skeleton showed in numerous places about its body.

I did not wish to let it get to where it could make noise and attract others so I quickly pulled out the pistol and attached the can so that I could make quick and quiet work of this thing. I was happy that there seemed to be only one of them. Once I was sure that I had not misthreaded the suppressor, I chambered a round and started shooting. It took two shots to bring the thing down, the first shot hitting the neck and the second hitting the bridge of the nose. The thing fell and I examined it from the safety of the loft window to determine if it might have anything of value. It had nothing left but a leather belt holding up rotting pants, and I decided that whatever the thing had in its pockets it could keep. While eating my last can of chili cold in the loft of the barn, I noticed that I had only one more item of canned food left (beef stew). I think I might save it for a couple of nights.

Canned food was getting old, and I despised it cold, but eating it was giving me the excuse to listen to my surroundings before climbing down the loft ladder. I didn't want it to seem like I was doing that for my own sanity. I sat and dined and nonchalantly listened for any sound that would keep me in the loft any longer.

I set out this morning knowing that the Project Hurricane coverage must be abating, as evidenced by the fact that I was now seeing the things in close proximity. This really put me in a bad mood as I began moving and forced my mind to wander to my most recent good memory of hot chili. I suppose a good meal is the only thing I have to look forward to and the one guaranteed motivator I have to get home. I remember deploying to the desert all those times. I remember the war and how much I missed home and how much I always had something to get me through. The thought of camping with my family or the thought of purchasing that new rifle with the tax-free money I had earned from the tour I was on or the idea that I'll actually get a weekend off someday if I just keep my head down and get the job done.

I'm reduced to thinking about warm food. That is my pick-me-up for today. Tomorrow perhaps it will be that I can lament the fact that the helicopter I crashed in had substandard maintenance and was built by the lowest bidder with no living certified mechanic for hundreds, possibly thousands of miles. Chip light. I was forced down in nearly uninhabitable territory because a flake of metal in the engine casing caused a catastrophic failure in the aircraft's ability to remain in the air. Any landing is a good landing if you can walk away from it, unless you walk away from it dead.

Tonight I found shelter in an abandoned gas station, the type of oasis that was out of business long before the fall. No sign of life but the remnants of rats from months or years before. The place was cleaned out. Looked to be decades old and had probably been a profitable place back in the day. The pumps were analog readout and there were no security cameras installed above them on the roof. Under the old wood counter inside the store was what looked like an old shotgun rack from days gone by when that was perfectly acceptable.

Like today.

There was an old used set of snow chains that worked well to secure the entry points. They would slow a human assailant and downright stop one or two undead. I set up shop in an area with visibility to both access doors. From either heavy door I could see fifty feet to the tree line. The grass was very tall beyond the old, cracked blacktop parking spots but afforded enough visibility. The wind is howling and I hear an old piece of tin barely flapping on the gas pump roof. It is getting colder and I think that this winter will be a challenge if I make it that long.

17 Oct

0800

I slept poorly after waking up to a series of disturbing dreams. I dreamt of hundreds of different things but could only remember two. It seems like the ones I really wanted to remember escaped my grasp. I was on the top of a hill looking down on millions of undead. There were several 20mm gun emplacements manned by what looked like U.S. military personnel in various different types of uniforms. I looked at myself as if I was a third-person spectator and looked into my own eyes as I gave the order to fire. The undead were still a mile in the distance but the 20mm barrels were spitting shells downrange so fast that a moat appeared below the feet of the disintegrated ghouls. I saw AC-130 gunships flying low and taking out thousands with their guns. Old F-4s and A-4s flew low and dropped napalm, decimating the enemy, but they still moved forward. I flashed to the next dream, inside

Hotel 23 with Tara. She was alone in the environmental room crying as she looked through a box of my belongings. As the tears slowly dropped from her cheek I heard her say, "Where is it?" and I faded from my subconscious back into the reality of the situation. I had tried my best not to think of her since the crash. It only complicates my situation.

Waking up, I was reminded that I was down to only one can of vegetable beef stew, which in a way is good news as that is the last of the heavy food besides the two MREs that I have broken down, throwing out the heavy cardboard to lighten the weight. I lit the candle once again to cook the can of beef stew. I didn't feel well this morning and I could not decide if it was the broken sleep or the onset of a cold that made me feel weak and aching all over. I drank half my supply of water and consumed the entire can of food before repacking my pack for the day's travails.

1200

I have made good time today despite my apparent weakening condition. I'd love to drink a gallon of orange juice right now, as that always seemed to help in a less fucked-up world. About two hours into my hike this morning I spotted a glint behind me from the direction I had come, just a subtle reflection. Pulling out my binocs I could see nothing. The wind was blowing colder by the day and off in the distance at around a thousand yards there was no sign of movement besides the swaying foliage. In case there is a call, I have the phone hooked into the solar charger hanging from my pack as I make my way toward the bottom of the map. I've accepted that they are not daily occurrences.

I spotted random pockets of undead in the past two hours and observed them in the various fields and areas around me. None seem aware that I am in their vicinity. I keep scouting ahead, readjusting my course to maintain safe distance from the enemy. Anything closer than a hundred yards would most likely result in contact with them, depending on the wind and their level of decomposition. I have the pistol and suppressor at the ready, strapped to the outside of my pack, in the event I need to neutralize one of them. I can't take the chance of making noise if I am being followed or tracked.

1600

No call today. I feel that my paranoia has cost me some time, as I kept looking over my shoulder to see if I could catch a glimpse of my alleged follower. I could see no sign. I feel as if I am being watched, but it is difficult to tell if the feeling comes from the warning or if it's a bona fide sixth sense. Hell, it could be both. To-night I take refuge in an old tavern right off the road. I took shelter early, as I feel I am about to be stricken very weak by this bug I have caught. I cannot eat but I am forcing myself to drink the rest of my water. I hear thunder on the horizon and the feeling of approaching rain is in the air. Numerous bottles of alcohol remain on the shelves, never looted. I picked out a dusty bottle of Maker's and unsealed it, drinking directly from it. It stung but soothed my throat and made me feel warmer than I actually was. I sat in a corner booth in this old hole-in-the-wall tavern known only as River City Liquor and Eats. Some people preferred a booth when going to eat out. I suppose I'm a corner-booth man.

I know all these bottles of alcohol have medical value for disinfection and pain killing. I wish I had the room to take more than a small fifth of whiskey. The wind is kicking up and the rain should follow, not long after this sentence.

18 Oct

0900

I was able to refill my water supply three times last night due to the heavy rain. Checking the drawers of the manager's office, I discovered a bottle of prenatal vitamins. I checked the back label to make sure they wouldn't make me grow breasts and popped the top and took a double dose. They were about to expire, meaning they were probably weak in effect. I needed vitamin C in my current condition. My appetite was down but I kept forcing water into my system (two-hundred ounces since last night). It seemed like I was at the tavern door with my rifle in one hand and my gun in the other taking a leak every fifteen minutes. I feel it prudent to make River City Tavern my home for one more night so I can regain some strength.

1500

I was outside, weary and shaking, waiting on the call that never came. Leaning against an old derelict vehicle in a ditch just up the road from the tavern I spotted one of those things. It spotted me too and started shuffling quickly toward me. I had no time to pull out the suppressed pistol. I leveled my rifle on the thing and put the red dot on its forehead and squeezed the trigger. That was that, only it was very loud and no doubt would draw them to my location. After the satellite window came and went I quietly made my way back to the tavern to think this through. It was becoming more difficult to think as time went on. I felt my fever go up by the hour. I noticed when I got back to the tavern that a propane tank in the shape of a huge aspirin sat in the back. It was possible that this place had the resources for cooking and such. All that was left in my pack was the dried food and MREs.

2200

The propane system in the tavern works. Using rainwater and an old skillet, I made some of the dehydrated food and forced it down. It tasted pretty good despite my body telling me that I was not hungry. It was dark outside, so I decided to get more practice with the M-4 optic using NVGs. I dialed the red dot to the first setting and it seemed to work just fine with the NVGs. It would be fine for a limited engagement, but the muzzle flash would give me away after one shot, maybe two, depending on the observer's distance. At least I have the capability to use it at night if necessary. As I was peeping through the optic with the NVGs I saw movement out the window. It was pitch black inside so I knew that the things could not see me. I kept my weapon trained, focusing on the dot, making sure that any threat could be neutralized. Then I saw them . . . ten to fifteen of them. They were moving about on the road seemingly aimless. I held my breath and watched them and talked myself out of checking the action on my weapon at least thirty times. I might not survive if they find out that I'm in here. I was weak from a cold, and a night engagement in these small confines would give them the advantage. Too many ways to die here tonight. Remaining low and quiet and unfortunately awake.

19 Oct

0645

The morning looks as if it will develop into a clear day. The creatures left the immediate area around 0200. I didn't force myself to sleep until 0300. I am operating off of three hours of sleep and I feel like I have a hangover. I continue to drink water and I even found some old sealed-up coffee. Not the best thing in my condition but I need the caffeine this morning. I will not stay here another night. I move today or I may not be moving anywhere again. Where there is one there are two and where there are fifteen there are a hundred. I'll attempt to do ten miles today.

1200

I'm resting at the military crest of a ridge, with rocks covering my back. I have made a somewhat gruesome discovery. There is what looks like an old grain mill about a klick down into the valley. I would have missed the structure if it were not for the smoke rising from what appears to be living quarters near the mill. There is a separate building that looks to hold livestock or possibly prisoners. I have set up a nest here with the sleeping bag as my hideaway. My gear is safe in the waterproof pack, covered by some branches, and I am observing the area closely, deciding what to do.

There are people walking about, perhaps roving guards. I need to monitor their movements and document their patterns.

Guard 1 (crossbow man): Observed leaving living quarters randomly between 1030 and 1130.

Guard 2 (fat woman): Observed patrolling grain grinder every fifteen minutes between the hours of 1030 and 1130.

Guard 3 (AK-47): Observed standing guard fifty yards from structures, seems attentive. Did not leave guard shack.

1300

Situation: Close observation over time revealed that an armed hostile party is holding captive at least one civilian. Grain mill has been modified to utilize human power. They are using creatures to turn the mill. Not certain if the mill is for grain or for pumping water. Creatures are secured to the mill with harnesses. No mouth restraints, but they are fitted with some modified form of horse blinders. They are stimulated to walk forward by the fat woman, who comes every fifteen minutes.

1330

Observed an uncovered military troop transport truck approaching the compound with only two individuals in the back and one driver in front. They seemed to be part of the staff here at the compound. In my binocs, I could see the fat woman's mouth open up to a shrill scream at the men after they offloaded what looked like a body (really dead).

1400

So much for making ten miles today. I am going to take the diplomatic approach with a five-hundred-pound LGB (laser-guided bomb). I decided this after I observed them attach a living person to the grain mill wheel to further entice the undead to move forward. Stick and carrot. I plan to find a place to hole up for tonight, then observe their daybreak routine and execute preemptive attack. It seems as if they are trying to keep a one-to-one ratio of living to dead on the wheel. They are tied so close to the dead that I thought I could make out one of the ghouls actually touching the back of the living person in front of it with its bony fingertips as they made their rotation in perpetual circles.

Part of me wants to drop high ordnance on them right now, but if I don't find a place to hole up for the night, I will become even more ill or could succumb to undead attack in my sack here on the high ridge ground. I'll take out the one in the guard shack first with my rifle. He's the only threat to me at this range, from what I can see, and one person is not worth the bomb. After taking out the guard, I'll lase the structure that I deem hostile and try not to cause collateral damage to the wheel containing the assumed friendlies and scattered undead. It's only a plan at this point. At one point today I witnessed a flash on the opposite ridge but could not spot movement with my binocs.

Another morbid but beneficial aspect of all this is that I can test the functionality of the Reaper flying overhead on an actual target worthy of an LGB. If all goes well I can take out the bad guys without getting within four-hundred yards of the structure. It's raining and I continue to feel ill and continue to refill my water and drink it to the point of wanting to puke. I have no choice, as there are probably no sterile IVs or saline within a hundred miles not guarded by a thousand undead. No call today, but I did attempt to trickle charge the SATphone with the solar charger while I continued to observe the compound below.

2000

Left some gear at my hiding spot near the mill and found a hiding place for the night in an abandoned unlocked car sitting on a hill. It was a stick eighties Volkswagen Bug. I picked this vehicle because it was off on a side road at the top of a hill. I got inside and checked for keys—there were none. I released the emergency brake and the car quickly started to roll. I only let it go for two feet before I put the brake back on. I could safely sleep inside the vehicle and if I were attacked by the undead in the night I could simply release the brake and roll down the hill. If the car were not a V Bug, I'd attempt to hotwire. The decade is right for the job, but I don't know where the essential parts are located, as the engine is in the trunk. Last time I did this it was Detroit steel. Wish I had that Buick Regal right now. Sleeping with one hand on the e-brake tonight.

20 Oct

0800

Up early this morning planning the attack and analyzing Reaper documentation. Double-checked the beacon and double-checked the Reaper coverage times. Would have attacked at night if I had the coverage. I slept relatively well with no unwanted interruption besides the local wildlife. An old owl kept me awake for a bit. What I would give to be able to fly right now like that wise old owl.

Change of plans: If I shoot the man in the shack and then the Reaper doesn't work as advertised, I could be a dead man. I wish I could remember how many inches a 5.56 round dropped at five-hundred yards from a sixteen-inch M-4 barrel.

The Reaper should be on station already or shortly. I tested the laser and heard the beeps resonate. Batteries check good. Aimpoint checks good too—1× magnification will do no good so I'll need to get to about four-hundred yards to increase my chance of a hit on the guard. No way his AK-47 is more accurate at that range, so I'll take the chance. Found an old Chevrolet station wagon (bonus cool points for the wood paneling) not far from the V Bug. Checking my surroundings, I popped the hood to check the belts and hoses. Some were cracked but overall serviceable. No keys but I could work with this. Using the same technique I had used months before I should be able to get this old battle horse running all the way to Wally World. I had the phone and charger with me, but I had left the fuel treatment at my observation area just below the ridge line. I needed to scavenge some wire. Disconnecting the battery using my knife I pulled it out of the car and carried it to a clearing just out of sight of any foot traffic. I unfolded the charger so that the cells would get full exposure to the sun. The instructions to charge the phone were to only expose one cell. This was a big battery. The solar cell unit had no name brand markings, which I thought was odd.

I covered the battery with a plastic shopping bag scavenged from the back of the wagon, leaving only the unfolded charger exposed to the elements and the partly cloudy morning sky. I'm taking off in a few "mikes" to do more reconnaissance and possibly bring the pain down if need be.

Sniper

1200

Enemy structure is leveled and on fire. I arrived on site this morning at 0850 hrs and prepped for my incursion inside five hundred yards to the target. The manpower situation was the same as was observed yesterday. I saw the fat female slice the back of one of the living slaves tied to the wheel, probably in an effort to entice the thing behind him and turn the wheel faster. The wheel only had one living being. Looked to be a middle-aged man. There were scratch marks on his back from the fingernails of the creature behind him. There was no doubt in my mind that the man was already dying from infection at this point. I carefully watched the wheel to confirm that he was the only living creature walking in a circle.

At about 0930 hrs I lased a spot of ground between the wheel and the living quarters of the people that were running this place. After approximately six seconds I got a steady tone on the device. I kept the device true on target as the LGB impacted . . .

I was flat on the ground but the blast still blew my hair back and popped my ears. The structure shattered into oblivion and the grain wheel flew into the air like a Frisbee at least a hundred feet from where it originally stood. Obviously the infected male was now dead. The blast blew the guard shack over like an old outhouse, leaving the guard dazed and confused. He eventually got to his feet and started running around shooting in all directions.

After wasting five rounds I eventually brought him down to the ground. I have been waiting here for any sign of movement for thirty minutes now. It's probably best to let anything alive bleed out. I'm about to go scout the area for survivors and make

411

sure everything that is dead stays dead. In a slight hurry, since the blast was loud and pretty difficult to miss no matter what your heartbeat status.

1350

As I walked to the only structure that didn't get destroyed or heavily damaged I noticed bodies on fire that still walked. Bringing the M-4 up to my shoulder I waited until within fifty yards before taking them out. Killing seven in all, I approached the building and unlatched the door. The structure was slightly damaged and leaned a little to one side. Jerking the door open, I felt a swift wind of flies blowing past my head. It was at this moment that the SATphone went off while fifteen ghouls started to flow out the door. I sprinted back the way I came with the things in tow. Right hand held the M-4 and the left hand on the phone . . .

Shooting as best I could, I tried to fight and read the screen. I suppose this was the end-of-the-world version of driving down the freeway with a cell phone and coffee while you shave.

All I saw on the other end was: "SITREP: Unidentified male closing your posit. Armed. Reaper LGB battle assessment: Thermal indicates only two living bipeds in area. Project Hurricane Ex . . ."

The rest was garbled.

I danced with the ghouls for a good bit and had to change magazines and run in circles like an idiot to keep them a safe distance away. That's when it happened: I put the red dot on the forehead of one of those things and its head exploded before I pulled the trigger. Then a shot rang out. As I watched the creature in front fall, I didn't notice the one behind. It was almost close enough to put its teeth around my neck. In the corner of my eye I caught its head explode and decayed pieces of bone hit me in the shoulder as the shot rang out in delay once again. There was only one left, so I waited and kept my distance, trying to find some cover.

I hid behind a moldy hay bale and watched another head explode, then another. The report came less than a second after the head was impacted, not totally destroying the head, but taking a good-sized piece off. I reached for my binocs and scanned the area all around. Nothing. No sign of the shooter. I crawled until I couldn't stand it anymore and ran as fast as I could to my gear cache up on the ridge.

To my surprise I did not get shot in the back of the head on the way up. The smell of smoke and bad beef jerky was in the air, making me even more nausated than I already was from being down with a cold. I sat up on the ridge line scanning all around the valley floor and surrounding areas. After about forty-five minutes of this I caught a glint of something. I could barely make out the outline of a torso at least five to six hundred yards away on the opposite side of the valley. The person was holding a small reflective mirror or piece of glass of some sort. Then he started walking and I could see that the man was wearing some serious camouflage on his legs and was carrying the top part of the ensemble in the hand opposite his rifle. Every now and again he'd signal, then check my area with binoculars and signal again to indicate spotting me.

After a few minutes of this, I decided that if the man had wanted to kill me he would have done so already. I kept my gear hidden and walked down to the valley floor with only my M-4 and sidearm. At two hundred yards we dispensed with the binoculars and closed the gap. At pistol range we stopped and squared off. He was wearing a light burlap ghillie suit and had dark skin and dark black hair and a beard. The man put his weapon and signal mirror down on the ground in front of him and stepped back a few paces. My pistol was tucked in my pants behind my back so I felt safe enough to lay the M-4 down and step back.

He yelled over to me in a heavy Middle Eastern accent and said: "My name is Saien; I mean you no harm. I have been tracking you for days."

I noticed that the weapon in front of the man was an AR-type sniper rifle.

I asked him why he had been following.

"I'm trying to get to San Antonio and you were going in the same direction."

I informed Saien that under no circumstances was I headed to San Antonio for at least a few hundred years. He frowned at this but understood as he replied: "Are you sure?"

I said that I was and that I had escaped the city in January right before they dropped the nuke. He began to reason his way out of that by stating that he had heard that some of the cities listed were not destroyed. I had to flat-out tell him that I saw the blast from the airport tower I was hiding in at a safe distance east of the city.

"Have you seen the special ones? The ones that move faster?"

"I saw one of them for sure. On a ship in the Gulf of Mexico. They are lethal and need to be avoided."

"I agree, my friend. From my apartment one hundred miles south of Chicago I witnessed them do things that I did not imagine were possible. Later down the road as I was leaving Chicago, I saw them open unlocked car doors and even sprint . . . but not far or long. They came out of Chicago, I'm certain. I saw the blast out my window last January. Two weeks later they came south. They chilled me—is that the right word?"

I chanced a half smile and told him that it was, I supposed.

"I saw those things go door to door, or so it seemed. One of them even rang the doorbell and turned the knob. More dead birds fell from the sky around the time they arrived. The dead were dumb animals, to be sure, but some memory remained. Do you know why?"

I responded with one word . . .

Radiation.

"I heard the same on the AM radio from someone in Canada working from an AM relay. I observed one of them standing at a door for a month before it moved. It just stood there barely moving, almost sleeping . . . until a raccoon happened upon the porch. The thing fell on top of it and devoured the animal, leaving nothing."

I asked the man what he wanted in San Antonio, and he replied that he had many brothers there. I saw him reach behind and touch a blanket that was strapped to his back. He saw that I had noticed and withdrew his hand. As I stared at him, his response was: "Allah has left this place. Many days since the fall of man I have questioned my belief and lost him. I no longer believe."

In my heart I felt that Saien was genuine and did not wish to harm me, at least today. It was another level of surreal, talking to a living human besides myself.

I inquired, "Do you have more gear?"

"Of course I do, it's hidden, just like your gear is hidden in the hill behind you."

He then said: "Sir, I have tracked and watched you before you found this foul place . . . I do not understand how you placed the explosives on the buildings. I never saw you infiltrate. Did you go at night?"

"I brought the explosives in early this morning."

It technically was not a lie. Trust is to be earned over time, never given.

My turn to ask the pointed questions, and I inquired where he learned to make head shots from a thousand yards.

"Afghanistan."

"Fair enough. What brought you here?"

"I was a freedom fighter, or I thought that I was. I came to Illinois to help my brothers. Before I could do this, the dead began their dance."

I decided to probe no further, as it was a good trade for discussing the origin of the explosion or any detail regarding Remote Six.

I suggested that we check out the rubble for anything of use and he agreed. We walked over to the building where Saien had saved my ass from the creatures. Some of those things were hanging on meat hooks with random limbs missing. A large cooking pot (like a witch's caldron) was in the center of the room. This was fucked up to the fifth power, but it appeared these people were eating the dead. The creatures gazed at us and snapped their jaws. I saw nothing of use in this building, so Saien and I set the place on fire and went to gather our gear.

I asked if he had any wire, as I needed it to secure transportation. Confused, he replied that he did not, but he was sure that we could find some in the abandoned cars. He was right, but something about leaning under the hood scared me to death. I thought of the monster with the hatchet that nearly cleaved me up the middle. We gathered our gear and made for the solar charger. Walking with Saien had reinforced the need for diligence. He seemed to stop every ten steps, listen, and sweep the distance out front with his scope. This is probably the reason he is still alive. I noticed that Saien had an oversized M-16. I asked where he got it. As he handed it over so that I could check it out, he told me that he liberated it from an abandoned FEMA camp tower on his way south from Chicago. Upon closer inspection, I noticed the rifle was chambered in 7.62 with a bull barrel, an SR-25. The scope had a small holo sight mounted on it. He told me that the glass was no good at much less than a hundred yards. The holo sight was for the closer encounters. The weapon was extremely heavy compared to my M-4. The ground where we are standing is a long way from Chicago, and I can't even fathom how he made the journey. I've almost been killed ten times since I crashed less than a hundred miles from here.

We walked and listened all the way back to the area where the wagon sat in derelict condition, as it had for months. I enjoyed the light movement without my gear and strained at the weight of my pack as we returned. Saien and I quickly split up the duties. He disconnected the battery as I went hunting for wire. Here was the problem. We could not add the fuel treatment without first knowing if there was gas in the tank. It would be a waste of the solution. We had to connect the battery and get power to the dash, then check the manual to calculate how much fuel was in the tank so that I can put the proper mixture inside. Too much public math.

I left our base of operations just as Saien was lugging the battery back to the wagon. I had a multitool and my suppressed pistol. I made for the V Bug to cut her guts out so that I could start making time south. The explosions and gunshots worried me. Since January, I've never seen noise fail to draw the attentions of those creatures in some way. There was always cause and effect. Approaching the Bug I observed one of them on the road facing the other direction beyond the car. The day was cloudy and it looked like I was in for a nagging drizzle. Miserable morale sapping weather.

The creature stood there in the center of the road facing away from me. I arrived at the V Bug just as a loud clap of thunder rang out. The creature stirred and looked about, as if looking for the thing that had created the noise. Foolish thing.

I popped the trunk to get at the wiring around the engine compartment. I used more thunder to disguise my work as I cut enough wire to perform the wagon's starter bypass. It felt like I looked up every five seconds to make sure the creature was still unaware of my presence. It started to walk up the main highway to where Saien and the wagon were. Yanking the last bit of wire from the Bug and stuffing it in my pocket, I drew the pistol and started walking quickly to intercept the creature. I was on a side road off the highway. I then heard Saien scream out, "My friend, you need to hurry!"

The creature broke into a trot in the direction of Saien. I had to run to catch the creature. It was moving faster than any of them I had seen. Not sprinting pace, but fast enough to *chill me,* as Saien would say. It was now that I found out how difficult it was to sprint and shoot accurately with a pistol. The creature kept a stiff-legged pseudo-jog going until the suppressed round I fired hit the thing in the shoulder, knocking it down. I took advantage of this and kept up the chase so I could close the gap and get the head shot. Despite the shattered shoulder, the thing was on its feet as quickly as any sacked quarterback would be. It snarled and started a stiff-legged jog in my direction. I aimed my weapon and emptied three rounds into its head before it fell to the ground twitching.

I sprinted for Saien and was so out of breath by the time I reached him that I was seeing stars. He pointed down the road and handed me his rifle. It was damn heavy, which reinforced my respect for Saien's constitution. He was obviously a tough son of a bitch to carry this thing a thousand miles. I braced the large sniper rifle on its bipod on the hood of the wagon and peered downrange through the looking glass over a mile in the distance. Past the reticle, I could clearly see battalions of those creatures moving along the highway in our direction. The scope was powerful enough to let me know that we would have a lot of company soon. I asked Saien how far they were. He said "two thousand meters." This gave us thirty to forty minutes at best. Saien looked nervous so I didn't think it would do any good to tell him that one of the radiated dead had been about to run up and bite his ass five minutes earlier. In the back of my mind, I knew I had one five-hundred-pound laser-guided bomb left on the Reaper orbiting over my head. I was thinking that there were at least fifty of those creatures in that group. I asked Saien what he thought.

He laughed in my face and said: "No, what you see before you is well into one hundred infidels approaching."

Working quickly, I explained to Saien what I was doing, ". . . plug wires to the coil wire . . . attach the wire to the . . ."

Saien interrupted with, "Yes, yes, my friend, I know . . . positive end to the positive side of the coil. We must move faster."

Saien alternated between helping me with the bypass and judging the range of the *infidels* approaching.

"Eighteen hundred meters."

"Roger."

I told Saien to run to my pack and pull the treatment out of the side pocket. Now that power was to the dash, I could see the fuel gauge. I quickly turned off the headlights and the heater to save power. I checked the dash. Half a tank. I then disconnected the circuit to save power. I pulled out the owner's manual and determined that the wagon had about nine gallons of fuel remaining in the tank. Doing the quickest math I could, I calculated that the amount of treatment to add to the tank would be less than one-quarter of the bottle. The gas had been sitting in this tank for at least nine months and was probably nearing a year old. I didn't guess it to be too far gone, so I decided to put one-eighth of the bottle in the tank. I quickly did this and shook the vehicle back and forth to slosh the solution into the gasoline as best as I could.

Just as I read "must wait one hour prior to combustion" on the bottle, Saien called out:

"Fifteen hundred meters."

We didn't have an hour left. Saien didn't respond when I asked him how it looked. He just shook his head and kept one eye glued to the optic. I was able to see them with my naked eye. It had drizzled and they were still kicking up debris from this distance. Judging from the time it took the creatures to transit three hundred meters, I estimated that we had thirty minutes of useful time before the first wave was on us. I quickly reconnected the solar panels to the battery and laid the panels out on the roof of the wagon. Thirty minutes may not do much but it was better than nothing.

I located the starter solenoid just as Saien called out:

"Twelve hundred meters."

Everything was set and it all depended on the battery charge and the gasoline treatment. I frantically packed my things to be ready to go in the event the vehicle failed to start. I had everything prepositioned except for the solar panels on the roof of the wagon. If the vehicle didn't start I would use my remaining minutes to shoulder my pack and move as quickly as possible out of the area. Saien would be of little defensive use with his sniper rifle. With a nineteen-round magazine and a twenty-four-inch barrel, the .308 isn't nimble enough for what was headed our way. Nothing really was, short of a GAU cannon.

I started to gather Saien's things together to place them in the rear of the vehicle for easy access when he told me to leave his bag at his feet and that he would take care of it.

"One thousand meters."

The creatures were well inside a mile and moving directly toward us on the highway. I felt a strange energy in the air and thought I could hear them crushing debris and moving forward like an undead tank division, hell-bent on destroying everything. I reached into my pack, pulled out my binoculars and hung them around my neck. Cleaning the body grease and dirt from the lens with my T-shirt, I peered through them and saw the fifth dimension of hell.

The creatures were moving forward at comparatively high speed and zigzagging back and forth across the highway as they moved forward as if sweeping and searching for something. Obviously this was not the case but the creatures were moving with a purpose. I dropped the binocs to hang around my neck, disconnected the solar panels and reconnected the dashboard circuit. I then completed the connection between the starter and the juice and the car turned over a couple times but didn't start.

It had only been twenty-plus minutes since I administered the additive. I disconnected power and reconnected the solar panels to at least get back some of what I had just lost in the start attempt.

"Seven hundred fifty meters."

His voice was louder and displayed a bit more nervousness than last time. I raised my binocs and had another look. The creatures appeared to be in similar stages of decomposition, but this stage was not nearly as bad as it should be. They looked relatively fresh, not like something that had been dead for nine or ten months. This fact, combined with the fact that they were moving faster than the undead I had experienced in the past, led me to believe that the radiated *scout* (so to speak) I had neutralized earlier was only the beginning trickle. A river of lethal undead was approaching.

I checked and double-checked my M-4 three times and tested the laser device for beeps just as Saien called out, "Five hundred meters."

I could hear them. Wailing moans and unearthly sounds were getting louder on the air. I could not keep from looking. Through the lenses I could see them scan an abandoned car for any signs of food and move to the next. The car down the road shook from side to side as the army bumped by. Saien reached down for his pack and began to open the top so that he could get at something inside. I didn't have time to wonder what he was doing but I knew that he couldn't hold off the undead with the weapon he was using.

He then started shooting.

I screamed at him, asking him what the fuck he was doing.

"Taking out the fast ones."

I told him to fucking stop and that he would just let them know for sure we were here. I think I was right, as the sound in the air modulated to a different tone after the report of his last shot stopped echoing.

"Three hundred fifty meters!"

I shook the vehicle, ramming it with my shoulder, thinking somehow it would help the treatment work faster in the tank if I kept it sloshing inside. The creatures were getting close enough that I could hit them with my rifle. I made the decision to deploy the Reaper. It was our only chance to buy some time for the treatment to take effect. Using my binocs to judge the range, and bouncing my estimate off Saien, I lowered the optic down to the creatures. As I peered through the glass I could see that Saien's estimate of the number of creatures that were headed our way was better than mine.

I activated the laser device . . .

Beep . . . beep . . . beep . . .

. . . a constant tone. Drizzle and sweat was running down my forehead and into my eye, causing it to sting as I kept the device steady on a piece of ground fifty meters behind the front mass of the creatures.

I thought I saw the warhead for an instant on a ballistic trajectory straight down into the mass of creatures. The explosion rocked the ground two hundred meters in front of our wagon, and most of the creatures hit the dirt in the blast.

I screamed out to Saien that I would explain later, and he nodded and checked his pack again. He kept looking through his sniperscope as I once again made an attempt to start the car. I checked the crowd and estimated that at least fifty creatures were getting to their feet and once again lurching forward in our direction. I ran through the hotwire procedure again, checking to make sure that all wires and points were connected.

"One hundred fifty meters! Hurry!"

Saien was getting very nervous, and this raw emotion was being transmitted to me. My hands started to shake as I checked the wires and began to connect power to the dash. Saien threw his rifle into the backseat and reached into his pack and pulled out a suppressed MP5.

He then said in his Middle Eastern accent: "Get the car started, Kilroy!"

I connected the power to the dash and turned the car over again, probably using every bit of energy the battery had left. The car jacked over once, twice, and on the third time the engine came to life—the sweetest sound I had ever heard. I slammed down the pedal to get the juices flowing in the engine, thinking that it might speed the battery-charging process. I jumped out of the car, grabbed the solar panels and chucked them in the back on top of Saien's gear.

Just as I got settled into the driver's seat, Saien opened fire on the approaching undead. I had my pistol in my lap with extra mags ready. Slamming the vehicle into reverse, I started to back up and told Saien to fall back and get into the car.

He acted like he did not hear me as he kept firing at the undead, taking out the fastest one so that another fast mover could replace it. The creatures were very close. We would be overrun in seconds if he did not get into the car. I screamed at him as loudly as I could and threatened to leave him if he didn't stop.

He finally snapped out of it, fired one last round into a fast mover less than fifty feet in front of our car and jumped in, riding shotgun. I slammed on the gas, driving by rearview mirror, increasing the distance between the creatures and us. Nearly in shock, I made a comment to Saien about how fast those creatures moved.

He replied callously with only, "*That* is not fast, my friend."

He didn't elaborate, and I really did not want him to.

I flipped the car around, put her into drive and put the pedal down to escape the advancing mob. The sun was getting low in the sky by this time and we needed to find a place to park the vehicle. As we drove Saien told me of how he saw the C-130 drop and how he observed me moving the equipment around and entering the abandoned house where I reorganized my gear. He had been tracking me for quite some time. Saien was vague about his survival and also about his time in Afghanistan. The Reaper UCAV bombing I triggered with the laser never came up in the conversation, but the man seemed intelligent enough not to miss something of that magnitude. I kept scanning the engine and fuel gauges to ensure that this old wagon would hold up during our journey south.

It seemed that every five to ten miles we had to stop to assess a roadblock. Some of the wreckage was easy to navigate around and some of it nearly stopped our progress altogether. Optimally we'd need a larger truck with a winch or good towing chain to pull debris off the road. The third and fourth roadblocks we came to in our search for shelter were obviously intentional, a throwback to bandits and highwaymen long dead. Large-caliber bullet holes riddled the vehicles, and skeletal remains occupied the defending side of the wreckage. Two rusted AK-47 rifles lay decaying on the ground. We had to stop the vehicle anyway to assess how we would get around the wreckage so I hopped out and picked up the salvageable AK (the other was all but destroyed). The only damage to the weapon was a bullet hole through the wooden stock and rust all over the metal components of the weapon. I couldn't get the bolt back, so I slammed it against the wrecked car. After two attempts the bolt flew back and a round ejected from the weapon. I walked over to a wrecked motorcycle, smashed the oil indicator viewer on the side of the engine and flipped it over to spill out the motor oil. Reaching down, I filled my hand with oil and liberally splashed it on the bolt assembly of the AK-47.

I took out the mag and jacked the slide back about ten times. I put the ejected round back into the mag and threw the weapon in the back of the wagon. The mag was full. I salvaged the mag from the wrecked AK and tossed it into the back with the other. I'll take the extra weight, since I'm not humping it. Just as I closed the back door, Saien came around the wreckage and told me that we could make it around with no trouble. As I got back into the vehicle, in the back of my mind I was thinking of how the sun was getting low and that my Reaper UCAV was now empty and probably returning to base. As we weaved slowly down the road we continued to pass remnants of last stands. Some cars contained the caked leftovers of undead corpses still moving inside their clear caskets even though sun-baked and rotting.

As we drove along the side of the road we came to a new-car dealership. The cars still sat in neat rows along the road. Before the world fucked itself up, car lots seemed to have a uniform look with vehicles lined up in perfect rows. A car lot had held a very neat and clean appearance. Fast-forward to now and many of the cars have flat tires and the once-even rows now look like a staggered collection of cars in a junkyard. Hail damage and the rest of the elements have taken their toll. It was going to be dark in about half an hour. Saien and I made preparations to park the wagon in the showroom of the dealership so that we could sleep in relative safety and still be able to drive out of the building with assumed lower risk if we were swarmed as we had been before on the road. Using my hatchet and some of Saien's tape, we were able to unlock the sliding door to the showroom floor. We set up the ramps and swept the showroom for danger. Saien had my abandoned

MP5, and we began to systematically go room to room through the sales offices. There was no sign of anyone in the entire dealership. We secured the back doors by placing office debris (old boxes full of paper, and so forth) against the doors so that nothing could find its way inside while we slept.

The main back door had a place for a two-by-four as a barricade for after hours. Before setting the plank I opened the door to see what was back behind the showroom. The maintenance area was housed behind but we didn't have the daylight left to properly clear it. I shut the door and put the plank in the slot, securing the door against anything short of a battering ram. I backed the wagon onto the showroom floor and shut and locked the large sliding glass doors, cutting Saien and me off from the rest of the world for the night. Before retiring for the evening I will ensure the solar charger is connected to the phone in anticipation of the morning sun and tomorrow's possible contact.

I rounded up some paracord from the drop and, using tape, I made some magazine pulls so that I can easily pull the M-4 magazines from stowage in the event that I'm running and gunning my way out of somewhere. Tomorrow Saien and I will need to visit the garage so that we can acquire the raw materials we'll need to get the wagon prepared. I've noticed that there are road atlases in a stack in the corner. They were probably gifts for the new-car customers here. They are dated for last year but something tells me that there has not been a huge number of roads constructed since they were last printed.

In my spare time in the dealership I checked out some of the maps that were in the drop. They were overlaid with a military grid. The map was laser jet printed and some obscure machine language was present. There was a legend on the back and I found myself flipping the map over and over. Then something clicked and suddenly a light bulb went on in my head.

The area where the supply drop occurred was marked with an S, presumably for supply. The letter S had a diagonal line through it, probably signifying that the drop had already occurred. There were other places on the map with an S that seemed to follow a logical path south to Hotel 23 (within twenty miles either side of a straight line). They did not have the diagonal line through them, which could indicate drops we would find ahead of us. There were areas marked with a radiation symbol. Dallas was one area marked, as were random other areas along our path that probably gave off enough radiation to trip national sensors. It could in theory be anything large and dense, such as a crane or a fire truck that had absorbed enough radiation to hold and emit a residual amount. It could also be a large group of those things, like those we had seen today, although I doubt the relatively outdated (in real-time terms) map would be useful in pinpointing the location of a mass like that.

Random items of concern: Charge the phone, rewire the wagon, garage, reorganize gear and distribute sixty 9mm rounds to Saien.

Sticker Price

As my eyes gained focus on the light reflecting off the dusty showroom floor, I saw Saien lying belly down on his drag bag with his rifle scanning the area in front of the dealership. It would be absurd to attempt a head shot through the thick glass, so I wrote this off as him just making sure that things were kosher in the area. The man remained alive, despite traveling hundreds of miles through an apocalyptic wasteland to where he is today. I'm not qualified to question his methods, and even if I were, I am too jaded to care.

I cleared my throat to get Saien's attention. It took him a few seconds, and then he whispered over his shoulder, asking, "What do you want, Kilroy?"

I didn't want to argue that Kilroy was not my name, nor did I wish to give Saien an American history lesson, which would be about as valuable as a lesson on the Mayan civilization.

I said, "Saien, we need to clear the garage area and scavenge some wire so that we can reliably wire the wagon for the journey."

Saien looked at me as if I were an idiot and asked, "Why do we not charge the battery and treat the fuel on one of the new vehicles on the lot?"

Fighting off embarrassment, I had to admit that his suggestion made more sense than spending an entire day wiring an old wagon. Using a factory ignition method would be more reliable, and using a new vehicle could save us a potential breakdown in no-man's-land.

Despite what he said, we would still need to charge the battery on the vehicle that we would liberate from the dealership. There

427

was a selection of hybrid vehicles on the lot but they were mostly smaller in size.

"Another question, Kilroy: Why do you write in that book? What is so important that I see your nose buried in it when we stop? You are going to die writing in that, you know."

I wasn't sure how to answer. I just told him, "It helps." I think he understood what that meant.

Saien and I debated about vehicles and decided that although the hybrid vehicle would save us from scavenging gas by the order of half, we would need an SUV with a towing package and tow chain to get around all the cars and debris blocking our way from here to our destination. During our discussion I noticed that the sleeping rug that he had rolled and attached to his pack was very ornate. It appeared to be an oriental carpet. I didn't know Saien, so my first assumption was that he was Muslim and this was his prayer carpet. He has seemed troubled since the action died down and I could see conflict in his eyes.

I suggested that we pick out a vehicle so that we could start the charging/fueling process, and he agreed. Before finding our ride we decided to check out the garage and maintenance office area of the dealership for any threats that might lurk there. Saien put a fresh mag in the MP5, and I was at the ready as we opened the door. Nothing was out there but the apocalyptic silence that still tortured my nerves. The back end of the dealership was fenced off with chain-link. Saien and I walked around the perimeter and saw nothing outside the maintenance area but the corpse of a canine that hadn't been able to get out of the fenced area to keep himself alive. For some reason this caused me more grief than I had felt for some time. I imagined the poor animal thirsty and unable to eat or drink and just dying on the ground in misery.

With this on my mind I didn't notice the creature approaching on the other side of the fence. The screeching sound of the creature's reaction broke me from my thoughts, and I instinctively raised my weapon and put the red dot on the thing's forehead. Of course, there was no reaction from the creature, and it just advanced into the fence, striking it and falling straight back to the ground. I lowered my weapon, let it hang down on my sling and asked Saien to pop the creature with the MP5 to avoid the noise that my M-4 would create. Right before he carried out my request, I told him to wait. I wanted some more practice with my Glock. I attached the suppressor and gave the creature two to the chest and one to the head, Mozambique style. There was no particular reason I wasted the first two rounds; I just felt I needed the practice. One of the rounds that I aimed at the creature's chest damaged the fence but still had enough energy to penetrate the creature's ribs.

I kept my carbine slung and walked the perimeter with the pistol at the ready. There were no other creatures in the immediate area. I did look farther down the field adjacent to the dealership with my binocs. I saw two of the creatures, but they were walking away from my position. If we practice vigilant noise discipline we should be fine—unless we get swarmed like before.

The door leading to the administration portion of the garage building was locked. Saien and I both peeked through the window and stayed there making sure nothing was moving about. My head was planted to the window so long that the glass fogged over, making standing there useless. If there was anything in there it was not moving or was really dead. Saien pulled a small rectangular leather zipper case from his pack and out came a lockpick and tension wrench. Through his clenched teeth, holding another shaped lockpick rake, he asked me to cover him while he worked. Within a few seconds he had the door unlocked and his gear put away. We readied our arms and went inside. I called out quietly, asking if anyone was inside. Of course, I knew that no living thing would be here, but if there was a functioning dead thing inside it would no doubt react to my voice, giving away its own location.

Dust, mold, and a corkboard were the main showpieces of the office. On the corkboard were handwritten notes and messages dated the first week in January. One of the handwritten notes stated, "The End Is Here" and "The time to repent has come and gone." There were internet printouts of the major headlines broadcast when the world started to crumble. They ranged from, "How Will the Dead Affect the Economy?" to "If Anyone Is Left, This Is It."

The latter article, printed from the *Wall Street Journal* homepage, I saw fit to read, and I attach it here:

If Anyone Is Left, This Is It

Hello everyone, I'm . . . well, who cares who I am . . . with the *Wall Street Journal.* I'm not a columnist or a writer or a newsman of any kind. I'm the *Wall Street Journal* system administrator. Our generators are at 37 percent fuel capacity and I feel that if I do not get this out the story will never be told. We lost power in the New York metropolitan area early on in the epidemic. Our grid is so fragile it's a wonder it was working before this happened but I must digress.

Why am I still here? Great question. I was told by corporate that the situation was under control in the building and that I would be receiving a nice promotion for tending the server farms and network issues during the crisis. My family would be taken care of and the company was sending armed security personnel to my home to assist. By the time I figured out that no one was really in control, it was too late to leave.

My family is no doubt dead, as is the rest of the city. I'm safely locked in the server farm here and I can honestly say that I'm very happy that we have thick steel doors as a server physical security precaution, because they would be destroyed by now if they were anything but thick steel. I'm slowly going mad because of their methodical (debatable) and relentless pounding. I ran out of water yesterday and had to bring one of my water-cooled servers down so that I could scavenge the water from the coolant tubes. They hold exactly 1.25 gallons of closed-circuit H_2O. It tasted bad but has kept me alive. I'm currently devising a way to evaporate my urine using the generator heat to create water for drinking. With one of the telephoto lenses and a digital camera that I acquired before I locked myself in here, I can see through my window down into the streets of ~~New~~ Zoo York.

I have spotted nothing living down there in a week. The last living thing I saw down there was a police officer running. I snapped a picture of him with my camera as a souvenir of the last living thing in the streets of New York City.

On the overseas news wire I am reading interpreted

stories of Europe being actually worse off than the United States, if you can believe that is possible. The U.K. is no different. Apparently their decision to disarm their citizens decades ago did not pay dividends when the anomaly occurred. Of course I am compelled to be unbiased and apolitical in my writing here, but I would love the feel of a rifle in my hands at this very moment. If any of you reading this are safe anywhere with your weapons and prepared, I envy you. I do not think I'll make it from this ivory tower. There are dozens of floors below me that I'd have to traverse before reaching the street, and for what? The second I hit the street I'd have to start running, but to where?

Did the government information czars cover up any news? Hell, yes, they did. I am an eyewitness to that. We had gag orders as early as January 3 not to report on the anomaly overseas or the situation on the Eastern Seaboard. We had our own "man in black" here in the building personally screening every piece of news that went out with his black Sharpie marker cutting up the First Amendment as if it were a Scrabble rule.

That's old news, and the average family sitting at home knew the writing on the wall. You can censor the news but you can't effectively censor the internet. Video and social websites were buzzing with mobile phone footage and photos of the real story. I have archived as much of it as possible on server NYT2 located off-site at our mirror server farm in Wichita, Kansas. That server is solid-state and should protect the data long after the lights go out in the Midwest. There were pictures taken that still jump out at me. I remember America complaining about gas prices before all this. One cell phone image of a gas station sign I saw had gas sitting at twelve dollars per gallon. A week later reports of it going for a hundred dollars per gallon were rumored. A woman sitting in a news van in Chicago uploaded her last days to the net via her phone. She was surrounded and overrun and one of the windows to the van was smashed and three of those things were stuck in the window trying to get in. They were eating the driver as the reporter cried and said her last words before opening the back door and jumping into the crowd in an attempt to escape.

I am all that is left alive on my floor. There is no way down and no escape. Good luck to all of you out there. If any of you see this and are in the area, please stop by for a visit and end it.

Staying alive,
G.R., System Administrator,
Wall Street Journal IT Department.

Saien and I checked every nook of the maintenance office area and moved on to the maintenance bays. After checking the maintenance bays and scavenging some small items that were light and could be of use, we made for the dealership's key locker to pick out our next ride. After assessing the pros and cons of the various vehicles, Saien and I decided on an extended cab diesel pick-up truck. It was new-looking and seemed in decent working order, other than the tire on the right front being a little low. The compressor in the garage obviously wouldn't work without electricity, so we will have to find one of those cheap car lighter compressors at some point along the way or we'll have to jack the truck and use a bicycle pump.

Amazingly, there are no jumper cables anywhere in the area and even if there were, jumping another vehicle would be too decibel-costly. Saien stood watch as I pulled the battery on the Ford and set up a charging station. I wanted to siphon the gas from the wagon but it would have no use on the diesel. Looks like we may be stuck here for at least a day while this battery charges in the sun. I placed the solar charger on top of the truck and put one of my dirty pairs of skivvies underneath to tilt it south. After a full, uninterrupted charge the battery should be suitable to start. I really wish I had access and skill to weld some bullshit over the windshield *Mad Max* style so that Saien and I could have something durable for our trip and something we could shoot out of without worrying too much. I continued to check the vehicle over where I could. The oil seemed fine and at the proper level and the key from the key box fit the ignition with no problem. The spare underneath the truck bed was full-sized and was full of air. I kept checking my watch. I didn't want to miss any possible communications during the satellite phone window today. Since the solar charger is being used for the truck battery, I'm forced to keep the SATphone turned off to conserve the battery until the window.

An air of strangeness surrounds Remote Six. Nothing checks out in my head. The odd gas treatment, the Reaper beacon technology and the remarkable solar panel that seemed to charge batteries faster than my commercially bought home panels ever could.

The sticker price on the truck was $44,995. The sticker also stated that this rig got 17mpg on the highway. The owner's manual said the tank would hold 26.2 gallons of diesel fuel. Using mental math, I calculated that that was over four hundred miles per tank. Hotel 23 was over two hundred miles from here. A full tank of diesel would get me home.

I studied the owner's manual, specifically on the tire change. Sometimes manufacturers used some ignorant proprietary means of loosening the spare tire or something else. Sure enough, this truck required the owner to assemble some device to crank the tire from the bed frame through the back end of the truck. I saw no value in this and knew that it could mean that we would be in for some trouble if we had to pull a NASCAR pit stop on a road somewhere. I detached the spare and threw it in the bed of the truck, as there was plenty of room. I also took some time to verify the jack lift points. I found a towing chain in the garage and threw that in the back end of the truck to make it easier to clear roadblocks. I also spotted a coffee can full of old spark plugs and asked Saien to gather as much of the ceramic from the plugs as he could and to try to keep the pieces as large as possible. The ceramic pieces could prove useful later for a little B&E.

In a fleeting thought, I disconnected the charged battery from the wagon and took it over to the truck. They were not the same model battery, but I thought I'd give it a try anyway. Saien was using vise grips to crush the ceramic from the old spark plugs while I tried my science experiment. Before I got too involved in this, I walked the perimeter once more to ensure that we were not in any immediate danger of being overrun. Back at the truck I set the wagon's battery in the spot where the dead battery was. I haphazardly connected the vehicle wires to the battery and went to the driver's side to see what I could see. I flipped the ignition to power the dash so that I could see the fuel level. I was very lucky to see nearly a full tank in the truck. Diesel was not as refined as gasoline, meaning a longer shelf life, so I decided to see if I could get the truck started without fuel treatment.

I told Saien what I intended to do so that we could discuss the pros and cons of starting up a vehicle out here and possibly drawing attention. It was around eleven when we loaded up the back of the truck to attempt to start it up. Our thinking was that if no undead came to the noise, we'd stay a little longer to make sure our gear was packed properly and that everything else was in order.

I keyed the ignition and the truck sputtered for about five seconds before turning over. I then had a thought about the battery. With gloves, I reconnected the factory-new battery to the truck while it ran so that the alternator could do its job instead of the panels. The vehicle alternator would charge the dead battery much faster than the sun, no matter how efficient the panel.

After reconnecting the truck battery and quietly shutting the hood, I walked the perimeter once more. I saw no sign of activity in any direction around the car dealership. Checking my maps, I estimated about 230 miles or so until we'd reach H23. We should be in radio contact before that time, depending on the transmitter we used. John would be monitoring the aviation distress frequency, so that would be the best way of reaching H23 at the soonest possible time. The trouble would be finding a serviceable VHF radio to make the transmission. It would take about thirty to forty-five minutes to get a decent charge on the battery, so I thought I'd double it to at least an hour to make sure. I opened the door and took in the new-car smell that still lingered despite months of abandonment. Flipping on the heater, I enjoyed the feel of artificial warmth flowing over my hand. It had been a while. With our gear stored in the back, it would be possible to catch some sleep in this vehicle if we picked good spots to hide during the night. On another truck we discovered a bed cover that could easily be transferred to this truck. That seemed useful to keep our gear dry and any undead stowaways out of the back. The next order of business was to take the bulbs out of the tail-lights and remove all the reflectors from the truck. The only lights I wanted were the headlights if I needed them. The undead were not the only enemy. I covered all the exposed areas with duct tape to avoid any chance of an electrical short. The truck would never be road-ready without a professional welder's help, but it would have to do for our trip. I flipped on the radio and scanned both AM and FM bands.

Nothing.

Nothing to mark the existence of what once was a bustling medium of information flow.

Consulting the overhead maps, Saien and I plotted our next leg southwest. We are not far from Carthage, maybe fifteen miles. It looks like we need to keep it that way. We would need to head down Highway 79 and veer south to intercept 59. The priority will be to stay on county roads as much as possible and dip into larger roads only when necessary. When I estimated 230 miles, it was a straight-line estimate. Looking at the road schematics overlaid on the imagery, I saw that this could add some time and distance to the trip. We must also consider that we will not be able to main-tain the speed limits of a year ago with all the debris and other dangers that lay waiting for us along the way. My cousin James hit a buck in his truck a couple of years ago, totaling the vehicle. That deer couldn't have weighed more than 150 pounds. Hitting a two-hundred-pound corpse could end our day quickly. Corpses do not try to get out of your way. They are like bugs to a zapper. They don't care what is between them and the light, they just go.

With the imagery I had received from the drop was a trans-parent sheet of plastic with two oblong orange circles, another asymmetrical orange shape and a radiation symbol in the bottom right corner. I then realized the purpose. I put the transparent sheet over the map of the region and it showed the fallout areas covering Dallas, San Antonio and New Orleans. The Dallas and San Antonio areas showed extensive damage, but the New Or-leans fallout areas indicated a decimated area covering southeast-ern Louisiana, southern Mississippi, part of southern Alabama and the tip of the Florida Panhandle. After a minute of my jaw hanging slack Saien asked what was wrong. I told him I had friends in all these areas and that I was taken aback to see proof that they were most likely dead. He said he was sorry for my loss and took the overlay from the map, prompting me to move on with the planning. I was confident we could make the outskirts of Carthage in a day if we worked together.

As we sat there discussing our plan, I kept catching Saien glancing down at my rifle. I knew that he wanted to know how I caused the explosion from the day we met as well as the explosion on the advancing undead when we were getting the wagon running. I finally broke down and told him a sanitized version of what I knew. I told him that the drop was from the government and that I had been in previous contact with what was left of them. I explained to him that there was a Reaper UCAV orbiting overhead watching our every move and waiting for me to lase my target with the device mounted to my rifle. I saw no reason to inform him of the beacon device or the fail-safe associated countermeasure.

I showed him the iridium phone and told him that the only time it would be usable would be between the hours of 1200 and 1400 due to the degraded satellite orbit. He asked me who was on the other end, and I informed him that it was always a mechanical-sounding recording with a text situation report (SITREP) and that he knew as much as I did on that subject. I told him that I was headed to a place in the vicinity of Nada, Texas, and that he was welcome to help me get there if he so desired. As San Antonio had been destroyed and that had been his original destination, his silence told me that he had no other place to go. It being late October, we decided to build a fire in the maintenance courtyard for warmth. The October chill was definitely in the air, and last night I was very uncomfortable as I tried to get my few hours of sleep.

Before all of this I loved my eight hours of rest per night. Now I am lucky if I get five hours. I only take what I need as the thought of sleeping away what little life I have left disturbs me. The SATphone is on and I'm just waiting for the call.

A message arrived today at 1350 instructing me to proceed to the next drop point marked on the chart, southwest of my current position, and that the drop will occur tomorrow at 1500 hrs. No mention of Saien or anything else in the message. I checked the chart and circled the next point along our path southwest with the letter S designating the location. The imagery I had in my hands indicated that the area was over a small airport. The drop was located east of Carthage just off highway 79. We have made preparations to leave in the A.M. to increase our chances of finding the drop point. I am not sure how I am expected to pinpoint and navigate to the area on the map with so little detail about exact area/coordinates at which the drop is to occur.

A few hours ago Saien and I decided that we should start a fire to fend off the late October cold. I gathered firewood from outside the fence just as the sun began to set. We stacked the wood and Saien tore a page from a book he was carrying in his pack. I noticed the title, *Milestones*. The cover was simple, and it appeared that this was not the first page he had torn from the book to make a fire. The book looked as if it was missing about half of the original pages. We cooked some of the last remaining heavy foods and filled our stomachs for the long day ahead tomorrow.

"There you go again, writing in your book."

"At least I'm not tearing pages out of it."

"Goodnight, Kilroy."

"Same to you, Saien . . . one eye open, man."

"Both eyes, my friend."

Buggy

We have been on the road since 0700 weaving in and out of wrecks. We've had to get out of the truck half a dozen times to tow cars out of our path. Half of those times we've had to kill undead. Most notable was the corpse that still lay waist-strapped to its gurney in the back of an ambulance unbeknownst to me. It posed no threat, but it severely freaked me out when I tried to attach the towing chain to the back of the ambulance and the damn thing sat up in its bed like Dracula and reached for me, mouth agape. I had no idea that it was inside. It was of course hideous and decaying and will be one of hundreds of horrible snapshots I'll carry in my brain until I die.

I pulled my sidearm, punched a hole in its head and shut the ambulance doors before its back hit the bed. After hearing the suppressed shot, Saien ran over to the ambulance and asked what happened. I told him not to worry about it and to be glad he wasn't on chain duty for this round of roadblock fun.

We have taken a break in an open field on top of a hill. Saien is on watch while I calculate our current location and how far we are from the airfield. Highway 79 is the shortest route, but a smaller county road may be our fastest considering the volume of cars that have been left abandoned on the highway. As I tuned through the AM and FM bands to see if I could hear anything from the high ground, I cleaned up the salvageable AK-47 as best I could. Using some oil and sandpaper taken from the maintenance bay of the dealership, I dismantled the weapon and removed the rust from it. I must say that it really does look like baling wire on the internals of the weapon. I took my knife and cut the jagged wooden edges where the bullet passed through the stock and sanded it down as best I could. The hole wasn't in a bad spot and the weapon didn't have a sling, so I used some of the paracord from my knife sheath and fashioned a makeshift sling for the weapon through the hole of the stock. It was now fully serviceable, with approximately forty-five rounds loaded between two magazines. I again coated the exterior liberally with oil and threw it in the back of the truck with a round in the chamber and safety engaged.

I scanned the area with my binoculars and saw no immediate threat from any direction. The morning sun was beating down but it didn't quite cut through the chill of the fall. For some reason it felt considerably colder than past Octobers I remembered. After catching the supply drop east of Carthage, the next high-density areas will be Nacogdoches, Lufkin and then Houston. Even in the helicopter, Baham didn't dare fly over downtown Houston. It's the nearest megacity that didn't get the nuclear treatment and could still have human survivors as well as potentially millions of undead. There is no doubt that I would be either dead or undead if we had crash-landed inside the Houston city limits.

1900

I'm on the roof of the airport administration building at the south end of the runway with Saien. My thoughts drift back to the tower with John months ago, but there is no tower at this airport. The drop occurred just as planned today at 1500, with one complication. The aircraft lost control and crashed at the north end of the runway a little less than a mile from where we are. Just after the gear left the cargo door, the aircraft seemed to have trouble stabilizing its center of gravity and went nose-down toward the runway.

I could see the nose start to pull up but it was too late to recover from the stall. The aircraft hit hard and started skidding down the runway until one of the wing tips snapped off and fuel started spraying everywhere. This caused the aircraft to wobble as it skidded, making the other wing dig into the concrete and cause the airframe to spin around like a top. By the time the aircraft came to rest it had lost both wing tips and two engines had been thrown about a thousand feet back in our direction.

Disregarding the gear that had just been dropped near our position, Saien and I made for the wreckage. I found it remarkable that the aircraft was not in flames and thought at the time that whoever was piloting the aircraft was a lucky bastard. That was until I made it to the front of the aircraft. There were no windows on the plane. The aircraft resembled a porcupine, as its spine was covered in antennas but there were no windows anywhere on the aircraft. The back cargo release door was still open where the aircraft had just dropped its payload. I asked Saien to boost me up so that I could peek inside. After getting inside the cargo bay and fanning away the fumes from the aircraft fuel, which will stick to my clothing for at least three days, I made my way to the front of the plane. On the way I noticed that the standard C-130 open bay toilet (with curtain) was not present, another indicator of what was going on with this aircraft.

I was over the center of the fuselage now. It was difficult to walk with the intense fumes and the fact that the aircraft was canted to one side, resulting in a funhouse affect. There was no door to the cockpit, only an olive drab curtain. I felt as if I were about to meet the Wizard of Oz as I swept the curtain aside, only to find what I had suspected since viewing the exterior of the plane—no pilots.

This aircraft was not an air breather, it was a modified C-130 UAV not unlike the Reaper orbiting over my head at this moment. The aircraft controls were still present, but there were no seats and no windows to the outside. There was a rack of computers with a fiber-optic connection leading into the avionics. No manufacturer markings were present on any of the equipment in this aircraft. There was no cabin pressure indicator on the instrument suite, and I saw no auxiliary oxygen tanks. This aircraft seems to have been stripped down to minimize weight for maximum unmanned endurance. Assuming this aircraft burned about four thousand pounds per hour at optimum burn bagged out with full fuel, it could have come from anywhere in the United States. The exterior had no unit markings or BUNO/BORT-type tail number.

It was painted in a dark-blue urban camouflage color scheme and appeared well maintained.

I went back to get Saien to see what he made of the aircraft and the situation. We both went forward to check out the cockpit again. Saien agreed that fiber-optic connection to aircraft avionics was not something he had ever read or heard about. The fumes were starting to get to me at this point, causing me to forget cause and effect once again. It was very dark in the interior of the aircraft, with only red lighting, probably so that the recovering maintenance crew could see the interior to accomplish a proper postflight checklist after landing.

Using the cargo webbing left over in the bay, I fashioned a quick ladder so that I could get out of the half-closed cargo door without twisting an ankle or worse. As I climbed down the ladder, the fresh afternoon air hit me and my brain started to recover from the fumes that were in the aircraft.

I watched in a relative daze as Saien climbed down.

I thought about the crash, and then I realized that it had made considerable noise and there was no doubt we'd have company by nightfall at this location. We hopped in the truck and got the chance to hit a hundred miles per hour on the runway with no obstructions in front of us for over four thousand feet. As we cruised back toward the supply drop we discussed again the unmanned aircraft and the implications of the crash. We got to the crash site and immediately noticed two pallets—one small and one large.

The large pallet had a vehicle sitting on it wrapped in plastic. The only marking on this drop were the letters DARPA engraved into the metal portions. Saien and I pulled out our knives and began cutting the plastic wrap and gathering the spare paracord and webbing and other parachute materials.

The vehicle was a desert sand buggy with a heavy roll cage and thick metal screen welded over the passenger/driver area. There was a place to stand on the back above the engine with a harness-type mast structure welded on the frame to keep the rider from falling. There were also what appeared to be two machine-gun mounting points. The vehicle could hold three people, with minimal gear, if any. There was a cylindrical "beer keg" tank on the back above the engine and heavy off-road tires all around. I entered the vehicle and started it up with no trouble, then drove it over behind the airport administration building near the roof access ladder and jogged back over to the smaller drop. Saien was already cutting into the cargo by the time I arrived, very much out of breath. I didn't think we had much time before more of the dead started to trickle in. The crash was much louder than a gunshot even from nearly a mile away and the engines that the aircraft threw are still popping and cracking somewhere in the distance.

The smaller pallet contained two large black Pelican cases that required a two-man lift and a heavy crate marked *Auto G Rounds*. There was also a smaller case in with the other cases. The large cases were stenciled *Auto Gatling A* and *Auto Gatling B* respectively. We heaved the cases into the back of the truck and hauled ass back to where I parked the buggy so we could think of our plan for the evening. I brought the case marked *Auto Gatling A* up to the roof with Saien's help, leaving case B in the back of the truck. Instead of parking the truck near the buggy, we parked it a hundred yards on the backside of the building in the event the undead swarmed the ladder area. We'd at least have two chances at an escape from the confines of the roof. The smaller case contained what was described by enclosed documentation as a long-range Geiger counter, enabling remote Geiger measurements.

The buggy is parked right under the ladder in plain view of the road, but the truck (with most of our gear) is parked in a less obvious position. After getting our essentials to the rooftop (food, water, shelter, weapons), we opened up the Pelican case to determine if it was worth the weight and trouble. Inside was a weapon that I had never seen before. It appeared that Remote Six was going to great expense to give me what I needed to stay alive. This weapon was a miniature baffled Gatling gun that fired small-caliber linked rounds. The instructions that came with the unit were similar to the Reaper lasing device instructions—they got the point across but that's it.

The unit included a low probability of intercept (LPI) radar that worked inclusively with a thermal-imaging sensor to act as an undead deterrent. The thing was built to last, and the diagram indicated several deployment options. The instructions stressed that the gun was not suppressed, only baffled (whatever that means).

Option one was to simply open the case and face it in the directions indicated by the arrows and flip the on switch, similar to claymore instructions. Anything moving below the temperature of ninety degrees Fahrenheit would be designated hostile and neutralized immediately at the rate of four thousand rounds per minute but preset to one-hundred-millisecond bursts. The onboard radar used a very low-power emitter (less than half a watt) and was stated effective for target acquisition out to two hundred yards.

The second mode of operation was buggy-mounted. The instructions were to loosen the twist screws and lift the unit out of the case (radar, fire computer, battery and weapon were attached to one steel bar that fit onto the buggy mount). The third mode of operation used the magnetic and suction trimounts included in the case. A diagram showed a schematic of the units mounted in tandem on top of a semi-truck trailer facing opposite directions in figure one of the manual and a schematic of the units using the mounts as tripods in front of a building in figure two.

The specifications claimed sustained operation for one hour between charges if under continuous firing conditions and twelve hours if in radar and thermal scan operating condition only. The manual went on to list vague limitations of the system.

The system was said to have a known issue of shooting at moving water, windblown tree branches and flying birds. The last was due to the thermal sensor's inability to pick out the avian heat signature due to size and the radar cross-section limitation of the system. There was a warning next to this section stating that use of the system when ambient air temperature reaches ninety-four degrees Fahrenheit is not recommended. No reasons were given for this warning in the documentation. The sun was about to go down at this point, so Saien headed down the ladder (with me covering) to fetch some ammunition for this weapon so we could see how option one works out tonight. If this thing uses radar coupled with thermal for target acquisition the night will have no effect on its operation. One final warning stood out ominously:

WARNING! The Automated Gatling system is a prototype weapon and shall not be relied upon for primary defense.

After reading the manual and putting it back into the case (loading instructions were printed and affixed to the lid), Saien returned with two cases of ammunition from the crate and we loaded the weapon, pointing it in the direction most likely to see undead incursion—the road.

I flipped the toggle to the on position and listened to the gun calibrate to its surroundings with a whir. The LPI radar made a sound similar to a camera click, probably acquiring an initial 3D map picture for ranging and elevation, and the system immediately went dormant. The only indication of activity was a dim glowing green LED on the rear of the gun.

The sun was nearly down and it was time to build a small fire in a coffee can to warm up some water for our dry food. Saien tore another page from *Milestones* and started the fire in the coffee can. I slid on my NVGs and walked opposite the fire looking over the edge of the roof out to the road. I did see movement in the distance. The movement was at the very edge of the capabilities of the goggles, but it was present. I could also see infrared indications of a small fire, probably where one of the aircraft engines landed after the crash. It was not visible without night vision and was probably contained to the internals of the engine. I whispered to Saien to angle the weapon left a few degrees to better engage the area I thought the threat would flow from. The radar recalibrated immediately after Saien stopped moving the system and the gun did one full gyro check before going dormant again. I kept my eye on what I thought would be the threat and saw nothing.

Saien poured some water into my canteen cup and I made my dinner for the night sitting Indian style with my NVGs pulled up above my eyes.

Saien asked again, "What does this writing do for you, how does it help? I'm sorry to ask again."

"No trouble, Saien. I don't mind. Much better than talking to myself."

I didn't really know what to say or how to answer his question, so I started at the beginning and told him the whole story of my vantage point and how it began for me. I told him that it was a resolution of mine to keep a documentation of my life because I felt that life was quickly passing me by, even though I was still relatively young in years. The last time I ever spoke to my grandmother was last year during vacation. She was old beyond her years and I loved talking to her and listening to her stories. She told me that the older people get the more they lose track of time, so a person should do everything he can to slow it down.

"Time here is finite, Junior," she said.

She was getting old and I thought in the back of my mind that this could be the last time I would see her. We ended our discussion with my memories of my great-grandmother, her mother. I told my grandma of how I remembered that great-grandmother was still sharp in her eighties and told me stories of how she crossed the mountains between Fort Smith and Fayetteville on a covered wagon and remembered when men rode horses to town and carried guns on their hips. She died the summer after she told me of the old frontier Arkansas.

Saien saw more now, I think. He understood that my grandmother was trying to get me to slow down and be aware of life and living. I suppose documenting all this is my only link to what I was and to what she was. He said that what he missed most was his sister. The last time he spoke to his sister was via email a month before all of this. She was living in Pakistan with her husband and was having a baby. Saien was going to be an uncle. He smiled as he said this and I kept my morbid, defeatist thoughts to myself as I wanted him to cherish his memory of his family. Saien drifted off to sleep after dinner and I hoped his mind was with his loved ones.

Lights Out

The rooftop is littered with spent casings. I was so exhausted last night I thought the ripping sound I heard was a dream. It was not until Saien was slapping the NVGs off my head that I woke to the sound of the mini–Gatling guns blazing away and hot casings hitting my face and neck. Saien put on the goggles and just stood there watching in the darkness. It was approximately 0300 hrs. After about five minutes of random gun bursts the radar recalibrated the weapon gyros and the system went silent once again. I asked Saien for the optics so I could see the battle damage. I checked out the roof first and noticed hundreds of rounds (not even a dent in the ammo supply) scattered all over the roof. Walking closer to the edge I could see scores of creatures on the ground. One of the creatures was still writhing on the ground but seemed to move without purpose or logic. Gun B seemed to jitter in response to the random movement on the ground so I decided to pull my sidearm and attempt a suppressed shot to prevent the gun's gyros from burning out. It took three shots to fully neutralize the creature. This was a small group of undead, but the sentries had made short work of them.

It seems that these devices could be worth their weight. After trying to go back to sleep for the final morning hours, Saien and I thought it a good idea to discuss how we would logistically handle our new gear. I told him that I thought it to be smart for the buggy to run point, followed by the truck. We both agreed it was sound to deploy an automated Gatling on top of the buggy until I thought of the operating limitations of the weapon. What if I turn on the weapon and it tracks Saien's truck? The truck is moving and would therefore be targeted by the thermal/radar sensors. If we rolled in a convoy we could not deploy the buggy while moving. We could not risk getting taken out. We'll also need to charge the batteries in the device using either the jumper cables and the truck or the solar panels. It was decided after discussion that I would drive the buggy and run about a quarter mile ahead of Saien to scout any potential bottlenecks in the highway. Saien would have the MP5 and AK loaded and ready in the event I got stuck or broke down in front. It was very cold in the mornings so I had no choice but to bundle up if I was going to go riding down the highway in basically a steel cage with four wheels. We'll wait until sunup before we pack our gear so that we can see if the guns missed any targets before they have a chance to get up and return the favor.

27 Oct

_0630_

We have been on the road for a few days since we acquired the buggy and automated weapons. There has been no contact via SATphone. The going has been very slow due to wreckage and the typical mayhem of undead corpses moving about on the highway. When either Saien or I clear wreckage, the other must cover the area with full attention. We have saved each other from attack numerous times recently. Days ago (or was it just yesterday?) we came upon an old hulk of a semi-truck jackknifed on the road. The trailer was riddled with high-caliber bullet holes and shrapnel marks, which piqued my curiosity. After establishing a moving perimeter in a circle around the wreck we moved in. We checked all possible angles and upon closer inspection discovered that this was a feed truck. The feed inside was long ago ruined by water damage and summer heat. Saien covered me as I jumped up on the running board and peered into the cab. Abandoned. No sign of trouble inside and no sleeper cab to hold surprises. This rig was meant for short haul. The owner probably lived not more than a hundred miles from where he abandoned his rig long ago.

This unknown blue-collar contributor to the dinosaur that was the U.S. economy could still be holding out somewhere, his back to a barricaded door.

Inside I noticed a CB radio. What caught my eye was that it appeared to be installed on a whim, wires still hanging out under the dash and around the gearshift. Following the antenna wire outside the cab I noticed that the antenna wasn't very tight either. I headed back to the truck bed to find the tin of spark plug chips so I could get inside the cab and see about salvaging the CB radio.

As I approached the truck, Saien whistled and pointed behind me. One of the creatures methodically approached, eyes locked on us like a lion stalking prey. Its hands were slightly bent and it walked in a half crouch, carefully moving forward. When I drew my sidearm the creature snapped into offensive mode and moved forward more quickly. I slowly squeezed my trigger and took its right cheek off. It kept coming, causing me to step backward until my retreat was stopped by a minivan. I kept squeezing off rounds until the creature fell not more than a foot from my boots. It still twitched for a few seconds, the last bit of evil seeping from its miserable frame.

I shook this off and went at the semi. With a small handful of spark plug ceramic I gave the driver's window a slow overhand pitch. The window shattered with very little sound. Most of the sound was a result of the broken glass hitting the running board and tank. The truck smelled very old inside. Months of mold and sun-bleached fabric particles whirled around the air inside the cab. I picked up the pieces of ceramic that I could find and went to work on the CB radio with my multitool. I checked to make sure I was being covered while I worked, as I had no choice but to keep the door open so I could get under the dash to remove the wires. This process took about fifteen minutes, as I wanted to avoid damaging the radio or the wires. As I removed the radio I noticed another radio under the seat, wrapped in its original wiring. The trucker's original CB must have given out, forcing him to purchase another and perform a truck-stop install.

I took the radio out of the semi and put it in the backseat of the pickup along with the antenna. Grabbing my binocs I went back to the truck and climbed up on top of the trailer. Scouting in all directions, I noticed that it seemed there were more undead about than in the days before. I yelled down the situation to Saien and we traded spots. Saien agreed that there seemed to be more undead in our area. Saien covered as I attempted to wire the CB radio to the truck. Salvaging parts from the surrounding vehicles, I was able to install the radio better than it had been installed on the rig. Finally, I checked the rig's fuel tank and determined that there was enough fuel inside to top off the truck. Saien and I worked to do this as we continually checked our surroundings for danger. After siphoning the diesel, we attempted to test the radio. The receiver worked, but we didn't know how effective our transmission was because there was no reply to our broadcast sent out in the blind.

I had the CB set to channel 18 so Saien could hear any transmission that might occur while we are on our convoy. Later in the day we came upon a small town, the same type of town you see in a Norman Rockwell painting. Although no living testament to Americana was present as we made our way down Main Street, there was an air of tension, and I felt that something watched from the windows. Something wicked. I kept scanning the second-story windows as I idled through. Since the outbreak occurred in the winter, the windows were closed. All but one—a second-story window above a flower shop. I stopped the buggy, jumped out and signaled Saien to cover while I secured the immediate area. A light breeze blew the thin curtain of the open window. Upon closer inspection of the area I noticed that the cars looked as if they were victims of a vicious hailstorm. Huge dents pocked the horizontal surfaces and the windows were all cracked from a great force. It didn't register logically in my brain, so I kept looking and noticed that the faces of the buildings were all damaged as if someone had pulled a great anchor chain along the side of them.

The place had been swarmed. It appears as if the huge mass that swarmed the streets of this small town had long since moved on, bringing the original townie ghouls with them in all the noise and commotion. I estimated that thousands had moved through here, so many, in fact, that they were climbing on cars and grinding the building fronts to get through.

Thinking of the radiated undead, I stayed clear of any dense metallic objects to avoid unnecessary exposure. There appeared to be a makeshift roadblock consisting of midsized cars at the other end of Main Street. Amazingly, the fronts of the cars had been pushed outward, away from where I was standing. Whatever size this swarm was, it had moved in the same direction Saien and I were headed. I can only hope it was months ago. Saien and I agreed that there was no advantage to checking out the second-floor room above the dead flower shop. We drove off toward the old roadblock and saw remnants of corpses with half their torsos in the street storm drain, and half out . . . just waiting to rot enough to fit down the drain and be washed away forever.

28 Oct

2100

We found shelter in an old power plant west of Nacogdoches, Texas. My maps give telltale indications that Nacogdoches was once a moderately populated area. The plant was completely surrounded by a tall chain-link fence, excluding the front and rear parts of the structure. In these areas a swing gate stood, designed to stop vehicles from entering without authorization. The gates looked newer than the rest of the plant and were probably a result of post-9/11 security measures. Saien and I had not seen a need to deploy the automated Gatling guns since our night on the airport rooftop. We had spent most of the nights since then sleeping on top of linked railroad cars, parking one vehicle near our position and one vehicle a few hundred yards farther down the track as a backup means of escape. This was how we found the power plant. The rain was coming down as my watch alarm went off, warning me it was two hours until sunset. Just as we were about to give up on finding a set of rail cars to provide shelter for the night, we came upon "Anaconda." Saien and I had been staying sane by playing stupid games like naming the trains after snakes, depending on color and how many rail cars were linked together. The past few nights were black snake and garter snake. We also tried to find as many states as we could represented on the license plates of abandoned vehicles. Approaching Anaconda, we could verify it was a very long train. Most of the green hopper cars were filled with heaps of coal for what seemed like miles.

We drove alongside the tracks counting cars. The ground under the cars was stained black from the months of rain seeping through the coal and hitting the ground. Nearing the end of the line, we saw the massive mountain of coal near the power plant and the rusting hulks of bulldozers used to move the black rock. One bulldozer was overturned and the rest were parked in a row. We counted 115 rail cars, not including the propulsion locomotive. Fog was rolling in as we neared the front access gate. I pulled the buggy inside and Saien followed in the truck. I got out and pulled the gate closed behind us, latching it into the hole in the ground with the T-hook. Saien was already doing what I was thinking. He pulled out the Gatling and we set it up at the access point. Setup took three minutes. I parked the buggy in a spot that would facilitate a quick getaway, and Saien and I drove to the back of the plant to set the second Gatling. It was raining and miserable and I was happy that these prototype devices depended on radar and thermal for target discrimination, because I couldn't really see that far in this mess.

As the sun moved lower behind the dark clouds I thought the same thought as I did many nights before. The Reaper UCAV overhead would soon be headed home along with my two five-hundred-pound laser-guided bombs. Finding a secure room with two exits didn't take long. We didn't have time to clear the area before night fell so we had to make the best of it. I've not heard a peep from the Gatlings and I like it that way.

29 Oct

1200

Saien woke me up this morning for no good reason—just to take a piss. Although I was annoyed by this, we had already agreed that neither of us should go anywhere without the other person in visual range. Grudgingly, I stepped outside behind him in the cold October morning. The sun was out and I realized that I needed to answer nature's call too. Saien faced the forward gate and I faced the aft gate as I helped to fill up a mud puddle from last night's rain. Looking out into the distance toward the cannon, I noticed that it was canted to the left. When I left it yesterday evening it was calibrated facing straight forward toward the access road. Putting away my gun and shouldering my rifle I stepped toward the gate. I walked for a few seconds before I heard Saien's steps behind me. As I got close enough I noticed the wind rolling the spent casings around at the base of the system. Only a few. Looking out into the street I could see two dead birds. I ran over to them and saw that they were ducks. It was then I realized I had walked into the field of fire of the Gatling and yelled for Saien to turn off the weapon. I picked up the two ducks by their necks and we rushed to get them ready to eat. No need to waste this golden opportunity for fresh meat.

I lopped off their heads with my knife as Saien ran off to get some coal from the massive black mountain. After forty-five minutes or so of preparation they were good enough to cook. We set up a campfire with the coal and kindling and had some duck for brunch. After eating most of the duck we began clearing the power plant and looking for anything of use in the area. I was getting sleepy with such a full stomach but I had no choice. I didn't want to waste the meat. As we attempted to add method to our area-clearing we came upon the stairs leading to the main control room on the second floor. At the top of the stairs was a corpse. It was so long dead that it looked like a sea bag full of bones. It was dark, forcing me to turn on my weapon light and use my muzzle to flip the remains of the corpse. I could barely make out the embroidery on the coveralls, but the man's name was Bill and he was a lead boiler mechanic. Walking up the stairs with Saien covering I could see gore marks on the heavy steel door. The door was locked. Saien asked me to cover him as he pulled out his pick set. Under his breath he complained that a rake would not work for this lock. He'd need to pick it pin by pin. After ten minutes he had the door unlocked and his foot planted to keep it closed if something was inside that wanted to come out. I knocked on the door and then put the muzzle of my rifle inside. No reaction. Saien swung the door open and our bright lights penetrated the darkness of the defunct control room, cutting through the floating dust. There was a wall of windows that offered a view down into the generator level below. It was so dark that I could see only the rounded generator tops. They looked like large round steel bales of hay in a field. After shining my light into the abyss I could see movement below. There were creatures on the generator floor. Number unknown. All observed were in coveralls.

We were relatively safe here above the mess below. A thick layer of dust covered the computers and switches and various mechanisms of the room. A large green logbook was sitting at the main desk in the center of the room with an ashtray, desk lamp and pen. I opened the book. It started with the date January 1985. After a few weeks of entries in 1985 the last 1985 entry read, "Log being decommissioned due to new computer logging system installation implementation, Signed, Terry Owens, Plant Manager."

The book was decommissioned in 1985 with only a couple dozen pages filled in. The next entry read:

Log recommissioned by Bill. End of the world. Computer systems unreliable. —Bill

January 15—We have sixty days of coal remaining and a train on the way to the plant.

January 16—Coal train arrived. No conductor aboard. Parking brake set.

January 17—We are down to 50 percent crew. The Department of Energy has authorized shutting down infested grids. We will be receiving the list soon.

January 18—List of deactivations received.

January 20—Using only 15 percent previous consumption.

January 21—We have one bulldozer operator remaining. Without her, we will be unable to feed the burners and generate juice. We have hired a walk-in to sit with her and shoot the things that keep trying to climb on the dozer.

January 31—Government announced city destruction plans. *Cities match January 18 DOE list.*

February 1—We're still here.

February 5—Plenty of coal, not much to do with it.

February 6—We are down to one burner and generating power for the plant only.

February 20—They are at the door. Getting out through vent below control panel. Shutting plant down. Only one left.

Lights out. —Bill

30 Oct
0700

The automated weapons have been going off all night. We have heard strange noises outside in the darkness that can only mean an undead posse in the vicinity of the front of the plant. We are packed and about to recon the area now that the sun is up.

0900

Automated weapons are spent and knocked over. Through Saien's scope we can see that the ammunition has been depleted and dozens of bodies lie around the emplacements. Some of the creatures still thrash about, their brains damaged enough by the Gatling to render them useless but not completely neutralized. We decided to hide the technology so that raiders with bad intent cannot salvage it. Leaving the plant soon.

Bridge of No Return

After countless hours and countless trials since the coal plant, Saien and I had one more major obstacle between the last stretch to Hotel 23 and us. Upon surveying our maps carefully, we only really had two options:

1. We could trek north and perhaps find a way across the river that lay ahead.
2. We could take the Livingston Bridge.

Most likely the bridge on our charts would be two lanes wide, based upon the highway it served for crossing.

Going north could put us close to a larger city as we attempt to go around the lake. The only drawback to option two was the unknown material condition of the bridge. After discussing various pros and cons we decided the bridge option made the most sense. Yesterday in the A.M. we adjusted our course south and a little west to rendezvous the bridge. I was taking the lead with the buggy as Saien trailed not far behind. The landscape was so monotonous that it barely warrants description . . . abandoned wrecks, packed SUVs, scattered emergency vehicles and of course the dead. Many times I have caught myself canceling them out like an expensive noise-canceling headset—a dangerous habit.

When the sun reached its highest point in the sky, I signaled from the buggy that it was time to pull over. I picked a spot at an abandoned group of rail cars. This system of shelter had not let us down to date, causing Saien and me to rely on it when possible. We attempted to warm up as we sat in the sun on top of a boxcar marked "Northern Railroad." The exterior of the car was decorated with much precollapse graffiti. Gang signs and cryptic hobo signals made up the bulk of the markings. After I finished inspecting one side of the car and started on the other, Saien called for me to come up. As I climbed the ladder to the car and looked up over the top I spotted Saien lying on his drag bag staring out to the east. I came over and asked him what was up.

He extended his bipod legs, rested the butt of the rifle on his jacket and said: "Look."

Peering through the powerfully magnified Japanese glass, I could see the reason for Saien's concern. Out to the horizon I could see a great cloud of dust swirling about. Without looking through the optic of Saien's rifle, one could mistake the dust cloud for a small rain cloud surging on the horizon. It seemed that we were seeing firsthand a possible undead swarm. It would be nothing like what we had encountered the day I met Saien. The mere presence of a swarm roughly ten miles in the distance did not mean they were headed directly to our position. It would be prudent to assume that they would be moving southwest in our general direction and upon contact with the river's edge would move either up- or downstream. The river could cause them to funnel in our direction or they could move upstream as a collective. We spent the rest of our shortened lunch attempting to verify the direction and speed of the mass, without success.

Later//

We made the best time we could to the ingress point. Stopping short of the bridge on a high knoll we conducted some reconnaissance. A rusting Abrams tank was pulled crossways in the road right in front of the bridge. The paint still held, but rust marks streaked down the thick armored steel portions. Shooting a reading with the Geiger revealed that the tank was emitting medium amounts of radiation. It was nothing immediately deadly, but I would not want to spend a few nights inside. There were gore marks all over the tank and civilian vehicles in the vicinity were heavily damaged, much like to the old town Main Street we had passed through days before.

Before heading down the hill to the bridge we surveyed the dust cloud. The cloud was visibly growing and there were very faint sounds on the wind that unsettled me to the point that I had to make a conscious effort to remain in the game. Moving down the hill, I was demoralized by the size of the bridge. It was so long that the vehicles on the other side looked like specks in the distance.

Nearing the rusting Abrams's hulk I could see that the hatch was barely open. I jumped onto the tank and strong-armed the hatch. Geiger readings remained constant. I shined my light inside, causing a bird to fly out of the opening, scaring the hell out of me. The tank was clear.

There was no way to get our vehicles past the tank without moving it. Towing the tank was a nonstarter. Its weight was many times that of the truck. There were operating manuals tucked into a storage cabinet near the controls. I followed the instructions and was able to start the turbine after three attempts. The tank was still operational, but it seemed that the jet fuel inside was contaminated, as I never got the turbine speed up to optimal operating temperature as indicated in the manual. This caused all movements to be delayed and sluggish. The controls on the tank were like bicycle bars with a hatch open light, master caution, panel dim, reset and master warning light mounted above the steering controls. Right below the handlebar was a small lever with R, N, D and L transmission settings.

After a short warm-up period I put the tank in D and activated the throttles, causing the tank to lurch forward. The smell of burning jet fuel permeated the tank and everything inside it. After stopping the tank I was able to leave it running so that I could help Saien get the vehicles onto the bridge.

After getting the buggy and truck safely on, I ran back to the tank to repark the beast. As I approached I noticed that someone had spray-painted the word "TROLL" on the side of the turret. I climbed back in and attempted to put the tank back. I destroyed the guardrails on both sides of the bridge and nearly drove off into the water before giving up and accepting a 90 percent solution. There was a gap large enough for a motorcycle to squeeze through on one side. Before leaving the tank, I flipped on the radio and put on the headset. Every frequency I tuned in on the SINCARS radio returned with static not unlike a jamming-type signal. I could hear RF energy but nothing was being relayed. I sent out a distress call on 282.8 MHz and 243.0 MHz to Hotel 23, letting them know my situation and position. If this area was being jammed it did not mean H23 was also. For jamming to be effective, the jamming emitter must be directed at the receiver, as jamming the transmitter would do nothing on the receiving end.

I repeated my transmission three times before shutting down the gas turbine and heading back to the vehicles. The dust cloud was still present on the horizon. I thought of the tank and how useless it would prove as its lack of fuel economy, coupled with its crushing weight, rendered it a hindrance. I doubted the bridge could take the weight. We were halfway across the bridge when we first made visual contact with the swarm. The sound billowed like great tubas reverberating in my chest.

In a stroke of merciful luck they broke into view two miles upstream. On Matagorda Island during my stint at the docks, I observed the creatures standing at the water's edge, hesitant to enter. I know that when they hit the shoreline they will follow it until they come to a crossing point. Saien and I kept clearing the bridge roadblocks, fitting the wrecks where we could on the left or the right. It was like the old sliding puzzle game where you tried to fit fifteen tiles in chronological order with only one empty space with which to rearrange the numbers.

When we were three-quarters of the way over the bridge the creatures hit the water's edge. The wails and moans jabbed at the front of my brain and nearly knocked me off my feet. There were thousands. Later I would discover via SATphone text message that over five hundred thousand undead were part of Swarm T-5.1 as designated in a cryptic Remote Six message text.

As the head of this long, terrible viper hit the water in the distance upstream, I could see the wake of white water, and the wails of frustration and primal hate intensified. Saien and I kept working, careful not to make too much noise. Using my multitool, I disabled the horn on the truck so that it could not be accidentally pushed during our clearing operation, as has happened before.

An armored car with four heavily damaged run-flat tires was giving us trouble because of its weight. We worked the problem for nearly thirty minutes as the legion of undead built up on the shore upstream. Their radius was growing so large that I could make out individual creatures in the distance. While attaching a tow chain to the old Ford next to the armored car, I heard a familiar shrill and instinctively reached for the M-4 slung across my chest. Checking the clear plastic viewport on the polymer mag I knew I was as ready as I could be.

I scanned the area around the vehicles and heard the undead moans loud and overlapping. Some of them sounded like gurgling. I stepped to the guardrail of the bridge and peered over. In the deep-flowing, chilly water below I could see dozens of creatures thrashing and moaning. Water had freely seeped into their dead lungs, causing their sounds to be even more frightening. Looking upstream I could see the waterway heavily dotted and clumped with the creatures flowing downstream from the mass and under the bridge where I stood.

A handful of the creatures drifting at the whim of the river current caught sight of me standing above them. Their clawed hands reached skyward as they passed below the bridge. Despite our best efforts we were unable to budge the Ford, as the armored car was wedged too far into the other lane. The cars that we had repositioned behind us gave room to retreat but there were too many undead to consider that option. The number and size of the swarm less than two miles upstream was growing in our direction and soon we would no doubt be in detection range, if we weren't already. I made the decision and instructed Saien to put the vehicles in a line in front of the repositioned cars, giving me a clear shot to the armored car. If we could not make it over the bridge without our vehicles the undead would pace us indefinitely and eventually get us.

With only my M-4 and extra mags I sprinted back to the other side of the bridge. Leaving the hatch open I jumped into the tank and started the massive turbine engine. A Christmas tree of fault lights illuminated: "Low Turbine Temp. Hatch Open." Pushing the throttle, I steered away from the bridge, impacting the metal guardrail. The screeching of metal was deafening even over noise from the undead.

The sound caused an audible retort from the creatures below and I forced myself not to waste valuable time looking at the physical reaction of the mass. I took the gamble and rolled the tank onto the bridge, pushing the throttles forward to gain momentum. I could feel the bridge shake below the treads as the vehicle's speed reached 30mph. I clipped one of the cars as I sped past Saien on a collision course with the armored car.

Throttling back to 10mph to avoid injury, I was reminded of physics and the mass differential between the puny paperweight of the armored car and the behemoth tank. Like brothers at a poolside cookout, the war machine easily pushed the car over the guardrail and into the river.

I made every attempt to throttle back to idle but the spin-down time of the turbines was not responsive like that of a car or truck engine. What I thought were the brakes only complicated my problem by yawing the tank at an awkward angle.

The tank followed the armored car into the deep below.

Time slowed to a crawl as the steel brick of a vehicle rolled over the guardrail, tipping like a seesaw. As the tank free-fell ten feet to the water's surface, I tried to leap through the hatch. I was halfway out as the cold water rushed inside, holding me in place, taking me into the green murky abyss of the river.

After the water flow equalized and the immediate shock of the cold water abated, I swam to the surface, following the air bubbles. I could make out the bodies in the water, their legs moving as if they were trying to walk as they floated down river. My rifle slapped my back and head as I sidestroked to the surface. When I hit the air I wiped the water out of my eyes, brought my rifle above the water and took shots at the undead around me. After killing three I noticed the river was taking me under the bridge. I screamed for Saien to move the vehicles off the bridge as I made for the shore, kicking and brushing past the corpses that I had just shot.

After I hit the beach I could see the horde approaching the bridge. The tank crash, the gunshots and the truck noises obviously had had a hand in making them crazy. Saien had parked the truck and was making for the buggy to get it across. There was no time. Whistling loudly, I signaled him to fall back and cover me. The buggy would be an acceptable combat loss.

Taking cover behind a deadfall on the bank, I surveyed the bridge. Carefully picking a spot between support pillars on the undead side, I lased the target. Forcing my body to stop trembling from the cold water, I held the dot on the bridge as the tone increased in frequency until it was steady. Four seconds later a five-hundred-pound bomb rocked the bridge, collapsing a section of it forever. I was sitting there surveying the damage when I was startled by a corpse hitting the rocks ten feet behind me, a half-second before I heard Saien's shot. Saien waved and signaled me to come toward him up the bank.

The river seemed to be full of bodies as I ran up the bank to the truck. Through my binocs I witnessed numerous joggers on the opposite bank, many with severe radiation burns to their exterior, verified by Geiger.

Rally

Today marks the first contact with Hotel 23 personnel in over forty five days. A week has passed since our departure from the bridge, and we are currently sitting northwest of Houston, Texas. We started monitoring the CB radio at night after noticing that there was less static present. Last night Saien and I found a telephone company utility building surrounded by a high chain-link fence. After picking the padlock (with a tire tool) we spent the night inside the perimeter sleeping in the truck, listening to the fading static. At about 0100 hrs we heard the signal key but no voice. We instantly keyed back with a distress response. There was no intelligible reply for an hour but we kept transmitting.

The signal faded in at about 0215 with: ". . . this is Gator Two on search and rescue in Sunny Side Texas over . . ."

I replied with the Dragonfly call sign and was greeted by Corporal Ramirez, United States Marine Corps.

"Sir, good to hear your voice. We picked up your distress signal on the ninth and departed the following day in the direction of the coordinates you relayed. Movement has been slow due to the large groups of those things we have encountered and road wreckage. What's your position?"

After I gave my position to Ramirez he gave me instructions to sit tight while he planned a route for the two-vehicle convoy to meet. I asked for an update over the radio of the situation at Hotel 23. The corporal replied by telling me that it was not a good idea to give the update over the radio and that there were some things happening that he needed to tell me about in person.

After some radio silence, Corporal Ramirez came back up on the CB.

"Sir, time for payback. I get to save an officer's ass, just like before the world went to shit. The rally point I recommend is San Felipe, not far from your position. I propose we meet at the north end of town at the 1458 before the bridge. There is a field three hundred meters southeast of the bridge. The town is small and there should be a minimal hostile footprint."

I consulted my maps and agreed to the rally point, in a non-joking manner, on the radio.

1200

We rallied to Corporal Ramirez at 1000 hrs. After a short firefight with a dozen or so of those things, we set up a small perimeter and debriefed for a bit in the safety provided by the LAV. While the gunner manned the crew-served weapon, Ramirez told me of the oddities going on back home. From the armored vehicle, he took out a small binder of written reports and a few photographs. I recognized John's handwriting. Ramirez stated that a few weeks back an aircraft started appearing in the skies above Hotel 23. I immediately identified the aircraft as a Global Hawk UAV. The picture was marked as having been taken with a handheld digital camera with an 18-200mm lens and I could just make out something large mounted under the fuselage. The picture was not clear enough for me to identify the payload, and I didn't remember the Global Hawk being weaponized.

We continued to generally debrief and I introduced all the Marines to Saien and told them the stories of how he had saved my life more than once since we had met. The Marines seemed to be very friendly toward Saien, but he was visibly nervous around them for reasons that I could not waste time trying to discover. I also warned the Marines that there was an undead mass unlike any they had ever seen about eighty miles northeast of where we were now. We had destroyed a section of the bridge and tried to line cars up in roadblocks behind us along the roads we traveled when possible. This would slow them down but not stop them. I told them of the C-130 drop plane, dead drops and the unusual equipment that I had attained from a group known only cryptically as Remote Six.

This prompted everyone into action, and we decided to roadblock the 1458 bridge with abandoned cars before we did anything else. Using the LAV, we put four cars into position and smashed them together. This would slow any oncoming mass of undead and increase the gap between us. This bridge was too close to Hotel 23 to destroy, as it may prove logistically valuable in the future. I saw a billboard a few hundred yards away, threw Saien my binocs and asked him to climb the board and check out the area. One of the Marines went with him for backup.

I asked everyone to pull back from the bridge a few hundred yards south. After Saien returned he told me of a dust cloud at the very edge of his visibility to the north. We decided that this could mean the mass of undead or it could simply be weather. We were roughly fifteen miles from Eagle Lake Airfield, according to the map in the LAV. Incidentally, we were also close to Interstate 10. Before nightfall we'll attempt to cross the I-10 threshold and head south a few more miles to add a safety buffer from the interstate.

2100

It had been seven months since I had been on foot in this area of Eagle Lake. Not much has changed. The moon illuminated the road and abandoned cars and airport tower and also the more frightening things in the dark. Earlier today when we caught sight of the I-10 overpass in the distance, we sped up, weaving to avoid the wrecks. The LAV was moving at 60mph in front of us and we were keeping up. As we roared under the overpass I heard a thump hit the truck and looked back. One of those creatures had walked off the overpass, hit the closed tailgate of the truck and tumbled behind into the ditch. As I kept driving more of them fell from the overpass. Some got to their feet and some didn't.

After we put I-10 far behind us, things got a little easier. We stayed on county road 3013 until we were on the outskirts of Eagle Lake, very near the airfield. I consulted the notes I had on the area and we decided to convoy into the airfield complex, set up a perimeter for a couple of hours and then plan the rest of the short trip back home. Upon arrival at the airfield and exploration of the hangar, I saw the dark smudges of the remains of the creatures I had killed months ago still under a blue tarp in the corner. The summer heat had really done a number on the remains. Using my flashlight, I could see the deformed copper-jacketed bullets that I had fired sitting in the rotting liquid goo of the dead.

I was reminded by my journal that I should also be watchful for any living human enemies that may be present in this area. I remembered the large crosses I had discovered, months ago, on my last trip en route to this area, with creatures crucified upon them. We sat under the illumination of a red-filtered M-4 light and planned our route home.

Home

16 Nov

0430

We've traveled to Hotel 23 from Eagle Lake under cover of darkness. The place looks dramatically different, with the concrete barrier complete around the perimeter. The civilians and military have succeeded in working together and salvaged enough of the concrete highway barriers to form a formidable wall. I doubt that even the tank I sent to the bottom of the river could get through this wall without getting stuck. More to follow after I have fully debriefed John and especially Tara.

17 Nov

0500

My sleep schedule is ruined because of the change in my surroundings. Tara is sleeping next to me. I'm ashamed to have blocked her out of my thoughts for so long during my period of mechanically induced exile. This is something that only a veteran can really understand. Sometimes before and during deployments you seem to detach yourself from the ones you love just to make things hurt a little less.

Using the notes in my journal I spent the entire day resting, rehydrating and debriefing John, the Marines, Tara and anyone else who wanted to listen. Saien quietly listened, and I could tell he was absorbing my debriefing. John had not sat idle in my absence and had penetrated several different networks on the military mainframe. He also confirmed what the Marines had hinted at when we met at the rally point. Despite only getting the Cliff Notes version from Ramirez, I still discovered that someone had been jamming my receiver. John said he could hear my transmissions and did in fact pick up my distress beacon coming in loud and clear on October 11 as well as the distress call made on November 9.

I'm still in shell shock and can't overstate how great it was to see everyone. Laura asked how my vacation went, and I told her that it went very well and thanked her for asking. She asked me if I brought her a souvenir and I told her that it was not a fun vacation but more of a working vacation. She understood what had happened to me—I could see the intelligence in her eyes. Her parents did a good deed by shielding her, but she knew. Danny walked up, punched me in the arm and said: "Good to see you!" He then proceeded to give me a hug. Little Annabelle even gave me a bark and a lick on the nose to signify that she had missed me or at least noticed my return. Dean immediately tried to feed me and had noticed that I had dropped quite a few pounds since she last saw me. I suppose it was true. The man I saw in the mirror looked like one of those guys from a reality survival television show after a couple of weeks in the wild. Multiply that by ten and that was about where I was—wild-eyed and hairy.

1100

After a shower and a shave (my first real cleansing in over a month) I felt much better. I had a horrible rash on my waist and legs from sleeping in my clothing for so long. I suppose the last wash for my clothes had been on the sailboat millennia ago. Tara said that she needed to talk to me later today after I was finished debriefing John. Something wasn't right. Something I didn't notice until this morning. Dean found me this morning around 0630 and forced me into a haircut. I now felt fairly presentable, with the only visible evidence of my absence being minor cuts, scars, bruises, weight loss and the slight limp I have incurred from my severe shin splints.

This morning was spent with John, Saien and the senior enlisted Marines. I flipped back and forth in my journal and went over key incidents during my time away. I showed everyone to the best of my knowledge where the original crash site was as well as Saien's and my rough route back to Hotel 23.

We then went into discussions about Remote Six. I passed around all the hardware I had obtained since being exposed to this organization as well as the provided documentation that I had retained. The materials passed around were: the maps of eastern Texas with the drop locations and other symbology, the M-4 with attachments, the automated Gatling manuals, iridium SATphone, experimental fuel treatment and a few other odds and ends. We deliberated the entire morning over the materials, the documents and the notes I took on all communications with Remote Six via the SATphone.

One of the ideas we came up with was that Remote Six was some sort of secondary government, previously established in case the main government was knocked out. The term "Fifth Column" was also discussed as it relates to the data at hand. John pulled up the computer screen on one of the flat-panel displays in the secure compartmented information facility (SCIF) in which we were located. He pulled up a network file system that he had cracked not long ago, and this referenced many government facilities on a map that indicated "status GREEN." The only location out of the many on the list of active facilities that I recognized was the pulsing green dot sitting just outside Las Vegas, Nevada.

An hour into the meeting I was concentrating on the discussion when I felt a hand on my shoulder from behind. I jumped out of my seat and slapped my chest to reach for my sidearm. I wasn't wearing my load-bearing vest.

It was Tara. My open hand shook uncontrollably and I had no way to explain what I was experiencing. My mind was still out there in the void. Lost. I couldn't hold a pistol steady in my hand if I tried. Tara brought down some coffee for the group. I apologized to her and explained that I was still a little jumpy from my extended stay outside the wire. Of course she nodded and said that she understood and kissed me on the cheek and walked out.

I quickly summed up the major points of the meeting and went after her. I caught up to her in the passageway and she embraced me quickly.

"I honestly thought you were gone."

"So did I. There were times that . . ."

"Don't talk about it. Let's just enjoy the time we have now. The time we have been given."

"I think you are right. Let's try."

At this point John rounded the corner with a "one more thing" comment and Tara just laughed and told John he could borrow me but he had to return me in one piece.

John laughed and told her that he'd do his best.

John had found a networked program that was embedded in the overhead imagery system previously discovered. Although many of the satellites were not functional and have probably re-entered the atmosphere, some of the multimission satellites were still working. The radiation sensors seemed to still be operational, and the satellite broadcast indicated hot zones overlaid on a United States map. This system was able to finally give us the locations of most if not all of the fallout areas as well as intermittent hits on probable locations of undead swarms if they had been radiated or had come from areas that were.

John had spent the last few weeks cataloging areas and tracking movements of any hits that seemed to be mobile. He kept his documentation on paper in the event the system failed, as so many have before. The system name was "Wasteland." It was probably named by a cynical USSTRATCOM/NORTHCOM/DHS programmer before all of this happened, as a casualty assessment tool. John noted that this system had not been working for the past two days.

We were all concerned about the Reaper that was probably orbiting over the complex. I expressed that there was really nothing we could do about it as we had no offensive capability against airborne targets and the Reaper was never directed against me or Saien. I had little doubt that the aircraft was data-linked back to some command center and that it was receiving real-time video feeds of Hotel 23. John commented that the aircraft carrier had suffered an accident resulting in loss of SATcom radios, which is why we lost contact with them for a short period a couple of months ago. The SITREP was sent out over a secure network via the existing WAN between our two units that were set up via the working overhead Inmarsat network. We had acquired a few of these phones on a scavenging mission a long time ago and set up a communications network with the carrier in the event the main system went down.

The SITREP message reason for comm loss was: "SATcom system damaged due to failure of radiated undead containment measures." I cursed so loud it made everyone jump.

I said rhetorically to the group: "Didn't we warn those idiots about this?"

I asked John when the last time we received a SITREP from the carrier was. He told me that he had been unable to establish a good Inmarsat connection since my return. After he said this it was as if everyone got the same idea at the same time and the light bulb above our heads got bright.

The jamming signal was following me and had been since Remote Six located me. Now the whole compound seemed to be cut off from the outside world with no early warning systems or network access.

18 Nov

0500

We received a transmission on the SATphone yesterday. Since my arrival I had had a guard stationed topside with the phone from 1200 to 1400 in the event contact was attempted. It was the same mechanical voice instructing the recipient to look at the text screen. The text gave instructions to log into the network using my common access card (CAC) and initiate launch in accordance with Executive Directive 51. Sets of coordinates were given for the launch as well as the physical location of auxiliary control. John and I discussed this after the phone lost connection and spent the rest of yesterday investigating and analyzing the information.

By 1900 we had made a startling discovery. John, Will and I had originally thought that this compound held only one nuclear intercontinental ballistic missile. After going through the instructions and initiating the subroutines we found that there were two more nuclear missiles at the ready in silos a thousand yards to the west of the compound awaiting launch sequence. Apparently, the only way to launch the warheads is to initiate the proper coding sequence while my CAC card is in the card slot reader. There is a small chip on the card with encryption that acts like the keys to the system. I remember that my card was recoded months before during one of the carrier supply drops. We were given launch codes and coordinates via the Iridium, so in theory it would be possible to launch the warheads.

John wasted no time plotting the coordinates given on a chart. They coincided to a location within six miles of the flag-ship carrier's position of intended movement as indicated on their last situation report. They were operating in a location in the Gulf of Mexico west of Florida and conducting replenishment operations. Remote Six was seemingly trying to destroy the carrier battle group, for reasons unknown. I did not refuse to comply during the text session and the screen continued to provide instructions on a loop with the final text question: "Have you initiated?"

The loop flashed four times until I finally ended the call. We then went searching for auxiliary control. The Marines found the door to the second control node first.

The doorway resembled an old cellar bulkhead. Heavy foliage and deception netting concealed the entryway. The door was made of steel and required a cutting torch to get inside. I saw no need to stay while the Marines secured auxiliary control and left them to the task of ensuring that no former residents of Hotel 23 remained inside.

18 Nov

1900

The text repeated again yesterday and today ordering the launch sequence to be initiated. The only difference was that the coordinates given varied by a couple of dozen nautical miles. They were adjusting for the movement of the carrier fleet. I asked the communications officer to send a message in the blind to the carrier to attempt to warn them again. He will be repeating the message every hour until I rescind the order.

The team sent to AUXCON breached the door and discovered that it was just a carbon copy of Hotel 23's main control center, living quarters and all. The only problem was that no subterranean tunnel connected the two control centers. There was a passageway reported in AUXCON that indicated an egress tunnel similar to the main control center layout. It was not yet known where the AUXCON egress tunnel let out in relation to the main egress tunnel. I was briefed that there were a few items of interest in AUXCON that I needed to see and that it was safe and clear for visitors.

Jan passed me in the hallway and asked how I was doing. I told her that I was fine and that I needed to talk to her about the status of medical care at Hotel 23. We sat down for a bit discussing the new (to me) military personnel she was working with and I found that they were very well trained and had seen a lot of battle in the past few months. She had learned a few things from the enlisted medics and they had learned a few things from her.

They had successfully conducted a few scavenging trips to secluded hospitals (both human and animal) in the area. She described one particular supply run, to a small-animal hospital a few miles away. Being the resident doctor, she had volunteered to go on the medical raids with the convoy to help identify useful items. The marines had cleared out the Happy Paws clinic minutes before Jan entered with Will. He insisted he go with her, and what husband would not? The stench was of course of dead flesh, which put the operators on high alert. They held their suppressed SMGs tight to their shoulders with flashlight on full one-hundred-lumen setting. One operator was positioned in front of Jan and Will and one behind, in pincer formation. That is how it is done. They entered the kennel area, and to their horror found cages with dogs long dead inside.

Some people take it really bad when seeing the evidence of an animal's suffering. I am no different. Hearing her story wrung my gut, and hers too, as she told it. Her eyes strained as if peering off into infinite space as she told of the cages with rotting dog corpses and the broken teeth and bloody claws from the dogs' using their last bit of strength in a vain attempt to bite and scratch their way out of the metal cages. The kennel was not full, only about 40 percent. The charts on the sides and floors near the cages showed the same story. Owner on vacation and will return at so and so time. All the dates were January. In her description I could see the animals lying in their cages with eternal snarls of agony penetrating the wire metal doors.

Hurricane

We were attacked.

It is very dark outside now. We sent the word out to the battle group in the blind over radio warning them of the intentions given to us on the SATphone. We had no way of knowing whether the ship had received our communiqué. The radio-jamming signal continued throughout that morning, as it had since my return and before.

We lost dozens the morning the device was dropped on us. Retribution for not launching? Even if we had launched, they would have likely hit us anyway. What would be the point in leaving us alive? Nothing makes any sense.

The now-deaf topside observers wrote on a whiteboard what they had witnessed. A whistling sound—getting higher in pitch— was the last sound they heard until the javelinlike Hurricane beacon slammed down into the ground, splitting one of the civilians in half from shoulder to hip.

The device immediately started transmitting its deadly payload, a sound so unimaginably loud that it immediately caused deafness in anyone who was above when it hit.

The device was reminiscent of a huge bee stinger—the magnified view of the top of the stinger pulsating, pumping poison into the arm, the ground. The device was stuck deep into the earth, slightly canted to one side, and was louder than words can describe.

We could clearly hear the barrage of noise and feel the vibrations through the thick steel and concrete from inside the bowels of Hotel 23. John immediately turned his available turret cameras onto the device and the other cameras to the perimeter areas overlooking the visible horizon. It was only a matter of seconds, maybe minutes until the sound reached the hardened internal ear canal hairs of the dead hundreds of miles away, turning their attention to this location.

They would geolocate the compound like a fleet of FCC vans hunting a pirate radio station. John transmitted an emergency message in the blind requesting help and a brief situation report on what had happened.

All available men and women in a position of leadership met and discussed alternatives. No one was allowed topside without good reason and double hearing protection. Even with the added hearing protection the sound was louder than standing next to the speakers at a rock concert. Watching the video surveillance, I could see that the sound disrupted and tilled the ground. The intense sonic energy moved the lighter civilian vehicles parked near it, not unlike a cell phone vibrating around on a coffee table. The device must have lodged itself twenty feet or more into the ground on impact.

All attempts to destroy the noise mechanism ended in failure. It seemed to be constructed from thick case-hardened steel or some other alloy. The internals at the top of the javelin were sealed. An already deaf Marine volunteered to try to destroy it by climbing to the top with a tool bag and a grenade. He didn't make it off the ground when he attempted to bear hug his way up. The device vibrated at such a resonance that every part of bare skin that touched it was sheared off in layers. Shots were wasted at full auto attempting to penetrate the top of the device. LAVs were systematically rammed into it.

Nothing worked.

I was in one of the LAVs. The beacon sound was barely dampened by the thick armor. The sound was so intense that it seemed to steal every breath. We established a perimeter with backs to the device, waiting for the undead to appear on the horizon. There were no indications at first. I peered through the thick-layered glass of the armored vehicle just as another object slammed into the ground two hundred yards from my position, nearly hitting one of the other LAVs. Shortly after the crash, I heard the distinct sound of supersonics overhead and caught the wing flash of an F/A-18 Super Hornet. After the small explosion subsided and the fire died down I could see by the wreckage what the craft had been—a Reaper UCAV, probably the same aircraft that had shadowed me for all that time after my crash and until my return to Hotel 23.

Immediately, the radio light flashed inside the vehicle, indicating a valid signal. Putting the headset on I could hear a voice speak clearly and concisely, warning repeatedly that there were A-10 Thunderbolts rolling in on our position from Scholes International in Galveston. The "Hawgs" were targeting the barrage beacon with 30mm cannons and they were asking all friendlies to rally east of the target so as to minimize fratricide.

Time to on top: twenty-one minutes.

After the Hawg controller finished transmitting, I could hear a faint signal and a voice identifying itself as the carrier air boss. He was ordering a division of F-18s to drop dumb iron bomb payloads on our position to complement the more precise optically aimed Warthog 30mm cannon strikes. With the jamming signal apparently destroyed along with the Reaper UCAV, I transmitted back to John and the others on a discreet channel what I had heard and that we were going to rally east a few hundred yards. The command center tuned in to the action on the radio as we started the engines and rolled east. We sat on a knoll overlooking the compound. There were dozens of undead already drawn to the beacon from the front of the compound area near the large steel double doors.

From our vantage point we saw iron hell rain down all around the compound via a division of F-18s dropping iron bombs onto pockets of undead. One F-18 used its airframe as an offensive weapon by going supersonic a foot over groups of undead to rip them apart or disable them with concussion. Explosive forces violently shook our vehicles as John reported in via radio below that the lights were flashing underground. After ten minutes of bombardment I overheard the codeword "winchester" on the radio, signifying that the fighters were out of ordnance and returning to mother. The sonic beacon had survived the bombing runs with no damage. The cursed device continued to transmit our position for all the dead to hear for miles around. Of course, the fighter supersonics didn't help our cause much either.

The LAVs remained in formation east of the beacon as the first of the Hawgs rolled in hot, conducting a first pass before slamming the beacon with a mix of tungsten and depleted uranium 30mm rounds. Gaping up at the A-10s I could not help but wonder how they could fly so slowly.

The vulcan cannons began to grunt loudly, causing something that I had not expected . . .

The Hawgs cut through the sonic beacon javelin device as if it was paper. It was utterly disintegrated into shards, except for a few feet of alloy nub sticking out of the ground. The immediate silence shocked my system more than the overhead air strikes. I flung open the hatch, yanked the brass out of my ears and watched the rest of the strike from the top of the LAV. I could see Saien doing the same thing a few dozen meters to my right. He had his rifle sitting on the turret and I could see him scanning to the distance in the direction of what was quickly becoming a vast dust storm on the horizon.

Getting back down inside the LAV, I turned the vehicle optics to my face and looked out to the horizon. The dust plumes looked identical to the cloud surrounding the horde that Saien and I had encountered previously. There would be no stopping them. Not with a thousand A-10s loaded for bear. I immediately radioed down to John and the rest to prepare for evacuation from the facility immediately.

There were hundreds who needed evac. The carrier was steaming at full speed to rendezvous the coast to conserve helicopter fuel. Only the women and children and those who were injured would evacuate via simultaneous multihelicopter trips from the facility to the ship. The Hawgs were given instruction to intercept the horde just a few miles away and swarm around above them in an attempt to stall or draw the undead in another direction. We do not know if this tactic will work, as there are only three aircraft with enough fuel to attempt the distraction operation. Over the radio, I heard one of the A-10 pilots say that he had to switch to manual reversion for his flight controls and that his hydraulics system had experienced a catastrophic failure. He declared an emergency and a few seconds later I saw him buzz over our heads, scramming back to base. I hope he makes it.

I'm sitting on back of a deuce and a half waiting on the remaining carrier helicopters to pick up the rest of the high-value assets before we roll. The current plan is to convoy southeast to the Gulf of Mexico and then rendezvous the USS *George Washington* via small boat. We have multiple hard cases full of intelligence to be analyzed onboard the carrier. John backed up the entire H23 mainframe before we welded the doors shut, turned off the lights and bugged out. The intelligence was marked for immediate review and dispatched with the first available outgoing helicopter.

CVN

The carrier is in poor shape. There is red rust everywhere, much more than the expected haze gray of a well-maintained warship. There is no safe way to perform material condition maintenance, as every dry dock port will most likely be overrun with the creatures. The convoy operation to the carrier did not come without a hefty price. We lost dozens of good men. We were being attacked on all fronts as we cleared countless old roadblocks and wrecks. Most casualties occurred as a result of waiting for the small boat that would take us to the ship. With the carrier's large size, she could not berth near the shore. She had to anchor out a distance and send smaller craft to extract us at a rate of two boats per trip.

The operation was delayed an hour due to choppy seas. We were forced to defend ourselves against hundreds of undead with our backs to the Gulf. Many retreated by jumping into the water, choosing the cold waters over being eaten. We set up chain-linked islands of LAVs floating offshore, providing crew-served weapon support from the water's haven. We did what we could until the boats arrived. The dead we were fighting up to this point were likely the leading edge of Swarm T-5.1. The information previously transmitted by Remote Six suggests that they have somehow tagged the known swarms in the United States and seem to be attempting to designate and track them from a distance. A rotating sortie of Hawgs did what they could to draw a line in the sand by cutting the horde down by about 0.001 percent at a time. In the end it might have saved our lives by buying us those extra few seconds we needed to board the boats. The pilots reported an undead stream for miles and miles.

We kept fighting, expending all small-arms and crew-served ammunition. We could hear the powerful sound of the small-boat diesel engines behind us as the undead broke our fifty-yard perimeter kill barrier. Just as they were overtaking our position and reaching our front-line defenders, the boats arrived. We quickly boarded. Some had to fight the undead hand to hand with bayonets and empty weapons to board. I tossed my Randall knife to one of the Marines just in time for him to unsheath it and brutally decapitate two nearly skeletal and naked creatures clawing for his flesh. He yelled a hearty thanks, wiped the blade off on his pants and gave it back as he boarded the boat.

We were safely moving in the water toward the carrier, stopping only briefly every few hundred yards to pick men out of the water who were still alive but going into shock. Some had already turned and reached for our rescue personnel as they attempted to save those that they could.

The day we arrived a mixture of military surgeons and volunteer AmeriCorps doctors that were onboard immediately checked us out. Although they were not military, they were happy to be here instead of on the mainland. As they patched us up they told us that the life expectancy in some areas of the mainland was one hour at most. Another sailor onboard told me that they had to make dangerous incursions hundreds of miles inland to places like Redstone and Pine Bluff arsenals to replenish ordnance and critical repair parts from time to time.

Tara and I were berthed in a stateroom together on the O3 level. I was more than happy to see her and find out she had made it onboard without problems. She gave me the stateroom numbers as well as deck and frame numbers of all former Hotel 23 residents, and I made a mental note to visit everyone I could when I had the time. When I was not writing an operational intelligence report on the past year's goings-on I spent all my time with her. She has seemed much more emotional lately. This is completely normal, considering the stress everyone has been through.

I truly missed her during my absence, and I finally had some time where we both felt safe enough to let our mental guard down a bit and have real conversations about what happened to me out there.

I'll never forget her words: "I can't believe you are here in front of me. I missed you so much. You were bringing back what *they* took away from me."

As we were moving deeper into conversation a messenger knocked on our door and asked me to follow.

My debriefing in the Aircraft Carrier Intelligence Center (CVIC) took an entire day and a half. I was going over documents with John and Saien when the ship's acting intelligence officer appeared on deck. He introduced himself as Joe from the Central Intelligence Agency. He wore one of those olive-drab "shoot me first" photographer's vests, gray T-shirt and cargo pants with desert combat boots. Using my journal, I pored over the details I thought would be of significance. I was told that the acting Chief of Naval Operations would be summoning me to his office soon, as he wanted to meet me and get firsthand ground truth about the situation on the mainland and speak about an upcoming mission that may need my consultation.

Joe quickly redirected me to anything and everything regarding Remote Six. I explained to him the nature of the technology I had seen—everything from the weapon laser designator that I still had to the button beacon and even the UAV C-130. When explaining the fiber-optic boxes connected to the avionics of the C-130 I was compelled to tell Joe that I felt the unusual technology was years ahead of the mainstream technologies that were commercially available at the time the dead started to rise. He took careful notes and asked precision-guided questions regarding the technology. It seemed he was much more interested in the communications and the technology coming out of Remote Six than in the undead situation on the ground.

Another subject of interest was the condition in which we had left Hotel 23. I explained that every piece of valuable intelligence was exfiltrated with the evacuation and that we had welded all access doors closed to prevent tampering by anyone or anything. Over his shoulder he ordered one of the intelligence personnel to ensure that the CVIC "keeps an eye" on Hotel 23 in the event that an attempt is made on the systems inside. He stated that it was worth diverting assets for at least a while.

I told him of a list of compounds that John had gained access to via the computer systems inside Hotel 23. I said that there were at least a dozen locations, and that the only location in the database I had recognized was Groom Lake, Nevada. I asked Joe if there was any significance to that location and why it would still be manned and in the green. He said that he did not know, but it seemed to me that he was being deceptive. While telling him about Project Hurricane technology, I had witnessed that he was interrupted by a phone call.

After nodding a few times and saying, "Yes, sir," he hung up the phone and said simply: "You're on."

I dropped off the debriefing report that I had invested the last two days writing and followed Joe to the admiral's in-port cabin. After I had stubbed my toes on three knee knockers and nearly hit my head on a leaking low-pressure steam pipe, we eventually arrived. There were two Marine guards standing in front of the cabin door and they stepped aside after seeing Joe. We knocked once and a gruff voice responded with only, "Come." On entering the cabin I saw the admiral sitting at his mahogany desk with a bottle of Chivas scotch and three glasses. I walked toward the admiral and stood at attention eighteen inches in front of his desk. I didn't recognize him. I introduced myself to the admiral and stated that I was reporting as ordered.

He laughed and said, "Sit down, son, I was only a senior full-bird captain a year ago. The stars were, how should I say—battle-field promotions?"

I sat down and he poured three glasses and handed two of them to Joe and me. He introduced himself as Admiral Goettle-man.

He proceeded to offer his account of the past year—tales of his flotilla of small-boy ships and the littoral war against the dead that kicked off in the early weeks. After some major cities were destroyed by tactical nukes, his ships were charged with clearing operations. They would draw the dead to the coastline near major population centers and prosecute via full barrage for hours at a time in an attempt to thin the herd. There were times his destroyers and cruisers would sit at anchor for days with the ships' horns blaring intermittently to attract the dead in order to ensure high effect. He had personally witnessed .50 cal gunners throw red-hot barrels over the side into the water only to replace them with new cosmoline-coated surplus steel scavenged from various military arsenals around the United States He then looked solemnly into the distance—not at me but through me.

"Intelligence estimates credited my group with less than a one percent disposal rate. We got half a million at least. I know this 'cause we expended well over a million rounds. It turns out, the littoral war was of no more value than the nuclear campaign."

He then asked about my story.

After I had presented an executive-level debrief on my experi-ences of the last year, he took a long pause and then took a long drink of scotch and filled his glass back up three fingers. He went on to stroke my ego by saying that there are not a lot of men who could have saved so many people and survived that long on the mainland. He then stood up, walked over to the liquor cabinet and pulled it from the wall on one side. Behind the cabinet a safe was hidden. After spinning the dials back and forth he pulled out a thick file and placed it on his desk. As he unwound the string binding the folder, he informed me that he had a special team that he had put together for a very important, nationally sanc-tioned operation.

"The USS *Virginia,* a nuclear fast attack submarine, is cur-rently en route to the Pacific side of the Panama Canal from the waters of Baja. Of course the Canal is derelict and nonfunctioning, but it is still the thinnest land mass between this ship and the USS *Virginia* on the Pacific side. I'll cut to the chase: We are sending an incursion team to China. Reliable intelligence suggests that the source of the anomaly resides in a defense research labora-tory on the outskirts of Beijing. Our scientists think we may have a chance of finding a cure or at least a vaccine if we can locate and extract patient-zero or the research data associated.

"You and the civilians under your leadership survived for nearly a year on the mainland. The operators on this team I'm putting together can't boast that kind of experience statistic and probably wouldn't want to. China is, unfortunately, many times

487

denser in undead population than the United States, and over two-thirds of their undead population is walking on the eastern coast. In saying that, it is prudent to mention that they didn't deploy nearly as many nuclear weapons inside China to neutralize the dead. Luckily, Beijing was not destroyed. Taiwan was not so lucky. It was completely wiped out by the chicoms and will remain hot for years to come.

"The plan is to move the carrier to the thinnest point of the Atlantic side of the canal and fly the incursion team over the Panama land mass into the waitin' open hatches of the USS *Virginia*. She's relatively new and in much better shape than this ship. She has fifteen years or more until scheduled refueling of her reactors and currently has 'nuf food onboard for a six-month run."

I was starting to realize at this point what the admiral was leading up to.

"We intend to have the *Virginia* in the Bohai in three weeks. We've located airstrips with probably serviceable Chinese military helicopters at three different airfields near Beijing. Since the *Virginia* has no tactical requirement to run below periscope depth we can remain in constant data contact with her as she transits from CONUS to Pearl Harbor, Hawaii to the Bohai. After arriving in the Bohai, the *Virginia* will make her way upriver to Beijing and to the airfields we've identified. After arriving in the vicinity of the airfields, *Virginia*'s crew will launch Scan Eagle UAVs to recon the airfields and determine the best candidates for rotary-wing repairs and deployment.

"I'd like you to ride the *Virginia* to China as a technical consultant for the incursion team."

After letting the admiral's request (see: order) sink in for about ten seconds, I mentioned to him the obvious fact that I was no special operator. I am a naval officer and not a door-kicker or commando. I had no experience in this type of operation.

He replied callously with only: "I have been briefed in your background and I have decided that you will ride the *Virginia* to China and you will support this operation. I know about what you did in Texas. We screened all military message traffic leading up to the anomaly. Your name came up as, shall I say . . . *missing*?"

A line of seriousness appeared on the admiral's forehead and then he said: "Can't say that I blame you, son. There was no way to win at that time, but there may be a way to win now. There's space on the helicopter as well as the boat for an extra body, if you want to bring someone you know and trust. I'll leave that to you. You leave in three days' time. That is all, Commander."

All I could mutter was, "Aye, aye, Admiral."

. . . Then dismiss myself and walk out.

Leaving the cabin in a confused daze, I didn't realize until Joe congratulated me on my new promotion that I had been bumped up two ranks to commander. He also handed me the appropriate collar rank devices and wished me better luck than the man who had held these oak leaves before me. I tossed them in my pocket, never planning to wear them, and made way to my quarters.

TS//SI//SAP HORIZON

BT

CRITIC FOLLOW-UP/I+274/

BT

Be advised this is not a finished intelligence report. Numerous COMINT intercepts originating from the People's Republic of China (PRC) leading up to the event reveal the probable anomaly source.

BT

One year ago VORTEX received communications revealing that the PRC had recovered something of great technological interest from the ancient ice of the Mingyong glacier in Yunnan Province. An object of ovoid shape (see separate enclosure 01: AURORA overflight imagery) about the size of a large passenger bus was discovered by the local population and reported to the local authorities. Chinese web precognitive awareness predictive language supports this intercept.

BT

At first the Chinese radiometrically dated the unknown alloy of the object back greater than six billion years (a geological impossibility). That was until they calibrated their instruments to the alloy's true decay rate. After instrument calibration, it was discovered that the object had been in the ice for approximately twenty thousand years.

BT

The vehicle (as it turned out to be) was not without damage to the outer hull. Imagery analysis indicated a two-meter hole in the top of the object that allowed the elements to slowly enter the inside of the vehicle during its glacial interment. The immense pressure of the ever-contracting and expanding glacial ice and the vast time span from crash to recovery was a direct factor that likely caused the outer hull to warp over the centuries. After weeks of careful excavation the Chinese advanced to the cockpit of the vehicle (see separate enclosure

02: HUMINT handheld imagery). It is unknown by this agency why the Chinese chose to excavate in the direction of the cockpit and not the assumed advanced propulsion systems of the vehicle. In the cockpit the excavators discovered what is known in the transcripts only as a creature assigned the Chinese code name CHANG.

BT

When discovered, CHANG was restrained in the cockpit seat wearing a thin exoskeleton of unknown technology that Chinese researchers postulated could function as a conventional astronaut environmental suit [REF 243B2]. CHANG was still mobile and seemed to react to the excavator's presence by moving its head from side to side inside the exoskeleton's helmet. CHANG was also encased from the chest down in ice. The scientists and security personnel were initially very disturbed by the movement of the creature and were given orders to keep it restrained by any means necessary. They were also given specific instructions not to remove CHANG's cranial helmet.

BT

TACNOTE: Some of the researchers were executed when central military commission cyber-defense agents discovered that they had PGP encryption keys installed on their personal computers and were in intermittent communication with unknown [to PRC] persons outside the PRC (covered in separate agency correspondence).

BT

According to intercepted initial magnetic resonance imaging, the creature is bipedal and has the rough appearance in mass and appendages of a young adolescent human.

BT

After securing and removing CHANG (still at this point in a relative block of ice), the Chinese began to excavate the rest of the vehicle. They discovered numerous artifacts, some destroyed by the ages and immense glacial ice pressure and some still very much intact. Most notable were the advanced propulsion systems that the Chinese recovered and took back to the same research facility in which CHANG was being examined (probably in Beijing). At first the Chinese took great interest in reverse-engineering the advanced magnetic levitation, propulsion and inertial dampening systems as well as the exotic power plant of the vehicle. The vehicle appeared to possess what PRC researchers hypothesized as a *crumple drive* module that might allow the vehicle to distort or crumple the space directly in front to an area twenty meters out (single-source HUMINT report). Also recovered were numerous handheld directed-energy weapons. Utilizing a transmission electron microscope with half-angstrom resolution capability, the Chinese were able to perform a cursory examination of the artifact internals. Much of the inner workings examined on the smaller artifacts indicated subnano technology advanced circuitry. When the PRC quickly came to a technological impasse with reverse-engineering attempts, their focus turned to CHANG.

BT

CHANG was being kept in a biohazard containment vault in the compound (probably in Beijing). He (unknown gender) was under constant security and observation but seemed to exhibit very little intelligence and made no attempt to communicate with the scientists or military officers charged with interrogation and study. It was decided after deliberations by Chinese presidential authority that CHANG be removed from ice and observed.

BT

The last communications intercept contained a distress call from the research facility that held CHANG (confirmed to be in Beijing, PRC, by this timeline of reporting). All HUMINT sources inside the facility have since gone dark.

BT

Remote viewing data is available via separate compartmented reporting channels.

BT

Assessment: This agency assesses that CHANG was infected with the Mingyong Sickness somewhere in transit between his star system and Earth. Judging by the acquired photos taken at the glacier site, it appears that the vehicle was at an abnormal attitude in the ice, which suggests an inverted crash landing. The hull damage score marks possess melted and deformed edges, which could indicate a blasting event by some great force, possibly a separate energy weapon event.

BT

Also of intelligence value: It is assessed that due to the timeline of the anomaly and the extreme complexity of the subnano circuitry, the Chinese were unable to effectively reverse-engineer the propulsion systems of the vehicle or even develop a theory about how the systems function. Beijing was the first city to be overrun by the creatures, thus halting research and development of advanced systems. Home Base and Utah Site 84-026 concur with this assessment.

BT

TF HOURGLASS is standing by to provide operational intelligence support to the Beijing incursion.

BT

TS//SI//SAP HORIZON

BT

DECLASSIFY ON: MANUAL REVIEW

BT

AR

Iridium
G 2hrs. Reopen(?)
WTF.

0.9 NM

2×500LB LGB

Remc? ¿¿
- controls UCAV
- SatPhones
- DARPA Tech?
- Reason?

i-9-10! what is it? from hru ...netdms hrym

Stores

M-4/AimPoint MP5SD - Cached
→5.56× ~~500~~ 400   Cause
G-19/Suppressor [2×⬚(?)] - GOD(?) - MAN
L→9mm× ~~200~~ 210
H^2O-100 oz
→TP
Two
20-Hi Pri-

- Sleeping Bag
- 2x chili (Heavy, eat 1st)/Dry food
- 1x MRE
- PRC-90/283.8:243 - Dead
- Binoculars
- Waterproof matches
- Lighter
- 2x Rat traps (old house//Bad)))
- 3X AA Batts.
- Triple Antibiotic (expired)
- TP
- Hatchet
- Watch - G-Shock: RADIOActive?
- NVGs
- Flares
- Common Access Card (CAC)
- SunGlasses
- Pens×3

Last Words Box

Staying Alive

- Move at night (when)
- Press Check weapon
- Sleep off the ground (high)
- Stop, Listen, use Binos
- Parallel Roads//stay off HWY.
- Store water in Belly.
- Keep weapons Lubed (motor oil OK.
- Move FAST in open (Jog 10, WALK 10)
- Protect eyes.
- If Population Sign >30K AVOID!
- If must sleep on ground level, sleep in car on Steep hill, hand on e-brake.
- Some of them Require 2 shots to Dome.
- Eat when you can, heavy fats 1st
- Change Socks often
- 100 MPH tar works as moleskin
- You ARE NEVER Alone. (they ARE)
- Stay Quiet, engages last resort NEAR
- Brush, Floss
- Don't hunt without suppressor.
- The creatures can kill with only a scratch.
  → Avoid hand-to-hand
- Some books Are worth the Weight. (Atlas, SAS, etc.)

- Wish I had a .22LR Pistol
- Bathe when able or suffer.
- Minimum 2 ways out at all times.
- Set trip wires, gives warning
- all dogs are now Feral, except Annabelle.
- Kill humans at first sign of hostility.
- 10 miles per Day, or Risk Attracting too many.
- the creatures hibernate, Do not be fooled.
- Radiated creatures are FAST. Avoid. They emit RADS.
- If it has Moving Parts, it will Fail, or Crash.
- Witnessed one use a tool. Not good.

Miles

— Witnessed one use a tool. Not good.
— Boots, boots, boots. Have two pair.
— a good knife is minimum SURVIVAL gear.
— a good compass is a modern day Rolex in value.
— ~~have nothing~~

— When there is doubt, there is no doubt.
  ↳ Risk only when crucial.
— Dead eyes Dont reflect BACK in NVGs.

Caddo Lake

DOG RED 2øø

DOG GREEN 5øø

Sick Shit
The book — creatures
"Milestones"? — Pulling grain
Significant — wheel, human bait.
  — Claudia.
  — HATCHET thing

I have seen them
move fast. Not human
speed, but I am not ~~fast~~
~~too~~ shoot on sight
inside 25 meters.

I need to consider the poss.
that I ~~may~~ not survive this.

Too many of them. Raining
hard. Keep hearing strong noise, like
the sound of a small engine.

The rain has caused me to catch a
cold, but it has also taught me something.
My suppressor is much more effective
wet. Dropped SMG in water, picked it
up and shot one of them in the face. conf.

House
ø822, ø948, 1816.
ø838, 1923.

~~16ø~~ "Beware the
~~188~~ talented tenth."
~~11øø~~
  ⊙ 9 øø

Miss her.

Western group.
5 at moving N↑

HWY 59(?)

Dragonfly ✓

‖LL HELP ME
HERE

Last Words Box

Visitor

HOME

||||| ||||| |||||
||||| ||||| |||||
||

If You Can
Read This...

The Lone Star State capital fell to the undead three weeks after the first U.S. infections were documented in Maryland. Texas held out longer than most other states, but the infection juggernaut spread quickly, knocking out infrastructure, killing military, police, fire and medical personnel first. The same scenario played out everywhere, all around the world in HD. When the lights went out, the dead quickly filled the vacuum in alliance with the darkness. Those fortunate enough to live near a body of water with access to sea transport had a chance at survival, albeit small.

Eugene, until recently, had been a bagger at the Seadrift Grocery & Bait. He had filled and lugged thousands of bags of groceries since age fifteen to purchase his first car. That was three years ago. His whole life was ahead of him.

He had big plans like any other eighteen year old, at least until those things took out his town and, according to the news, every town. That was the wake-up call that hit him like a bolt of lightning; his big plans were now and probably forever a nonstarter. Welcome to the rest of your life, Eugene old pal.

His sister, Brook was all that remained of that life. Eugene's dad, mom and little brother Jake were killed by a raging fire while the family hid in the attic from the creatures below.

I couldn't have saved them.

Eugene had repeated that more times over the past few weeks than he'd asked his customers "paper or plastic" in the past few years.

The fire's smoke and heat in the attic that night was unbearable, its acrid thickness choking the life from him. The thermometer in the attic couldn't display temperature above 140; it must have been closer to 200 when he and Brook kicked out the attic vent and took a chance, blindly jumping two stories. Luckily, there was no undead mosh pit below to greet them. Both he and his sister survived the fall; Brook suffered a minor sprain, Eugene a few cuts from the holly tree.

The creatures closed the distance fast, some of them emerging from the burning house, on fire, still determined to feed. Eugene's screams for his family hastened the creatures' steps. He kept calling for them, but the only response from above was a blast of dark smoke shooting from the attic, resembling the rhythmic exhaust of an old locomotive. No screams echoed from above. The sounds of collapsing timber briefly abated the unholy calls of the undead. Eugene put out his hand for his sister and fled, never looking back. That was over a month ago.

"Got the keys, Genie?" Brook teased, her skinny frame hanging half out of the sleeping bag, unkempt dark hair everywhere.

"For fuck's sake, will you please stop calling me that? Like I don't have enough shit to stress about," Eugene snapped back.

"Seriously, Genie. Got 'em?" she persisted.

"Which ones? The store or my car?"

"Stop being an asshole," Brook said, punching his arm.

"Yes, I have them, go to sleep."

"I'm just making sure. Besides, don't forget, I popped out of Mom five minutes before you, Genie." Brook giggled quietly before turning over in her sleeping bag for the evening.

She was compensating, trying to stay ahead of the terror she'd endured. Eugene knew it, as he was doing the same thing. They had both been there—both forced to leave their family to burn.

Eugene and Brook had sprinted away from the burning home into the darkness, through hedges and behind fences, dodging the undead. Hands shot out of the voids like fast jungle traps, grasping for flesh. Eugene feared he had surely been killed when he thought a creature scratched him. He felt warm blood drip down his arm and panicked until he saw the piece of broken fence and a rusty nail had fallen against him in their haste. He'd live, with tetanus maybe.

Luck combined with a club fashioned from stair railing got them to Eugene's Buick and subsequently to the Seadrift Fire Department. Two creatures remained inside; firemen. Eugene clubbed them hard over the head, swinging with hate and fury, wishing the firemen had been alive to do their job. All the trucks were gone, abandoned around the city a month ago while fighting infernos like the one that killed his family. He pulled the Buick inside and shut the bay doors. His car looked absurdly small, parked where massive fire trucks once stood ready.

After clearing the fire house, Eugene seemed to get into a rhythm. He'd found a radio downstairs with 12 volt DC input and began scavenging car batteries. He'd left his own car untampered, of course, but the ten or so cars up and down the street outside were fair game. The batteries were heavy. Eugene lugged two at a time back to the station, taking breaks in between to make sure the creatures didn't hear and respond in full force. The Halligan breacher bar helped him get under the hoods and proved to be a pretty good weapon against the small number of stragglers that came calling in response to the noise. A tool designed to help firefighters breach doors, its spike penetrated skulls almost effortlessly, much more effective than the stair railing club. Wasn't long before he was an old pro with the tool.

He had nightmarish visions of the fat, bloated dead thing stuck in an Explorer, angry with him for prying the hood open. It was once a woman, he was pretty sure at least. He'd left it there, but it played hell on his nerves while he tinkered under the hood. The putrid creature shook the car back and forth, punching the window and slapping the door, wanting so badly to get out and have at him. He felt lucky that she never hit the horn, at least she didn't until after he pulled the battery and left her there to rot for all time. Her battery was dead, he should have known.

Eugene also attempted to scavenge gas from the cars on the streets, but the garden hose method he'd seen on TV didn't work. There was something stopping his hose from getting down into the tank. They never had that trouble on TV.

Eugene felt sure that tonight would be just like last night and the night before. He allowed his sister to sleep and slid down the fire pole for his nightly radio check. It had become sort of a routine, a break from the maddening silence. They slept high inside the firehouse, in case the building was overrun. Eugene didn't think it likely since they'd been real careful, except for that radio volume hiccup last week.

Eugene cupped his hand over his flashlight to dim the beam as he approached the dispatch station. On his tiptoes, he peered out the high bay door windows. *Good*, he thought, *there are only a few outside; lots less than before.*

He pulled a fresh car battery from the pyramid stack in the corner and attached the cables from the radio to the positive and negative leads. The radio's LCD display came to life, illuminating the immediate area with a dim blue glow. Eugene cringed, second guessing that he might have forgotten to turn down the volume the night before.

Thankfully, loud tuning static did not blare out, bringing the dead. He'd learned that lesson last week at the cost of a night's sleep. The pummels against the metal doors from cold hands wanting in brought vivid conscious nightmares.

Eugene turned the radio volume up slowly and began to spin the tuner incrementally along the spectrum. He listened, ear close to the speaker, for any sign of intelligent life that might be surviving, anywhere. A loud thump from behind caused Eugene to jump from the chair and reach for his heavy flashlight.

"It's only me, Genie, I can't sleep. Hear anything?" Brook asked.

"No, nothing yet. I'm going through a battery about every night. At this rate, we'll need to find more batteries this weekend."

"What's a weekend?" Brooked said sarcastically.

"Good point."

Brook brushed past Eugene and sat down in the dispatch chair. "Mind if I try for a little while? I could use a little static, if you know what I mean."

Eugene nodded, "Yeah sure, I know exactly what you mean. I'm going to take a shower. Stay quiet, I'm serious."

"Yes sir," Brook whispered, smiling, saluting with her middle finger.

Thankfully, they still had fresh water. The above ground storage tank had been a boon in their staying clean and hydrated. It was winter in Seadrift and the shower was cold, probably not as bad as up north, but still. If he thought they would stay through the winter, he'd paint the water tank black to help warm the water from solar heat. The hand soap definitely wasn't body wash, but it worked fine if you didn't get it in your eyes. Eugene converted some fire hose into a wash rag. It felt like sand paper but, like the soap, it did the job. The icy water made him gasp for air as he rinsed off. His eyes were closed tightly under the chilly stream when a hand slapped him on his shoulder, pulling him from the shower. Eugene nearly punched his sister in the throat. You didn't sneak up on folks in the shower even before the dead walked. Not cool.

"What the fuck, Brook!" Eugene said a little too loud, wrapping his naked body with the wet, mildewy shower curtain. Looking down, he realized the curtain was clear and let it fall.

"I hear something, Genie! Hurry up!" she whispered, running back to the radio.

Eugene struggled to put his pants on over his wet legs and fell twice to the cracked tile floor before getting them to his waist. He didn't bother with his boots. His wet feet slapped the floor while he ran in pursuit of his semi-frantic sister.

"What? What's the emergency?" Eugene said quizzically.

"Listen," Brook said, turning up the radio volume slightly.

The tinny voice spilled from the small but powerful speaker: *"Anyone out there? Repeat, anyone out there? We are . . . Matagorda Isl . . ."*

Eugene attempted a response multiple times but the signal soon degraded and faded out to garbled gibberish almost as he sat down to transmit.

"What did they say, Brook? Did you write any of it down?" Eugene asked excitedly.

"I didn't have any paper but I wrote down what I could on my arm. Look."

MATAGORDA ISLAND MARINA

"See, Brook, told you a boat was a good idea. That's practically swimming distance. Well, ten or fifteen miles south of Seadrift anyway. We could make it to the marina grocery store in the Regal and the rest of the way on a boat," Eugene said, tracing the words on her arm with his index finger.

"Your piece of shit car?" she said.

"That car saved our asses and got us here, didn't it," Eugene said defensively.

"Yeah, it's fast, I'll give you that, but the passenger side window won't roll up. Sort of a bummer during this little crisis, don't you think?" Brook said.

"Maybe for the passenger," Eugene said, grinning.

Brook slapped Eugene on the arm and said, "Besides that, the *Regal from Hell* is running on fumes."

"Sure, but we can stop at Old Reliable for gas. I can start up Reliable's hurricane generators with that five gallon can of diesel over there and work the pumps. It's barely a quarter mile from the marina. We can fill up the car, grab some food and then see about a boat."

"Let's sleep on it, Genie," Brook suggested.

"Okay, we can do that for one more night, maybe two, but we're about out of food and neither of us have much fat to live on. Keep that in mind. We'll talk more about it in the morning over our feast of stale crackers and peanut butter. Sound good?"

"Goodnight, brother," Brook said, walking up the spiral steps.

"If you say so."

Eugene unhooked the car battery and followed his sister up.

The next morning, the siblings awoke hungry. Brook and Eugene shared the crackers and remaining peanut butter. Brook broke the bottle afterwards so they could carefully lick every atom of peanut butter from the shards.

"We go tonight." Eugene said to his sister. "We're completely out of food, and we'll starve in a week if we don't find or kill something."

"Genie, I'm scared. I feel safe here. Are you sure about this, I mean do we have to go, leave this?"

"Yeah. I've seen more of them out there lately. I know it's hard to tell unless you've made a point to pay attention, but since that bright flash in the sky, there have been more of them in the streets. I have the keys to the store. There was still lots of food on the shelves when I locked up. Most of the town died before they needed it and right now *we* need it."

Brook kept her head and eyes low, staring through the floor as she listened to her brother speak. She was confused and scared. They were to be graduating together in a few months. This wasn't supposed to happen. As the smallest girl on the squad, she was the goddamn top of the cheerleading pyramid. Now she wished she had bought a gun at eighteen instead of that laptop for college. After all, this was Texas.

"Okay, let's go over the plan one more time Genie," she said, reluctantly.

"Okay, here goes. We pack up the Regal while we still have sunlight coming through the high windows. After the sun goes down tonight, we start her up, throw open the bay doors and haul ass to Old Reliable for a fill up. You take care of the nozzle and be ready to gas her up while I run around back and start up the storm generator and the pumps. After we fill her up, we peel out for the grocery store a quarter mile away and hole up inside for a night or two while we scavenge some food and get some rest. We'll need to find a boat while we're at it. I've never worked a day at the store where there wasn't a big boat or two docked. I remember there being at least one docked when I shut the lights off. When we find one that runs, we shove off for Matagorda. That's it."

"I don't know. It's gonna be really dangerous. You saw what they can do. All those people . . . "

"Yeah, I saw what they can do, but the way I see it we either die slow in here or take our chances out there. They haven't seen what we can do. We might die, but know this. They'll take me before they get to you, I promise."

Brook hugged her brother and started to cry, thinking back to when they were kids and all the dumb practical jokes he played on her. The stupid invisible thread joke when he convinced her he was telekinetic and she might be too, twin powers and all. The time he jumped out of her closet wearing that old Bigfoot costume when she was making out with Herby . . . it all played back in her mind. Eugene was a shithead but she loved him nearly as much as she trusted him. She may not be telekinetic but she did share a bond with him, something only twins know.

"Okay, Genie, if you say it's our only shot, then let's do it."

They organized, packed, and made ready for the maelstrom that followed.

Eugene was behind the wheel when Brook threw the bay door open. Five creatures flowed in from nowhere, spilling into the station. He reacted by stomping the accelerator. The car's turbo kicked in, catapulting it forward, nearly hitting Brook. The heavy car flung the hungry creatures in all directions. One walking corpse struck asphalt twenty feet away, its head scraping along the concrete, leaving bits of brain like a pencil eraser on a notepad.

"Get in, goddamn it!" Eugene screamed, reaching over to fling the door open for Brook.

Dazed, Brook jumped to her feet and sprinted for the car door. One of the creatures Eugene hit reached out, grabbing Brook's pant leg, yanking her to the floor. She hit the ground hard, thumping her head on the cement, making a melon testing sound. Seeing stars, she began to black out, her vision narrowed to a small tunnel. The last thing she remembered before waking up in the car was Genie's face, rageful and unforgiving as he wrestled and stomped the creature's dim lights out.

She screamed, "Did it get me?! Did it get me, Genie?!"

"No, sis. Close, but it didn't get you. Relax, we're almost to the station. You still up to the plan?" Eugene said.

"Yeah, I'll be fine." Brook said, assuring herself more than Genie.

Eugene pulled into Old Reliable gas station sideways, skidding to a stop near pumps number one and two. There were creatures about; Brook saw them briefly in the headlights. The firemen's bar was in the back seat; Eugene reached for it, telling Brook to duck as he brought it over her head to the front on his way out of the car. He grabbed the diesel fuel and swung his door, stopping it before it closed.

"Stay in until it's time, Brook. You'll know when I get the generator running," Eugene said.

"Okay, hurry."

Eugene disappeared behind the station.

Long minutes ticked by. The passenger window was stuck half way down, as it had been for months. Genie was too cheap to fix it; she wished he had. The gap in the window had the psychological effect of a big hairy tarantula or a growling T-Rex maw in the dim moonlight. She moved to the center of the front seat, away from it. The doors were locked but that didn't matter. She'd seen what they could do. Brook had witnessed mobs of them break down doors, smash windows and lay waste to her neighborhood.

She heard the generator turn over a few seconds before the overhead lights flickered on, illuminating the area, revealing a baker's dozen of undead just at the edge of the light.

"Shit! Shit!" Brook hissed, watching the creatures as they craned their necks in reaction to the new stimuli. They hadn't yet spotted her. The creatures seemed to know something was here; something out of place, not present before. The creep show began to enter the full glow of the fluorescent lights shining down on her.

Hurry, Genie, she thought over and over as the creatures walked about like viruses under a microscope, looking for living cells to infect.

She tried not to stir too quickly, fearing they might see her inside and surround the car. They'd crawl right through that window, at least the smaller ones would. She saw a few of them, children. *Damn you, Genie, cheap bastard.*

She heard a loud thunk and saw one of them hit the ground, Genie standing behind it. He was holding that big spiked thing. She dashed out of the car and grabbed for the gas nozzle. She frantically searched for the fuel door, cursing. *Goddamn this car!*

The undead began to take notice of them. The metal roof over the pumps acted as an antenna, amplifying the creatures' hellish cries. Genie was fighting his way to her, swinging and hammering at the undead. Kneecaps, teeth and skull fragments lay scattered about. There were too many.

The license plate, she remembered.

Running behind the car, she flipped down the plate, revealing the gas cap. She unscrewed it, tossed it aside and jammed the nozzle into the tank. She squeezed the trigger, but nothing happened. Realizing that she hadn't pulled the pump lever, she ran back, nearly hitting a creature as it rounded the front of the car for her.

"Fuck! Help, Genie!" she screamed.

Genie fought like a Spartan. Brook managed to flip the pump lever but was chased a few yards away, near the road. The breaching tool he swiped from the station served him well on the way to Brook. Genie—the Norse god—came down from above with both hands, splitting the skull of the creature attempting to murder his sister. They could both smell the gasoline filling the tank but it was too late, dozens of them surrounded the pumps. There was no way to make it to the car and get away without being bitten—or worse.

In a split second decision, Brook screamed, "Run Genie, let's go!" She reached for her brother, the siblings once again sprinting into the night in escape of walking death.

They ran for what seemed like a distance, but Eugene knew where he was. The moon was fully overhead, and he could hear his sister's feet behind him on the road. Eugene smelled the water before he saw it glimmer in the moonlight. He looked back, seeing Old Reliable's pump lights behind them and could even make out the undead mob that was forming under those lights. A few creatures moved away from the pumps in their direction, disappearing outside the glow in spite of the station's generator noise.

Winded, Brook said, "Genie, the keys."

"Yeah, front pocket."

I spent three years of my life at the store, paying for that car, now those things are crawling all over it, he thought angrily.

At the front doors, he reached into his pocket for the keys. Like a bad horror movie, he dropped them on the ground at his feet.

The jangling sound on the rubber floor mat was reciprocated by loud crashing noises from the parking lot. Eugene knew the sound, he'd heard it before—*shopping cart. Those don't fall over on their own and it's not windy*, he thought, bending down for the keys.

A cart was being dragged across the lot; the noise was getting louder, closer. Eugene couldn't see anything; a tree cast a shadow over the lot, shrouding the lunar light.

"Oh God, Genie! Hurry, it's close!" Brook said frantically.

Eugene turned the key, disengaging the lock. He swung the heavy glass door open into complete darkness. The all-too-familiar smell of decay slapped his face. He and Brook dashed inside. Eugene locked the door behind them and slid to the floor, back against the locked door, holding his head in his hands.

"Genie?" Brook whispered.

"Down here."

Brook stumbled into him. He'd left his flashlight on top of Old Reliable's generator; she'd left hers in Eugene's car. They were virtually blind.

"Genie, something's in here. I hear it," she whispered.

"Yeah. I can hear it too. Follow me," Eugene said, using the breaching tool to help him to his feet. "Take my arm," he whispered.

Using the dim blue light from his watch, he found the flashlight aisle. They were plastic, cheaper than the aluminum D cells they lost back at the gas station.

"Fill 'em up, sis, they need batteries, hurry."

Another sound interrupted the silence. Something fell to the tile floor. Eugene stood up, weary from battle. He readied the breacher tool and faced the sound. A can rolled, hitting the base of a shelf. The noise stopped.

"Here," Brook said, hitting Eugene in the leg with a flashlight, giving him a charley horse.

She'll pay for that later, he thought.

He shifted the heavy breacher into his right hand, gripping the flashlight with his left. His thumb felt for the switch. He pointed it, but was hesitant to turn it on. He was afraid.

Maybe if I don't look, it'll stop.

"What are you waiting for?" Brook whispered loudly.

The sound returned and Eugene switched on the flashlight. He panned the beam around, squinting when it reflected off the round convex security mirror in the corner, blinding him a little.

"I don't see anything," he said to Brook.

She filled another flashlight with batteries and joined Eugene. Both lights were panning around the store now. Something fell again on the other side of the store.

"That's automotive," he said. "Let's go."

Eugene led the way. Their confidence returned with the light. Rounding the aisle, they saw something. A path of congealed blood and innards wrapped around the corner, into the automotive section. They followed the repulsive trail, their flashlights jerking at every sound, real or imagined.

Eugene stuck his head around the corner and shined his light. He immediately turned away, dry heaving into his elbow.

"Don't look," he said between the heaves to Brook.

"How bad can it be? I mean, haven't we seen it all?"

Eugene's stomach was empty, running on half a tic tac. Still heaving, yellow acid bile soured his mouth.

He pushed the vision of what he saw from his mind enough to speak. "It's torn up pretty bad, but still moving. I gotta kill it."

Brook tried to lean past Eugene and sneak a peek. He crossed the breacher tool in front of her, blocking her attempt.

"Listen, I'm serious, Brook. It isn't like the ones we've seen—it's little. Stop, unless you wanna kill it yourself. Believe me, you don't."

Brook quickly backed away at those words, letting Eugene deal with it. Trying not to look down, Eugene stepped around the corner and slammed the spike down on the creature's head.

"I'm going to the back to get an apron and some gloves. We're gonna have to clean up. You want to come with me?" he asked.

"No, I'm good," Brook said, rubbing her head. A nice knot was forming where she'd hit her head earlier. "I'm a little lightheaded, I'm going to rest for a minute."

Eugene nodded at his sister and moved quickly to the back of the store and through the double doors he'd used countless times to clock in and out. His apron still hung on the peg where he'd left it. He'd moved up a few pegs of seniority over the years and was rather proud of that. Eugene threw on the apron, tying it around his back. The receiving area was in disarray, boxes and plastic wrap strewn about. The bay doors were closed and secured. *That's a bonus,* he thought.

"Okay, gloves, bucket, mop, water, soap . . . check," he said aloud, rolling the bucket with the mop through the double doors.

The doors swung back behind him when something moved in the corner of his eye, something fast. He turned to react, but was thrown to the floor hard with only the mop in his hands for defense. He'd left the damn breacher tool in the receiving bay, leaning against the deep sink.

"Brook!" he screamed.

It was strong. Brook's flashlight shone on the thing, illuminating it briefly. Eugene caught a glimpse of the patch on its work shirt, *San Antonio Locksmith, Inc.* The creature was just about the most horrible thing he'd seen, except for the dismembered toddler corpse he'd rekilled a few moments before. It had burns over most of its arms and face. Boils filled with clear pus popped as Eugene struggled with the creature.

Brook appeared over him holding a tire tool and took a swing, hitting its neck. The creature turned its head and growled, drool dripped from the corners of its mouth when it bared its teeth at her. The creature pounced and Eugene was forced to watch in horror as the creature quickly tore into his sister's neck. Just before her eyes went blank, he read her lips clearly . . .

Sorry, Genie.

Miraculously, Eugene temporarily flipped off his emotions, grabbed the flashlight from the floor and sprinted back to the double doors. He heard the terrifying sounds of the creature's pursuit. As soon as he cleared the doors, he turned off his flashlight, using his memory to guide him back to the deep sink. After a few seconds of darkness, he listened to the thing impact the double doors and fall to the floor, growling.

Just a few more steps, he thought. Reaching blindly, he felt the cold tubular steel—his Excalibur, the Halligan breaching bar. He switched on his flashlight and aimed it at the doors. The creature was on its feet, flailing about with its back to Eugene. It turned in reaction to the light and seemed to size him up for a moment before charging, faster than the others he'd seen before. Eugene waited for the right moment and swung hard, striking the creature in the head, sending it crashing into the deep sink.

"Fuck you, motherfucker!" he screamed, knees locked; revenge tears streaming down his face.

He missed the brain with the spike. The creature returned to its feet quickly and charged. Eugene parried, attempting to gain some distance to attempt another swing, this time with the spike. He stepped back, the creature giving no quarter, advancing, gnashing its teeth and howling for flesh. Eugene chanced a close attack but the creature lashed out, catching his weapon midstrike. He dropped his light on the concrete floor, shattering the bulb. Two sets of hands gripped the breacher tool now—his and the creature's. They danced in the dark as Eugene struggled for the weapon, the creature for Eugene.

Eugene sat bleeding in the cooler alongside his dead sister, or what remained of her. He'd bested the powerful creature, but not before it chomped his right ring finger from his hand.

He lost track of time, not knowing how long since the skirmish with the undead thing, or how long since his sister drew her last breath. His fever was high, the walls began to change pattern before his eyes—hallucinations.

The milk in the cooler had gone yellow, curdling in gallon jugs sitting in the racks above his head. He could feel the sickness inching up his arm now, a dreadful pain. He'd already taken a handful of painkillers from the shelf, no effect. His finger was bleeding badly. Black and poisoned veins branched up his arm, on a journey to his heart.

Eugene tried to escape, to let his mind roam. His imagination travelled momentarily back to happier times, but his sister's twitching returned him to the cooler. She was beginning to move.

Won't be long now.

He looked down upon his apron, the white canvass that it was, and began to write words by fading flashlight in his own blood.

He managed seven.

if you can
Read This
Kill Me!

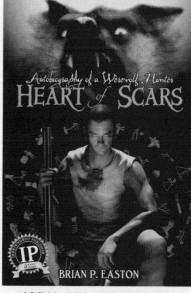